M000207215

THE BETRAYAL

ILLICIT LOVE
BOOK THREE

ASHLEE ROSE

Ashlee Rose

Copyright 2024 Ashlee Rose

First Edition

The author has asserted their moral right under the Copyright, Designs and Patents Act, 1988, to be identified as the author of this work.

All rights reserved. No part of this publication may be reproduced, copied, stored in a retrieval system, or transmitted, in any form by or by any means, without the prior written consent of the copyright holder, nor be otherwise circulated in any form of binding or cover other than that in which it is published and without a similar condition being imposed on the subsequent purchaser.

This is a work of fiction. Names, characters, businesses, places, events and incidents are either the products of the authors imagination or used in a fictitious manner.

Any resemblance to actual persons, living or dead, or actual events is purely coincidental.

OTHER BOOKS BY ASHLEE ROSE

STANDALONES:

Unwanted

Promise Me

Savage Love

Tortured Hero

Something Worth Stealing

Dear Heart, You Screwed Me

Signed, Sealed, Baby

DUET:

Way Back When Duet

NOVELLAS:

Rekindle Us

Your Dirty Little Secret

A Savage Reunion

RISQUÉ READS

Seeking Hallow

Craving Hex

Seducing Willow

Wanting Knox

Pursuing Hartley

Tempting Klaus

Valentine Belle

ILLICIT LOVE SERIES

The Resentment

The Loathing

LOVELOCK BAY SERIES

Wildest Love

All available on Amazon Kindle Unlimited

Only suitable for 18+ due to nature of the books.

READERS NOTE:

Xavier, Royal, Amora, Reese, Dex and Sage are British, you may find some different phrases and spellings for certain words and scenarios, but please be advised these are grammatically correct for a British person.

Titus, Kaleb, Keaton, Nate, Connie and Arizona are American.

All of the Illicit Love books are interconnected standalones and I do recommend reading them in order, although not necessary.

FOREWORD

I always like my readers to go into my stories blind, but if you wish to check trigger warnings, then please do so on the next page.

TRIGGER WARNINGS

Depictions of Sexual Assault
Depictions of Rape
Late Twin Miscarriage/Stillbirth
(not in detail and off page)

For all those who wished their dad's best friends were hot, I've got you.
Dark hair, green eyes, tall, handsome as hell and a killer smile.

PROLOGUE
ARIZONA

Excitement bubbles inside of me; my dad is finally home.

The weeks had rolled into one, work kept me busy and when I wasn't at work I was at home with Keaton. We were like passing ships in the night. I liked living with him though, he was fun to be with. When I had the odd evening at home, we sat and watched cheesy love movies. He said he hated them, but I know he secretly loved them. The way his face went all soppy, eyes wide as he took in every scene and the random tear that rolled down his cheek when the main couple got their happily ever after gave him away, but I never told him that I witnessed that.

It was another secret that I swore I would sew to my heart and be buried with.

My heart drums a little faster in my chest when I approach the bar, I pause for a moment and inhale sharply. Pushing on the door, the loud room rings in my ears and I see Keaton before anyone else. His eyes seeking me out. I hold my hand up and I see my dad standing next to a redhead. My skin prickles and I wonder if that is Amora. The smile that was so prominent on my lips begins to slip,

1

and I stand dumbfounded behind him when I watch the shit storm unfold in front of me, the words like a hurricane barrelling towards me and no matter how hard I try and barricade myself, to protect myself, it is useless. I am at its mercy.

"This is Amora, my wife." My dad's voice is loud and proud as he wraps his arm around her waist and pulls her into him and I see everyone smile, all eyes on *them*. "Oh, and Keaton," my dad calls out, a hint of laughter lacing his voice, "I think you may have put a dud condom in my bag as Amora is also pregnant."

And that's when everyone sees me. Their faces falling and I watch as Keaton shuffles in his seat. Their eyes widen and I can feel the tension grow thicker in the air, wrapping itself around me, slowly suffocating me second by second.

The air is knocked from my lungs as I try my hardest to breathe through the shock that zapped me, my brows furrow and rage fills me as molten lava pumps through my veins and every ounce of decorum leaves me.

"What the fuck!?" I shout out, my bag slipping from my fingers and hitting the floor with a thud, the contents tumbling out.

"Ari," Connie stands, her hands over her mouth as her eyes pin to mine while the shock is painted across her face.

I can't move. Grounded to the floor. Anchored.

"Sunshine..." my dad turns around and I can see the worry and shock that is etched onto his face, "we were coming to you next," he stammers, and I see the way Amora stares at the side of my dad's face.

"Well, Keaton thought it would have been nice for me to *surprise you*, but it seems I am the one that is surprised." I shake my head from side to side as laughter bubbles out of

2

me. No idea why. Shock again? I fall to my knees and collect the shit from my bag and stuff it back inside in a hurry.

"Ari... please," My dad steps towards me which causes me to look up at him.

"Don't *Ari please* me. I am angry with you." I snap, standing quickly and holding my hand out in front of me to stop him coming any closer to me. I am furious and heartbroken all at the same time.

"This... me and Amora..." he sighs heavily, and I watch as his shoulders shrug, rolling forward in a stance of defeat.

"Yeah, you fell in love, knocked her up, blah blah blah... whatever," I shake my head from side to side and turn to walk out the bar, not once looking back and with every step, my chest feels a little heavier, my heart aching a little bit more. Once outside, I suck in a deep breath, filling my lungs with the air they so desperately burn for.

I let my head fall back and the tears roll down the side of my face, disappearing under my chin.

"Ari..." Keaton's voice blankets me and I turn to face him, watery eyes focus on his beautiful green ones.

"You knew?" I swallow down the lump in my throat, betrayal lashing at my skin like a whip.

"Hey, don't be mad at me. It wasn't my news to share," his tone was a little curt, but wrapped in the truth. He steps forward cautiously and my heart stutters in my chest.

"What am I going to do?" my voice trembles, chin wobbling and I hate that I'm a mess. Broken into tiny pieces. Wilted and dishevelled.

"You're going to go home," my eyes widen at his words, and he continues, "not home, *home* Arizona. I will be back shortly, and we will spend the night talking."

I nod, unable to speak. Not really much to talk about

though was there really. Pettiness coats my tongue and I bite it for a moment.

"Don't shut your dad out, it wasn't his intention for you to find out this way," Keaton tries to put a band aid across the gaping wound.

"Well, he fucked that didn't he. I don't want to hear the poor excuses. I'm done," I step back, and a laugh vibrates through me.

I can't do this.

I won't.

I turn from him and walk away. I needed out.

And once he was out of sight, heaviness crept back inside my chest.

I felt *betrayed.*

I AM NUMB.

I have already been forgotten by one parent and now I am going to be replaced by another. No one is going to give a shit about poor, little Arizona.

Sure, I wanted my dad to find love again but not with a girl my age. Even worse, he married her and knocked her up.

Worse than that!? He told his friends before *me.*

But don't worry daddy... you're not the only one who kept a secret.

Switching my laptop on and making sure the door is bolted, I open up my webchat.

TallDarkandHandsome has entered the chat.

I smile.

My favorite fan.

YourGoodGirl: *Good evening handsome.*

I type on my keyboard as I give myself a once over in the mirror. Red, laced bralette, a matching suspender belt with ivory stockings and crotchless panties.

Just like he wanted.

I wasn't in the right frame of mind for tonight, but at the same time, I needed out of my head, and this was guaranteed to help.

I glance over at my toys laid out on the bed and excitement thrills me.

TallDarkandHandsome: *Evening Vixen.*

Okay, so I'm not a doctor.

Far from it.

The only thing we have in common is I see a lot of people daily.

But enough about that now.

Now was time for my revenge and Mr *TallDarkandHandsome* was the perfect antidote for that.

Like I said, they weren't the only ones with a secret.

BETRAYAL WAS BEST SERVED HOT WITH A SIDE OF YOUR DAD'S BEST friend.

CHAPTER ONE
ARIZONA

I LEAN ACROSS THE BAR, PERSPIRATION BEADING ALONG MY hairline, and I feel a trickle run down my spine.

"Good set," Lance, the bar guy, gives me a wink as he slides a glass of water over to me.

"Thanks," I smile, my eyes lifting to the time. It has just turned ten p.m.

I have worked at *Prestige* since last year. The club is pretty cozy. Black walls with chrome lights bringing a dim ambience to the space. Large ceiling lights hang, but of an evening, the brightness is turned up a little more, so everything is a lot more visible. No hiding away in the corners when they're on. The sofa booths are wrapped in grey leather where expensive suits sit while smoking on their cigars. Off the main floor you have four red, metal doors. Behind the doors are private rooms with beds, sofas, toys, cameras. Occasionally we have to do online cam work, though it's very rare. But if someone wants you all to themselves, that's where they'll take you. Then at the end of that hallway is a cigar lounge. Only the richest go in there. They offer extras to the girls and me, but I have never been brave enough to cross that threshold yet. I am comfortable here.

I like what I do.

I sigh, thinking about how much everything has changed in the last six months.

The truth was, I did graduate early. I did get into med school way before my peers.

But I failed my first-year exams.

The familiar prick behind my eyes reminds me of how I felt back then. Disappointment surges through me and I hate that I lied to my dad, not as much now as he lied to me too, but it still stings.

But he doesn't need to know.

I'll go back one day, but just not yet. The thought of having to work under my class as their intern was too much to bear. I was embarrassed.

Little Arizona King.

Top of her classes.

Flew through school years ahead of her friends.

Gets into med school.

Fails her intern exam because of a careless mistake.

I shake my head from side to side as I turn to face the stage, Roxy is giving the guys a hell of a show.

Roxy, Lucy, Autumn and April. The ones that took me in with open arms with not an ounce of judgement.

Don't get me wrong, I love Connie and Reese, even though they're slightly older than me, they're my friends and I know if I spilled my truths, they would be there for me.

But *my* girls here?

They know everything and I have no secrets with them.

I can be who I want to be here; when I am with Connie

and Reese I have to slip back into old Arizona, and I am starting to dislike the old me.

"Hey," a soft voice pulls me from my thoughts, and I turn to see Sage.

Long, black straight hair that sits under her ribs, beautiful tattoos covering her arms and midriff. She wears a black fitted crop top and wet look leggings. She is curvaceous and simply stunning. Her piercing green eyes sparkle like sapphires under the club lights.

"Hey!" I call out, placing my water on the bar next to me as she stands from her stool and envelopes me in her arms. "I didn't know you were coming over!" I pull away and step back, my smile wide.

"Last minute trip; Dex and Rhaegar had some business..." she trails off and rolls her eyes.

"Ah," I laugh, and follow her eyes as she focuses on Roxy.

"She is something," Sage whistles.

"She is, best of the best."

Sage lives in England with her fiancé Dex Rutherford. I would never tell her this, but Dex is hot as sin. Tall, dark haired, covered in tattoos and muscles that ripple under his glorious skin. They're a match made in heaven.

From what I have heard through the club walls, Sage used to dance at one of Dex's clubs and she was dating his dad, Rhaegar but left him for Dex. I mean, don't get me wrong, Rhaegar is the definition of silver fox, and I am sure that he was very much like his son back in the day, but Dex...

"How are you getting on?" She asks me and I turn my head away from the stage and push my thoughts to the back of my mind.

"Yeah okay, things seem to be picking up a little more now which is good," I smile as Roxy finishes her set.

"That's good," she takes a sip from her tall glass.

Prestige is one of the most upmarket Gentleman's Clubs here in New York. Members only and no touching unless a private dance has been booked. You get the few familiar faces here and most of them are respectful.

"Little One," I hear the low rumble of a man's voice and my eyes fix on how Dex wraps his large arms around Sage's body, nuzzling his nose into her hair. She giggles, her cheeks turning crimson.

I look away, suddenly feeling a little nosy. I sit quietly enjoying the music until the next set is due. I am on the floor for the next couple of hours which suits me. I like walking around and taking in the ambience of it all.

"Arizona," Dex's voice is cool as it breezes over me like the cool spring air.

"Oh hey," I wave softly at him. I would have said hello before, but I didn't want to interrupt.

"Nice to see you again, you okay?"

"I'm perfect, thank you," I nod and turn my gaze away. I am definitely not perfect. But no one needs to know just how broken I am.

I've met Dex and Sage a few times as they come over every few months to check in, but it never looks good if you're ass licking the boss now does it.

Sasha comes bounding over, hands on her hips.

"Ari, sweetness. Move your little tush and get going, you need to get changed and out on that floor baby girl," she rolls her eyes in an overexaggerated manner, and I give her a small smile.

"Sorry," I shrug my shoulders up and wave off Sage and Dex as I begin to walk towards the changing room.

I dress in a silver bra and thong, finishing the look with nude fishnets with diamantes on each cross over. Slipping into black, killer platform heels that finish my look. My dark brown hair is in its natural curl. It's shoulder length but when straight it sits just under my shoulder blades.

Rubbing bright matte red lipstick across my lips I roll them and rid the excess, so it doesn't mark my teeth.

"Hey Arizona," Sage walks round the corner and into the changing room. My brow furrows.

"All okay?" I breathe as I open my locker and grab my phone to check it.

"Yeah, fine, I was just wondering whether I could do a set with you? I haven't been on a pole in *years,* and I don't know, watching you and Roxy up there earlier, well, I just thought that you could show me a few things and vice versa."

My mouth falls agape for a moment.

"You want to dance with me?" I half giggle, thinking she's joking.

"Well, yeah," she smirks, eyes bouncing between mine.

"I'm better on the floor I think, my pole needs a little more work."

"Then let me teach you? I am here for a few weeks. Dex and his dad are going to be in back-to-back meetings for the next couple of days. If you don't want to its fine, I will ask one of the other girls."

"No! of course, I would love to."

"Cool, I'll catch up with you later," she winks at me before turning and walking out the room.

"Did Sage just come on to you?" Lucy pipes up from the sofa and I spin quickly, my brows pinching.

"No, well..." I stammer for a moment, "no," I shake my head laughing, "no, she didn't."

Letting my eyes fall down to my phone, I click the screen and see a message from my dad. I sigh, ignoring the begging and apologetic spiel and lock my phone. I don't want to hear his excuses. I am done with him. Hands washed clean.

I swallow the bitter taste down and ignore the way my stomach rolls.

Putting my phone back into my locker, I slam it a little harder than intended.

"Ready," I turn and plaster a fake smile on my face.

"Are you?" one of Lucy's brows lift. Her long, blonde mermaid wavy hair cascades down her sides. She is wearing a white bra and hotpants which are covered in sequins. She is tanned and lean. She's one of the favorites.

"I am," I give her a small nod.

"Man, you get to dance with Sage. I have such a crush on her," Lucy tsks.

"She is something... but so is Dex," I whisper the last bit in case anyone hears me.

"I mean, yeah, he is hot, but out of the two, I would take Sage, nah, Dex..." Lucy stands, hands on her hips, "you know what, I would take them both." She wiggles her brows and licks her lips.

"Why don't you try and initiate a threesome?" I smirk as I begin to head for the main floor.

"Don't tempt me," she slaps my ass as she catches up with me.

Lucy is probably my best friend out of the girls here. She took me under her wing when I arrived. I was so nervous. This is not the job I thought I would be doing, but things change and well, I actually really enjoy it.

Me and Lucy walk hand in hand as we begin to scope the floor, stopping at the large tables with the expensive suits sitting there. They're loud and drunk as they lean across, one of them reaching me and pulling me onto their lap.

"Hello sweetness," he purrs, and he smells expensive.

"Hey," I smile, ignoring the way my heart is thrashing inside my chest as I try and push off him, but he pulls me back down.

"You're not going anywhere, how about a little private time for me and you," his dark eyes fall to my parted lips and then to my heaving chest as his hands curl around my hips, smoothing over my skin.

"I have to work the floor first," I breathe, my heart ricocheting in my chest.

"You'll earn more with me than you will on this floor sweetie."

I half laugh, half choke as the smell of his whiskey hits me. Heat blazes across my cheeks and I know he is telling the truth. I would earn a killing if I took him up on his offer.

"No touching," I hear a deep voice boom behind me, and I freeze.

"Sorry man," said suit drops me quickly and I stand to rebalance myself on my stilettos.

I turn and see Dex standing there, arms crossed as he looks between me and the guy. I give a small smile, then tuck my head down as I begin walking, Lucy hot on my heels.

"Fuck," I gasp, looking over my shoulder to see Dex leaning down and talking to the guy.

"You okay?" Lucy asks, her brows pinched.

"Yeah, fine," I nod, letting out a deep sigh.

I'm not okay. Far from it. I don't really get called for privates and honestly, I am fine with it. There are some things I am keeping to myself and not giving away at work.

"Okay cool, come, let's keep moving."

After an hour of walking and flirting, we take a moment and slip our notes into our pouches behind the bar. We don't like to keep walking when we're full of small notes. We feel it puts people off, plus, the really drunk ones forget that they tipped you.

Lance takes our pouches and puts them away before giving us both a water.

"Slow night, isn't it?" Lucy puffs her cheeks out.

"A little," I half shrug.

"I need a fuck; I slept with that pretty little redhead I met at the bar last weekend," she smirks, "she was a rocket in the bedroom."

"Was she now," I hum, my eyes skating round the room.

"Mmhmm, knew what she was doing. She acted all shy at the bar, but once we were in that bedroom..." she trails off then mouths *wow*.

"So hot," Lance groans from behind the bar, "shit, I would have loved to have been there."

Lucy spins, her eyes pinned to Lance, "You couldn't handle me," she winks.

"Try me," Lance bites back.

Lucy becomes quiet for a moment. "Don't tempt me, I'm horny as hell and I've seen your dick before; I mean, I've had better but yours is definitely adequate enough to get me off," her blue eyes trail up and down Lance's body as she slowly licks her top lip.

I giggle as I watch the both of them going back and forth when suddenly I am frozen on the spot. I hear him before I see him.

"Well, this is a funny looking hospital."

Shit.

CHAPTER TWO
ARIZONA

I can't move.

I am anchored and my eyes are pinned to my dad's best friend.

The guy I have been staying with the past few months.

Shit.

His eyes burn into mine; his jaw is tight and I want the ground to swallow me up. Whole.

He steps towards me, and I feel myself shrink. My heart is racing in my chest and I know he is going to rat me out to my dad; no doubt he'll throw me out on the sidewalk with all my stuff.

"Ahem," Sasha clears her throat, her foot tapping on the floor, her eyes moving between me and Keaton. "If you want to have some time with Arizona, you need to book a private room. I have room four available for the next thirty minutes. Would you like that?" She asks, tapping her long nails on the bar as she waits.

"No thank you, he was just leaving," I try and swallow down the bile and ignore the thickness in my throat.

"Like fuck I was," he grits, his teeth baring for a

moment, and he finally lifts his eyes from mine and I choke on my intake of air. "Give me the room," he pushes his hand through the side of his dark hair, and I know he is frustrated.

"No, honestly, we don't need it." I shake my head from side to side as I move closer to Sasha, but her ice blue eyes flick up to mine and she pouts as she reaches for the keys. It's too late. She drops the keys in Keaton's hand, and he grabs the top of my arm and pulls me towards him.

"Hey, don't touch her like that!" Lucy shouts out, following us.

"I'm not a fucking client, she *shouldn't* be here," Keaton snaps. "Now back the fuck down and stop following me." He growls, tightening his grip and continuing to drag me down the narrow hallway towards the private rooms.

"Keaton," I hiss, trying to drag my arm from his grasp but he just tightens it. "I can't walk that fast in these heels," I stammer out.

"But I bet you can dance just fine in them can't you," his tone is sharp, and I ignore the sting at the back of my eyes. He drops me from his grip, unlocking the door and pushing me through before he slams it behind him which makes me jump.

I stand, fingers interlocked, head dropped, standing there like a naughty fucking schoolgirl who is waiting to be told off.

Keaton just paces up and down the room, one hand in his suit pant pocket, the other covering his mouth.

After what feels like hours, he stops pacing and looks at me. I can see the disappointment that is laced all over his face. Sharp jaw line, pouty lips and stunning green eyes. The devil dressed in Tom Ford.

"What the fuck Ari!?" his temper is valid.

I slowly lift my head up, my wide blue eyes on his.

"Please don't tell my dad," I whisper, because if I speak out loud, he will hear the crack in my voice, and I'll break.

His mouth drops open as if the request I have just asked is out of this world. Is it? I watch his large hand push through his shiny, dark hair, the odd strand of caramel shimmering through. He always looks so hot when he does that. Weak at the knees hot.

"Ari..." he pauses as he looks around the room I'm in. I mean, we pretty them up but they're basically sex rooms.

"Have you used all of this?" My cheeks flame scarlet red and I am mortified. My silence tells him all.

"Shit," he hisses, and now he is back to pacing.

The tension grows but he finally stands in front of me, clasping my face in his large hands and my heart stutters in my chest.

"I won't tell your dad... but in return, I want you to introduce me to Lucy." He licks his lips and they twitch into a soft smirk and my eyes flutter shut as I let out a shaky breath.

I nod.

"Good girl," and my stomach flips as his low, growly voice rasps over me.

He lets me go and I walk towards the door, not looking back as I go to find Lucy. My head spins quickly as thoughts whizz through.

All my dad's friends are hot.

I wasn't blind.

But there was always something about Keaton that I gravitated towards. It's a no-go zone for both of us.

He was my dad's best friend.

It was always the five of us. Me, Dad, Nate, Keaton and Kaleb. The men that helped bring me up.

But Keaton would never help with diaper changes or anything like that. His help was solely on occasional school drop offs and he was my dance recital cheerleader, but that was only if my dad couldn't make it and it was rare that my dad wasn't there.

My dad always said Keaton wasn't a *kid* kind of guy. Plus, he was married to a witch, and he was with her most of the time so I very rarely saw Keaton until I was in my teens. He had sacked his wife off, or so he says, and he was around a lot more.

He was the definition of tall, dark, handsome.

Beautiful green eyes that looked blue in some lights. Dark, long hair that had a light curl when it grew too long, his skin was lightly tanned and he had a killer jaw. Angled and defined. Sharp and chiselled. Moulded perfectly. He always had girls falling at his feet. He was confident and that oozed out of him.

Lucy runs towards me, a glint of a smile on her face.

"What the fuck, who was that hunk?" she looks past me.

"My dad's best friend..." I trail off.

"*The* dad's best friend..." she wiggles her brows in a knowing manner.

I nod.

"Well... shit," she rolls her lips.

"He said he won't tell my dad," I shrug, "so I suppose that's something."

"It is."

"But..."

"But what?" her eyes are bouncing back and forth between mine.

"He wants me to introduce you to him; for him to keep my secret, that's what he wants."

"Little fucker," she laughs softly, "and you're okay with that?"

"Yeah of course," my voice jumps a little higher, "go for it. Come, I'll take you to him."

I ignore the burn in my throat, the way my stomach coils and tightens as I get closer to where Keaton is waiting.

Knocking softly, I push the door open. He stands with his back to us, Lucy slips past me and Keaton turns to face her.

"Here we go," I hold my hand out and move it up and down showing Lucy's presence.

"Thank you, Arizona," my name rolls off his tongue easily. He steps closer to us, but his eyes are not on me, they're on her.

"So, I couldn't help but hear your little conversation, I am assuming you're bisexual?" Keaton goes straight for her throat, asking her a personal question but Lucy laughs it off.

"Wow, forward much?" she looks at me, her eyes widening before she focuses on Keaton again.

"Well, thought I may as well just ask the question that has been sitting on the tip of my tongue."

"Fair enough. I don't like to put a label on it," Lucy shrugs. "Just if I like someone, regardless of their gender, I'll go for it." I scoff as Keaton stares at her. "But hey, you wanted an introduction. I'm Lucy and I love pussy and dick," she holds her arm out, her small hand right in front of Keaton. I watch for a moment and after a second or so, Keaton shakes her hand.

"Nice to meet you, Lucy." Keaton's lips twitch and I take that as my cue to leave.

My fingers curl round the door handle as I tug it down but as soon as my foot oversteps the threshold, I hear

Keaton call out, "Go home Arizona, you don't work here anymore."

I raise my brows. The fucking nerve.

I turn round and plaster a wide smile across my lips.

"Fuck you Keaton," I flip him off then storm down the hallway.

Fucking asshole.

I am seething. Anger consumes me whole as I march back onto the floor.

"All okay?" Sasha asks and I hold my hand up at her.

"Put me on the stage with Sage."

"Sorry?" She gawks at me.

"You heard me, put me on the god damn stage."

I surge forward, my legs weighted as I continue. I seek out Sage, sitting at the bar and taking a mouthful of her drink, Dex sitting next to her, his large hand resting on the small of her back.

"Dance with me?" I am fully aware that I sound crazy. But I need out of my head. I can't think of Keaton fucking Lucy.

"Now?" Sage beams at me before looking over her shoulder to Dex.

"Yup, Sasha is getting the stage ready. I need out of my head, please..." my voice cracks on my plea.

She sees the vulnerability all over my face.

"Okay baby face, let's do this." She jumps off the stool but spins and kisses her beautiful beau before she links her fingers through mine and drags me out back to the changing rooms.

Sage has borrowed a pair of black platform stilettos, and she looks every bit amazing in her high waisted wet look leggings and black cropped top. I'm still wearing my silver bra and thong. My chest heaving, my breasts spilling over the flimsy material.

"You okay?" Sage asks, sensing my mood.

"I will be," I smile.

"Okay," Sage goes quiet for a moment as Sasha begins talking.

"You okay with just dancing? We can work on pole tomorrow?"

"Sounds perfect," she beams just as Sasha calls us out on stage as *Worth It – Fifth Harmony* begins playing.

My skin prickles and my heart thumps but I swallow all of that down as I'm pulled onto the stage by Sage.

"Follow my lead," she whispers, and I nod, "eyes on me." A small smirk lifts at the corner of her mouth and she winks slowly. Her fingers lace through mine as her hips begin to sway and I hear the cat calling start.

Sage owns the stage. She knows what she is doing.

Spinning me off her arm, my hips begin rotating slowly as my fingers skim across the soft skin on my throat, trailing between my breasts as I tease the guys in the front row. Sage drops down on all fours, crawling to the edge of the stage where Dex is standing center. Swinging her legs round, they hang off the side and she reaches for his hair, pulling him between her legs as she lowers her mouth over his.

My heart thumps.

She swings around, standing quickly and pressing her body against mine. Her head dips into my neck, her lips brushing lightly across my skin. I let my head fall back, my arm snaked round her waist as I let her take the lead. Her hot mouth moves across my collarbone, down my chest and her hand presses against my sternum. I lean back, molding to her silent commands. Her mouth is off me, and I roll myself up and turn so my back is against her front. Sage's hands grip onto my hips as my ass rolls against her and I lower myself down, hands pressed against the floor as I continue wiggling over her. Rubbing her hand over my bare ass, she slaps it gently which causes a little roar from the expensive suits and I smirk.

Rolling my body up in a slow, seductive way, Sage spins me round to look at her, her head pressed against my forehead as we pant. Stepping apart, legs part slightly as we roll our hips, lowering to the floor. Knees pressed against the cold surface, we widen our knees, dropping down so our chests are low, our asses in the air for just a moment. Sage stays in the downward dog position, but I lay flat, legs straight and roll onto my back. Perching myself on my elbows I smirk at her and I see her lips widen into a smile. She drags herself across the floor, moving to her knees as her head rolls round, her long, silky black hair cascading down her back before her eyes land back on me. Turning my head to look at the crowd, all eyes are on us. But then I see his.

Sparkling green eyes shining and standing out in a room full of people, and they're all I can focus on.

Hard jawline. Tight and wound.

Eyes ablaze with something dark and hot and I feel myself quiver.

"Eyes on me," Sage snaps me out of it and I nod softly and quickly so it's only her that notices.

Her small, soft hands rest on my legs that are stretched out in front of me before she tightens her grip, pushes them up into my chest and spreads them wide. Her body is over me, her hips rolling as her hand pushes against my heaving chest so my back is flat against the floor. Turning once more, my eyes seek him out and my lips part, but her fingers grip my chin softly and she turns my face towards her.

"Stay with me, nearly finished," she dips down, our lips brushing, and a giggle slips past my lips as her hair veils us from their greedy eyes. "It's all an illusion baby girl, they have no idea what is going on between us," she winks and seductively pulls her hair away from our faces, then drags it over the other side of her neck so now they can see everything. She lowers her finger on my bottom lip, trailing it slowly until her spare hand is curled around my neck as she leans across my body, her ass vibrating and twerking to the music. The last chorus of the song wraps around the club and her body rises and so does mine. I arch my back off the floor but leave my head so it's hanging as Sage's fingers grip onto the small bit of material between my bra, dangling me as she kneels between my spread legs. Her grip loosens and I push myself back, scissoring my legs in rotation as I roll onto my front, and Sage is there, behind me, gripping my hips and pulling my ass into her. One last roll of my ass against her and I slowly lift from the floor, both on our knees, my back against her heaving front as we turn to face the audience, my chin lifting off my shoulder a little more as she edges her lips closer to mine. Before our lips can even touch the curtain falls and the men cat call, a thunderous applause filling the room and I spin to face her, laughter consuming both of us.

"Shit, that was..." I stammer.

"Hot!?" Sage beams, standing and holding her hand out for me to take which I do, gladly.

"So hot," I blush and nibble my bottom lip.

"Well gentleman... how about that for your Thursday night? What a treat for you all!" Sasha's voice booms through the microphone.

"You did amazing, thank you for dancing with me." Sage gushes as she pulls me in for a cuddle.

"Thank *you* for dancing with me," I laugh, "I don't think I have ever felt that confident on stage before so honestly, thank you."

"You're an amazing dancer," she lets go of me and my cheeks pinch.

I step back and inhale deeply.

"So who got your attention in the crowd?" she asks and my mouth pops open before I close it again.

"Um, it's complicated," I laugh as I push my fingers through my hair and away from my face.

"When is it not?" she raises her brows, "Mine and Dex's relationship was complicated, but look at us now," she smiles and her eyes glass. Do you know when you just look at someone and can tell how in love they are? Well, that's Sage and Dex.

The curtain pulls open and Sasha holds her arm out as we walk towards her.

"I think we need to make this a tradition. Frisky Thursday? Thirsty Thursday?" Excitement consumes Sasha, she can hardly control it. "Thirsty Thursday!" Sasha calls out again, "I think I like that, would you guys like to see some more of what Sage and Arizona put on stage tonight again?" and the guys clap. "Then it's settled; Arizona... get me a song list and we will see if I can make Thursday evening yours," she gives me a soft nod before she turns her mic off and the DJ puts low background music back on.

"Check you out, possibly your own spot," Sage nudges into me, bumping my shoulder with hers.

"I know," I whisper, and I finally let my eyes lift to where Keaton was standing. He hasn't moved. "Not sure if I can do that again with someone else though," I admit.

"Of course, you can, we can practice whilst I am here. I'm sure one of the girls would like to dance with you."

I just nod. His eyes are still on me and I can feel the tension brewing thick and fast between me and Keaton.

Letting my eyes drop, I turn towards Sage when I see Dex whisk her up, Sage's legs wrap round his waist as he carries her off stage and I smile.

Letting out a deep sigh, I move to the side stage and make my way to the locker room. I needed a moment to catch my breath.

Keeping my head down until I am away from the stage, I press my back against the wall and let the cool walls blanket my skin in a cold chill. My eyes flutter shut, my breaths shallow and my erratic heart finally begins to slow.

I don't even need to open my eyes to know he is here. I can feel him. My breath stutters on my intake.

"What the *fuck*?" he rasps, and I don't know if his tone is angry or shocked.

I turn my face to look at him, my eyes roaming up and down his stupid body.

"Why are you even here? I've been here a year and never seen you," I hiss.

"Someone I know mentioned it, kept telling me about this pretty, curly haired beauty that has caught his attention and for some reason, I was curious."

I roll my eyes.

"And you came to check her out, did you?"

He says nothing.

I scoff, shaking my head from side to side.

"I didn't enjoy seeing you up on that stage," he steps closer to me, but he is cautious.

"I don't give a fuck," I shrug my shoulders up and turn to face him, his eyes roaming over me and suddenly I am conscious that I am in nothing but fishnets and lingerie. Spinning, I unlock my locker and grab my stuff, dropping my bag to the floor and pulling out my sweats and oversized tee.

Silence gravitates around us whilst I dress. I need to get home. I need to get away from him.

"You're not doing that again, I don't care if Sasha gives you the slot. I'll keep your little secret about you working here, but I will not have you up there doing that again," his tone has bite to it.

My eyes widen.

Slamming my locker shut, the loud bang echoes around the small room as I step towards him.

"Sorry?" I raise my brows high in my head.

"You heard me, I don't need to repeat it."

"Fuck you Keaton," I close the gap between us now, "you're not my fucking *daddy*. Fuck off," I barge past him, intentionally knocking into him as I walk down the hallway and out into the dark night.

Asshole.

CHAPTER THREE
ARIZONA

I'M SHOWERED AND DRESSED IN BLACK MATCHING LINGERIE. THE lace bralette just about covers my chest, my nipples constricted against the thin material. The matching thong panties are crotchless, just like he always asks for.

Extensions pull at the root of my hair as I make my shoulder length hair skim down to my waist. I've covered my skin in a light shimmer moisturizer that smells of salted caramel and sandalwood. Sweet and musky. It smells amazing.

Placing my laptop down on my desk, I reach over and grab my backdrop from the side of my bed, pulling it up and hanging it from the small hook on my ceiling to cover the headboard and back wall of my bedroom. A light yellow now covers the once greige wall and my black metal headboard.

Sighing, I turn to face the door and quietly slip the lock across. Not that Keaton ever comes in unannounced, but you never know.

I still for a moment when I hear heavy footsteps followed by a slam of his bedroom door.

What a prick.

Shaking my head, I switch my laptop on and reposition the camera, then step back to the edge of my bed to make sure I am in the screen.

Perfect.

Standing once more, I quietly move to my bedside drawer which now sits behind my back drop and I grab the medium size, leather washbag from inside of it and drop it onto my bed. I unzip it and see a small selection of my toys.

Small crystal dildo.

Bullet.

Blindfold.

Handcuffs.

I bend down, reaching for the bigger bag under my bed and grab my white vibrator.

I inhale a deep breath and my laptop beeps to let me know he has entered the chat. My skin prickles. Stepping towards the laptop, I click into the screen and slide open the drawer of my units, reaching for my mask, then laying it down carefully next to my laptop. It's always been this way. I can't see him. He can't see me. I pick up my contact lenses, opting for dark brown and place them in, hiding the true color of my eyes.

Picking up the black mask, I slip it on and tie the silk ribbon ties under my hair and around the back of my head. Stepping aside, I give myself the once over in the floor length mirror. Black lace bralette that hugs my full, round breasts. Suspender belt wrapped around my waist and thin, satin ribbons attached to stockings. I'm bare under my crotchless, lace panties and I feel sexy and brazen. Something about slipping into a hidden identity makes me feel so much better. My eyes lift and focus on the pretty masquerade mask. One side of my face is completely

28

covered, the black decorated in a pattern with glitter that trails down and around the eyes of the mask and onto the cheek. The full lips of the mask are coated in glitter and sparkle under the dim spotlights of my bedroom. The right side of the mask is open, but covers my eye and shapes off over half of my cheek. It's pretty and makes a statement.

Inhaling on a shaky breath, I collect my laptop from the side unit and place it on the bed desk, where I sit and brace myself for my evening. I love this job, the money is good, and I like that it's a secret; well, Lucy knows but no one else does.

Hovering my fingers over the keyboard, I see *TallDarkandHandsome's* message.

Evening little vixen, how are you?

I smile while typing a response.

I am great, looking forward to spending some time with you.

Let's get started then shall we? ;)

My cheeks pinch and I know I am going to have my work cut out tonight. He always pushes for that little bit more and honestly, I love it. I love playing into his hands, I love that he is dominant and I'm submissive to him. Even alone in my room, he is the one that controls everything. I lean forward, clicking my webcam on and it takes a moment for it to kick in.

There she is. My girl. Kneel up, let me see what you're wearing.

He types and I shuffle back, kneeling up so he gets me in full view.

Simply stunning.

My cheeks turn crimson beneath my mask.

So beautiful, show me love, show me how beautiful you look whilst your fingers play with your pretty pussy.

I fall back, one elbow pressed into the mattress and my legs wide so he can see all as I slowly begin to trail my hand down my neck, skimming my fingertips over my collarbone. I tease him as I let them skim over my hardened nipples that are straining against the lace material of my bralette and my head rolls back, my eyes fluttering shut for just a moment as my breath catches. My fingertips glide past my sternum, dipping into my belly button then skating them lightly across the front of my pubic bone before letting them slip between my pussy lips as I rub softly over my clit. Lifting my head, I hear the ping of his messages.

Fuck. So fucking pretty. You're glistening.
Such a good girl listening to my instructions.
Eyes on me Vixen.

My dark blue contact covered eyes connect with the camera and I moan as I slide my fingers into my wet opening.

Does that feel good? Just imagine I'm there with you, knelt behind you as you lay between my legs, your back

*to my stomach. My fingers slip in and out of your tight
little cunt with ease, teasing you as I rub your clit. I
would have you in front of a mirror, watching as I get
you off.*

"Fuck," I moan out. I have no idea what this dude even
looks like but still, my chats with him get me hot and
bothered, turning me on in an instant and causing a puddle
of mess on the floor.

My chest heaves up and down, I can see everything on
my screen and my skin prickles in a cool sweat.

Keep going Vixen, let me see that pretty, wet pussy come.

I force my eyes shut and let my mind wander to a place
it shouldn't, but it helps push me to my climax, my fingers
rubbing in slow, lazy circles.

I need you to come little Vixen.

My eyes focus on the screen, re-reading his messages
and feeding off his desire when I hear a bang on my
bedroom door, my head snapping to the side as they
widen.

"Arizona!" Keaton calls, banging a little harder now and
I see that my little companion has signed offline.

Shit.

Slamming the lid of my laptop down, I grab my dressing
gown and wrap it round my slender body and turn back to
look over my shoulder at my toys, I toss my blanket over the
top of them then rip my mask from my face and kick it
under my bed.

Bang bang bang.

I rush for the bedroom door, pulling it open slightly, my cheeks flustered with a shade of pink as my eyes catch his.

"Hey, what's up?" my tone is cool. Too cool for someone I am seething with.

His eyes burn into mine, his jaw wound tight as he stands defensively.

"Your dad..." he pauses for a moment, one of his large hands rubbing round the back of his head, and I can tell he feels awkward.

"Not interested," I go to slam the door on him but his large, booted foot slips into the gap, stopping me.

"Ari, you can't freeze him out much longer..." Keaton pauses, and I watch as his throat bobs.

"Watch me," my brows pinch as I place my hands on his chest and shove him back. He tumbles, losing his footing just enough for me to shut the door in his face. "Stop trying to fix it Keaton, it's not your job to fix it!" I shout through the thick partition that separates us.

I don't miss the growl that vibrates through the floorboards, and I can't help the small smirk that pulls at the corner of my lips.

I'm not having my dad thinking he can use Keaton as a mediator. I will talk to him again, but only when I am ready.

I press my back against the door, and I rub the ache out of my chest.

"Ari," I hear the exasperation in Keaton's voice.

"Please," I beg, forcing my eyes closed and a tear escapes, rolling down my cheek and off my chin before it falls into the carpet beneath me.

"I'm just trying to help."

"I don't want or need your help, Keaton." I'm exasperated too and I hear him heave a sigh. "You want to help?" I finally say after a long pause, swinging my bedroom door open. "Stop trying to make things right between me and my dad and leave me alone," I don't miss the way the hard façade slips off his beautiful face. He sinks back and as much as I want to beg him not to leave me alone, I don't. I slam the door in his face and try to forget this wash out of an evening.

CHAPTER FOUR
KEATON

IT'S BEEN THREE WEEKS SINCE I LAST SPOKE TO ARI. IT WASN'T AS if we weren't talking per se, but we didn't go out of our way to spark up a conversation. I didn't want to fall out with her, I didn't want to fall out with Titus and somehow, I have got myself caught in between their feud.

Scrubbing my face, I grab the keys off the side table and slam the door behind me. I have no clue if Ari is at work or whether she is asleep upstairs. Glancing at my watch as I walk down the steps onto the sidewalk, it's just past eight a.m. Unlocking my car, I slip in and start the engine. Another monotonous day at the office with my three best friends. Work was slow, and after the epic fuck up with Wolfe, we all had targets on our backs. Titus is trying to keep Amora safe, but at the same time be there for us with work. We can't find him without Titus and until he gets his head fully back in the game we can't really focus on the job in hand.

Kaleb has decided that he doesn't want to take on any new clients until this is rectified and honestly, I don't blame him. We have no idea just what extremes Wolfe will plan to get to Titus and Amora. Hoax jobs, fake clients... the list is endless.

Pulling onto the quiet side road, I drive on autopilot towards the office, but all the time Arizona clouds my mind. I don't want to fall out with her, but I don't want to go against Titus because of her. My loyalties lie with him. He wants to make things right and I know deep down he deserves that. I have loved living with her, a little bit too much if I am honest with myself. I don't love that I can't bring girls home freely, but it's a consequence I can get on board with.

She is a ray of light, and she brings a little bit of warmth into my life. I know people may find it weird seeing as she is one of my best friend's daughters, and yes, I knew her as a baby, but I didn't get involved in any of that. I made it clear from the get-go that I would be on drop off duties and the occasional ballet class ride as well as her cheerleader for when her dad couldn't make her dance recitals. That's as far as my *parental* duties went. I had a wife at the time, unlike the other three assholes that I call my family.

A lot of my time was taken up by Satan, so I kind of feel like I am living my young, carefree single days now when I am forty-seven.

Kaleb is settled with Connie.

Titus is cozy with Amora.

And then there is me and Nate.

I like to think we are lone wolves and will keep that title, but me and Kaleb think that Nate has a little side gig going on, but you would never know.

That kid keeps things locked down.

Even *if* you did find out and saw it with your own two eyes, he would still deny it.

Sneaky fucker that one.

I scoff a laugh as I pull into the underground garage, my eyes scanning to the three spaces next to mine.

Kaleb. Nate. Me. No Titus.

Probably running late. Possibly tangled in the sheets with Amora.

Most likely the first one.

Locking the car, I pace towards the elevator and ride to the office in complete silence.

It's not a long ride, but it's enough to appreciate the quiet for a moment or two. I like the silence, my mind is busy most of the time.

As soon as my foot slips over the threshold I see Kaleb's head pop up from my desk, Nate doesn't lift his eyes from his screen, but he does hold his hand up in a shit attempt at a wave.

"Morning fuckers," I run my tongue over the front of my teeth and give them a goofy grin, dropping my bag next to Kaleb and wait as patiently as a toddler for him to move.

"Morning," Kaleb yawns, stretching up and taking far too long for my liking. Leaning closer to him, I give him a quick jab to the ribs which has him folding forward and cursing like a god damn sailor.

I chuckle to myself as he clambers out of my chair then rubs his rib.

"Oh, give over you big pussy," I roll my eyes in the same exaggerated manner as Kaleb reacting to a playful fist.

"You're a big dick," he spits out.

"I have a big what?" I throw a wink at my brother, and he returns my stupid, childish comment with his middle finger.

"What's new?"

Nate finally looks over his computer screen at me and shrugs a shoulder up.

"Not much," Nate's nose scrunches, his messy brown hair wild and he pushes his glasses up the bridge of his nose.

"You're a bunch of boring fuckers; how's the wife Kaleb?"

"Are you that bored Keaton? Seriously, I'm in no mood for your shit."

I turn slowly to face him.

"What's eating you? Connie still refusing to peg you?"

And I hear a low chuckle from behind Nate's screen.

"Don't," Kaleb warns, shaking his head from side to side, hands fisted in his pockets.

"It's all about communication," I continue, ignoring the burning eyes in the side of my head, "you don't ask brother, you don't get." And that's when Titus walks through the door, hand scrubbing at his face, rough stubble across his chin and mouth.

"Nice of you to join us big fella."

"Ignore him, someone put two cents in him and wound the asshole up."

Titus just stands, fingers wrapped round his bag as his eyes bounce between me and my brother.

"What the fuck have I just walked into?" he groans, shaking his head softly as he pulls his chair out and slumps into it.

"A very happy workplace," I chime as I wait for my emails to load. "You okay?" I ask, my brows furrowed as I stare at Titus. He looks tired and washed out.

"I will be," he groans, another hand scrubs over his face.

"Arizona?" I ask, ignoring the way my blood burns when her name slips off my tongue, the way my heart beats a little faster. Should probably just ignore it. Absolutely ignore it.

37

His silence gives me the answer to my question.

"She will come around."

"It's been a while... we're halfway through Amora's pregnancy and they still haven't met."

"Technically a lie, they did meet."

"Keaton," Kaleb warns but I ignore him.

"That's not what I meant," Titus stiffens in his seat.

"I know, but she isn't ready yet," I shrug my shoulders up.

Silence bubbles between us for a while before Titus speaks.

"Is she okay?"

I roll my lips.

"If she wasn't I would have told you, my loyalty lies with you. You're my best friend..."

I hear Kaleb and Nate both clear their throats.

"And you two, for fuck's sake, but I'm not talking to either of you, am I?" I turn in my seat to look at my brother and I see a tug at the corner of his mouth.

Titus searches for something from me but I don't know what.

"She is okay; she is busy working, and when she isn't working, she is studying or sleeping." I'm annoyed at how easily that lie rolled passed my lips.

Titus gives me a gentle nod and a heavy sigh leaves him.

"Is there anything else?" I wanted to double check; he doesn't seem his happy go lucky self.

"I'm tired of this Wolfe shit. I should have killed him when I had the chance, but I fucking spared him and I don't understand why," he slams his hand down on the desk which causes Nate to jump.

"We will find him," Kaleb beats me to it, like a wise old owl who only comes into the conversation when relevant.

"I want him gone before our baby is born," his face tilts down and he runs his index finger over his wedding band.

"Then we better crack on." I give him a weak smile. None of us know where he is. Xavier—Titus's father-in-law and the reason we have an issue with Wolfe—has no idea where he is either. Xavier worked in ways that we never understood, but since he was working with the police he can no longer partake in this little investigation how he normally would.

The silence in the room blankets us as we lose ourselves in the files that we have checked numerous times to try and find something we may have missed.

But alas, like always, we have no luck.

CHAPTER FIVE
ARIZONA

I CLOSE MY LOCKER AND EXHALE A SHAKY BREATH. NERVES WERE rippling deep inside of me and everyone could tell my mood was a little sour.

"It'll be fine, you've got this," Luce pulls me in for a hug and holds me a little tighter.

The thing is, and don't laugh, but I am still a virgin. It has just never happened. And yes, I know I work in a *gentleman's* club, but let's call it what it really is, a strip club, dressed up and wrapped in an emerald, green bow.

I am grateful for Sage, Dex and Rhaegar, but this is not what I had envisioned for myself when I was the little girl in my doctor costume and stethoscope wrapped round my neck.

"I don't feel like I have this," a nervous giggle bubbles out of me as Lucy lets me go. Tilting her head to the side I see a slither of sadness weave through her opal eyes.

"Do you not want to go there?" she asks as she turns her head to look behind her to the narrow corridor that leads towards the back exit.

"I do… but I don't," my head is nodding towards her, but my insides are crippling with anxiety.

"Ross will be on the door, three bangs and you're out."

My nodding grows a little faster, my pulse racing under my skin.

"You're right," I stand a little taller and roll my shoulders back, "it'll be fine," I swallow the large lump down and ignore the way it burns as it lodges itself in my windpipe.

Dressed in a light pink bra and G-string, I pull a white silk kimono over my body and wrap myself up as if it's my security blanket. Taking two small steps, I look at myself in the mirror and blink away the tears that are threatening to leave.

I know what is expected of me in that room. My eyes drag down my body to my silver platform heels before they glide up and focus on my face. Heavy make-up, hazel contacts, long extensions making my hair end at my waist.

"You ready?" Lucy asks as she stands beside me, giving me a warm smile.

"Ready as I'll ever be."

"That's my girl, the car is waiting out back," she gives me an encouraging slap on my bare ass cheek. I turn and begin walking away when she steps up beside me. "Don't forget…"

"Three knocks, yeah I remember," I give her a reassuring smile and disappear down the corridor towards the back of the club.

A blacked-out Mercedes is waiting, and a driver opens the door for me. I give him a curt nod as I slip past him and nestle myself into the seat. My door closes softly before the engine starts and he drives me across town to the smaller club that hosts these kind of private sessions.

The ride isn't long, but it feels like a million miles away when you're nervous. We pull curbside and the driver lets me out and walks with me to the hostess. My eyes land on her for just a moment, my lips part ready to announce my name but she looks down at her tablet in her hand.

"Mr Tall, Dark and Handsome told me to escort you to the room." She gives me a smile and nods goodbye to the driver who disappears behind me.

With each step that brings me closer to him, my heart beats a little harder inside my chest causing my whole body to vibrate with every pound.

My nerves settle slightly when I see Ross. He bounces between both clubs, and I adore him.

He steps forward and gives me a curt nod. Tall, extremely handsome, too handsome to be working as a bouncer in a strip club. Dark curly hair, sharp jaw and crooked nose. He is every bit delicious.

"Ari," he smiles warmly at me, his dark brown eyes glisten as they sweep over my body. My cheeks blush. "When you going to let me take you out?" he asks just as I get to him.

"How about Friday, five o'clock? It's my day off," I give him a shrug of the shoulder as I try and fail miserably to act nonchalant.

"I'll see if I can get my shift changed."

"Perfect," I flash him a wide, toothy smile as he hovers his hand over the doorknob.

"Three knocks, remember?"

"Three knocks," my voice trembles as I swallow the nerves. I turn to face the dark green door, his fingers finally tightening round the gold brushed doorknob and my heart is in my throat.

"I'll be right outside."

42

I nod, because I can't say anything else. I need to get my game face on. I need the money, I can't live with my dad's best friend much longer.

I wanted the fresh start, and this was how I was going to get that start a lot sooner.

The handle twists and I step into the deep emerald green room, with low lighting, the bed in the middle of the room and my eyes scan to see where my mystery man is.

"Hello..." but the room is empty. I spin towards the closed door and look in confusion.

What the fuck was going on?

Turning back towards the bed, I slowly walk over and see a note, a black, silk blindfold and a single, black rose.

Reaching for the note, I flip it over and read.

Put on the blindfold and wait for me, xo.

Anxiousness swims around in my stomach but I do as the note says. Placing the blindfold over my head, I familiarize myself with the room before I cover my eyes and inhale deeply as I wait.

"So..." his deep voice floats across the room, "we finally meet, little Vixen." His soft an American accent rasps, and I shiver as an ice breeze dances up and down my spine.

"How did you find me?" I whisper into the room, wrapping my arms around myself.

"I have my ways."

I nod.

"Why the blindfold?" a nervous laugh escapes me.

And that's when I hear his shoes move across the floor, and within seconds he is behind me, hands on my hips as his fingers fumble to the tie that is wrapped around my kimono, his lips next to my ear.

"When you lose one of your senses, the rest heighten."

My breath catches at the back of my throat as his fingers dance across the bare skin of my stomach, teasing and skimming his fingertips along the hem of my G-string.

"I didn't want to see your pretty little pussy over a screen anymore," his whispers become more ragged, his chest rising and falling as he slips his hand into the front of my underwear.

My heart jackhammers against my rib cage, the blood thrashing and pumping round my ears.

"Just breathe, let me work your body little vixen..." he rasps as his fingers dip lower and press against my clit.

"We have the whole night, we don't need to rush," I pinch my eyes closed and I can't deny his fingers feel good. I may be a virgin, but I have definitely been touched before.

Widening my stance, a little, his fingers glide between my lips, teasing a finger at my opening and a moan slips out.

"Look at you enjoying this already, I've barely touched you... you're sensitive... just how I like them."

My head rolls forward as his fingers tease at my opening, my nipples harden against the silk material of my bra and I'm not even ashamed that I am enjoying this.

Whimpering when he pulls his hand from my panties, he leaves me standing alone at the foot of the bed.

"Here's what I am going to do to you..." his lips are back against my ear, "I am going to eat your pussy while burying my fingers deep inside of you and just when you're on the brink of coming, I am going to fuck you hard and relentlessly." I stiffen as his knuckles brush across my goose bumped shoulder. "I don't go soft and easy; I fuck how I want to fuck and you will come all over my cock."

He's now in front of me, his fingers digging into my cheeks as he brushes his lips against mine.

"Do you understand me?"

And I nod. Nerves cripple inside of me.

"Good," I don't miss the snarl in his voice as he pushes me onto the bed, his hands grip onto my knees as he widens them so I am at his mercy and within seconds, he is putting me through the paces, his tongue pressed against my clit, his fingers buried deep inside of me causing me to stretch and burn around him. Just when I feel everything in me wound so tight that my back arches off the bed, the sound of foil tears and as quickly as he pulls his fingers out of me, he impales his thick cock deep inside of me.

I gasp, my lungs burning and begging for the air that he so cruelly snatched from me when he shredded every piece of my virginity away with his harsh pounds, fucking me into the mattress. A hand is wrapped around the base of my throat, the other is pinching the skin on my hip as he chases his own high and I lay, mute. All pleasure gone in an instant and all I have is the burning ache between my legs and the escaped tear that rolls down my cheek.

He collapses on top of me, his face buried in my neck as he catches his breath.

"You were better than I expected," he grins against my skin.

"Thanks," I plaster on a fake smile as I reach for the blindfold, but he wraps his fingers around my wrist and tugs them away.

"Not until I am gone," he whispers as he pushes off of me and I hear him suck in a breath. "You were untouched, well, that's made this evening even better," and I know he is smirking over my body at taking my innocence, but I don't even have a minute to let it settle as he buries himself deep inside of me once more.

I SIT INSIDE THE BACK OF THE CAR COMPLETELY NUMB. IT'S ONE thing when you're behind a computer screen and getting yourself off, but to have them hunt you down and find you to basically use you how they want... maybe if I was more experienced it wouldn't sting as much as it does, but I feel hollow. My heart aches.

Yes, I did want my first time to be special, but that was before I got kicked out of medical school and wound up as a stripper. Once I was in this line of work, my virginity was somehow tarnished, and I felt embarrassed to still have it.

I am wrapped in the driver's coat as my body trembles into the seat. Even if I wanted to, I couldn't make myself stop.

"Ma'am," I see the smartly dressed driver look in the rear-view mirror at me, but I can't even look at him in the eyes. I feel somehow ashamed of what happened. "Are you okay? Do you want me to take you straight home?" I can hear the concern in his voice. He has every right to be concerned. Maybe.

Shaking my head from side to side, I keep my eyes focused on my clasped hands.

Ross ran for me as soon as I was out the room, but I didn't look at him. He grabbed me, a little too hard maybe? My face was stained with tears, and marks blemished my skin. He saw it all. He tried to stop me, but I fought him off, pushing and tugging at him until I was free of his grasp which lead to him walking into the room I had come from.

The car rolls to a stop and this time, the driver turns to face me.

"Are you sure you're okay ma'am?"

My bottom lip trembles and before I give in to the wave of tears that are building behind my eyes, I force my eyes wide and ignore the burn in my throat. My shaky fingers fumble with the inside door handle before I break free of the car and I run into the club, not once looking behind me.

I ignore the commotion and I am grateful that the lights are dim as I keep my head down and walk towards the locker room. I need out of this lingerie.

Not that there is much left of it.

The longer I am alone with my thoughts, the more I am working myself up. He didn't abuse me. He paid for my time. He paid to use me how he wanted. Yet I am letting it belittle me. He didn't do anything wrong.

The thought causes a sickness to roll through me. I throw my body through the door of the locker room and I see Sasha standing there, her eyes scope me in one movement before they focus between my legs. Lucy rushes over to me, her hands on the top of my arms as she searches my eyes for something, anything to give her a reason to why I am acting this way.

"Arizona?" Sasha walks towards me, the panic evident on her face whether this was her fault.

"I'm fine," I finally seem to wake up from my daze.

"Ari... I..."

"Leave me alone Sasha, I am fine. I just need a shower and I need to go home," my voice trembles but I ignore it. I strip out of my clothes in the middle of the locker room and I don't even care that they're all standing here watching me and witnessing me bare.

Willing my legs to move, my muscles ache but it's fine. Of course, it's fine. Even if it wasn't, it was my job, wasn't it.

And this man wasn't a stranger. I had bared myself to him numerous times over a screen; if anything, I was asking for him to find me and use me.

It won't always hurt.

It'll soon be a distant memory.

Twisting the shower faucet, the pipes bang before the water spurts out the head of the shower. I can hear Lucy and Sasha talking quietly amongst themselves, but I force my eyes shut and silence them in my mind. Stepping under the shower, I let the burning hot water scald me and I welcome the burn on my sensitized skin. Reaching for the soap, I scrub my skin until it's red raw. Next is my hair, I pull the clip in extensions from my hair and let them fall into the shower tray. Dragging my nails over my scalp, the pain radiates deep inside of me before I scrub the suds into my hair, letting it lather up before I rinse it.

Cutting the water, I step out and walk towards my locker. No one else is in here now apart from Lucy. My skin still covered in soap suds and silky from the water. My brown hair drips down my back and I let the shiver blanket me.

She stands and walks in front of me towards the lockers and pulls my towel out. I stand, numb to it all when she blankets me in warmth.

"Get dressed, I'll drive you home."

And that's when everything hits me, flooring me in seconds.

LUCY DRIVES ME HOME AND I AM INTERNALLY GRATEFUL. SHE'S pretty. Wavy blonde hair, the perfect little nose, beautiful freckles and killer lips that she proudly tells everyone are filled. She has the perfect pout.

She stays quiet and I know she is dying to ask me about the evening but I'm not ready to say anything yet. She is a little older than me, around twenty-seven, I think. More like Reese's age, my dad's friend's wife. I was the youngest. Then Connie. Only by a couple of months, I think. My mind drifts to my dad and I know how angry he would be if he found out just what my life was like now.

He would be so disappointed. And then seeing him disappointed would disappoint me. Yeah, it would. It would really disappoint me.

My stomach knots when we pull up outside Keaton's. I'm wearing an old, oversized sweatshirt with gym leggings. It's all I had shoved in the back of my locker. My hair was still wet and it's natural wave was beginning to show itself.

"Want me to come in?" Lucy offers as she puts the car into park.

"No, thanks." I grimace as I open the door and step onto the sidewalk. "I'll call you tomorrow okay?"

I don't wait around for her to answer. Nerves cripple me as I climb the steps to Keaton's, fishing around in my bag for my front door keys. Twisting my neck to look over my shoulder, Lucy is still sitting there, I would like to say she was waiting to see if I get in safely, but I can see her texting on her phone. Probably Keaton. Who am I kidding, it'll definitely be Keaton.

I turn a pretty shade of green.

Jealousy does not suit me, especially when the person I am jealous over doesn't even see me like that.

Sighing, I push the front door open, and I am met with darkness.

He isn't home yet and I'm not sure if I am sad or relieved.

Softly closing the door, I press my back against it and close my eyes. My mind becomes a lot quieter, and my heartbeat slows to a steady beat. I step forward, tossing my keys into the bowl on the side table when Keaton rushes through the door, his eyes wide and pinned to me.

"Oh, Ari," he looks confused, his thick brows pinch and form a deep V and I want to run my fingers over his fine lines to smudge them away into nothing.

"Hi," I breathe, my fingers locked together. Dread consumes me.

"I wasn't expecting you... I..." he looks at the closed door behind him before his eyes are back on me. His full lips open and close repeatedly but nothing comes out.

"I had a work thing," I roll my lips, sort of answering the lingering question that is no doubt hanging on the tip of his tongue.

"I didn't think you were working tonight."

"Something came up," I swallow the bile that is thickening at the back of my throat, "how about you?" I ask, my blue eyes volleying back and forth between his, but he breaks contact when his phone begins ringing.

"I had a private client across town," he sighs, clearing his throat and walks past me without saying another word.

A private client?

CHAPTER SIX
KEATON

I SEE THE CAR PULL AWAY AND FURROW MY BROWS, I DIDN'T recognize it. Climbing the steps up to my house, I unlock the door and knock it open with my foot when I see Arizona standing there. Damp hair, wide eyes and waiting like a lost little girl.

"Oh, Ari," confusion laces my tone and my eyes pinch as I take in her appearance. An old, oversized sweatshirt that is far too big for her delicate frame and worn-out leggings.

"Hi," her voice is barely audible as she locks her fingers together in front of her, and I'm ashamed to admit that I let my eyes linger a little longer as I stare into her crystal blue eyes.

"I wasn't expecting you... I..." I turn to look at the closed door, who dropped her off? Was she okay? My mouth parts and closes. I mean, she didn't seem okay but after the day I have had, I don't have it in me to even ask.

"I had a work thing," she rubs her lips together, and it's as if she is trying to guess what is going on through my head.

"I didn't think you were working tonight," I squeeze out as I drop my keys in the bowl, and I feel my body tense.

"Something came up," the words sound pained, her throat bobbing as she swallows. "How about you?" she asks me, her eyes bouncing between mine, but my phone rings in my pocket allowing me to break contact.

"I had a private client across town," I sigh as I fish my phone from my pocket and take that as my cue to leave, walking past her and not looking back.

Once in the kitchen, I gently walk to the doorway and crane my neck around the doorway to see her still standing there.

"Yeah," I say into the mouthpiece of my phone.

"Xavier wants a meeting tomorrow, does that work for you?" Kaleb asks and I can hear Connie singing in the background. I rub the tension from my temples, but it only moves it to the base of my neck before spreading towards my head.

"Sure, yeah," honestly, I wasn't paying attention. I was too busy trying to work out what was going on with Ari.

"Ten, Sarabeth's?"

"Yeah cool," and I cut him off mid-sentence. Leaving my phone on the countertop I pace slowly back towards the hallway, but she's gone.

Resting my hand on the ball of the newel post, I look up the stairs wondering whether I should follow her up. Probably shouldn't. My foot is already on the bottom step as I begin to climb and head for her room. I pause, lifting my hand to knock but retract it back.

Maybe I should just leave her.

Nah.

I knock on her door before I change my mind.

"Go away," and I'm not sure why, but her little temper makes me smile.

I ignore her, of course I do.

Pushing the handle down I walk into her room and see her sitting on her bed whilst cradling a bottle of tequila in her hands.

"That's my tequila," I frown, but my tone is light and playful, but all I get in retaliation is a scorned look over her pretty face.

"Tough," she shrugs her shoulders up and takes a swig, her nose scrunches as she winces.

Folding my hands into my suit pant pockets, I walk over to the bed. The oversized sweatshirt is loose and hanging off one of her shoulders and her leggings are nowhere to be seen.

It's not until I am standing at the side of her bed, my eyes graze across her and I notice red blemishes and scratches on her neck. My back is immediately up, and I kneel on the bed. She stares at me, all wide-eyed and shit. Like a doe trapped in headlights. Gripping her chin, I lift her face up and look a little closer at the fucking marks on her skin.

My blood boils in an instant, my rage simmering at the thought of someone hurting her.

"Who did this to you?" and I fucking growl like a possessed demon, protective over what is his.

She snatches my hand away from her skin and shoves the palm of her hand into my face, pushing me away.

"Don't worry about it," she shakes her head and lifts the bottle to her lips, taking another gulp. "I just want to drink and forget about today... it's not one I want to remember." I don't miss the stutter of her breath when she inhales. That's when I notice her eyes are swollen and red.

Fuck, has she been crying?

"Look..." I sit on the edge of the bed; my eyes focus on just her. "You might not want to tell me what happened, but it's clear that something has..." I pause for a moment and snatch the bottle of tequila out of her hand.

"Hey!" she lunges towards me and tries to grab it, but I stand, holding the bottle above my head and shake my head disapprovingly.

"But just know this," my voice lowers, my eyes darken, "I'll make sure whoever upset you never gets a chance to do it again, do you understand?"

She blinks at me.

"Ari..."

"Yes," she drops her chin, her eyes cast down.

"And I'm always here, if you ever wanna talk..." I try and soften my tone, but I am so fucking angry.

"Can I have my drink back?" she gives me her best puppy eyes along with a pout and my lips twitch, one side lifting into a slow smirk.

"Only if you let me have some with you?"

"Fine," she rolls her eyes in an exaggerated manner, "I didn't want to drink by myself anyway, what a loser." And that's when I see a ghost of a smile on her lips.

ARIZONA

"Oh, fuck off," Keaton bellows and a loud laugh fills the room. My cheeks hurt from laughing, and god, it feels so good to laugh.

"No, I'm serious," I sniffle for a moment as I reach for

my own bottle of tequila, Keaton has moved to scotch. Bad move Keaton. Bad. Move.

"I don't believe you," his head is dropped as he moves it from side to side.

"I'll show you," defiance burns deep inside of me.

"Go on then, show me," his eyes narrow on me and my stomach flips at the way the once light green that is so prominent in his eyes turns to a darker emerald as they dance over me.

"Okay," I clamber off the sofa and sit on my knees in front of him, one of his brows lifts and his lips purse.

"Mind out of the gutter, old man."

His head tips back as he laughs loudly and I swear, it's one of the sexiest laughs I have ever heard.

"Right come on, stop stalling," he shuffles, sliding to the edge of his chair.

Rolling my eyes, I ball my hand into a fist.

"You ready?"

One curt nod confirms his answer to my question.

Placing my hand by my lips, I slowly open my mouth around my fist and make it disappear behind my teeth and Keaton just sits, wide eyed, jaw lax as I sit on the floor with my fist in my mouth.

"Well, fuck," he slaps his thigh just as I maneuver my fist from my mouth, my jaw clicking.

"Ouch," I rub my cheek and get a burst of giggles. "Told you."

"Okay," I sit down next to him on the sofa and take a swig of my drink, it's going down far too easily now. "Truth?" I fire the question at him, and he turns to face me.

"I've never been in love," he takes a mouthful of his own drink and I just stare at him.

"Oh, piss off, you were married to...." I pause for a moment and scratch my head. I have no idea what her name is, to be honest, she was never an important part of my life. "Satan," I settle on that, it is what Keaton and Kaleb call her anyway.

"So? Didn't mean I had to love her."

"So, you just existed in a loveless marriage?"

"Seems that way," he puffs out his cheeks.

"That's pretty pathetic really," I shrug my shoulders up.

"It is, but that's all in the past. I'm not made for love anyway. I'm happy just fucking," and the crudeness of his words makes my cheeks burn.

"Too much info," I smirk, crossing my legs underneath me.

"What about you? Truth?" he asks, taking a mouthful of his scotch.

"Errrr," I think for a moment, "I slept with someone for the first time tonight and it was a fail," I half laugh, half cry. I shouldn't have said that. I know I shouldn't have. I hurt myself a little bit, and Keaton is staring at me weird.

"First time as in with that person or...?" and I know this is strange, this whole evening is fucked up. I'm talking to my dad's best friend about my sex life.

My cheeks burn and I can't look at him. So I drink. And drink.

"No," he whispers, but it's so loud.

"Mmhm," my eyes are still cast down.

"Boyfriend?" his question comes out tight, as if his jaw is clenched, his teeth are gritted.

"Work," I squeak and I know it's going to cause uproar.

"Ari," but the way my name falls from his lip is soft and sweet, and not at all angry like I expected.

"It's fine," I swallow.

"It's not. Do you want to know what it is?" his fingers

grip my chin, and my head is tilted back so I have no option but to look up at him and try not to lose myself in his deep green eyes. The warmth of his breath dusts across my face, the smell of scotch comforting in some way.

"What?" I whisper.

"It's a fucking travesty."

I didn't get a chance to respond. He was in front of me, my face in his hands.

Our lips locked, our teeth clashing and all I can taste is our alcohol mixing as our tongues dance together.

And that's when everything blurred into one.

CHAPTER SEVEN
KEATON

Oh.

My.

Fuck.

I force my eyes open, everything is blurry and hazy, my fucking head is pounding and that loud, high pitched ringing is not helping.

It takes me a minute or three to come to and realize it's my phone.

"Ughhhhhh," is all I can muster.

My mouth is drier than the desert, my heart is racing and my head hurts.

Reaching across to my side table, I see three missed calls from Kaleb, and then I clock the time.

My eyes widen.

"Shit!" I groan.

My phone screams in my hand and I hold it to my ear.

"Where the fuck are you?" my idiotic brother bellows down the phone.

"On my way," I grunt, cutting the phone off and tossing it on the bed.

I stand a little too quickly, my head spinning, and I steady myself. Hand pressed to my forehead, my chin drops.

What the fuck?

I rush forward to my bathroom and get myself showered. I shouldn't have drunk on an empty stomach.

Towel wrapped around my waist, I storm into the bedroom and that's when I see her.

My best friend's daughter.

Lying in my bed.

Next to where I was just laying.

Beautiful wavy brown hair fanned behind her while lying on her front.

Fuck.

I'm by the bed in three long strides and I delicately lift the duvet to see that she is completely naked.

Double fuck.

It's fine.

I reason with myself.

When I know deep down this is far from fucking fine.

I grab my phone, watch and rush to the dressing room.

IN TEN MINUTES, I AM IN MY CAR BOMBING IT TO MY MEETING. Fuck the speed limit. I am late.

Nothing happened between me and Ari. We both just drunk too much and passed out.

That's all.

Too drunk to get into our own beds.

So I offered up mine.

No, I would remember.

Last thing I remember was her showing me how she fit her fist into her mouth.

We must have gone to bed after that.

Yeah, cool, it's fine.

We just went to bed.

Pulling into a parking space outside the restaurant, I reach for my sunglasses. My eyes are like pissholes in the snow. And I stink of scotch.

Jesus Christ.

Kaleb is going to be so pissed.

Climbing out of my car, I slam the door a little too hard and wince as the noise echoes. Storming towards the entrance of Sarabeth's, I ignore the hostess and head for the large table in the private area.

Kaleb stands up and claps me at my attendance.

Condescending cunt.

"Give it a rest," I lift my glasses onto my head.

I look over to see Titus smirking. *Wouldn't be smirking if I were you after what I just left behind.*

Nate is Nate, a small shrug of the shoulders and a wave.

Kaleb is fuming. Standard. Totally understandable.

And then there is Xavier.

"The man, the myth, the legend..." I smile at him, strolling towards him and holding my hand out. "Or so I have heard," he claps his hand into mine and gives it a firm shake. "So, you're the father-in-law," I chime, trying to keep my mind busy. "Titus didn't tell us just how strappingly handsome you are, Xavier."

"Is he always like this?" Xavier turns to look at Titus completely unimpressed and Titus just nods.

"Unfortunately. But then again, he reminds me a lot of you."

"I have never been so offended," Xavier rumbles beside me and I take my seat.

A hot little waitress walks over, hovering for a bit as I browse over the menu.

"Have you fuckers already ordered?"

"No, we were waiting for you," Nate says deadpan not lifting his eyes from the menu.

"Sorry about this morning, was a bit of a weird one." I shake my head.

"I'll have the French toast," Nate says.

"Scrambled eggs with spinach," Titus mutters, "black coffee too."

"I'll have a grapefruit juice," Nate interrupts.

"Avocado toast and a black coffee," Kaleb passes his menu to the waitress.

She eyes Xavier, holding her pen on her pad.

"I'll have the buttermilk pancakes with a side of bacon. White coffee too please."

"Never heard the word *please* leave your mouth before," Titus is on his phone as he throws a little dig towards his father-in-law.

"Don't get cocky, Titty."

Snorting a laugh, I realize the waitress is waiting on me.

"Omelet and a bloody Mary," I close the menu and hand it to her, "and a black coffee too," I show her a toothy grin but she is not impressed.

Probably can smell me.

I can smell me.

The alcohol is seeping through my pores.

"Perfect, I'll get that put in for you," she smiles at the table then walks off.

"So, what is this all about?" I ask, this hangover is killing me.

"Well," Kaleb shuffles in his seat, "if you wouldn't have cut me off last night I would have explained."

"Touché"

"We think Wolfe is in New York," and I don't miss the way Titus stiffens opposite me.

"How come?" I ask just as my drinks are placed in front of me. I am fucking parched.

I down the bloody Mary in one.

Fuck, I needed that.

"I got a ping from his phone."

"Right?" my eyes move between them all.

"Well, that's it," Kaleb snaps and I give a simple 'huh'.

I stare for a moment, their chatter falling a little quieter around me as I see an image of Ari.

Lips touch, tongues dancing.

"I think we should send someone to his hotel," I hear Titus say but I ignore it.

Hands clasped and fingers entwined with hers beneath me.

"I think Wolfe is playing a lot smarter than we think, he wouldn't just show up, he knows where we are," Nate pipes up.

Breathy moans as my body slips between her legs, lips on her neck and feeling her pulse throb beneath them.

"He is right, Wolfe is far from silly. He is calculated and has eyes everywhere. You would never know who worked for him, he has fingers in many pies," Xavier's thick British accent floats around the room.

Exploring mouths and fingers, pulsing and rubbing.

"Why didn't you just put a bullet between his eyes?" Kaleb asks Titus.

Our bodies moving together, skin shimmering in perspiration.

"Because you didn't hear the way Amora was crying. It

wasn't a normal situation. He had a doctor trying to rectify her pregnancy, then he was dead on the floor next to her..."

Moans; erotic, heavenly moans. Dimmed lights but enough to see just what we were creating. Pure magic.

"It was her wedding day, I had to do something..."

Back arching, fingernails clawing down my back, my name slipping off her lips as she...

"Fuck, I left Arizona in bed," my eyes widen, my heart thumping as the realization hits me.

"What the fuck do you mean you left Ari in bed?!" Titus roars across the table.

"No! Oh my god," I scrub my face, "not like that, no..." I shake my head, "I was meant to wake her for her shift, but I was in such a..."

It was exactly like that.

"Who's got the pancakes?" a new waitress asks as she holds the food.

"Sucks doesn't it Titty having a man your age in close proximity to your daughter..."

Might have fucked her after all.

Fuck.

"Can we focus on Wolfe?" Titus snipes.

"Of course," I nod, swallowing the thickness.

I left her in fucking bed. Like a dirty one-night stand.

But it wasn't a one-night stand.

"Do we think Wolfe is after you or is it Titus and Amora?" Kaleb asks, but his eyes are zoned in on me and only me.

He knows.

Stupid twin power shit.

"What the plan then?" Not even sure if I have already asked that question, not even sure if I care.

All eyes are on me.

"We put a fucking bullet between his eyes," Titus groans before the guys agree in unison.

My phone beeps, face up on the table and my eyes glance over at what it reads.

Arizona
Didn't peg you for...

Titus looks thunderous as I snatch the phone up.

"It's not what it looks like," I warn before pushing away from the table and walking out of the restaurant.

Turning the engine on, I sign into my chat app and see that she hasn't been online in a couple of days. Unlike her.

Tossing my phone into the driver's seat, I need to get home.

CHAPTER EIGHT
ARIZONA

JESUS. MY HEAD IS THUMPING, MOUTH DRY AND BODY ACHING. Letting my eyes open slowly, I blink a few times and that's when I realize I am not in my own room.

I roll, keeping the sheet tight to my body and see that I am alone.

In Keaton's room.

"Shit," I whisper, sitting up quickly as my mind whizzes to try and piece some of the night before together.

There was drink. A lot of it.

I burp and feel the burn of tequila rise up my throat.

Gross.

There was also kissing. Also, a lot of it.

Fingers, hands, lips, bodies moving together in a way I've only ever read in my romance novels before being twisted in the bedsheets together.

And yet I have woken alone.

What did I expect? To be wrapped in the arms of my dad's best friend after we slept together.

Double shit.

How could I have been so stupid.

Climbing out of bed, tugging the sheet with me and keeping it clasped to my body, I pad across to my room and find my phone.

And suddenly, I felt angry.

Furious.

Dramatic I know, but here we are.

Snatching my phone up, I click on Keaton's name and type a message.

> **Me**
> Didn't peg you for a runner. Shocking.

I watched the ticks change to read.

Hoped I would have felt a little better. Didn't though. Annoyingly.

Tossing my phone into the bed, I fall into the duvet. I decided right then and there I wasn't going to work today. The thought of walking back into that place and having to explain what happened. Resting up onto my elbows, I see my laptop and my stomach twists and turns.

Not ready to turn that on yet either.

Last night with *TallDarkandHandsome* was not what I was expecting.

I was always in control, until last night.

Blindfolded and used to his advantage.

Even worse he took my innocence.

I wasn't precious about it, just would have rather not had it taken like that.

But now it's gone.

Crumpled and broken.

Falling back again, I lift my arm above my head and fish for my phone. I hadn't even noticed that I had unread messages.

Lucy. Ross. Sasha.

Ugh.

I opened Lucy's first.

> **Lucy**
> Babe, you okay? I'm off today. Wanna hang? Xo.

> **Ross**
> What happened in that room Ari? The driver came back and told me he was worried about you. I'm off tomorrow, want to get a drink?

> **Sasha**
> You stay in Prestige now, no more wandering over to that private club. I need eyes on you at all times. Whatever happened in that room shouldn't have. Whoever that was who summoned you stayed anonymous...

I gave up reading her essay. I was over what happened last night in that room. I was fine. I had my moment yesterday, then I forgot all about it when my dad's best friend's dick was inside of me.

Dropping my phone, I cover my hands with my face and shake my head.

So stupid and reckless.

Don't even know if we used a condom which was even more stupid.

I need to shower. Yeah. I'm going to shower then put this shit show behind me and move on.

Two reckless decisions.

A banging headache and awkward tension between me and Keaton from now on, no doubt.

Dropping the sheet, I walk for my bathroom and scrub myself clean. Flashbacks play over of me and Keaton and I'm not mad about it. My skin feels hot, my breath ragged as they play out in front of me.

Our fingers interlocked, his lips grazing across my jaw, my neck, my collarbone until they're back on my mouth again. Legs wrapped over his hips, our bodies molded into one. Perspiration glistens over our skin, my lips parted as I enjoy every moment. He moves slow, riding me until we have nothing left to give.

Tension is wound tight and I'm mad that I was too drunk to even remember how he felt. How *we* felt together. It's no secret that I crushed on Keaton, but he never knew. I was a pity fuck, I knew that. He knew that. There would never be anything more than this drunken night between us.

Maybe it was hotter in my head. Maybe these flashbacks are just a fantasy and instead of creating magic and sending me to heaven temporarily, maybe we were a sloppy mess who both fell asleep on each other.

Probably more like it.

First—and potentially only—time sleeping with my dad's best friend, and I can't remember it.

What a travesty.

Leaving the shower, I sit on the edge of my bed wrapped in a towel and dry myself. Grabbing clean panties, I slip them up my legs and discard the towel to the floor.

Memories float before my eyes once more, heat blossoming between my thighs. I press my thighs together to try and relieve some of the pressure that is building but nothing stops it.

Trembling fingers reach inside the bottom drawer, fumbling for my vibrator. I'm on the edge of my bed, in just my panties because this hangover is no joke and everything is taking twice as long. But not my want, nor my need.

I tease the head of my toy over my pantie covered sex, and I am aching for release. My stomach tightens into a knot, my skin pebbles in goosebumps as I slip between my folds, teasing at my entrance. Wetness pools inside my panties and my cheeks pinch crimson.

Pressing the on button, I slip the panties to the side and massage my clit softly with the head of the toy. My head rolls back, my hips buck and roll on top of the bed as I slip the vibrator through my pussy, teasing at my entrance before focusing back on my clit.

My mind is loud and heavy and messy with a fantasy of me and Keaton.

A fistful of my hair, one knee on the bed, the other widened as he stands behind me. Back arched, breasts pushed out as he guides his thick cock into me, slowly at first, warming me up.

I moan, my free hand rolling my nipple between my fingers.

Curling a hand round my hip, he holds me still and slips his cock in and out of me with ease, pulling to the tip before filling me to the hilt.

I am stretched and full, tightly wrapped around him and enjoying every moment. My fingers rub over my clit as his pace quickens, fucking me with harshness and I feel everything inside of me wound tight begin to unwind, pressure building until it has no choice but to explode deep inside of me.

Crying out, the vibrator is inside of me, my fingers are on my clit and I come.

Hard.

My body trembles, my head rolling forward, my lips rubbing together as I perish into nothing, but a pool of mess made by my own doing.

Placing my used toy on the bed, I feel so much better. Slowly rolling my head around, my heavy eyes flutter open to see Keaton leaning against the doorway, thick, muscly arms crossed against his chest, eyes so fucking dark they instill a fear deep inside of me.

But I crave his touch. His lips. His eyes on me, burning into the depths of my soul.

"Arizona..." he rasps, and I shiver as his voice fills my room, "what have you done?"

CHAPTER NINE
KEATON

THE WHOLE DRIVE HOME, MY MIND REPLAYED LAST NIGHT OVER ON repeat. I couldn't get her out of my head. Was it as good as my mind was portraying or were we like drunk teenagers who sloppily fell into bed with each other.

Titus was going to kill me.

Never had I thought of Arizona as anything more than my best friend's daughter and yet, here I am, racing home because I need to make sure she is okay. I need to make sure I haven't fucked us up.

Look at me using *us*.

There is no us.

I moved her in with me while Titus was working away. Now, well, somehow, we are this messy, complex and fucked up situation that I have no idea how to navigate. I made the first move. I was the one who made the mistake. Not a mistake though, not in my eyes.

Shit, see, I am so fucked up over this.

I've forgot what right and wrong is, even though deep down I know how wrong this actually is. Of course, it is wrong. It's hardly right, yet I can't seem to stop wanting it to be right. Begging for it actually.

She is all I want to taste. All I am craving. She is all I want to touch, to feel her caramel silky skin under my fingertips knowing she is forbidden. Forbidden is always more fun, right?

Just not when I have a six-foot four best friend who would knock me the fuck out. I'm kidding. He would fucking bury me.

He wouldn't hesitate.

Bam.

Dead.

Gone.

No one would know. They would be told I had gone to live on a farm or some shit, bit like the spin you tell kids when their dog died but you don't want to tell them that their dog died.

"It's okay little Jimmy, Fido went to live on a farm far, far away with all of his doggy friends."

Never got it myself.

Suppose I never had to.

Never had a dog.

Pulling curb side my phone vibrates and I see a message from Lucy.

Fuck it.

Cutting the engine, I snatch my phone out of its holder and read the message.

> **Luce**
> Still on for dinner tonight? Looking forward to that promise you made me a few weeks back.

Scrubbing my face, agitation ignites inside of me.

> **Me**
> Might have to take a rain check, shit loads of work.

A lie.

But fuck it.

I'm over it today already, I don't need to be worrying about her at the moment. Good oral game, pretty face, but not sure if I want to pursue anything more.

Running through the front door, taking the steps two at a time because I needed to find her. I found her easily, but hadn't prepared myself for what I did see though.

Wearing nothing but little white panties, pulled fully to the side exposing her, her fingers circling her clit and a vibrator edging her. Her face is turned up, head rolled back and she is too lost to even notice she has an audience.

That heavenly moan passes her lips and my body reacts in a way it never has before. Craving her. Wanting her.

Leaning against the door frame, my arms are crossed over my chest, my dick hard.

Finally, her head rolls forward, satisfaction painted over her pretty face and after a moment or two of her enjoying her post orgasm bliss, her eyes open and land on mine.

Possessiveness wraps around me like a tailor-made suit. Eyes darken to almost black as I look at her through my lashes. Heart thrashing in my chest, high on adrenaline.

"Arizona..." I rasp and fuck her name sounds a little too good dripping off my tongue. Her doe eyes all wide and wanting, glistening with lust. Her pouty, pink lips parted and wanting to be kissed. "What have you done?"

"I... I..." she stammers, her eyes falling from mine to look at the used toy on the bed. Her trembling fingers skim across to try and cover herself but there is no fucking chance I am missing out.

I am in front of her in three steps. Closing the gap.

Her head tips back, her wondering eyes bouncing between mine as I wrap my hand round her wrist and pull her hand away.

"What are you doing?"

"Enjoying every fucking second of this before I realize what the fuck I am doing..."

I sink to my knees, hands on her hips as I pinch her skin and that's when I notice a deep purple pinch mark on the curve of her hip; I growl. My eyes scan up her body to the marks on her neck.

Anger burns my blood, my hands push inside her thighs as I part them further and bury my tongue inside her pussy, not giving her a chance to try and stop me. Wouldn't let her anyway.

"Keaton... we shouldn't... Oh, fuck, yes... shit," she whimpers into the room, and I smirk.

Sucking her clit, my tongue rubs softly, head moving side to side as I enjoy every fucking second of this.

Looking up at her through my lashes, her lips are parted, cheeks all fucking rosy in a soft pink, just like the cherry blossom trees that line the sidewalks.

Teasing a finger at her opening, her hips roll, silently begging for me to fill her.

"Beg me," I groan, lifting my lips from her for just a moment and seeing how my lips are still connected to her pussy, a string of her arousal tying us together.

"I don't beg," she whispers, her eyes watching with intent.

"You don't come then Blossom." Where the fuck did that come from? Not mad about it though. "It's that simple." My lips brush softly on the inside of her leg, soft, wet kisses coating her warm skin.

"Don't," her voice trembles as I glide my fingers up and down her pussy, avoiding her swollen clit.

"Don't what?" playfulness laces my voice.

Her cheeks flame a deeper pink.

"Tease me," she pants, squirming in her spot.

"Then tell me what you want me to do, there is no point being shy baby. My mouth is inches from your pretty pussy. We're way past shyness." I kiss her clit gently, my fingers caressing her delicate skin.

Not going to lie, I am so close to giving in. Her pussy is my drug. Highly addictive. Craving it constantly.

"Keaton..." she whispers, my warm breath dancing over her sensitive clit.

"Beg," my voice comes out needy and I am the one on my knees begging for her to let me continue eating her cunt. I am famished. "Beg me baby, I *need* to taste you again."

She quivers, her bottom lip being dragged in by her teeth.

"Taste me, fill me, just..." and she doesn't even get a chance to finish her plea as my tongue is on her clit, my fingers slipping slowly into her tight pussy. "Yes," she pants, her fingers tightening on the ablaze sheets beneath her.

I coax her orgasm, the tip of my curled fingers rubbing her g-spot causing her back to arch, her tits pushed out. Kneeling up and instantly regretting moving my mouth off her pretty pussy, I lock my tongue round her pert nipple and treat it to the same attention as I did her clit while my fingers are still buried deep inside of her.

"This can't happen again," she whispers against my lips and the need to fuck her barrels over me.

"I know," I murmur against the skin of her chest, gliding my lips up to her neck.

"We need to promise."

"Promise," I muster, and I have already decided that I am going to break that promise. A lot, most likely.

Her fingers fumble at my fly and I remove my fingers out of her, pushing them to my lips as I suck them clean.

Her eyes widen when she frees my cock from my pants.

"Condom," she licks her lips, breathy moans filling the room as I take a moment to just admire her.

Turning, I walk towards my bedroom and give no fucks that my cock is resting against my stomach as I raid my nightstand.

This is not what I had planned when I drove home from work.

I wanted to actually sit and talk to her.

Yet, here I am again. Crossing every fucking line. Man, what am I talking about; there is no fucking line. The line is gone, I crossed that line hours ago. It's nothing but a mere distant memory.

Kicking my pants off as I walk into the room, I toss her the condom as I fumble with the buttons of my shirt. She is up, on her knees resting on the bed as her small hands skim up my chest and I don't miss the way my skin burns at her touch. In a good way though. Her hands travel up as she pushes my shirt off my shoulders.

My hand clasps her face, eyes falling to her begging lips. They're not begging long.

This is intimate. Too intimate but I don't care.

My lips are on hers, her arms locked around my neck as our bodies are pressed together, heart thrumming under our skin. She trails her hands down my body until she's rolling the condom down my hard cock and I am foaming at the mouth to be inside of her.

Laying her down, her legs parting, my hands fall either side of her head.

"This time, I am going to savor every moment," I whisper against her lips just as I slide into her in one, swift hip roll. She gasps, her hands on my cheeks as she pulls me down to her lips, legs wrapped around my back and possessiveness riles up inside of me as I ride her into the mattress. Hard and punishing but not in a 'I hate you' way.

No. More in a 'I can't get enough of you' way.

The best fucking way.

CHAPTER TEN
ARIZONA

It had been a week since my encounter with Keaton. And we have kept to our promise, sort of. It's more him than me. But there has been no sex. Just everything in between.

I took a leave of absence from work and to be honest, it has done me the world of good.

I like my job, I don't love it, but I am comfortable there, but after what happened I just needed a break and as long as when I go back I am only up on the stage and with the girls, I'll be fine.

Walking towards the entrance of *Jack's Wife Freda*, Connie had arranged lunch, and I am *sooo* looking forward to it. It's been a hot minute since we have had the chance to sit down and catch up.

The autumn air is beginning to get a nip to it, and I miss summer already. Yes, it's hot and humid, but I would take summer over winter any day.

Pushing through the door, I undo my light trench jacket and search the restaurant. I'm wearing a black skort, knee high heeled boots and a white blouse vest. Maybe a little over done for lunch but I felt like I had a spring in my step.

I spot Connie straight away.

Long brown hair that sits at her waist, beautiful dark hazel eyes and a figure to die for. Sitting next to her is Reese. Honey blonde hair and opal eyes with glowing tan skin. Tall, lean, hardly any boobs but I'm a little jealous. No need for a bra and she can lay on her front with no problem.

Walking up to the table, Connie stands up with a glisten in her eye as she pulls me in for a cuddle.

"Oh my god, Ari you look amazing!" she compliments me, and I hug her back.

"As do you," I beam, and she does. She's wearing a little capped sleeve scallop necked cream tee, high waisted skinny jeans and chunky doc martens. She looked good. Happy. Glowing.

Loved that for her.

Reese scooted out of her chair and wrapped her arms round my neck, embracing me.

"Totally gorgeous. We've missed you. Brunch just hasn't been the same without you," she sticks her pouty bottom lip out as she steps away from me and takes her seat opposite me, her British accent thick. She wears a white long-sleeved bodysuit, high waisted mom jeans and white sneakers.

"I know, I've just been swamped with work."

Not technically a lie.

"We get it," they both nod in unison.

Reese works with Killian, which is Connie's dad, but also her husband. I scrunch my nose up at my thoughts. And Connie was their nanny for Celeste, which was her baby sister.

"So," Reese browses the menu, her perfectly shaped brows lifting, "how are things?" she peeps over the top of her menu, nose turned up, eyes cast down.

In other words; *have you sorted it out with your dad yet*?

"Standard," I half shrug, picking my menu up and looking for what I fancy.

Unfortunately, six foot five, dark and handsome dad's best friend isn't listed under lunch, and I let out a sigh, suppose I'll have to settle for the prego roll.

Crying shame really.

"When will you sit down and talk to him?" Connie asks very blasé, as if the question is a routine one and not one out of nosiness.

"No idea, not interested to be honest."

"I don't believe that," Reese lays her menu on the table, blinks a couple of times and I chew the inside of my lip.

"I love my dad, of course I do. Adore him. I'm just not ready yet. He hid stuff from me, he could have picked up the phone and been like '*oh hey, guess what...*'"

Connie puffs out her cheeks.

"Do you know what bugs me more is that he told *everyone* else before me. That's what cuts me up. It isn't about him being with Amora. I am glad he has found someone, I really am. He deserves it all," I pause for a moment, "but he could have told me, yet he chose not to. I was forgotten about."

"I get it..." Connie reaches across and places her hand on top of mine.

"Oh yeah, I forget that Reese was fucking your dad behind your back."

And Reese chokes on her water, spitting it out onto the table, eyes wide.

"Ari," Connie rolls her eyes, lifting her hand and grabbing some napkins to mop up the water while Reese is trying to catch her breath.

"I didn't know he was her dad in my defense."

I laugh, shaking my head from side to side just as the waitress comes over.

"What can I get ya?" she looks between the three of us, smiling as she jots down our order.

We fall into more casual conversation while eating, and it's so good to catch up with them without it being too heavy. By the time lunch is eaten, we're on our second pitcher of margaritas.

"Let's not leave lunch so long next time yeah?" Connie says filling her glass to the rim.

"Work has just been kicking my ass," I say, sipping my own drink. I mean it's not a lie, it's just not at the hospital.

"Well, you need to make sure you're getting a breather, having fun..." she wiggles her brows.

"I am having lots of fun I'll have you know," and that gets both of their attention, their eyes pinned to me and I give them a half shrug.

"Ohhhhh, I see," Connie purses her lips.

"Is he a hot doctor?" Reese edges closer, elbows resting on the table.

"Who knows," I keep my answers vague.

"Is this a potential boyfriend or just casual?"

Pouting my lips I look at both of them. I can't say what I want to, which would be *casually fucking my dad's hot as fuck best friend*.

"Just a casual thing, quick hook ups, that kind of thing," I sit back against my chair.

"Well, cheers to Ari having hot, casual sex." Connie raises her glass just as I see Reese's eyes widen behind me. Connie abruptly sets the glass back down, slamming her mouth shut.

I feel my skin prickle as I slowly look over my shoulder and I want the ground to swallow me up.

Kaleb, Keaton, Nate, Killian and you guessed it, my dad.
Oh. My. Fuck.

I slide down in the chair, cheeks flaming red.

"Oh shit," Reese whispers, but gets a nervous giggle and I kick her shin under the table. Connie hides behind her menu.

"No point fucking hiding, they have already seen us," I hiss through my teeth.

"How did they find us?" Connie whispers to Reese, her eyes not moving from the men in front of her.

"Killian has that find my phone thing."

"Course he does," I roll my eyes, "fucking possessive demon man."

"Ladies," Keaton's dark, delicious voice licks at my skin like a flame, marking my cheeks in crimson.

I ignore him, sitting a little taller.

"Hi," Connie squeaks just as Kaleb walks across, leaning down and smiling at her, his lips pressing against hers.

"Hey baby," he croons.

"No public affection with my daughter, thank you," Killian reaches for Kaleb's shoulder and pulls him up.

Kaleb just chuckles and shakes his head.

"Ari..." My dad's voice floats across and I stiffen.

"So, this was real nice but I think I am going to chip off now," I smile, reaching into my bag for some dollars to throw in the middle of the table.

"Hey, no, don't go... I'll go," my dad's voice trembles, and I close my eyes, ignoring the burning lump in my throat.

I ignore him. Putting my money on the table, I scoot out of my chair, and walk straight for the door, not looking back.

I stand on the sidewalk, arm out as I try and flag a taxi.

"Hey, hey," Keaton jogs up behind me, reaching for my elbow he tugs me round to face him.

"Was this some ambush plan? Walk into where we are having lunch like some coincidence?" I tug my arm out of his grasp.

"No, it wasn't like that," Keaton closes his eyes for a moment, head hung low. I cross my arms across my chest.

"Do you know what? I'm tired. I have work tonight, just go in there and enjoy your lunch." Exasperation is evident in my tone.

"Blossom..." Keaton's eyes widen, his head up and hand tucked round his neck.

Heat rises within me at the nickname. He only called me that during sex. Sex with Keaton is... hot as fuck sex.

Ugh.

Stupid Keaton and his perfect dick.

It's all I can think of.

Maybe his dick imprinted on me.

I see a taxi coming, my arm is stretched out as it slows and pulls against the sidewalk.

"I'll see you at home," I don't even look at him as I slip into the back of the taxi.

He just stands, hands folded inside his suit pants, but his eyes don't leave mine until we're pulling away.

KEATON

"Blossom..." the nickname rolls off my tongue and I instantly regret it.

Do I?

She just stares, absent for just a moment and I hate that

she felt ambushed. I mean she was, it wasn't a coincidence but she knows that. Of course, she does.

"I'll see you at home," her voice is soft as she turns her body away from me and slips into the back of the waiting taxi and I have to stop myself from climbing into the back with her.

But what do I do? I stand, hands tucked deep into my pocket and watch her drive away.

Kicking the toe of my brogue into the sidewalk, I inhale deeply. I knew it wouldn't work. But hey, what do I know.

Turning, a grimace apparent on my face as I walk back inside the restaurant and see everyone sitting at the table. Titus's eyes find mine and I can see the desperation seeping out of them.

I shake my head from side to side and he drops his.

"Fucking stupid plan," I grunt towards Killian and Kaleb, sitting smug as shit with their arms tucked around their partners.

"It was worth a shot, at least they were in the same room for a moment," Killian pipes up and I glare over at him.

"You fucking ambushed her. She knew it wasn't a coincidence that me and the fucking cast of the Muppets rocked up." I ball my fist and sit next to Titus.

They say nothing.

"Just let me fucking deal with her. All you've done is push her further away." I sigh, slipping my phone out to see if she had messaged but she hadn't.

Titus rumbles beside me.

"It'll be okay," I wrap my arm around his shoulder, giving him a pat on his shoulder blade.

"I know," he softly nods.

Silence creeps across the table and I take that as my cue to leave.

"Would say this has been lovely but..." I shrug a shoulder up and stand. "Catch you on the flip side fuckers," holding my hand up, I walk out of the restaurant and wait for a taxi.

CHAPTER ELEVEN
ARIZONA

CHASE ATLANTIC – INTO IT PLAYS THROUGH THE SPEAKERS. MY body rolls to the beat, across the floor and round the pole. I lose myself in the music, shutting everyone and everything out whilst I work my routine. Hanging upside down, fingers fumble and slip dollars into my baby pink G-string, and you always get one that tries to dip his fingers a little further than needed.

Scissor kicking my legs around, I hook my knees behind the pole before I am on the floor for the saxophone instrumental. Crawling across the floor, I drop to my front, ass up and slowly roll onto my back.

Arching my back from the cool floor, the back of my head tipped back, my knees bent and on the last beat I drop my body down before the lights darken. Heart thumping, I stand quickly and rush out the back and into the changing room.

"Loved that, slow and sensual, seemed a crowd pleaser," Sasha says as she pops her head round the door frame.

"Thanks," I smile at her, rummaging through my bag for my second outfit.

"See you on the floor in ten," she winks and disappears into the evening.

Pulling out a black, lace bodysuit I pop into the changing room and slip my set off.

A couple of the girls are off, Roxy, Luce and new girl Chloe. April and Autumn are on leave.

Of course, there are more girls that work here, but we don't really talk. I have my little friends here and I am happy with that.

Walking towards the mirror, I glance at myself.

Extensions make my hair long and wavy, in perfect beach waves. My blue eyes glisten as they roam over my body. Lace floral detail stitched into the body, mesh breast cups finished off with lace and just covering my nipples. A run of my caramel skin shows down the center and there is a mesh, denier bottom half leaving little to the imagination. Twisting round, I look over my shoulder at myself. Straps tucked over my back exposing my skin before they clasp onto the thong of the suit.

"Well, look at you." Spinning, my eyes find Ross leaning against the door frame.

"Ross," I breathe, pushing my fingers through my hair as I walk towards him in my ridiculous heels.

"You okay?

"Yeah, thanks," I breathe, stopping in front of him and placing my small hand on my racing heart.

"You?" my eyes bounce between his.

"I am now that I know you're okay."

I give him a sweet smile, "Thanks for checking up on me."

"Always," he leans in, and I turn my face quickly, his lips pressing to my cheek.

"I better get going," I whisper, letting my hand fall.

"Want to get that drink soon?" he asks, hopeful.

"Maybe, yeah..." I trail off as I walk down the corridor and to the floor.

Turning the corner I bump into a hard body. Tilting my head up I see Keaton's boyish grin spreading across his lips.

"For fuck's sake," I swat him, slapping my hand against his chest.

"What?" he chuckles.

"What are you even doing here?" I hiss. "Go away," I stomp my heeled foot like a bratty child.

"Hey, no pouting. I am just keeping watch," and he winks just as his arm wraps around behind me and rests his hand on the small of my back. "I am allowed to, right?" his voice is raspy, my eyes glued to his, my lips parted, and I hate that he makes me feel this way. Giddy and dizzy. Wanting and needy. Horny. All the god damn time.

"Sure," I grin, my lip curling over my teeth. "Enjoy *watching* me," I snap out of my hypnotic gaze, push him back and walk past him, hips sashaying side to side.

"Fuck, you look gorgeous... your ass..."

"Fuck off Keaton," I flip him off, but what he doesn't see is my huge smile.

COLLAPSING ON MY BED, I DON'T EVEN HAVE THE ENERGY TO TAKE my make-up off and I know I'll regret it in the morning. By the time my face is buried into the pillow, I'm out cold.

Groaning, I roll over to my phone buzzing. I'm a light

sleeper. Hate it. I reach around for it and see Lucy's name flashing.

"What?" I snap, sleep evident in my voice.

"Wakey Wakey, you promised me coffee today," she sings down the phone.

"Shove your coffee up ya ass, I'm wrecked," I moan, and my body aches.

"That's not nice, look, I'll be a couple of hours and I'll come pick you up. Go back to sleep for an hour or so then get dressed. See you later bitch." She hangs the phone up and I face plant the pillow.

Why the fuck do I make plans after I've done an eleven-hour shift?

I try with all my might to get back to sleep, but I can't.

"Thanks Luce," frustration fills me and I am pent up.

I spend twenty minutes scrolling my phone and I see a picture of my dad and Amora. I sigh, they make such a lovely couple.

I would probably get on with her quite well.

Shame really. Oh well.

Tossing my phone into the duvet, I clamber out of bed, all limbs as I notice the make-up imprint on my white pillowcase.

Shit.

Stripping it off, I throw my bedding into the corner of the room. Peeling my clothes from my tired body, I pad heavily towards my bathroom and slip under the hot water.

Hair washed, body washed and moisturized. I felt so much better.

Placing a foot on the bathmat, my eyes widen when I see the empty towel rail. Fuck it. Rushing for the storage cupboard in the corner of the bathroom, I tug the door open and moan with frustration. Empty.

What an idiot.

I'm gonna have to shout down to Keaton.

Opening my bedroom door, I poke my head out, my skin is silky and wet and I internally curse myself for not checking before.

"Keat!" I shout and wait a moment.

My hair drips down my body, running over the curve of my breasts before rolling off and into the carpet.

Nothing.

"Keaton!" I shout a little louder and I hear his footsteps closing in, his head popping up through the stair railings and his eyes light up. "Fuck off," I warn, hiding behind the door.

"Don't be like that, you obviously called me for a reason... baby," his voice is deliciously deep and my insides quiver.

"I need some towels." I grit.

"Oh dear, should have checked before you got yourself all..." He pauses for a moment, and within two strides he is in front of me. Close. Too close. "Wet," he growls and I clench.

My skin isn't the only thing that is wet.

Annoying.

I mean, a little bit of weakness never hurt anyone right?

No. No.

No more of Keaton's perfect dick.

You're an addict.

Could be addicted to worse things, I counter with myself.

"Please," I whisper, my fingers curled around the door.

He exhales heavily.

"Fine..." his tongue runs across his top lip slow and

seductive, and my teeth are in my bottom lip without me even realizing.

"Stop undressing me with your eyes, you want me?" he chuckles, "Just say the words."

"I want a towel, now shoo," I brush him off with my hand, ushering him on.

Rolling his eyes, he disappears and within a minute, he is back with warm and fluffy towels. I snatch them, slamming the door shut and wrap myself up.

Once warm and dry, I make myself wet and messy thinking about him.

CHAPTER TWELVE
KEATON

HARD.

Rock, fucking, solid.

Her silky skin. Her wet hair framing her pretty fucking face, her plump lips and all I could think of was how they would look wrapped around my cock.

Slamming my bedroom door, my sweatpants are down round my ankles and fisting myself within seconds. I jerk myself off hard and fast, all while my eyes are closed, head tipped back as I fantasize about sinking my cock inside of her again.

I come in two minutes.

Shameless.

No fucks given.

Cleaning myself up, I open my bedroom door the same time she steps out onto the landing, our eyes meet and her cheeks pinch that pretty blossom pink.

"Flustered?"

"Hardly," she rolls her eyes, bedding in hand.

"Make a mess with your hand and vibrator?" Tongue in cheek I rock up on the balls of my feet.

"In your dreams baby," she teases, and I let out a low chuckle.

I follow behind her, eyes on her peachy ass in her high waisted black jeans. She slips into the laundry room, and for some reason I follow her.

Shoving her bedding into the washing machine, I lean against the door just watching.

"What's the matter? Want a lesson on how to work the washer?" she spins, tongue slipping out the corner of her mouth, teeth pinching the thing I want running up the underside of my cock.

"I'm just thinking how pretty you'll look whilst I eat your wet little pussy." Risky move, I know but I can't curb my tongue around her.

Her eyes bug out. Her lips open as her jaw falls lax.

"Keat..." she pants, her eyes roaming over me.

I step closer.

"We said no more..."

Pushed up against her tight little body, my neck cranes down at her, my eyes burning into hers.

"I know, but you're just too much of a temptation," I whisper, my lips hovering over hers.

"We promised." She moans as I curl my fingers round the base of her throat. She likes it. Her pulse dances underneath my fingertips.

"Promises were made to be broken." Skimming my hands down her body, both curling round her hips and I lift her onto the washing machine.

"Not our promises," her hands press against the cool metal of the washer.

"One last taste..." I rasp, widening her legs and slipping between them as my lips brush against hers.

"One last..." she whispers and the doorbell rings.

And that's all it takes for her to snap back into reality. Shoving me off her, she jumps down.

"You and your dirty mouth," she scowls, skipping out the laundry room and down towards the door.

Fuck it.

My cock aches between my legs and I shut the laundry door to give myself a moment.

Or five.

Walking back out and into the kitchen, I see Lucy and Ari sitting at the deep oak dining table.

"Morning," I greet her, and switch the coffee machine on. "Drinks?"

"We should really..." Ari starts.

"We would *love* one," Lucy answers before Arizona can even get her words out. My back is to them so I smirk.

"Oh, Arizona," I look at her slowly over my shoulder, "don't forget about your bedding in the washer."

She stays mute, pushing away from the table and into the laundry room.

"Do you take cream? Milk? Sugar?" I ask Lucy.

"Cream, no sugar," she says sweetly.

Ari is back in the room, while I make her coffee. Little milk and two sugars. It's mad to think that she has been living here for only three months. It's a home with her, but I know this won't last forever. She will go back to her actual home. So, until then, I am going to enjoy every minute.

Turning, I waltz towards the girls and place them down. They fall into easy conversation, and I join them. Arizona eyes me.

"Do you mind?"

"Nope,"

Ari's tone is curt and I know I've rumbled her.

Don't care.

Will still try and devour her again.

Her pussy is too good.

"Lucy, how's work?" I ask, brows lifting as I bring my cup to my lips. Who would have thought, me, Keaton fucking Mills would be sitting here on my Saturday morning with two—this is going to sound harsh, but it's also true—strippers.

I mean? Is that the right term?

"Not too bad, was nice to see a familiar face last night," she gives me a smirk, cheeks blushing, and I feel a swift blow to my shin.

Fuck. My teeth grind.

"Private dance?" Arizona's body is turned towards Lucy.

"Something like that," she drops her face, and I don't miss the sly smirk on her lips.

Arizona glares at me. Fuck's sake.

"It wasn't anything like that," I take a mouthful, burning my tongue and instantly regret it.

"What was it like then?" Arizona's elbows perched on the table, hands resting under her chin and her eyes are burning into mine.

"She danced. Didn't touch her. Was literally just a dance; Lucy, tell her,"

Lucy rolls her eyes and looks at Ari.

"It was just a dance," she huffs, "I tried pushing for a little more but mister grumpy over here wasn't having any of it," she flicks her eyes back to mine.

"See?"

"Why does it matter to you so much?" she asks, and Ari stays quiet.

"Probably because I'm her dad's best friend... little close to home maybe?"

Ari's cheeks flame a shameful pink.

"And what?" Lucy's brows pinch, "Is it because you have a *crush*?" she taunts.

Oh, Arizona.

"Luce!" She slams her cup onto the table, spilling some coffee and her eyes widen at her friend's admission.

"What? It's true, you've had a crush on him for what feels like foreverrrrr," she drags out the last word.

"Don't listen to her," Ari crosses her arms in front of her chest.

Too late.

"Well, well, well..." I shuffle in my seat, "you know this can only stay a crush though, right?" I goad her and I know she is reeling inside. "We're forbidden, taboo..." I pause and have to ignore the growing bulge in my pants.

"Obviously," she brushes it off, but I don't miss the crack in her voice.

"But you're not forbidden or taboo to me," Lucy slides her hand across the table and my lip curls.

"Goldie, you're sounding desperate. It's not attractive," I side-eye her, my brows raised.

"Keaton!"

"Yes," I chime and if looks could kill. I would be dead.

Six-foot underground.

Done for.

"Luce, let's go," Arizona huffs, the chair scraping along the floor and Lucy nods. She grabs her bag from the floor, swatting me round the back of the head as she walks by me, but not before lowering her lips to my ear and whispering, 'call me'.

I turn in my seat, watching them walk down the hallway and I call Arizona.

"Hey, Ari... come here for one sec." I stand up, finger wrapped round my cup, the other folded inside my pocket.

She sulks towards me. Pouty bottom lip. Eyes wild. Hips rocking side to side.

"What?" one hand on her hip, her eyes dance with mine.

"You're never taboo or forbidden to me... I'll prove that to you once you're home," and her breath trembles. "Have a nice lunch, I look forward to enjoying you later," I smirk but she doesn't budge.

"I'm not yours to enjoy... bye Keaton," she spins on her heel and walks towards her friend.

Defiant little madam.

CHAPTER THIRTEEN
ARIZONA

I HAVE TRIED TO AVOID KEATON AT EVERY OPPORTUNITY. IT'S BEEN hard. I mean, it's Keaton.

He is sex on legs.

But I haven't given in anymore apart from those two times. Yes, we've done bits, but no sex.

I wrap myself in my coat as I walk towards *Prestige*. I was in no mood for work, and I am grateful that I am only working till five today.

As soon as the hour hits, I am going to run out of there like a bat out of hell. I want a self-care evening. Face mask, bath salts, chocolate and a chick flick.

It really does sound like the perfect evening.

I nod to Jerry on the door and slip down the corridor to the dressing room. When I enter, April is sitting on the sofa scrolling her phone.

"Hey," I wave, dropping my bag by my feet, "how was your vacation?"

"Oh, it was perfect, Bora Bora was beautiful. If you ever get the chance, go," she nods at me, all wide eyed and giddy.

"That would be a dream," I sigh, opening my locker and lifting my bag into it.

"Can't believe I am back here though," she whines, her head dropping back.

"Mm, Bora Bora is definitely more appealing." She nods in agreement. "Hey, how about next time your dad wants to book an all-inclusive trip, he can take me too?"

"Sure thing," she winks and pushes up from the sofa. "Well, the show must go on," she places her phone in her locker and walks out the room and into the busy club.

I take a moment to fold my clothes and get changed. I was over work already and suddenly I felt desperate for a holiday.

Walking the floor, I am a little grateful I'm not on the stage tonight. I honestly don't think I have it in me. I feel exhausted, my head is pounding, and I am silently praying the Advil I took a while back kicks in soon. Rounding the room, I stop at a table of rowdy football players and give the captain some attention. His hands are on my hips as my body rolls over him, but I am careful not to touch him at all.

His head tips back, his eyes on mine as he leans up.

"Let me pay for a private..." he whispers against my lips, and I stiffen.

"Not working privates tonight," I smile back at him, then spin so my back is to his front. His large hands back on my bare skin.

Pulling me onto his lap, he tucks my hair over my shoulder and places his lips to the shell of my ear.

"I'll pay double."

And my body vibrates in laughter.

"She's not working privates." The deep British accent floats across me and my skin pebbles.

Dex.

"Fine, fine, sorry man, jeez," the football captain rolls his eyes and thumbs behind him to his mates as if to say *what's with this guy*.

"She told you once, don't make her tell you again," he steps closer, wrapping his fingers softly round the top of my arm as he gently pulls me away.

"You didn't have to step in," I half laugh, half scoff in annoyance.

"I know I didn't, but I can't stand it when drunk ass fellas ignore when you talk,"

his comment sounded directed towards me specifically, which I know it wasn't, but still.

I spin to look at him in the dimmed room.

His long, black hair pushed back. High cheek bones, beautiful eyes you could lose yourself in. Broad, lean, tattooed from head to toe.

"That wasn't aimed at only you by the way," he chuckles, rubbing his large hand over his chin, Sage's name tattooed over his fingers on his left hand, a crown on his wedding finger.

"I know," I sigh, dropping my eyes from him for just a moment.

"I just don't like guys taking the piss out of young women, I know it's a bit of a stupid statement to make seeing as this," he throws his hand around the lavish club, "but still, I'm a little protective."

I laugh when I see Sage roll her eyes as she stands beside him.

"You? Dex Rutherford, protective?" she snorts a laugh, "Not you babe," she adds as her arm tucks into Dex's.

"I have no idea what you're talking about," he turns his face down, smiling at her.

"Anyway, I better be going," I give a weak smile, wanting out of their little PDA and walk past Sage.

"Hey, Ari, wait a sec," Sage runs up behind me and grabs me by the elbow.

"Everything okay?" my brows pinch for just a moment.

"Me and Dex are flying out to Vegas in a couple of weeks, potentially buying a new club and well, I was thinking why don't you come with? I would love to get your opinion?" she stands hopeful, her eyes bouncing around excitedly.

"Me? Really? What about Sasha?" I place my hands on my hips and she shakes her head. Stepping towards me for just a moment she leans in and places her lips by my ear.

"She doesn't have the potential... plus, we're thinking of replacing her soon..." she pulls away and gives me a wiggle of her impeccably shaped brows. "So, Vegas? With me and Dex? You're welcome to bring someone with if you want?"

"Sounds amazing, I'll put my vacation request in."

"No need," she stands beside me, linking her arm through mine as she leads me away, "it's already approved."

I step out onto the sidewalk ready to hail a cab and I see Keaton parked and waiting. A soft smile graces my lips as I saunter over to him, the door unlocking as I approach. Slipping in he turns to face me.

"Well, hello you," my cheeks color pink as I buckle myself in.

"Didn't want you getting a cab."

"I am big enough to get a cab, you don't normally mind

when it's five a.m..." He chuckles, signaling to pull out onto the busy road.

"Okay, fine... I missed you. It's been a week and you've ducked out at every chance you've had," he licks his lips, brows furrowed for just a moment as we roll to a stop.

"I just thought it was best we kept our distance... we've not been very good at it recently," I sigh.

"What if I don't want to keep my distance?" he asks, looking at me for just a moment as the lights turn green.

"We both agreed it was a bit of fun, it was never going to be any more than that..." I rub my lips together and ignore the way my heart is jack hammering in my chest.

"Ari..." the way my name rolls off his tongue does things to me that I am too ashamed to voice out loud.

"Keaton," I spin to face him, "it needs to be like this. If you can't then... maybe I need to move out for a while. I'm sure I can crash on a sofa somewhere."

"What?" he hisses as we roll to another stop. Jeez. The lights are not on our side tonight.

"I mean..." I shrug, "it might be better for us. Just to *help* put the distance between us."

I don't want to move out, but the more the silence fills the car and I am alone with my thoughts, the more I think that this might be best for us. He stays quiet, fingers tightening round the steering wheel of his SUV.

"You can't help being a walking god and my lady boner can't take it," a slow smirk pulls at my lips and I know I shouldn't inflate his already huge ego.

At least it matches his huge dick.

Fuck, he has a beautiful dick.

"Can we talk about it at home? I am famished and need food," he groans, his eyes darkening as he pulls off the busy main roads and into the side streets.

"What you hungry for?" I ask as my own stomach rumbles.

"Your pretty wet cunt," and I choke on my intake of breath, "that's the only thing that will appease my appetite." He glares at me, and my eyes widen.

Shit.

He isn't joking.

My fingers grip into the seat as tension builds over the duration of our drive home.

And I would be lying if I said I wasn't excited.

CHAPTER FOURTEEN
KEATON

THIS ISN'T HEALTHY. I KNOW THAT.

She's one of my best friend's daughters.

I am sick. And the only thing that is going to cure me is her pussy.

Honestly, if I don't have her, I think I'll die.

Dramatic? Yes.

Cause of death; starvation of Ari's pussy.

That would be on my headstone. My lips twitch.

I eye her fingernails digging into the soft leather of her car seat and I can't wait to have said nails digging into my skin. I don't even care if I get off. As long as she is coming on my tongue, my fingers, my dick, that's enough of a high for me.

You're a sick, sick, bastard.

Pulling into my space outside the house, I am ravenous for her.

Famished. Starved.

Drooling at the thought that as soon as we're over that threshold, my tongue is going to be buried in her pretty little pussy. Cutting the engine, I lean over and unbuckle her.

"Keaton," she whispers.

I'm out of the car, my feet hitting the sidewalk hard as I open her door, nearly pulling it off its hinges.

"You're a mad man," tongue in her cheek her eyes are as wild as mine.

"I'm a starved man Blossom, there is a difference."

Dragging her from the car, I lift her before both her feet can touch the floor. I toss her over my shoulder, slamming the car door shut and walking towards the house.

She's wearing tight jeans and a little cropped top wrapped in a denim jacket. Fuck, I want to sink my teeth into her skin and mark every part of her.

We're in the house within seconds and as soon as that door shuts behind us, I place her feet to the floor. My eyes darken, her eyes frantic and I watch as her chest rises and falls a little harder than normal.

"Strip." I command, not lifting my heated gaze off hers.

She stands for a moment, her eyes narrowing.

"Don't be disobedient baby, acting like a brat doesn't suit you," folding my hands in my suit pockets, I widen my stance slightly.

She smirks and my heart thumps against my ribcage as she drops her denim jacket.

Kicking her shoes off, she then slowly unbuttons her jeans and slips them down her legs before discarding them down the hallway.

My hungry eyes roam over her.

Pretty white panties.

Silk.

Wetness already pooling on the material giving away just how turned on she is.

Next is her top, her fingers wrap round the scalloped

hem of her cropped tee and she lifts it from her head, balling it and tossing it towards me.

"Fuck, you are something else baby," I groan, taking in the low cupped bra that matches her panties and I may have died and gone to heaven.

She stands, knotting her fingers together.

"Lose the panties," my voice is full of gravel and I swallow the thickness that coats my throat.

Her thumbs slip inside them and she slides them down her pretty, long, legs in a slow and torturous pace. I stalk towards her.

One.

Two.

And I'm in front of her, my fingers plucking her panties from hers and I lift them to my nose, inhaling.

"These are mine now," I growl, craned over her.

Curling my hand round her hip, I glide it up and unhook her bra, watching as it softly falls down her arms and to her feet.

Backing her towards the stairs, I knock her back gently as she sits on the second from bottom step. Tossing my head from side to side, I nod up, indicating for her to shuffle up one.

She does and I am on my knees, fully dressed and in awe of the beauty that is sitting bare in front of me.

Lurching forward, my lips are on hers, tongue sweeping through her lips as she moans into my mouth. Fingers rubbing her clit, and my cock presses against the fly of my pants.

"Keat," she pants, pulling away, her body trembling, her breath quivering.

"Yes blossom?" I kneel back, putting distance between us.

She turns crimson.

"I'll let you eat…" she bats her lashes and I sense a but coming, "but you let me move out."

I take a millisecond to process her terms. That's all it took.

Fuck I am so weak.

A weak, weak, man.

"Spread those pretty thighs baby and let me eat, I'm starving."

And she does. She spreads them nice and fucking wide and her cunt is wet and ready.

"Crawl to me," she smirks, her fingers rubbing in small circles where I am desperate to have my tongue.

Fuuuuuck.

I do.

I fucking crawl like a dog, ready to listen to her every command.

"There's a good boy, now eat."

And I just nut.

Full blown cum in my pants.

I'm not even ashamed. I should be, but I'm not.

Possessiveness burns inside my chest and I lower myself down, my tongue rubbing against her clit as I lap up her arousal, my fingers spreading her lips to expose her. My hot breaths cover her, my mouth moving at a steady rhythm as my tongue devours her, eating her.

Her fingers lock in my hair, twisting and tugging as I bury myself deeper inside of her. She slips forward slightly, her hips lifting as she watches my tongue bring her closer to her undoing.

My fingers slip deep inside of her, curling and rubbing where she wants me.

Where she needs me. I nip at her clit and she moans,

her pussy tightening. Lifting my mouth from her slowly, I smirk as her arousal strings from my lips.

Sucking my bottom lip into my mouth, I take just a moment to bask in the sight before me. Her hands squeezing and kneading her tits, my fingers buried in her cunt.

"Fuck, you look so fucking pretty."

Her eyes roll, moans escaping her.

"Let me fuck you one last time. I promise... then I'll let you go."

I ignore the sting that sears through me. Yeah, I definitely need to ignore that.

"You eat pussy so good," she pants as she rolls her head forward, "I want your tongue on me." She practically begs.

I pull my fingers from her, both hands gripping the inside of her thighs as I widen them, her pussy glistening and my tongue is on her, gliding down her cunt, teasing the tip at her wet, hot, entrance before I am back on her clit.

"Yes, oh, please fuck." I do it again. "Yes, oh god, oh god," her fingers press to the back of my head as she pushes me deeper into her.

My lips lift for just a moment.

"That's it baby, call my fucking name," I groan, tongue buried inside of her.

"Right there, fuck yes, fuck fuck fuck you're so good," she cries, her moans strangled.

My cock hardens. "Let me come on your tongue Keaton, let me make a mess," she whimpers.

I'm going to bust again.

What is she doing to me.

Sucking on her clit, my tongue flattens and I slowly lick her.

My hands skim underneath her, lifting her ass up and I

fuck her with my tongue, her fingers on her clit and her beautiful blue eyes focused on me eating her perfect little cunt.

"Yes, oh fuck," her head tips back and her pussy tightens around my tongue and she comes hard, my tongue sliding up and down her cunt as I clean up her pretty fucking mess.

She's panting. I'm standing.

I am more than satisfied but I'm greedy.

"Let me fuck you," I groan, cock hard as steel in my pants, heart racing in my chest.

"Upstairs; condom," she breathes.

I nod, eyes closing for just a moment, and I lean over her, fingers swirling in her wetness.

"I can't guarantee you'll make it up the stairs..." I whisper against her lips.

"We shouldn't," she trembles, brushing against me.

"We shouldn't have done a lot of things baby..."

She trembles as I slip two fingers inside of her.

"Upstairs," she whispers.

"Upstairs," I nod, slowly pumping them in and out of her.

We stay like this for a moment, me bringing her close to another release but stopping before she gets there.

Slipping out of her, I push my fingers between her lips.

"Taste yourself Blossom, see why I am so fucking hungry for you all the time, see how good you taste on my tongue," I groan as she sucks my fingers into her hot little mouth.

I need my cock in her mouth. "Take my belt off," I order, slowly standing over her I smirk down at her.

Her fingers fumble at the buckle as she unbuckles it and I push my pants down, fisting my cock out of my boxers. She edges forward, pursing her lips at the head of my cock.

"Just for a moment," I sigh as she slips me into her mouth, taking me to the back of her throat and she gags. "Fuck, baby," she swirls the head of my dick on the tip of her tongue before she flattens it and takes me again.

I stand still.

Fighting with myself to not fuck her hot, wet mouth and ruin her pretty fucking throat.

I want my dick inside of her cunt.

Not her mouth.

I lean over slightly, watching her, her watching me. Grabbing a fistful of her hair, I guide her up and down my cock, my jaw wound tight as my eyes close, my cock slipping down the back of her throat.

She purses her lips, my cock sitting on her cushioned bottom lip.

"Fuck me," she whispers.

"With pleasure, I don't want to cum in your mouth, I want to cum in your pretty pussy," I whisper, and she stops, her eyes full of want and need.

Smirking at me, she turns and begins to crawl up the stairs. Her glistening cunt teasing me.

"Fuck it," I groan, reaching for her, and stopping her. "Teasing me Ari," I groan as I lean over her back, my lips by her ear.

She smirks, looking at me over her shoulder.

"Let me fuck you right here, right now," I plea, my cock weeping and pressed against her wet cunt.

"Just the tip," she breathes, her thighs squeezed shut, ass sticking out, her elbows pressed into the stairs.

"Just the tip," I pant, kneeling on the stair below her, I align my cock at her opening and press the tip into her and I groan. My hands are on her hips, holding her still as I edge in and out of her.

Her body trembles every time I pull out of her, and she is driving me wild.

Slipping a little further into her, she moans as I stretch her, her thighs still pressed together.

"Keaton," she pants, eyes wide as she looks over her shoulder at me.

"I know, but you feel so good," I admit, watching as I slip my cock in and out of her. I am desperate to fill her and fuck her.

"We shouldn't," she whimpers, "it's risky."

"I know," I nod, slipping out to the tip and refusing to move. I just stare at how pretty she looks. My hips rock forward and back gently so my head stretches her enough to make her feel it.

"Fuck," she cries, her hips moving with me, desperate for me to fill her.

"Baby..." I plead, tightening my grip on her hips.

"Please," she whispers and I still.

"Please what?" my brows knit.

"Fuck me Keaton, I can't wait," she cries, her hips rotating and rocking over the tip of my cock.

"Yes baby, yes," I grit, slamming my hips into her as I fuck her, hard. My cock slipping in and out of her.

Pound after pound.

"Let me ride you please," her voice cracks as I slow, slipping out. I fall down a step, sitting and watch as she lowers herself over me, legs over my thighs, her back to my front and my eyes roll in the back of my head as her pretty cunt stretches around me.

"Fuck you're such a turn on," I whisper. She looks over her shoulder at me, our lips brush turning into a messy kiss as I grip her hips, guiding her up and down my cock. "Fucking you on my stairs; you're too much," I nip at her bottom lip, her hips rotating over me as my cock fills her in slow, long strokes.

She fights against me, her head looking down between our bodies and she whimpers.

"Don't we look good together baby," moaning, my eyes lift to the mirror that sits next to the front door and I can see *everything*.

"Look at us Blossom, look in the mirror and see how good you look being filled with every inch of my cock."

"Keaton," she chokes, one of my hands wrapping round the base of her throat, her head against my chest.

"Look how good we are, look how well you take me."

She watches as I fill her to the hilt as she rides me, slipping up and down my cock.

"You're so big," she whimpers, and I nip at her neck.

"And your tight little cunt took all of me."

Her pussy pulses.

Her fingers are on her clit, rubbing as she slows, but I don't let her. My hands are back on her hips as I lift her up and down my cock, fucking her with hard and punishing thrusts.

"You're going to come all over my cock, then I am going to fill you full of mine," I groan, "do you understand?" She cries out, nodding as the back of her head rests against mine. "Let me take control, let me switch us up," I beg.

"Control me," she whispers as I slow, and her hips roll over my cock.

"Patience," I smile, lifting her from me as I stand, then I pick her up, wrapping her legs around my waist and walk her to my bedroom.

I drop her onto my bed, flipping her over and lifting her hips so her ass is in the air.

Pressing the head of my cock at her opening, she sucks in a breath as I fill her. Fingers digging into her hips, her head is pressed against the bed, her back arched as I fuck her how I want too. Hard. Fast.

"Come for me baby, come all over my cock," I beg her, my large hands on her ass cheeks as I spread them apart, stretching her out and I watch as my cock slips in and out of her.

"Deeper, fuck, yes," she cries out as she presses against me, and my cock rubs against her g-spot.

"Does that feel good Blossom? Tell me."

"So good," her eyes roll in the back of her head.

"Then show me how good and come for me."

I slap her ass cheek and dig my fingers into her skin, still spreading her and watch between our bodies.

"Slap me again," she cries out, her fingers on her clit and I do as she asks, slapping her ass cheek harder as my cock drills deeper and faster. "Yes, fuck, I am going to come." Her pussy clenches, pulsing around me as she rocks her hips.

"That's it baby, come all over my cock," my teeth are gritted and I see my cock coated in her arousal and I explode deep inside of her as I fuck her relentlessly.

Slowing, I catch my breath and when I am ready, I pull out of her and watch as our cum drips out of her pretty little cunt before I scoop it back up and push it deep inside of her, making sure she is full of me.

CHAPTER FIFTEEN
ARIZONA

WE LAY NAKED, LEGS TANGLED, MY HEAD ON HIS CHEST AND I listen to his steady heartbeat.

"I'm going to Vegas," my voice hazily skates through the room like a blade to ice.

"Are you?" he cranes his neck, lifting his head from the pillow but I don't look up at him.

"Mmhm," I hum, my fingers grazing across his dusting of chest hair.

"With?" his tone is cold for just a moment, and I smile.

"Dex and Sage; they want me to go look at a potential new club with them."

"I see," his fingertips dance up and down my spine.

"They said I can bring a plus one..."

"Lucy?"

"No," I breathe.

"No?" he repeats, and I can hear the surprise in his tone.

Lifting my head, I turn my face towards him. His green eyes settle on mine, they're soft and sleepy and I decide in this moment that this, right here, is my favorite. How his eyes are now, will always and forever be my favorite. As if they're holding my most precious secrets and memories, locked away behind the windows of his soul and I am the only one that can access them. Treasured and kept.

"I was wondering if you wanted to come with? I know it's an ask, what with work and my dad and I don't expect anything to happen between us but..."

"When do we leave?" he smiles at me and my heart thumps in my chest, leaping and pirouetting inside its butterfly cage.

"So that's a yes then?"

He cups my cheek in his hand, his thumb brushing against my cheek.

"It's a yes baby."

KEATON

Walking into the office, I have a little spring in my step.

Maybe it's because I fucked my best friend's daughter senseless and made her see the moon, the stars and the galaxies. Or maybe it's because she gave me a goodbye blowjob.

But, sadly, we have agreed that this morning was most definitely the last time. We've crossed so many lines, they've rolled into a sphere. A big, fucking sphere.

"Goooood morning," I sing as I dump my briefcase on my desk.

"Fuck, someone is in a good mood," Titus leans back in his chair and lifts a brow.

Because I fucked your daughter.

Little out of line. Even for my thoughts. Not anymore though.

No more fucking the forbidden fruit.

We both agreed.

I mean, I was hesitant... but she is right.

Crying shame. Pussy was insane.

100/10.

Would say I recommend it, but I won't. Because then I'll get jealous, and I can't afford to get jealous.

"I am in a very good mood," I turn my computer on and wait for Titus to appear at my doorway.

"And why is that?" he asks, leaning against my doorframe.

"Slept well, just chipper." I shrug my shoulders and I fight the smile that is trying to present itself.

"You got laid, didn't you?" he goads, stepping over the threshold of my office and I roll my eyes.

"A gentleman never tells," I scoff, sitting at my desk and resting my elbows on the surface.

"Gentleman!?" Titus roars a laugh, shaking his head from side to side. "Keaton, you don't even know the meaning of the word," he scoffs and for some reason, it pisses me the fuck off.

Blood boiling. Heart beating hard in the depths of my chest.

Narrowing my cold and intense stare on him, he curls a brow.

"Struck a nerve?"

"Never," a sly smirk pulls at my lips.

"Whatever you say bro," he laughs once more and walks away.

"Prick," I rumble under my breath as I wake my computer up and open my diary. I flick over the dates that Ari told me about and block them out.

I just need to think of a reason why I am out the office. Can't say I am going to Vegas with Arizona.

Fuck them. They don't need to know.

I'll take sick leave. Just need to get through this week and I'll be in Vegas with her.

Just me and her.

As friends, of course, just friends.

But still, away from all of it here.

Next week can't come any sooner.

CHAPTER SIXTEEN
ARIZONA

EXITING THE CAR ON THE TARMAC OF THE AIRFIELD, A SMALL WHITE private jet sits pretty waiting for us and I feel as if I should pinch myself. I never grew up not knowing what it was like to go without; I was privileged but grounded. I wasn't spoiled. My dad was comfortable but only because he worked hard for it. They all did. Keaton, Kaleb, Nate and my dad. They hardly took leave, they worked with what they had and built their little empire.

"I am so glad you agreed to come," Sage smiled, linking her arm through mine as we walk towards the jet. I glance over my shoulder at Keaton, his eyes on me as he talks to Dex.

"Thank you for asking me, I have never been away from New York, so this is amazing," I smile at her as she greets the captain.

"Miss James," he nods at her as we climb the stairs.

"This your plane?"

She looks over at me and gives a small nod, stepping into the luxurious interior.

"Mine and Dex's." I follow her to the set of four seats,

Keaton sits next to me, Dex next to her. He scoops her hand up instantly, pressing his lips to the back of her hand and you can see how much he adores her with every fiber. "I grew up with not a lot; I worked two jobs, and it was just me and my mum," her eyes cast down for a moment, "we got by, she couldn't work and I had to earn the money and I was more than okay with that. My mum gave me everything she could whilst I was in school, so it was only right I returned the favor." Her face turns up, a sad smile ghosts over her lips for just a moment. "Then I met Rhaegar," Dex scoffs beside her and she returns it with a roll of her eyes.

"He was her sugar daddy," Dex just comes out with it, his British accent thick.

"For a short while..." her cheeks turn pink against her pale skin.

"Wait," Keaton shuffles in his seat, his hand so close to mine and it's killing me not having his fingers locked through mine.

"Here we go," I mumble.

"You used to date his dad... how did this happen? Were you two exes, or was it just a coincidence?"

Sage laughs softly, letting her head fall back and rest on her seat.

"Dex was a client of mine; it was agreed with Rhaegs that I would still work and do my clients." Dex smirks.

"She did still *do* her clients—me, I'm her client," he laughs, and she swats him with the back of her hand.

"It got a little much, Dex became a little more obsessive and before I had formally met him, he used to make himself known. Bumping into me at my place of work, meeting me at the club, it got a bit weird..." she raises her brows, "then, I was set to meet Rhaegar's son. I was excited but nervous. I was young, twenty-three at the time and I was possibly going to be this kid's step-mum."

"Woah," Keaton whistles through his teeth.

"Oh, it gets better mate, trust me," Dex wiggles his brows up and I can't stop the giggle that bubbles out of me.

"So, I wanted to get him a toy, his dad said he loved trains so I got him this cute steam train. We arrived at the restaurant back home in London, and as we're shown to our table... guess who is sitting there with a smug as fuck look on his face," the excitement in her voice is present and Dex watches her, hanging on every word that passes through her lips.

"No fucking way," Keaton bellows, laughing. "Shit, so not only were you with his dad, you were with your sugar daddy's son too!"

"Yup, and well... things just sort of blurred from there. Dex helped my mum get the help she needed, and he helped me too. I didn't want to be a dancer, I didn't want to give lap dances. I had a dream and that was to have my own car garage, to be a mechanic. I love cars, and Dex helped me achieve that dream. I owe all of this to him..." she pauses for a moment and twists in her seat. "I owe all of this to you," her eyes glass over and Dex grips her chin, tipping her face back slightly.

"You owe me nothing Little One, this was all you." I turn to look at Keaton, a sad smile tugs at my lips. "You make your own fate..." he says softly, before whispering, "baby."

"But, I like to help out with the clubs. It's fun and I get to meet people who are so much more than a dancer, people who remind me of myself," Sage's eyes narrow on mine now, Dex's hand slipping between her thighs. "Like you, don't tell me your dream was to be an exotic dancer," her eyes lift to the announcement that croons through the jet, telling us that take off is imminent.

I rub my lips together and shake my head softly.

"Then chase your dream, Ari. Don't get stuck in a rut because it's easy. Your dreams are achievable, they're in your reach... you just need to not give up."

I nod, and then I nod again.

"Don't stop chasing," she leans over, placing her hand on my knee and I find comfort in her words.

WE'RE OVER HALFWAY INTO OUR FLIGHT, LUNCH HAS BEEN SERVED and the champagne is flowing.

"Are you two not married?" I ask, my brows pinching as my eyes bounce between both of them and Sage shakes her head. "I did think that when the captain greeted you with '*miss*'."

She laughs.

"Nope, not married yet. I mean, I want to... but it's not the be-all and end-all for me." She turns her face to look at Dex, "Where this man... he—and I make no joke—has weekly wedding magazines delivered to our house; he says he will take me shopping then we end up in a bridal boutique..."

"What? I'm a romantic." He bats his lashes.

"Yeah..." she pauses, a blissful sigh leaving her, "you really are."

"Apart from in the bedroom, of course," he declares and Keaton leans across and spuds him.

Honestly.

Children.

"What about you Keaton? A man of your age... married? Kids?"

And I feel Keaton shuffle next to me, my eyes pinned to his side profile, but he doesn't look at me.

Fuck, he is handsome.

"I was married once; never again." He shakes his head, dropping his eye contact with Dex.

"Bad ending?"

"Loveless marriage. She was a narcissist. Don't get me wrong, I wasn't a saint. Far from it, probably a bit narcissistic myself. But we brought the worst out in each other. We were toxic as fuck and that was not what I, or she, wanted. We parted amicably." He shrugs a shoulder up as if completely unphased. I had never heard this side of this story. Just that she was a bitch. He used to call her Satan. Never knew her real name. Knew her as Auntie Satan. She was a bitch though, then, when I was a teen, he told us they were splitting.

"Fair play," Dex nods a couple of times.

"Never been in love, don't think I am capable of such a feeling..." he pauses for a moment and swings his head round to look at me, blinks a few times and I see soft waves lapping against a beach, calmness. Complete stillness.

"Shit, this has got deep," Dex laughs and orders another round of champagne.

We hit a bout of turbulence and my heart falls from my chest, my stomach flipping and making me feel nauseas. Sweat beads on my brow, and even though it was merely minutes, it felt like hours. I have never been on a plane before; I didn't know what to expect.

Smiling, I excuse myself from my seat and walk to the back of the plane and with each step, my nerves make me feel sicker. Pushing through the door, I make it to the toilet just in time to throw up the contents of my stomach.

Shit.

This was not ideal.

I stand, my hands shaking softly as I turn the faucet on and wash my hands before splashing my face with cool water. Staring at myself, I look washed out suddenly.

I'm not alone long when there is a soft knock on the door.

"One minute," I call out, my voice quivering.

"It's me baby..."

And my skin pebbles.

Sliding the lock across, I pull the door slightly, his worried eyes on me, his brows creased.

"Are you okay?" he pushes through the door, hands cupping my face as he holds my gaze and I feel the sting at the back of my eyes.

"Motion sickness; the turbulence set it off... scared me to death," I whisper, and he pulls me into him, enveloping me in his embrace, my ear to his chest so all I can focus on is the steady beat of his heart.

"It's okay baby, I've got you."

And that's how we stand until I am ready to take my seat.

CHAPTER SEVENTEEN
KEATON

WE CHECK INTO THE BELLAGIO HOTEL AND ARRANGE TO SEE SAGE and Dex later on in the evening. I feel out of sorts and Ari hasn't been well since the plane, resulting in her being sick into her handbag in the car on the way to the hotel.

Once in the large room, I eye the two separate beds and it annoys me.

Walking into the bathroom, I run her a bath and fill it with bubbles.

"Ari," I call out softly and she is laid on the bed, curled into a ball.

Smiling, I walk slowly over to her and all I can do is stare at her. She really is beautiful. Too beautiful. Leaning over, I place a soft kiss on her cheek and pull a comforter over her body.

Couple of hours sleep should help.

Then we can have our evening.

Sitting by the window, the strip is alive and thriving beneath us and I am on my laptop working through this month's accounts. Titus and Kaleb haven't taken a job in weeks due to Wolfe and it's showing. We're okay, for the moment but we need something to keep us ticking over without diving into savings.

Cradling my scotch, I take a mouthful when I hear Arizona stir. Lifting my eyes from the screen, I watch her for a moment.

The room is dimmed with a low light but I can see her silhouette.

"Keaton?" she breathes, and I stand slowly.

"Over here baby."

Fuck.

Baby sounds too good rolling off my tongue.

"How long have I been asleep for?" she stretches up before climbing off the bed and walking towards me.

"About an hour or so," I smile as she wraps her arms around me, inhaling heavily.

"I needed it."

"Do you feel better?" I ask, pressing my lips to the top of her head.

"I do."

"Good," her head lifts, falling back gently as she looks at me and smiles. "Want a bath? I did fill it once but when I came out, well... you were asleep," a soft laugh falls from my lips.

"Would love one."

"I'll go sort that for you." I reluctantly pull away from her and disappear into the bathroom.

SHE SWANS FROM THE BATHROOM WRAPPED IN A FLUFFY WHITE towel and I am instantly hard.

Her skin wet and teasing me to touch her.

But I can't.

Well, I can.

But I won't.

"You getting changed?" She asks, hair wrapped in her towel as she unzips her suitcase.

"Are you feeling better?" I ignore her question completely.

"Yeah," she stands, tightening her towel round her beautiful body and I secretly palm myself under the table. "I am."

"Good, you look better."

"Now, back to my question... are you getting changed?"

I look down at myself and debate it for a moment.

Should have a shower.

Probably stink.

"Suppose I better," I groan as I push off the seat.

"You sound like an old frail man..." she taunts, and I see the teasing smile on her lips, her shoulders rolled back as she stands a little taller.

"Baby..." my voice is low and gravelly as I close the space between us in one, two, three steps. "We both know that I'm not old, or frail..."

She snorts a laugh.

"We will see how you fair after Vegas, darling," she sings pulling out a short, black mini dress and drops the towel.

I need out.

And to jerk off.

Dropping my head, I storm across the large room to the bathroom and shout, "No one likes a tease, Arizona," before slamming the door behind me and I hear her cackle.

After a jerk off or three, I'm dressed in a crisp white

shirt, black suit pants and brogues. We're out in a fancy restaurant tonight then moving to the casino.

Slipping my phone out of my pocket as I wait for Ari to finish her make-up, I get a message from Titus.

> **Titus**
> Drinks tonight? It is Friday and I could do with a few.

In other words, you want to talk about Ari and see if you can get shit out of me.

> **Me**
> Sorry man, on a date. Maybe next week?

I type back quickly when I hear the sound of her heels click across the floor. My eyes lift and *fuck me*. She looks phenomenal.

She always looks good.

Especially when she has been thoroughly fucked by me. Hair wild. Eyes glistening. Skin shimmering.

But here. Right now.

She's a fucking goddess and all I want to do is drop to my knees and worship every part of her. Wavy brown hair styled and sat on her shoulders, red matte lipstick and glowing make-up with cat eye liner.

A mini black dress clings to her body. Cleavage on point in a sweetheart neckline.

Tits look fantastic.

Always do.

Legs never ending. Hem of the dress sitting on the top of her thighs.

It's short.

Very fucking short. But who am I to tell her to pull it

down? Fuck that. Honestly, I don't even think it's short enough.

Will have to restrain myself tonight.

Probably won't.

"Fuck, you're going to be the death of me."

She fucking steps towards me, hands on my chest and her heels bring her from five foot four to five foot six.

"I know," she smiles, eyes fluttering closed before she turns and walks for the door.

And this time I do fall to my knees, holding my chest because she looks that fucking good.

She's a Queen.

ARIZONA

We walk towards the elevator, hands by our sides, mine only inches from his but touching feels too intimate. Casting my eyes down, I watch as his fingers flex before they relax and I am desperate to link ours together, but I do nothing.

Just ignore the tension that is slowly crackling between us, but we both made a vow that we wouldn't cross that line anymore.

We wait silently as he presses for the elevator and my phone chimes in my clutch. Keaton's brows sit up for a moment at the distinctive sound and my cheeks flame as I fumble to pull my phone out and I see a message on my cam app.

Shit.

Holding my thumb on the screen, I try to sneak a preview.

TallDarkandHandsome: *Where have you been? Do I need to arrange another private room for both of us if you're going to disappear on me?*

I swallow the sickly feeling that bubbles deep inside of me, my mouth watering and I squeeze my eyes shut willing for the wave of nausea to leave as quickly as it came on.

"Ari?" The rasp in Keaton's voice snaps me out of it, my head turning slowly to meet his worried gaze.

"I'm okay," I smile, "just come over a little queasy."

"We can go back?" he offers, and I smile at his kind gesture.

"I know, but I'll be okay... honestly," I whisper back just as the elevator doors ping open.

"Okay," he nods, walking forward and I follow as he presses the button for the ground floor.

Silence fills the small space, which gradually fizzles with soft voices of guests that join us on our descent.

Sneaking a gaze at Keaton, my heart thrums in my chest.

I shouldn't be feeling this way, but I do. Slowly falling into the forbidden territory which is my dad's best friend.

Slowly falling for him too.

Wish I could stop, but then again, I don't.

"Come," Keaton slips his hand into mine, our fingers entwining and my lips tug into a smile. Stepping out onto the floor, we see Dex and Sage waiting for us. Sage looks a vision and Dex looks handsome.

A red, provocative satin dress wraps around her curvaceous frame, Dex is dressed in a lightly checkered gray suit and a satin shirt which matches the darker gray line on his jacket.

"Well, look at you both," Dex smiles as he kisses me on

the cheek before turning his attention to Keaton, our hands slowly pulling from each other's.

Sage scoops me up in an embrace before sweeping her eyes over my outfit.

"LBD; classic," she winks before taking my hand as we head for *Picasso's*. I felt out of depth, we didn't do restaurants like this yet here I am. In the Bellagio, about to go into a fancy French restaurant with my bosses, boss's fiancé.

Like. Make it make sense.

Pinch me.

Because I feel like this is a little too good to be true.

"You look lovely, by the way," I say softly as I follow her lead.

"Thank you, babe, so do you," we slow as we stand waiting for the maître-de to acknowledge us.

After a beat, he lifts his head up and scopes us out.

"Evening, welcome to *Picasso's*, do you have a reservation?"

"Yes," Dex's thick British accent floats between us, "under Rutherford."

"Ah yes, Mr. Rutherford, please follow me. You're on the terrace overlooking the river," he wiggles his brows a little and grabs the menus.

This place is stunning, it's as if we've been transported somewhere entirely different as we look over the canal giving us Venice ambience.

"Lucian will be over shortly to take your drink order." He nods curtly then spins and walks away back to his station.

"Wow, this is..."

"Stunning isn't it. That's the thing with Vegas, you can

be anywhere in the world without ever having to leave," Sage smiles, resting her hand over Dex's.

Lucian appears within minutes and Dex orders a bottle of champagne and after checking with us all, orders the tasting menu for all of us, supplementing for the wagyu for our mains.

I only managed one glass of champagne before I politely refused and moved onto a mocktail. With how I was feeling, I was worried alcohol would make me so much worse.

My brows furrow when I notice that Sage hasn't once touched a drop of alcohol. She is drinking soda water and lime. I'm pulled from my thoughts when Sage turns to face me.

"Have you thought anymore about my offer?" Sage asks, reaching for her glass and taking a mouthful as Keaton tops my glass up.

"What offer is that?" Keaton asks, curiosity lacing his tone.

"About Arizona being manager of Prestige," she beams at me before her eyes bounce between Dex and Keaton.

"Is that what you want?" he asks me, and I can hear the edge his voice suddenly has.

"I don't know... I mean, it wasn't the dream I had once envisaged for myself." I admit, my fingers curling round the delicate stem of the champagne flute.

"What was it?" Dex asks, elbows on the table as he leans closer to me.

I scoff. "I always wanted to be a doctor..." I pause for a moment, my eyes moving across to Keaton for a beat.

"Then why aren't you?" He continues.

"Failed my first lot of exams. Didn't have it in me to beg

for another chance..." I sniff, "not that they would have given it to me anyway, I mean, life doesn't work like that."

"Surely you could re-do your first-year internship?" Sage asks the questions now.

"And work below my peers that I started with?" I shake my head from side to side, "I'm too proud," I half laugh, half choke on the breath that caught at the back of my throat.

"If it's your dream..." Dex says softly, his piercing eyes on mine and my heart drums a little faster in my chest. Dex, God of dream making.

"I don't know... maybe I have a new dream," I shrug one shoulder up and am silently grateful that our main course arrives.

Lucian places the tray down on a stand and serves our dinners up, Sage is the only one who has well done steak, the rest of us are medium.

I stare down at my plate, my stomach tightening as the smell of the meat wafts up and my mouth waters.

Not now.

I reach for my water and take a large mouthful, willing for the feeling to go away.

"Are you feeling sick again?" Keaton leans across to me, his voice low as his eyes settle on mine.

I nod but wave him away with a *'I'm fine'*. The less I just focus on me, the better it'll be.

Moments pass and so does the nausea.

"Are you okay?" Sage asks me, her hand on mine.

"Yeah, think I have a little stomach flu, been like it since the plane," I sigh, forcing myself to eat the dinner that Dex ordered.

"I have some stomach settlers in my room," she smiles, and I give her a gracious nod. Keaton catches Lucian's attention and orders me another glass of water.

My eyes glisten, but I blink away the tears that threaten to present themselves.

"Thank you," I whisper to him.

"Not a problem."

Once dinner is finished, Dex and Keaton are up and away from the table settling the bill and me and Sage begin walking to the casino, waiting for them to catch us up.

CHAPTER EIGHTEEN
KEATON

I'M TIPSY.

Not afraid to admit it.

Feels good to just be out in good company and enjoy a drink or five. Dex pushes an old fashioned into my hand as we walk from the bar to the Craps table where Ari sits all pretty.

I'm not one for gambling, but when in Vegas, I feel like you have to.

The croupier announces the game is about to start just as I stand behind Ari, my hand slowly slipping round the curve of her hip and I pull her into me.

I know we said we wouldn't go there again, but with the way I am feeling at the moment, I am ready to break that promise.

"You feeling okay?" my lips are pressed to her ear, my fingertips digging a little deeper through the thin material of her dress and into her skin.

"I am feeling much better," she turns her face to look at me and I place a soft kiss on her cheek.

"Good," I admit, lifting the glass to my lips and taking a mouthful of the delicious cocktail that sits in my hand.

We watch as the croupier calls for last bets and a young couple make a bet that if they roll a hard six, they get married tonight in the chapel.

My skin pricks.

Could you imagine... making a bet to get married. I scoff, but then my thoughts wander before I am brought back down to earth with a crash.

The table erupts as the couple throw themselves at each other, lips locked and bodies twisted as one as the hard six sits in the middle of the table.

The croupier laughs softly, shaking his head as he clears the table.

"Fancy a go?" I ask Ari, her eyes widening.

"Of Craps?"

"No, a bet to get married," I sway against her, the alcohol swims through my veins and I want more.

"Keaton," she spins to face me, eyes bouncing back and forth.

"Guys..." I hear Dex's warning tone but I ignore him. The fire in my belly is too much, my eyes are glued to her pretty blue eyes as I wait.

"So, what do you think baby?"

I tease knowing full well she will shoot me down into a ball of flames.

"You're on," her gaze steadies and focuses on me and my stomach falls out my ass.

Fuck.

"Wait, what?" I laugh, and it's nerves. I don't find this funny at all. But I mean, it could be worse, couldn't it?

"What's the matter, you chicken?" she crosses her arms

against her chest and challenges me and fuck, do I love a challenge.

"Not at all baby, I'll see you at the altar," my lips brush over hers as I tease her with a whisper of a kiss before I step back.

"You're on," she warns me, before calling in on the game.

"Hard ten," I shout out, placing my chips and rolling the dice.

And I shit you not.

I roll a hard ten.

Dex cheers, giving me a slap on the back as the croupier clears the table and hands out my chips.

I steady my gaze on her for just a moment, "You're on."

And my heart jackhammers in my chest.

CHAPTER NINETEEN
ARIZONA

WALKING THE CASINO FLOOR, KEATON'S FINGERS LACE THROUGH mine in total obliviousness of our surroundings. In this moment, it's just me and him. Dex and Sage are at one of the card tables, and after Keaton's small win on craps, we took that victory to the bar.

I lean against him as he steps towards the bar, resting his arm on the high gloss countertop.

I am happy. Blissfully.

"What can I get you?" the smartly dressed barman asks, leaning across.

"An old fashioned and a..." he pauses for a moment and turns to face me.

"Vodka soda," I nod and I see the barman eye me.

"You got ID?"

I nod, fumbling in my bag and handing it to him. His eyes flick up then back down again before he passes me my card back.

"Coming right up," he says as Keaton slips him our room card.

I turn, looking out at all the different kinds of people

that walk through the casino, but two people I definitely didn't expect to see here are Killian and Reese.

"Keaton," I whisper, tapping him on the top of his arm.

"Yeah baby?" he slurs; he is tipsy. Cute AF, but not when we're about to get caught.

"Killian and Reese," I hiss but it's too late.

They've clocked us.

"Oh shit," Keaton growls, but then explodes into laughter as he willingly walks over to Killian and shakes his hand.

"Arizona," Reese beams, wrapping her arms around me.

"Reese," I smile back at her as we pull away from each other.

"What brings you and Keaton to Vegas?"

I look over at Keaton, searching his face for an answer.

"A wedding," Keaton's lips turn down, his head bobbing.

"Of our friends, yeah, an old friend of mine," I interrupt.

Damn Keaton being drunk.

"Why are you here?" I ask, grinning wide as I pray that Sage and Dex don't come up and blow it.

"We fancied a few nights away and thought why not come back to where it all started," her hand rests on Killian's chest, looking up at her husband and smiling.

"That's lovely. Okay well look, we don't want to crash your romantic getaway, come on big fella, let's get you up to the room," I shove into Keaton trying to barge him, but Killian stops me.

"Why did you bring Keaton with you?" His brows pinch and I know he is trying to catch me out.

Not today Killian.

"Why not? I needed a plus one so I dragged him along."

"I see," Killian rubs his stubble and Reese rolls her eyes.

"Stop playing detective old man," she swats at his arm and a giggle bubbles out of me.

"Look, why don't we get dinner with you and our friends tomorrow night? How does that work?" I blurt out before I have even had a moment to register, but at least I have time to give Sage and Dex the low down.

"Sounds perfect, text me with the reservations yeah?"

"Of course, yeah," I smile at her and Keaton is just chuckling to himself beside me. Fucking idiot.

Killian leads Reese away and once they're out of sight I breathe out a sigh of relief.

"I need a drink, come on giggles, let's get drunk. Fuck it."

CHAPTER TWENTY
KEATON

WHAT THE FUCK IS THAT HIGH PITCHED NOISE?

Grumbling, I pat around the bed looking for something to silence it.

It stops for just a moment before it screams again.

Forcing my eyes open, the brightness of the day fills the room and my head is pounding, my mouth dry and my eyes burning.

I look across and see my phone dancing across the bedside unit.

"Someone had better fucking died to keep blowing my phone up."

Reaching for it, my brows furrow in confusion when I see Titus' name flashing up on my screen before it cuts off.

Twenty missed calls.

Twenty.

Shit.

My first thought goes to Kaleb, then Amora and the baby as I answer the call when it starts to ring again.

"Oh, hi Titus," I croak but still trying to keep upbeat. "You doing good?" He definitely is not doing good. "Look, as much as I am enjoying you perforating my ear drum, I'm a little busy at the moment," my lips twitch as I look over at a naked Arizona.

In my bed.

Again.

Oops.

He is still chewing me out. I have no idea what he is saying. I have just zoned out.

Best way.

"Yeah cool, I'll call you back," and I cut the phone off, tossing it into the duvet. I scrub my face with my hand and feel a coolness on my skin and my eyes widen. "Oh shit." I chuckle, but this is not the time to be laughing.

We actually fucking went through with it.

Fuck.

"Ari," I say softly, nudging her, "Ari!" panic claws at my throat as she stirs, moaning as she rolls on her back.

"Leave me alone," she swats at me.

"We have a problem." And she sits up, hair wild, make-up smudged and red lipstick stained over her pretty face.

"Problem?" she hums, and she still looks fucking pretty.

We must've fucked like porn stars last night.

The room is trashed, my muscles ache like I have run a marathon and she looks thoroughly fucked.

I hold my hand up which causes her to hold hers up and there it is, cheap yellow band with a pink heart shaped gem sitting proud in the middle.

"I'm going to be sick," she just about manages before she throws up in the garbage can next to the bed.

CHAPTER TWENTY-ONE
TITUS

THE LOW MORNING SUN IS SHINING, CRISPNESS TO THE AIR AND I am at home with my beautiful wife. It feels like the most perfect morning.

Sipping on my coffee, Amora's feet are tucked into my lap whilst I scroll my socials.

Bad habit, but I can't help but have a look hoping to get a little insight into Arizona's life that I am currently missing out on.

Aimlessly, I scroll past a picture in a Vegas chapel, and I swear I saw Ari.

Stop it. It's just your mind playing tricks on you.

I continue but then something niggles at the back of my mind.

I scroll back up and that's when I really see it.

Keaton and Arizona.

Him holding her in his arms like he is about to carry her over the threshold, and she holds up her ring, the caption reads:

Congratulations to our newlyweds, Keaton and Arizona.
We wish you a lifetime of happiness.

AND WHAT'S WORSE, I ZOOM IN ON THE IMAGE AND THERE, IN THE fucking background smiling all proud and shit is Killian.

"WHAT THE FUCK?!"

CHAPTER TWENTY-TWO
ARIZONA

"Ari," I hear the distant sound of Keaton's voice but I push it to the back of my mind and snuggle deeper into my duvet. "Ari!" I hear again, this time I am being shaken softly to wake me up. I roll over onto my back and throw my arm across, swatting him.

"Leave me alone," I groan, fuck, my head is pounding. Why did I decide to drink so much?

"We have a problem," and I don't miss the urgency in his tone.

I sit up, ignoring the way my head spins as I do. My hair is messy, my mouth is drier than the desert and I feel exhausted.

"Problem?" I hum, my eyes slowly falling heavy.

I squint my eye as I turn to face him and see him holding up his left hand, a wide ass grin on his face and I focus on the tacky yellow band that sits around his finger. Slowly lifting my own hand, my eyes widen when I see a yellow band wrapped around my ring finger with a large, pink heart shaped gem.

"I think I'm going to be sick," I just about manage as I

reach over and grab the garbage can beside the bed and empty the contents of my stomach.

Shit.

Flopping back in the bed, I pull the sheets up to my chin. I'm naked. Shock. No doubt had the hottest sex last night but I can't remember even a smidge of it.

"Your dad's been on the phone," and I facepalm myself, Keaton leaning towards me, playful green eyes, long unkept stubble and hair pulled in every direction.

We definitely fucked.

"Great," hitting my hands into the duvet I sigh in frustration. "Going to have to talk to him now aren't I? I can't be mad at him when I agreed to marry you. What were we thinking?"

"Vegas Keaton was thinking," he nods his head and my phone pings.

Turning my head to look at the bedside unit, my phone screen is lit so I reach for it and sigh when I see the numerous messages from my dad.

"I don't have the energy to speak to him."

"He has already screamed at me, give it a few hours," Keaton scoffs a laugh before his fingers wrap over my hand. My eyes focus there for a moment, the wedding band that sits perfectly on his finger makes my heart thump a little quicker.

"How bad have we fucked up?" I breathe on a whisper, lifting my eyes and settling on him.

My dad's best friend.

My *husband*.

"Depends how you look at it?" his thumb rubs back and forth over the back of my hand.

"And how are you looking at it?" I ask, genuinely curious as to what he will say.

"Like I have a hot as fuck wife on my arm..." he smirks and I let out a small laugh, "but, I know it's going to cause issues for you."

"Why for me?"

"Because of your dad. Titus will get over it with me, sure, he'll be pissed... but he'll be more pissed that you ran off to Vegas with his hot as fuck best friend and married him."

"Few facts wrong there but, I'll let it slide."

"Oh yeah? What ones?" he teases, pushing up onto his elbow and I miss his touch.

"The hot as fuck best friend..."

His brows furrow.

"I don't think you're his best friend anymore."

"And the hot as fuck..." he waits patiently as I climb out of bed.

"That's for me to know and you to never find out," I shrug, walking towards the bathroom completely naked knowing his eyes are me.

Once behind the door, I lock it and a small smile creeps across my lips.

Arizona Mills.

Does kind of have a nice ring to it.

MY HANGOVER HITS IN FULL FORCE AND I AM ALREADY OVER IT. Covering my tired eyes with black rimmed large *Gucci* glasses, I delicately sit down at the breakfast table and ignore the burning sets of eyes that are settled on me and Keaton.

"Well, well, well..." I hear Dex say and I internally curse. "If it isn't the happy newlyweds."

Sage elbows him and he lets out a deep rumble of a laugh.

My eyes move to Reese who is rolling her lips and Killian definitely looks worse for wear.

"So, is Titus pissed with you too Killian?" Keaton pipes up beside me and I roll my eyes behind my glasses.

"Pissed is an understatement," he grumbles.

"I say we just stay in Vegas," Keaton looks between us all as if this is up for conversation.

"Not going to happen," I sigh, reaching for the water in the middle of the table and I pour myself a full glass, drinking it in one.

"Thirsty, wife?" Keaton asks and I nearly choke on my intake of breath.

"Don't," I warn, my patience already wearing thin.

Killian chuckles softly and I watch as Reese swats him away and gives him a warning stare down.

"I'm starving, you guys eaten yet?" Keaton announces to the table and they all say no. I take that as my moment to gaze down for just a little while to see the gold band locked around his finger and my heart flutters for just a moment; but then real life smacks me in the face, hard. We need to get it annulled.

This isn't a real marriage.

It was a stupid, drunk bet.

Both of us are two pig headed and strong willed to be seen as the weaker person. So, we went through with the marriage.

Stupid.

Stupid, stupid, girl.

My phone buzzes on the table and I don't even look at it. I don't need to. I know it's my dad.

"Want me to speak to him? He is my father-in-law now..." Keaton licks his lips before they pull into a smile.

"I'm going to bury you," I seethe, cutting my dad off and pushing away from the table and walking towards the buffet table.

Nausea floats through me making my stomach turn, my mouth watering and not in a good way. Suddenly, I feel hot and clammy as I try and ignore the feeling. Mind over matter. *Mind. Over. Matter.*

I continuously repeat to myself.

A hand grips on my shoulder and I freeze.

"You okay?" Sage asks softly and I look over my shoulder at her.

"Yeah, this hangover is kicking my ass. Feeling clammy and sicky..." I pause for a moment as another roll of nausea consumes me and I can't help but turn my nose up at the smell of the cooked food.

"Hangover?" a brow lifts and I nod.

"Was so sick this morning. Could still be the back end of that stomach flu I had flying over. I thought it was motion sickness, it did sort of calm down, but I think the alcohol has made it worse," and I hate it, but I whine. I am the worst when I am unwell.

Sage reaches for my glasses and pushes them on the top of my head. Squinting at the bright lights I cast my eyes down.

"Why would they make it so bright when ninety percent of their guests are hungover?" I groan, reaching for my glasses but Sage stops me.

"I don't think it's stomach flu," she finally says.

"Sure it is," I half laugh, eyes widening when they bring fresh bacon out and I gag. "Don't be silly," I laugh her off and step away from the buffet table to take my seat next to

Keaton, but I don't miss a chance to look over my shoulder at her as she loads her plate up. Dex is beside her now, arm wrapped round her waist as he places a soft kiss on the side of her head.

"You okay?" Keaton asks me quietly as he stands from the table and I just nod, suddenly unable to speak. "Want some food?" I shake my head from side to side. My appetite is gone. "Okay," he says and hovers for a moment and I half expect him to place a kiss on the top of my head, but he doesn't and I can't help but wonder if it's because of Killian and Reese.

"You okay?" Reese asks, leaning across the table and taking my hand in hers.

"I will be once this hangover leaves."

"This feels like déjà vu," she smirks as she looks at a grumpy Killian.

"I bet... how did you decide about an annulment?" I ask, pulling my hand from Reese and filling my glass up once more.

"That's a story for another day, but I can point you in the right direction when you're ready." She smiles softly before standing from the table, tapping Killian on the shoulder and pulling him up with her and suddenly, I am alone.

My thoughts are loud, and Sage's voice is the only thing on repeat.

I'm not alone long when she sits in front of me, giving me a small smile and I cover my mouth with my hand as the smell of her food fills my nose.

"How far gone would you be if you were pregnant? Hypothetically speaking, of course." Sage's question catches me off guard and I focus on her, staring and in a state of shock.

"Sorry?" is all I manage after a minute.

"How many weeks late are you?"

I blink again, mouth opening and shutting like a damn goldfish.

"I'm not," I furrow my brow, shaking my head from side to side as I reach for my glass. I roll my lips, casting my eyes down for just a moment before rolling my shoulders back. A knowing smile sits on her face as she drinks from her own water glass.

"Are you?" I stare at her, waiting and hanging on for the words to slip past her lips.

She nods, and I see the happiness that is painted over her face. "Ah, Sage, that's amazing..." I pause for a moment when realization smacks me in the face, "wait, is that why you think I'm pregnant?"

She laughs.

"I don't think, I know. The way you're feeling and acting was how I was in the early stages of my pregnancy. So, how many weeks are you?"

I sit, dumbfounded and wait for the shoe to drop.

Pregnant?

If I was, I would be about three, four weeks if that... which means it could be either Keaton's or my web cam friend... shit.

"I swear I've had my period this mo..." and as soon as that sentence leaves me, I realize that I in fact, have not had my period. "Fuck," I put my head in my hands.

"It'll be okay," Sage's hand cups over mine, rubbing her thumb in slow circles across the back of it as I breathe through the crushing anxiety that has presented itself in my chest.

"Will it?" I whimper as I lift my head to look at her, tears threatening.

"Keaton seems cool enough, and now you're married... seems like fate, right?" I shake my head from side to side. "What?" she laughs, "he is not cool or...?"

"It may not be his..." and I'm going to throw up. Sage reaches for a napkin and pushes it into my hands as I empty the contents of my stomach in a somewhat discreet way and I am grateful my stomach isn't that full.

I am just grateful no one else is around us, they're all still over getting their food and coffees.

"Let's go pick up some tests hm?" Sage smirks and I want to cry.

"Not yet," I shake my head, "I just want to enjoy the rest of the morning without thinking or worrying about the possible human that will reside inside my womb for the next eight months," I puff out my cheeks just as Keaton sits next to me and places a coffee down in front of me and a bowl of cereal.

"I know how much you like cereal," he says softly as I try and hide the sick filled napkin.

"Thank you," my voice cracks at his small gesture and I manage to keep a poker face, but inside, I am full blown ugly crying.

CHAPTER TWENTY-THREE
ARIZONA

We walk back to our rooms and agree to meet at the botanical gardens in the hotel after we've freshened up; Reese and Killian as well. Nerves bloom in my chest, knotting my stomach and making the nauseous feeling more evident. Was Sage right? Could I be pregnant? Fear blankets me and inside I can feel myself trembling. I sit on the edge of the bed, my eyes pinned to the carpet of our room and I can't seem to concentrate on anything other than the possibility of a baby growing inside of me. How could I have been so stupid. I know I have used protection once with Keaton and *TallDarkandHandsome*, and I am on my own birth control methods so getting pregnant seems a rarity but not impossible. These things happen. I know that, not all methods are safe. No matter if you were double wrapped. Shit, what was I going to do.

Keaton didn't want to be a dad, and honestly, I didn't want to be a mom. Did I? Yeah, in the future I would love to be a mom, but not at the age of twenty-one. I had so much planned. Sure, my plans were derailed slightly with not passing my exams, but still, I was working and I know deep down I would love to go back to medical school and redo my internship. I just didn't have it in me to return with my year now above me. Maybe in a couple of years when they're further into their career, maybe then I could go back. But until then. I needed to just keep my job, save enough money and move out. I couldn't go back home. I didn't want to go back home. I didn't want to stay with Keaton forever either. He helped me out and was willing to let me stay while I needed to. It was getting to the point where I didn't need to be there anymore.

Fuck, and then we got married. What were we thinking? Both too strong headed to back the fuck down like we should have done. Neither of us wanted to be the loser. But now look at both of us. Married. Possibly pregnant with another man's baby and burning the once steady bridges around us.

Shit. This is fucked up.

Throwing my head into my hands I let out a heavy sigh. I didn't want to cry, but I could feel the burn in my throat, the sting behind my eyes like a thousand needles.

"Ari," Keaton's voice blankets me like a thick velvet blanket and suddenly I feel safe and warm. I look up at him, blue eyes glassy as I let them sweep over his wet upper body. Torso shimmering with shower water, dark hair flattened to his toned chest and a dusting of hair disappearing into his white fluffy towel that is hugged around his waist. My thoughts subside momentarily and are replaced with the thought of running my tongue over his torso, lapping up the droplets of water that run down his tanned skin. To feel the silkiness of him on my tongue.

"Yup," I look up at him, eyes burning into his beautiful green emeralds.

"Are you okay? You've seemed a little quiet since

breakfast," and I hear a small ounce of defeat in his voice. I nod.

"Just trying to wrap my head round all of this." A laugh catches at the back of my throat. "What the fuck did we do last night?" I shake my head from side to side and stand, Keaton closing the gap between us as his hand cups my cheek.

"We got married baby," he cocks his head to the side, a small smirk pulling at the corner of his lips and I lean into his hand, letting my eyes flutter shut for just a moment.

"We're stupid."

"Maybe," he chuckles softly, "but honestly, tell me... are you mad about it?"

My lids lift, my eyes widening as I stare at him, mouth opening and closing.

"Are you?" he presses, his tone dark and slow and delicious.

"No," I manage a whisper, "are you?"

"Not one fucking bit baby," he pauses for a moment as his thumb pad brushes against my flamed cheek. "But if you want an annulment, or a divorce... or whatever it is. Then I will do it. If that's what you want." His eyes dance with mine and I press up onto my tip toes and kiss him softly; my hand on his steady heartbeat, my fingers soaking up the now cold shower water and I let my nerves absorb every ounce of him into my soul.

He was an addiction that I knew I had to curb, but I couldn't. He was my drug and I wanted and needed him constantly, every waking moment my thoughts were on him, counting down the hours until my fingers were on his skin, our tongues were dancing together, our lips locked as our hearts entwined as one. We shouldn't work. But we do. I have never wanted anything as much as I want Keaton

Mills. It was wrong. We both knew it. But we were both addicts and we didn't want to quit.

I break away, stepping back as my stomach twists.

"I need to pop to the store, you stay here and I'll meet you back in the room shortly okay?" I rush out and begin walking to the door, grabbing my bag as I do.

"I'll come with you, hold up."

"No, honestly, I'm fine. I need some fresh air, Sage is coming with me," I give him a tight nod and grab my key card as I walk out the door, letting the heavy door close behind me.

I walk, head up, as I march towards Sage and Dex's room. Lifting my hand, I knock on the door softly, and within seconds, the door pulls open and I see a wide-eyed Sage.

"Er... did I interrupt?" I ask, my cheeks pinching red.

"Nope, well... maybe, but—"

"You did!" Dex shouts out and Sage rolls her eyes.

"What's up, is everything okay?"

"Not really, no. But, I need to go to a drug store or something. I need to grab a..." I pause, not sure if she has even mentioned it to Dex or not. I didn't want anyone else knowing about this until they had to.

"Sure thing, let me just..." she thumbs behind her and I give her a nod, stepping back as she closes the door. Bad enough I encroached, I didn't want to overstep more, so thought best to let her finish what she had started.

Nerves swirl like rapids in my stomach and my chest aches. What the fuck was I going to do? My dad would murder Keaton if I was. I was sure of it. Then he would lock me away.

Oh how ironic.

Dad and grandpa at the same time.

Sucks to be him right now.

I am pulled from my thoughts when Sage opens the door, dressed in a completely different outfit and large sunglasses on.

"Ready?"

"Nope."

"Good, then let's get going."

The autumn sun in Vegas was still hot and it felt so good to have the sun on my skin, I missed it. I didn't like the cold winters back in New York, but I loved the winter sun. The sunshine always made things better. Whether it would make this situation any better, we will find out soon, but normally, the sun does indeed make everything better.

The strip was busy, too busy for eleven a.m.

"How's the hangover?" Sage knocks into me and I let out what sounds like a growl. "That good aye?" I look over at her, narrowing my gaze on her but she wouldn't know that because I am hid behind my glasses.

"Sage what am I going to do?" I say quietly as we round a corner and down an alley where some shops are located.

"You're going to boss it. Of course, you are." She links her arms through mine, and I have never been more grateful than I am now to have someone by my side like Sage. What am I going to do when she moves back home? Fear claws my throat.

"Sage, I'm scared," I stop in my tracks and turn to face her, and I hadn't even realized a tear escaped, running down my cheek as I palm it away.

"Of course, you are, I would be worried if you wasn't." I nod, dropping my head for a moment. "How do you think Keaton will take it, hypothetically speaking..." she pauses.

"It's not just Keaton I have to worry about..." I focus on my chunky loafers, my bare legs out.

"Another man?"

"A one-night thing."

"Work?" her brows raise high enough to lift over the thick rims of her black sunglasses.

"I do cam girl work... well, did. One of my clients paid for a private room a few weeks back... I hadn't ever done anything like that before. He took my..."

I can't even bring myself to say the words when I feel my shoulders sag and a choked sob vibrates through my chest, my lungs burning and my eyes leaking with salty tears.

"Oh, my sweet girl," Sage breathes, pulling me into her arms and folding me into an embrace as I cry into her chest. "It'll be okay." Her hand is stroking though my hair as she lets me cry and soak her black peter pan collared dress.

"I am just hoping it's Keaton's."

"And if it isn't?" She asks the burning question.

"Then I have no idea," I whisper, lifting my head from her chest and pushing the glasses onto my head as I angrily wipe the tear stains off my face.

"Keaton is a good man... I think he will prove you wrong."

"I hope you're right, I really do," I tremble before she drags me back towards her and holds me tightly, not letting me go until I am ready.

WALKING OUT OF THE STORE WITH A HANDFUL OF PREGNANCY tests, I stash them inside my bag as we take a slow walk back to the hotel. I still couldn't believe I had gotten myself into this situation. I knew me and Keaton hadn't used protection a couple of times, so, given the odds of Keaton versus *TallDarkandHandsome*, Keaton was coming up trumps. But life doesn't work out that way does it. Life can be cruel, and given the hand I have already been dealt in this shitty life, chances were the baby would work out to be *his*, whoever *he* was. I was blindfolded that night, I heard the sound of the wrapper being ripped open but what if he actually never used it? It was my first time; I don't know how it should have felt.

Such an idiot.

We approach the hotel and I stop walking, looking up at the large building and my heart is drumming inside my chest at rapid speed as it skips beats.

"Whatever the outcome..." Sage says and I lock my hand with hers, our fingers linked as I give her a reassuring squeeze.

"Time to rip the plaster off..."

"Band-aid," I correct her.

"We say plaster," she scrunches her nose up.

"You're in America now baby, we say band-aid," and she swats the top of my arm and walks me back into the hotel where I am about to learn my fate.

And I think deep down I already knew what was about to come.

I just didn't want to believe it.

We said our goodbyes and I walked towards my hotel room, and with every step that drew me closer, my heart thumped a little harder in my chest.

Letting myself in the room, my eyes seek out Keaton who gives me a handsome smile as his eyes land on me.

"Was thinking you may have done a runner on me, wife?" he teases, and my insides knot at the word *wife* leaving his lips.

It has no right sounding as hot as it did.

"Never," I whisper, clutching my purse tightly under my arm.

"You okay?" his brows furrow as he steps closer to me and I step back, nodding.

"I just need to use the restroom," I drop my eyes from his, suddenly it feels too much to be staring into the window of his soul when I could potentially wreck his world in the next five to ten minutes.

I don't wait to hear what he says, just slip inside the room and lock the door behind me. Placing my purse on the countertop of the vanity unit, I curl my fingers round the edge and drop my head.

"Please, whoever is looking over me, whoever is guiding me down my path... please let this work out the way it should."

Finally lifting my heavy head, I stare at myself in the mirror. This is it. I needed to pull my big girl panties up and pee on the stick.

Giving myself a nod at my reflection, I reach for my purse and grab the small brown bag with the tests in. Sage told me to get a normal and a digital and to do both, so, that's what I was going to do.

Then come the waiting, and honestly, it was the longest three minutes of my life.

A knock on the door has me jumping back and spinning to face where the noise came from.

"Yeah?" I call out, nerves suffocating me.

"Are you okay?"

"Yeah, fine, just come over a little nauseous."

"Do you need anything?"

"No thanks."

There is so much more I want to say, but the words are struggling to fight through the thickness of my throat.

I turn around, heartbeat drumming in my chest, blood thumping in my ears when I finally allow myself to lift the tests up and read the results.

"Oh my god."

I stared at the two tests in front of me.

One with two pink lines.

The other with the words 'pregnant 2-3 weeks'.

Fuck.

Fuck, fuck, fuck.

This is fine. It's all fine.

Is it?

Shit.

No, it's not fine.

FUCK!

I slam my hands down on the work surface before wrapping my fingers back round the edge of the unit, my head tipped back as silent tears fall from my eyes.

Married.

Pregnant.

My life literally turned upside down in a day.

It's going to be fine.

I silently reasoned with myself.

Slowly letting my head roll up, I look at my blotchy face and tear-stained cheeks and smile at myself in the mirror. It had to be fine.

Because it wasn't just me anymore.

Dusting the tests into my purse, I then splash my face with water.

Standing up a little taller, I roll my shoulders back and walk out of the restroom and back to a pacing Keaton.

"Are you okay?" He rushes to my side, cupping my face in his hands as his eyes search my face for something, anything to give him an answer.

I nod, biting the inside of my bottom lip to stop the tears that are threatening to fall once more.

"Hey, hey, talk to me," he ushers, his thumb collecting a tear that escaped.

"I'm pregnant, Keaton." there is no point beating around the bush, no point stalling the inevitable. "It wasn't stomach flu, or motion sickness. It was pregnancy. I'm having a baby."

And I wait. And wait. And wait a little bit more for him to freak out. For him to start yelling and screaming about how stupid I am to get knocked up and how reckless it was of me to throw my life away so young with a pregnancy.

But he doesn't. I see the way his eyes soften, the way his lips turn up into a smile and then the light green of his eyes mists over.

"You're pregnant?" he whispers, my fingers wrapping round his wrists, and I nod, tears now streaming down my face, but then the harsh reality kicks me in the stomach like a horse hoof.

"But..." I pause.

"But," he hangs on my word.

"There was the guy before you..."

"But it was only once?" he looks at me confused.

"It only takes once, Keaton," and my tone is soft, our eyes locked on each other's gaze.

"But we have done it so much more," his brows wiggle in a playful manner and I couldn't love him more than I do in this moment.

"But..." I pause, "the buts don't matter Keaton. I can't promise this baby is yours... and I completely get if you don't want to—" he pushes his finger to my lips and shakes his head from side to side slowly.

"I'm not going anywhere Blossom, it's me and you," his lips press to my cheeks, soaking my tears up.

"But," my bottom lip trembles.

"The buts don't matter baby..." his hands slowly pull from my face and rest on my lower stomach as he recites my earlier words, "it's just the three of us. Genetics don't matter, it's you and me and our little baby. I'm not going anywhere. I promise you."

And I sob. Full on ugly sobbing as I throw my arms around his neck, holding onto him like he is my lifeline and I never want to let him go.

CHAPTER TWENTY-FOUR
KEATON

FUCK.

Pregnant.

Inside I am freaking out. But I don't want her to know that. I meant what I promised. I am not going anywhere. I am not going to let her slip away from me. She is pregnant, and sure, it may not be my baby, but it will be *my* baby.

My heart aches.

I always wanted to be a dad, but I never had it on my bingo card. It just didn't seem to come, there were so many girls, some I was careful with, some I wasn't, but they've never turned up at my door like 'hey, here is your kid'.

So I am pretty sure I am off the hook until now.

Fuck.

Titus is going to kill me.

Bad enough I've married his daughter, but now he is going to know I've fucked her too. More than once actually.

Odds are definitely in my favor.

I fucked her so hard that I am sure I put a baby or two inside of her.

My cock swells in my pants.

What the fuck is wrong with me.

Her arms are locked round my neck, mine round her back and we just stand like this, in complete silence as the world continues to spin, but in this moment ours has stopped. Frozen in time almost.

WE WALK TOWARDS THE BOTANICAL GARDENS OF THE BELLAGIO and Killian, Reese, Sage and Dex are already waiting for us. Sage glares at Arizona before her eyes land on me. Does she know? Did Ari confide in her before me? Not that it matters, of course it doesn't. Girl code and all that. Her and Sage have become closer which is nice, I know she has Reese and Connie, but they're linked to the drama that we left behind in New York, where Sage is like a breath of fresh air that we both so desperately need.

"How are our happy couple?" Killian asks, smiling at me before looking at Ari.

"We're blissful," I smirk, my arm linked around her back as I pull her closer towards me, my head turning as I press a kiss to the side of her head and linger for just a moment.

"Have you spoken to Titus?" He continues and I inhale heavily.

"No, have you? I'm sure you're on his kill list as well as me, old boy."

"Old boy? You're older than me." I shove Killian hard and he stumbles, losing his footing for just a moment.

"Fuck off," I chuckle, "I may be older, but time has not been kind to you my friend," and I watch as Reese looks up at Killian with concern on her face, her hand splayed over his heart and I want to kick myself. I know all about his health issues and now I feel like a class 'A' cunt for bringing it up. "Wasn't anything personal," I mutter and he gives me a knowing nod. I felt awful. Made my chest ache.

"I know it wasn't, you're a dickhead but not that much of one," and he smiles at me, pulling Reese into him and then I focus my attention on Dex and Sage who are talking quietly among themselves.

"We were thinking, seeing as we're talking about pricks," She smirks and Dex chuckles.

"Not actually talking about pricks are we though..." I breathe out and Ari giggles next to me.

"I booked us an early dinner at Pricks, the restaurant. We have one in England called Karen's and it is brutal, so thought, why the hell not."

"This is going to be interesting," I raise a brow and glance over towards Killian.

"Oh, it really is," Dex nods, taking Sage's hand in his and leads her towards the gardens, us all following like we're following our tattooed tour guides.

Dex and Sage are beautiful. Their tattoos, their edginess, their looks... everything about them.

Next to them I look like an old worn-out boot. Slightly broken in places and definitely glued back together in some.

Arizona's small hand tucks inside mine and we lose ourselves for just a moment as we walk through the gardens, taking everything in as Dex tells us the ins and outs of what's what.

"When are you going to look at the club?" Arizona asks as we sit at a small table for a coffee break, well, an iced tea break for Arizona.

"Tonight, got to be there for eight. Still okay to come?"

Sage looks at Arizona as she takes a sip of her milky coffee, Dex with his cortado.

"Yeah, sure, if you still want me to?"

"Of course we do, and the offer still stands. We want you as manager, if you still want it of course." she asks, a small milk froth on her top lip that Dex wipes away with his thumb, then pops it into his mouth and cleans it off.

"Yes, yes," she nods, a huge smile gracing her lips and Sage smiles back at her.

Quietness fills the table when Killian and Reese sit down in the two empty seats and it doesn't take them long to pick up the tension that is brewing because of the conversation that stopped so suddenly.

Reese looks around the table, then her eyes land on Sage.

"So, how did you guys meet?" Reese asks, taking a sip of her drink. Killian sitting with his arm tucked round the back of his wife.

"Work," Sage smiles and I see Arizona run her finger across her throat. Sage furrows her brows.

"Yes, Sage came into the hospital, and I was her intern with my attending," Arizona pauses for a moment, eyes bugging as she waits for Sage to clock on. "We just hit it off, and yes, I know, patient-doctor confidentiality and all that, but," she shrugs her shoulders up, "we met at the time I needed her most, things were happening with Dad, Amora was here, I felt bad making you and Connie choose who to spend your time with..."

"Ari," Reese looks at her, hand reaching across the table. "We would never choose, you're our friend and always will be. Yes, we have met Amora and she really is lovely. It's nice to have a few more Brits over here and on my side..." she pauses and gives Sage a wink, "but we love you, so so much and we will be here for you through everything. And when you're ready, we will be by your side when you want to see your dad. I know you're not ready, and no one is going to rush you, but just remember, you only get one dad and you're lucky enough to still have yours here and present in your life... some are not so lucky," she rolls her lips into a thin line and I grip Arizona's thigh under the table and give her a reassuring squeeze.

"Thank you," is all Ari responds with and I know that sounds cold and like she didn't give a shit what Reese said, but I know she would have taken it all in. Whether she acts upon it or not is another thing, but, baby steps.

Baby.

I would be lying if I said I hadn't thought about the other dude and I am praying that the baby is mine, but I did mean what I said. I was going to be a part of Arizona and this baby's life as long as they wanted me here. I made her a promise and I don't go back on my promises.

She is my wife.

And even though I haven't told her out loud.

I love her.

With every single fiber I have.

This isn't the way I expected my life to go at forty-seven, but here I am, married to my best friend's daughter and now she is pregnant.

But she is my life. Titus is going to hate me, but he would hate me even more if I kicked her to the curb and let her live out her life alone as a single mother, raising a baby by herself.

She will never be by herself.

She will always have me.

She will eventually have Titus and Amora. She has Dex

and Sage, Killian and Reese, Connie and Kaleb and of course, Nate.

She doesn't realize it yet, but she has a whole family waiting for her.

She will never be alone.

Ever.

I would make sure of that, until my last dying breath. And if, *if* the baby isn't mine and the dad decides he wants to be part of his baby's life, then she will have him too.

I won't step aside, but I will let him be a dad.

Because the baby deserves to know it's father.

Whether that be me or not. It'll break my heart, but it's the right thing.

CHAPTER TWENTY-FIVE
ARIZONA

WE WALK TOWARDS PRICKS, AND I FEEL AT EASE NOW THAT Keaton knows. I had no idea how he was going to react, but I couldn't have wished for a better outcome. He didn't walk away.

He still wanted whatever this was between us.

He wanted to be here for the baby whether it was his or not.

He still *wanted* me.

He promised he wouldn't leave me.

Promised he would be by my side.

My heart sung in my chest, leaping and pirouetting.

His fingers were laced with mine, and it's like all my worries slipped out from underneath my feet and we were floating. Killian promised not to breathe a word to my dad until I was ready, and I trusted him. Also, Reese wouldn't let him say anything. It's not that I didn't want my dad to know, I would tell him, but I needed to fix what was already broken before I threw something else into the mix. I wanted to call my dad and tell him everything and tell him I wanted to forgive him but it will just take me a little time.

Understandably. I felt betrayed in the worst possible way. My mom left me when I was a baby, and now my dad was married to a girl a little older than me and having another baby. I was his life. But now I wasn't going to be his everything and that was really fucking selfish of me to even be thinking these thoughts, but I didn't care. I already lost one parent, and now I was going to lose another one because he chose to move on and have another baby—which he was well within his right to do, obviously—but it still hurt. I was used to being his everything and now, well... I felt like I had been kicked to the curb and disregarded.

But I knew I hadn't. That's the annoying thing. My brain was constantly reminding me of what he'd done.

He texts me every morning and every night just like he always has done, but I leave him on read, because I am horrible.

My stomach knots and I feel instantly sad.

Keaton's thumb rubs over the back of my hand and tightens slightly which causes me to look up at him, giving him a sad smile.

It's like he can read my body language, any little emotion that I feel or show, he is there with me. I never believed in soulmates until Keaton.

I never thought I would fall in love with one of my dad's best friends, but here I am.

Married.

Pregnant.

In love.

We were so wrong, yet so right in so many ways.

Following Sage into Pricks, Reese and Killian were by my side and I was praying that I didn't feel sick at the table. I still couldn't believe I was pregnant.

I actually have a baby growing inside of me.

I know I am going to have to sign into my cam app and face *TallDarkandHandsome* at some point. I have been in hiding ever since that night. I never expected it to go the way it did, but yet, it happened. One of the worst nights of my life and I have had a few.

I never should have agreed to meet him. Should have just kept it online, in my bedroom. But I was stupid and did it anyway and now here I am. Pregnant. With either his or Keaton's baby and I really want it to be Keaton's. I know he says he will love it either way but still... will he?

"Ugh, what do you want?" the rude young server says to us, his eyes bouncing between the six of us.

"We have a table booked," Sage pipes up, walking forward and standing tall.

"How unfortunate for you," he rolls his eyes, scooping up six menus.

"Name?"

"Sage."

The guy blinks at her as if in disbelief.

"Sage? As in the stick they use to burn to rid of the unwanted dead?" She stays mute.

"By the looks of what you dragged in with you, it clearly didn't work."

She giggles and I hear Killian grunt.

"Come on Sage, lead your dead to the table and follow me."

We all follow him and sit on a long rectangular table.

"What the fuck is this place?" Keaton asks as the server tosses a menu at him, his arms flying up to protect himself.

"Your worst nightmare," the server says as he continues launching the menus around.

I laugh, lifting my menu up and scanning it. "My name is David, I will be your unhelpful server this afternoon," he sighs heavily, pulling out his notepad and pen. "Drinks?"

"I'll have a beer please mate," Dex says first.

"Mate? I'm not your mate. Wouldn't be mates with you if you were the last person on earth..." David looks Dex over in pure disgust and Dex laughs.

"What about you, Morticia, what do you want?"

"Sweet iced tea."

"Basic. What about you, Heffner?" he asks and faces Keaton and I want to die.

"Excuse me?"

"Sorry, I forgot you're hard of hearing. WHAT ABOUT YOU HEFFNER?" he now shouts across the table.

"I'm not deaf! Fucking hell man," he groans. "Beer," he huffs and tosses his menu into the middle of the table.

"And you, the quiet one who looks like she is sitting here against her will?"

"Sweet iced tea."

"Basic. Grandad number two and blondie?"

"Beer."

"I'll have a glass of wine please."

"Basic," he rolls his eyes, "let me guess, a chardonnay?"

"Sauvignon."

"It's a box wine, you get what you're given okay princess?"

She rolls her lips and hides her growing smile behind her menu.

"Well, that was painful, hurry and chose something to eat, I haven't got all day."

And with that, he turns and disappears out back.

"Well, that was awful," Killian groans looking over the menu.

"It's all good fun," Sage leans into Dex.

"Riveting."

And I laugh.

"Have you been here before Sage?" I ask as I scan the menu again.

"No, we have one like this back home in London, so thought this would be fun to come to."

"Fun is not the word I would use," Keaton groans beside me.

"Stop being a bore," and just as the words come out my mouth, David is back with paper hats for us all. He begins placing them on our heads one by one, but not before reading what he has written on all of them.

Sage: *High maintenance but swallows!*

Dex: *Pussy whipped coloring book.*

Killian: *Lets his wife peg him.*

Reese: *Daddy issues.*

Keaton: *A minute and half of pure pleasure*

Arizona: *My dad would be pissed if he knew how many dicks I've put in my mouth.*

And I am crying.

All of us are.

We all sit with our hats on for the duration of our meal and even take them home with us. I wasn't expecting to enjoy it, but I loved every second of it.

Saying our goodbyes, we slip into our room, and I feel exhausted suddenly.

"Let me draw you a bath," Keaton says as he wraps his arms around me and pulls me close.

"That would be amazing," he places a kiss on my forehead.

Stepping into the bathroom, the aromas fill my nose and I instantly feel relaxed. Lavender and eucalyptus wrap me in a warm blanket as I pull my dress from my body, and I let it fall to the floor. Once naked, I turn to face the mirror and look at my body, and I know it's impossible, but I already feel like I have changed from this morning. It's slowly sinking in that I am growing a baby, a little human who I am bringing into this world to love with everything I have. I have no idea how to be a mother, I have no idea how to love a child how a mother should, but I will do my very best. I had the best teacher in my dad, he was the best mom and dad there was, and I am so grateful. He was there for every cold, every tear, every bad dream and every fall out that I ever had. It was always him. Nate and Kaleb too. Keaton never really helped out when I was younger. He was only there if no one else could help, and now, being where we are, I am grateful for that.

Dipping my foot into the hot bath water, my skin breaks into goosebumps as I slip under the bubbles, and I hadn't realized how much I needed it until now. I feel my muscles relax under the water and with the bath salts. My eyes are closed, and I enjoy the silence until I hear the bathroom door go and a knowing smile graces my lips. Keaton kneels next to the bath, his hand slipping into the hot water, and I can feel him looking at me. Slowly opening my eyes, his green eyes are settled on me, scanning over my face as if he is trying to remember every detail.

"Stop staring," I say softly, my eyes falling heavy as I let them close once more.

"I can't help it, you're just too beautiful."

Cheese ball.

And I feel the heat creep onto my cheeks.

"Are you drunk?" I tease, eyes still closed, lips pulling into a smirk.

"Drunk in lo..." and he pauses, my eyes slowly opening.

"Same," I hum, not wanting him to think that he is the only one who is feeling something so much more than friendship.

"What's happening to us?" He whispers, his hand moving back and forth through the bath water causing soft ripples.

"We've fallen, we crossed the line..." I pause, his fingertips brushing the silkiness of my wet skin on my thigh.

"The line wanted to be crossed."

"It did..." I pause for a moment and my chest vibrates on my intake of breath. "Dad is going to be furious."

"So, he will get over it. These things happen. You can't help who you fall in lo..."

"I know," I nod, slipping a little further under so now my lips are under the water, stopping myself from saying the words out loud, but doesn't mean I can't mouth *I love you* under water where only I can feel it, only I know I am speaking it. "I do need to talk to him, I don't want to have this baby still being mad at him."

"I agree, he will be okay."

"I'm not so sure, I'm his baby."

"You are, but you're also a young woman who deserves to live her life and fall for whoever she wants. He will be madder at me, trust me. If I don't return, then send out a search party. I'll send my last location so it will give you a little hint of where he may have buried me. Plus, he has Xavier. There is no way I am getting out of this alive, Blossom," he smirks at me and I splash him with a little bit of water.

"Stop it, he wouldn't do that, he loves you too much."

"He did. Not anymore."

"That's how I feel."

And sadness blooms in my chest at my confession.

"Baby," he pauses, his wet fingers gripping my chin and turning me to face him, "he will never not love you. He may be mad, fuck, he may be furious, but he will always love you. You're his baby girl, he loves you so much Ari. He is worried but he knows you're in good hands..." he trails off and tilts his head to the side, "well you were before I married you while drunk and let you get pregnant."

I roll my lips.

"I want this baby to be yours Keaton, so bad."

"Baby, I've told you, this baby is mine. Blood or not, this baby is mine."

My eyes swarm with tears as they roll down my cheeks and I am so overwhelmed that everything inside of me aches with feelings I have never felt before. My heart is ready to explode in my chest and it's all because of this man that is knelt beside my bath, his hands buried in my water, and he doesn't even care.

I pull his lips down to mine, kissing him with all I have and he wraps his arms around me, pulling me from the tub and carrying me into the bedroom, laying me down on the bed. He finally looks at me, *really looks at me*. His eyes full of every emotion I have just felt as he slips between my legs, his hands linked in mine as he pins them above my head. His mouth drags across my jaw and down the column of my neck and my body reacts to him in a way that only he knows.

"Keaton," I whisper, fighting against his grip.

"Yes baby?"

"I need you," and he releases me as I grab the hem of his tee and drag it over his head. His fingers are wrapped back round my wrists, pinning them above my head but with only one hand now as the other roams over my body, worshipping me with his mouth and I am lost in this moment with him. We said we wouldn't do this again. But this is who we were. We couldn't help it. It was a chemical thing. A reaction maybe. A need and want all rolled into a beautiful addiction that only when I was with him did the need subside to nothing but a simmer deep inside of me.

His fingers rub in slow circles over my clit, fingers dipping and sinking into me before slipping out and focusing on my clit.

"More, I need more," I whine, and I know I sound needy but I don't care. My hips lift, as his fingers glide between my lips and slip into me once more, working me up before he drags my arousal back over my clit.

"I will give you everything baby, I promise," he kisses against my skin, his tongue licking out the fire that is spreading across my body.

His lips pull my nipple into his mouth, licking and sucking before gliding his hot mouth across my chest and onto my other nipple and giving it the same attention. I am writhing beneath him, his fingers buried deep inside of me, and I am too lost in the moment to think about anything else other than me and him. How perfect we were, but also how dangerous this game we were playing was.

"Keaton," I whisper, slipping my hands out of his loosened grip as I place my hands either side of his face, pulling him up to me.

"Yes Blossom," he whispers back, but I silence him by pulling his mouth onto mine, kissing him deep as our tongue entwine, his fingers still working me up, arousal pooling between my legs but he doesn't stop even though I am more than ready for him.

"I never want to know what it's like to not have you."

"You never will," softness wraps around his deep voice

and before he can say anything else, I drag him back towards me. I don't want to speak, I want to be lost with him forever. We were made for each other. He was everything I have ever wanted or needed. He was like the air I breathed. He came naturally to me but to not have him near me, to not be able to have him, scared me. My lungs burned at just the thought, and suddenly I feel like I am starved of oxygen. Fingers linked round the back of his head, I hold him in place just where I want him as he slips his fingers out of me and I hear his zipper go. My whole body tenses in anticipation and I need to feel full, I need to feel loved and worshipped by this man. The man who has giving me so much over the last year. He pulls away, looking down between our bodies and I push up onto my elbows, legs bent and wide as he lines himself up, green eyes devour me whole before they're back between where our bodies meet and slowly, so so slowly, he rolls his hips forward and slides into me until I am full of him. My mouth a gape as I relish in this feeling that has overwhelmed me wholly.

"Ari," he moans as he begins to move, slowly pulling out of me and pushing back into me hard. His pounds are punishing, and I know if he continues like this, neither of us will last long.

"You feel so good." My head tips back, fingers tightening on the sheet beneath me.

"You drive me wild, everything about you Ari, the way you were made for me, us fitting perfectly together," he growls. A hand skims down my body, fingers circling my clit to match the rhythm of Keaton and I can feel my orgasm teetering. My pussy tightening around him, clenching. "Fuck," he drawls out, head falling back for just a moment before he stills.

Pulling out of me, he falls to his knees, hitting the carpeted floor and his large hands wrap around my waist as he pulls me closer to the edge of the bed and rolls me onto my side. Resting on one elbow, my hand is still on my clit as I look down at him, wide green eyes hungry for more and I moan, wetness pooling and I am ready to explode. He edges forward, mouth hovering over my pussy before his tongue spreads through me, greedily circling my clit, matching the way my fingers are moving.

"Oh god," my head tips back, his finger teases at my opening as he licks and eats me like I am his last meal and he has been starved.

"How close are you baby?" Lifting his lips for just a moment, his fingers pulse deep inside of me, a third teasing at my opening which I am silently pleading for.

"Close," I whisper, fingers still dancing before his tongue joins in.

Slipping his soaked fingers from me, he pushes them into my mouth and I suck them clean.

"See how good you taste baby, see why I can't get enough," he groans, now standing and I watch as his cock bobs between his legs.

Snatching my fingers away, his large hands press onto my thighs, spreading them wider and pushing them down into the mattress.

"You've got such a pretty pussy," he smirks, looking down at me before spitting onto my clit. Not that I need anymore wetness but there was something so hot about it and I feel arousal trickle from me. Clenching my pussy, moans pass through my lips as he mixes us together. "Did you like that baby?" he asks, looking down at me like his prey and I nod, his fingers back inside of me, curling up and rubbing the heavy ache that is consuming me.

He does it again and I watch as he rubs it into me with his spare hand and he smirks when he feels me tighten around his fingers.

"My dirty girl," he groans, his fingers fucking me, and I honestly don't know how much more I can take of this.

I grind my pussy down onto his fingers, meeting his every thrust as I ride his fingers, hips bucking, and I am so needy for him.

My nipples are hard as I roll them between my fingers and he spits again, and I am fucking soaked. My cheeks flame red, my chest rising and falling as he rubs over my clit, fingers fucking my pussy and I am close to oblivion, my whole body trembles and just when I think I can't take anymore, his cock slips inside of me just as he pulls his fingers out and I lose it. Choked sobs leave me, his hands pinning my legs down as he rides me how he wants, my pussy clenching as the heat rolls through me, the deep ache that was once so prominent now slowly fading into nothing but calmness.

"Fuck, baby, you take me so well. I am going to—" he groans as he fucks me hard, and I have no idea how, but another orgasm explodes through me, taking everything I have and ripping it off me so I lay bare beneath him, showing him every ounce of my soul as he comes. Filling me, his moans fill the room and my whole body sings in tune with him as he gives me everything, fixing me back together after breaking me apart.

"That was..." I whisper as he lays on top of me.

"I know Blossom, I know."

Keaton stays back with Killian and Reese and I travel to *Laced Promises* with Sage and Dex. It's at the other end of the strip, tucked inside one of the hotels and the only way you get into *Laced Promises* is by buying your way in. This isn't any gentleman's club, this is the creme de la creme.

The best of the best.

It's prestigious and Dex and Sage wanted it.

"How did you hear about this place?" I asked as we entered the lavish hotel.

"My dad," Dex smiled, "he thinks it's a good investment and to be honest, it will always be booming here. Business is always good in Vegas but I have been thinking, maybe I need to invest in little wedding chapels," he throws me a wink and I roll my eyes.

"Still debating an annulment to be honest," I sigh, choosing to ignore the fact that we have consummated our marriage.

"Really?" Sage looks at me and I nod.

"I just don't know; my feelings are all over the place."

"That's understandable love, but don't throw it away yet," she smiles as we walk to the secret red door.

"Name?" The large doorman says, looking down his nose at Dex.

"Rutherford."

He checks his list, looking down his nose.

"In you go," he lifts the rope and all three of us walk into the club.

Walking down the staircase, we all stand as we look around the room, "wow," is echoed in unison.

"This is something else," Sage whispers, stepping forward.

The club is quiet, it's not open yet but I already love it. Red, velvet, long pieces of ariel silks hang from the ceiling, dim spotlights are evenly planted into the ceiling tiles, as well as small lights to make it look like a starry night. The stage is a large circle in the middle of the room, giving a circus tent feel. The bar wraps round the airy room, and upstairs is a balcony, that also runs around the room. I follow Dex and Sage upstairs and notice that five rooms have glass partitions, so you can see exactly what is going on in the rooms while in there and you can be standing on the outside getting hot and bothered.

"Well..." Sage raises a brow.

"I wonder if they're popular," I hum as we continue walking and I am intrigued by the rooms while my mind drifts to Keaton.

"I bet they are," Dex says as we walk up to black velvet covered doors with gold ornate keys hanging from the locks.

Twisting the matching gold doorknobs, it opens to a large room with a bed, sofa, television and an open planned bathroom. The walls are deep purple with gold wall fixtures, paintings and black wood floor.

"These all look new," I make an obvious observation. "Do we know why they're selling?" I ask.

"Nope, I think they've invested and now ready to sell." Dex shrugs his broad shoulders up, walking into the room and having a look around.

"I thought I heard voices," a deep British voice booms down the corridor and Dex turns to find a smartly dressed man wearing the perfect pin-stripe suit, waistcoat and shiny black brogues. Jet black hair is short round the sides, long on top and brushed back so it's away from his face and I can't help but focus on his dark brown eyes. "You must be Dex," he smiles, stepping into the room and shaking his hand.

"And you must be Wolfe."

"You are correct," he moves along to Sage, shakes her hand then looks at me, shaking my hand.

"I know who Dex and Sage are, but who are you?" he tilts his head to the side, eyes roaming over me and I feel myself flush under his gaze. But something about him creeps me out, maybe it's the way he is looking at me as if I am his next snack or the way his words hang on his tongue, hollowed cheeks and empty, soulless eyes.

"I'm Arizona, I work in one of the clubs back home in New York," I respond politely and I ignore the way a shiver dances up my spine.

"Well, Arizona," he steps closer to me, "it's a pleasure to meet you, would you care to join me for a drink after?"

I look at Sage and Dex, heart thrashing in my chest before swallowing the thickness down that is forming a lump in my throat.

"As lovely as that sounds, unfortunately, I have plans with my husband," and I am even shocked by hearing the word *husband*.

"That's a terrible shame."

I give a small nod and Wolfe turns around and stands back in front of Dex.

"How about we go and get a drink and talk business? The girls can go and have a spot of dinner somewhere else."

Dex side eyes Sage, then he gives her a small nod.

Sage steps aside, taking my hand and dragging me away from Dex and Wolfe before I even have a chance to say bye.

Climbing the stairs, we exit out the red door and both stand in the middle of the lobby.

"Was it just me..." Sage pauses and looks over her shoulder at where we have just exited from and where she has just left Dex, "or did he give you a weird feeling?" she asks.

"Oh my god, I am so glad that it wasn't just me. I thought it was because he asked me to go for a drink."

"Something about that man..." she pulls me a little further away before looking back over her shoulder again. "I just hope Dex gets wrapped up soon and gets the deal across the line."

I nod as we tuck into one of the busy restaurants across the lobby.

"Are you hungry?" she asks me as we sit at a table for two and I shake my head from side to side.

"I have plans with Keaton to meet him for some food, what about you?" I ask her but she is back looking over her shoulder to where she left Dex.

"Are you okay?"

She faces me and I can see the anxiousness that is on her face.

"Let's go back and get him," I nod but now she's shaking her head.

"I'm just being silly. I am finding that I am such a worrier now I am pregnant. My anxiety is awful, I worry and overthink every little thing," she sighs as she looks at the menu.

"You're not being silly, you're allowed to be worried. Even more so now you have a baby on the way," I give her a soft smile.

She shakes her head, then shakes her hands off.

"It's fine, all will be fine," she nods as she looks at the menu again.

"Are you eating?" I try and change the subject and hope it eases her worried mind.

"Sort of lost my appetite. Shall we just get a snack and some drinks?"

"Yeah okay," I nod and she calls the waitress over.

"Hey, what can I get you two?"

"Two sweet, iced teas and some nachos; you okay with that?" Sage asks as she pulls her worried eyes from the waitress and back to me.

"Sounds good," I hum, closing my menu and handing it back to the waitress; she nods, taking our small order and walking off.

"So," I ask, smiling at Sage, "when are you due?"

"May 8th," her hand rests on her non-existent bump.

"I feel like that'll fly by."

"I already feel like it's whizzing," she admits as the waitress brings our drinks over and she takes a sip.

"Will you find out the gender?"

"We're not sure, one minute we want to but I think Dex wants to keep it a surprise. He is old school," she laughs softly, her eyes dragging back over to where we walked from.

"I like the idea of a surprise, nine months of growing a baby, going through labour and then being told whether they're a boy or girl... I think," I smile and look down at my own flat stomach. "As if I am having a baby," I look up at Sage and blink.

"We can be bump buddies, our baby's will only have a couple of months between them."

"As much as that sounds amazing," I say a little sadly, "I'm not sure long distance bump buddies will work."

She looks at me with utter confusion on her face, brows furrowed as she lifts her iced tea to her lips.

"Long distance?"

"Yeah, you're from London. This is just a business trip is it not?"

"No darling," she laughs, "we've decided to stay. Prestige is doing really well and if we go ahead with this buy, then I would like to know that we're close enough if something goes wrong."

And I have no idea why, but I get teary.

"Oh Arizona," She stands and wraps her arms around my shoulders.

"I am just so grateful that I got to meet you, and I know this is going to sound really weird..." I pause just as she takes her seat, "but I never had a mom growing up, it was just me and my dad and he was amazing, and his friends all helped out when needed but I missed having a female for certain things if you catch my drift..."

She nods.

"And I know you're only a few years older than me, but you're an amazing mom figure and you have taken me under your wing and with everything that has happened and is going to be happening, I am so, so grateful."

"Arizona," she tears up as she reaches for a napkin and wipes a tear that rolls down her cheeks. "You're stuck with me now, I have never had a strong connection when it comes to girlfriends, but you, I don't know... there was something about you that just felt so natural. I never really had a best girl friend growing up, it was just me and Wes, my boy best friend but I feel like the universe gave us each other for that reason."

And now it was my time to blubber, just as the waitress walked over with our nachos.

"Are you both okay?"

"Yes, yes, we're fine. Just pregnant and soppy," Sage

laughs through her tears and the waitress just looks at us, giving us a nod and walking away as quickly as she came.

"Think we scared her off?"

"Probably?" I laugh, wiping my eyes.

"Love you Arizona."

"Love you too Sage," my bottom lip trembles as I push a smile onto my face.

"Why are you both crying?" Dex finds us, his brows furrowed as he looks between the both of us.

"Hormones?" I say, even though I probably can't use that excuse yet.

"Oh girls," he sighs, pulling us both up and enveloping both of us in an embrace. "How am I going to cope over the next few months with you two running the clubs and tearing up all the time, hm?" he asks, placing a kiss on the top of each of our heads.

"Wait, you said clubs?" Sage pulls out of Dex's embrace and looks up at him.

"I did baby, just signed on the dotted line."

Her eyes widen and she squeals, wrapping her arms around Dex as I slip back and take my seat and pride blooms in my chest.

"*Laced Promises* is yours."

"And you're happy for me to make it more... not, strip club like?"

"Yes, Little One, whatever you want to do with it."

"Love you," she kisses him softly before he kisses her back as if he has been starved of her for too long.

She sits down, Dex dragging a chair from a vacant table to sit next to us as we start eating our nachos.

"Will you still have your garages?"

"The ones at home I signed over to Hugo." I watch as

Dex stiffens and sits a little taller in his seat. "Calm down," she rolls her eyes.

I stare between the both of them.

"Mr Possessive over here getting all territorial over someone from years ago."

"Me? Possessive?" He places his hand on his chest as if he she has offended him.

"Was you not then?" She smirks.

"Okay fine," he rolls his eyes now and shakes his head from side to side.

"Was you?" I laugh, taking a sip of my tea.

"So bad. Used to..." he looks around before leaning into the table and lowering his voice, "stalk her."

"No, you did not!" and I am shook to my core.

"True story."

"Dex Rutherford," I shake my head in a playful manner.

"I know I know, but look, I couldn't not be with her. I knew she was meant for me, but she decided to date my dad instead until I stole her away."

"Thief."

"Only the best kind," he throws me a wink and a giggle slips from me.

"I'm glad you stole me away," she sighs blissfully, as he scoops her hand into his and brings the back of it to his lips as he plants a soft kiss.

The waitress clears our plates and Dex settles the bill before we all leave and walk back towards our hotel.

"Where are you meeting Keaton?"

"Somewhere called Fat Tuesdays?" I scrunch my nose up.

"Okay, let's head there. You okay with us tagging along?" Dex asks as he stops walking for a moment.

"Oh my god, of course. We wouldn't have been here if it

wasn't for you," my voice is soft, "and I wouldn't have married my dad's best friend, but hey, look, I'm not blaming you for that," I laugh.

"You couldn't blame me even if you wanted to, it was nothing to do with me, that was all you and Keaton."

"Shhhh," I cover my ears as I begin to walk again and I hear Dex and Sage let out a loud laugh and honestly, I have never, ever, been more grateful for two people coming into my life when they did.

They were so much more than friends. They were family.

CHAPTER TWENTY-SIX
KEATON

Turning my wrist to face me, it's just past nine thirty and I don't know why, but I have an uneasiness in my chest, an ache in my gut. Slipping my phone from my pocket, I check to see if she has messaged but there is nothing.

Me: *Hey baby, you okay?*

I place my phone screen up on the table of the bar we're sitting in just as I see Dex walk through the door with Sage and Arizona and my heart stills for just a moment. High waisted jeans, pretty ditsy daisy cropped top and high-top converse.

She always looks beautiful, but she is glowing tonight.

And she is mine in every sense of the word.

My wife.

Mother of our baby.

Mine.

Forever.

Never did I think I would be married again, but here I am. In Vegas, where anything could happen, and fate decided that I was ready for a wife that loved me as much as I loved her. Even though I know I love her so much more than she loves me, but we're not going to get into that right now.

She really was my world, and I know Titus is going to be upset with me, heck he will be mad and angry, but he only needs to see the way I look at her, the way that she is my priority and the way that she has molded me into a better person for all of that anger and upset to leave him. I really do hope he doesn't try and stop us from being together because even if he tried to put distance between us, it wouldn't stop me. I don't care if it'll rip our years of friendship into nothing more than shreds on the floor, I will always choose her. Always.

She's my baby.

My blossom.

My world.

She trumps all.

"Hey handsome," she wraps her arms around me, lips pressed to my ear. My heart thumps in my chest and heat swarms through me.

"Hey beautiful, I missed you," kissing her softly, I am grateful that I can be myself around her and there are people here who are on my side. I know this must be tough for Killian, but he is here. Titus is mad at him too and I am not going to let him take the wrath of Titus and I am sure that he wouldn't like me to take the full wrath of Titus either.

"I missed you more," she whispers, kissing me back and all I want to do is take her back to our hotel and love her with all I have. "You hungry?" she asks as she pulls away.

"Not for food," I wiggle my brows and she swats her hand against my chest. She tries to walk away but I reach for her, grabbing around her waist and pulling her back.

Just having my fingers on her beautiful skin is enough to make me hard and I am gagging for it.

She sits on the stool next to Reese and they fall into easy conversation and Dex gives me a pat on the back.

"You alright?" he asks, taking a sip of his manly looking cocktail.

It's not manly. It's sort of pink, creamy looking with a couple of umbrellas sticking out the top. Not going to lie though, it looks delicious. Might order it next.

"Yeah, I think so," I smile taking a sip of my mojito.

"Not sure if Arizona has said or not, but Sage is expecting too. She is a couple months ahead of Ari, so always here if you want to have a chat," he offers, and I am grateful.

"Thanks," I turn to face him, "I appreciate that man, it's so hard because Titus—Ari's dad—is one of my best friends... his wife is also pregnant, I think around four months? I don't know, he sends us updates every week but anyway, I'm falling off topic. So yeah, I would love to talk to him about it, a bit of common ground, but it's not like I can call him up be like *'hey dude, this has happened what did you do blah blah,"* cos I've got his baby pregnant."

Yes, I know it may not be mine, but it will be, I know it.

"Ah mate, that's tough, well look... I'll be your daddy friend if you want. I am learning each day and it'll be nice to speak to another man instead of having to listen to my wife talk about her baby chats she's in," he laughs. "Her and Ari seem to have really hit it off and I am grateful, because she has always struggled to make girlfriends, not sure why, but her and Ari seem very similar."

I nod in agreement.

"Ari has always struggled. I know she is close to Connie and Reese but that's only been since Connie started dating

Kaleb, my twin, and Reese came along with Killian as he is Connie's dad and Reese is Connie's best friend…" and I pause for a moment and Dex looks like he is trying to get to grips with what I have just said, as if playing on loop in his mind.

"I know, it's all a bit fucked up to be honest."

"And you married and got your best friend's daughter pregnant."

"Yup, sounds about right…" I take another sip of my drink.

"Wow." He runs his hand through his hair, "I thought it was weird when I stole Sage from my dad and my dad started dating Sage's old club friend."

"I dunno… yours is a bit weird."

"Mate, don't. Mine is not even close to being as fucked up as your situation," and he lets out a throaty laugh.

"Fair, fair," I nod.

"Still fucked up though," he shrugs his shoulder up.

"Totally."

The evening slips away a little too easily, but I am grateful to be back up in the room with my wife.

My wife.

Mine.

"So, wife, what would you like to do?"

"Ride you then sleep?" she purrs, and I definitely was not expecting that.

"Jump on baby, ride me good, milk me for everything I have, and I promise I will snuggle you all night."

"You're on big boy," she winks before slipping into the bathroom and closing the door.

She comes out dressed in white lingerie, looking like a damn angel. Not only did she promise to ride me which was more than good enough, she got on her pretty knees and sucked my cock until I came down her pretty throat. I feasted on her till her legs were trembling and I was sure she was going to squirt. She's got it in her, I just need to coax it out.

Then once she had caught her breath, she rode me like a fucking pro and took me for everything I had.

I filled her pretty cunt full of me, then made sure that every last ounce was pushed back inside of her. And as promised, once she had wrecked me not once, but twice, I spooned her all night and had the best fucking night's sleep ever.

TODAY WAS OUR LAST DAY IN VEGAS BEFORE WE FLEW HOME tonight, and I'm not going to lie, I was sad. I wasn't ready to go home yet. I liked that we were in our bubble and as soon as the jet hits the tarmac tonight, the bubble will be popped, and life will just go back to what is was before. Only now we were married, and she was pregnant.

The shit will be sure to hit the fan when we get home.

Big time.

"Anything you want to do?" She asks, her hand looped in mine and it's just the two of us. Killian and Reese are on their way home already and he promised me his lips are sealed.

"Just enjoy every single second before we're back home in New York," I sigh.

"It's been amazing... right?" she was hesitant to ask me that and I have no idea why.

"It's been more than amazing Blossom, one of the best damn vacations I have been on," and she spins round to face me, arms wrapped round my middle as she presses up on her tip toes and kisses me.

I don't want this moment to end.

But like everything, it must end eventually, whether we want it to or not.

On our way to the airport, my mind flashed back to our afternoon. Lunch at the Eiffel Tower and we had the most amazing views of the Bellagio fountains and I was sad that we were actually going home now. Four hours and fifty minutes of our bubble left.

That's it.

And I am truly gutted to my core.

Gutted.

Bubble well and truly popped.

CHAPTER TWENTY-SEVEN
ARIZONA

FOUR HOURS AND FIFTY MINUTES GONE IN A BLINK OF AN EYE.

I feel like we have been in our Vegas bubble for so much longer than four days.

And honestly, I am not ready for us to be back in New York.

Me back to work. Keaton back to work and more having to avoid my dad until I was ready to talk to him. Which at the moment, felt like never.

Keaton's hand sunk between my thighs as we rode the drive home in silence. Sage and Dex went in one car to Brooklyn and me and Keaton went in the other.

It wasn't an awkward silence.

It was just silence. Silence to appreciate the time we had to be completely ourselves, because when we're here and living our lives, we mask our true selves. Mask our feelings because we don't want anyone to see just how perfect we are together.

But when we're behind them doors, it's just us again.

Just the way we like it.

How sad are we.

Sighing when we pull down Hamilton Heights knowing that the car was going to stop at any moment. It was six Vegas time, nine New York time.

"You ready?" Keaton asks, leaning over and placing a kiss on my cheek and I lean into him.

"Nope, but let's go," I nod, opening the door and reaching out for Keaton's hand as the driver gets our small luggage bags.

"Home sweet home," he chimes, and the New York air feels even colder than it did before we left. "Fuck, it's cold," Keaton laughs as we walk up the stairs and I wait for him to unlock the door, and as soon as we are in, he locks the door and turns the heating on.

"I need a shower," I sigh, dropping my bags to the floor.

"Can I join you?" his arms are wrapped around me from behind, head tucked into my neck placing kisses over my pulse point.

"Always," I turn my face over my shoulder and kiss him on the cheek before I pull his arms from me and run for the bathroom.

We shower.

We fuck... obviously, because we have an illness where we physically can't *not* have sex. Then we climb into bed and order Chick-fil-A on Doordash.

"Are you ready to face my dad tomorrow?" I ask as I pop a fry into my mouth.

He sighs heavily, "Nope, not one bit."

"I'm sorry, it can't be easy for you."

"Baby," he turns to face me, "what are you apologizing for?"

"Because if you hadn't agreed to watch me, I wouldn't be here, we wouldn't have given into temptation, and we certainly wouldn't have got married. I can't say for certain whether there would or wouldn't have been a baby because... well, biology and all that."

He chuckles softly, his hands cupping my face.

"Well then I'm sorry too..." he smiles.

He kisses me slow while *Modern Family* plays in the background, and suddenly, all is forgotten for just a moment.

TUESDAY MORNING COMES WITH A LOUD CRASH AND BANG AS Keaton's alarm goes off and he forgets where he is for just a moment.

"Shit," he groans. I can hear the sound of water trickling and when I sit up I see he has not only knocked his lamp over and smashed it, he has also spilt his cup of water off the side that is now leaking over the edge of his bedside table and onto the floor.

He clambers out of bed, tired eyed and grouchy as he goes to find a towel to wipe the water up with.

"I'll get the broom," I twist and pad out of bed, but Keaton stops me.

"No, stay there in case you get hurt," he shakes his head from side to side.

"What? From a broom?" I laugh as I ignore him and walk out of the bedroom, moving my hips from side to side as I walk, knowing that his pretty green eyes are going to be on my ass.

Going to the cupboard under the stairs, I grab the broom and make my way back towards the bedroom and begin sweeping, Keaton on his hands and knees soaking up the water.

"What are you like?" I shake my head.

"I was having the best dream, then my alarm went off and I got used to not having it on for four days so it was a little shock to the system."

"What was this dream?" I asked, intrigued.

"It involved you, whipped cream, strawberries and ice."

"Sounds naughty," I chime as I sweep a neat pile in the corner of the room.

"It was, and messy."

"Well, maybe you can try it out one night, I do love strawberries and cream," I wink, leaning against the broom.

"Don't tease me baby, I'm rock hard and want to sink myself between your pretty little thighs."

"What's stopping you?"

"Work unfortunately, the boss is already fucked off with me."

"I thought you were the boss," I taunt him, lifting my cropped tee over my head then pushing my shorts down so I am standing naked.

"Well, there are four of us... so we're all kind of, technically the bosses?" he finishes with a question, but I am unsure why.

He is still on his hands and knees, and I saunter over to where he is, leaning over in front of him, gripping his chin and tilting his head back.

"Are you hungry?" I ask, humming with a need for him.

"Famished," he just about manages, his voice tight.

I lift a leg, placing my foot on the nightstand and keep the other firmly on the floor.

"Then eat," I softly order, and he does.

His tongue is on me, lapping over my clit as his fingers find my opening and dip inside of me and I steady myself by entwining my fingers through his long brown hair, tilting his head to the side as he eats me as if I am his last meal.

Moans fill the room, and he is still on his knees.

Fingers buried inside of me, rubbing my g-spot, the other is curled round my hip as I begin to ride his face.

"There's a good girl, take what you need from me," he murmurs, rubbing his nose over my clit, his tongue gliding through my lips as his fingers still fuck me at a slow and torturous pace. I tighten my grip on his hair, tilting his head back so his tongue is focused on my clit, his fingers deep inside me.

"Yes," I breathe as he fastens his thrusts, his tongue staying slow. "Just like that," I pant and he does as I ask. I come undone on his tongue and he doesn't let a single drop of me go to waste.

"You're a good boy," he helps me lift my leg down and I lean down, gripping his cheeks between my thumb and index finger, swiping my tongue into his mouth which switches something feral inside of him.

He pushes to his feet, lifts me into his arms and fucks me hard and raw against the wall, not letting up once as he covers my mouth the whole time until we're both coming.

CHAPTER TWENTY-EIGHT
KEATON

THE DRIVE TO WORK IS AN ANXIOUS ONE.

I know I am going to have to face Titus, I can't run and hide. I am a forty-seven-year-old man and I'm not going to lie, I am shitting myself just a little bit.

I deserve it all.

Still doesn't make it any easier.

Slowing when I pull into my parking space, I inhale deeply and give myself a moment or two before I finally step out the car, briefcase in hand. Suited and booted. Ready to have my ass handed to me.

Fair.

Pushing the button for the elevator, I count how long it takes to reach me.

Seven seconds.

Nine seconds to go back up.

Give or take.

The doors ping and I step out into the office ready to have my face punched, but it's calm. Nate sits at his desk. Kaleb is in his office, door pulled two and Titus's desk is empty.

Odd.

"Morning," I smile, nerves killing me on the inside and Nate's eyes widen.

"Keaton, you're back."

I nod, walking behind him and gripping his shoulder in a friendly way as I walk across to my office, pushing the door to.

Unbuttoning the top button of my white shirt, I run my two fingers inside my collar that feels suddenly too tight, strangling me.

Maybe just getting me ready for my friend's hands round my neck.

I'm not alone long when Kaleb pops his head round the door.

"My brother returns, I hear congratulations are in order for you and your beautiful wife," he twists his lips trying his hardest to not break into a laugh.

"I wish that was the worst of it," I mumble and yes, my answer could be coded. But I know what I am insinuating, Kaleb will think that I am on about Titus's reaction.

"Where is he anyway?"

Kaleb looks over his shoulder and puffs out his cheeks, "Should be here any minute, he ran out to get coffees."

"Cool," I sound very unenthusiastic.

"He is angry."

"No shit," I scoff a laugh and scrub my face when I see my emails popping in.

"I wish you luck, brother."

"Thanks," I salute him off my temple, elbow resting on my desk as he ducks out and goes back to his office. I think.

The elevator doors ping and I know that my minutes are numbered so, instead of angering the beast any more than I already have, I decide to walk out and wave my white flag in surrender.

All it took was one foot out of my office for his pretty blue eyes—that are almost exactly the same shade as Arizona's—to harden. Hers are more of a summer's ocean blue, his more like ice.

Sounds about right.

"Well, well, well..." he whistles, placing the takeout coffee on his desk and I swallow the large apple sized lump. "Look who has returned."

His eyes move to my left hand, seeking out the yellow band, but I fold it into my suit pocket in a poor attempt to hide it from him.

"Hey," I just about manage, "did you get me a coffee?" my voice is tight and fucking hell what is wrong with me. I feel like I am back in sixth grade when I used to get beat up at lunchtime.

"No," his eyes are thunderous.

"Standard," I nod.

"Don't get smart."

"Hardly getting smart," I scoff, rocking up onto my toes for just a moment and landing back on my heels.

"I'm warning you Keaton."

"Or what Titus?" I raise my voice. "You're mad, I get it, come and take it out on me. That's what you want isn't it? To lay punch after punch into my pretty face because I married your daughter."

Well, fuck me, it was like waving a red flag in front of his eyes.

If you need more clarification, I'm the red flag.

He is the fucking bull.

He charges at me, his arms around my waist as he

throws me to the ground and he knocks the fucking air out of my lungs as he winds me. I roll on my side, eyes crossing as I try and gasp for breath.

"You fucking married my daughter!" he shouts, and I swear spit flies out of his mouth and lands on me.

Deserved it.

If roles were reversed, I would have properly spat on him.

Inappropriate thoughts invade me for just one, split second at the thought of spitting, but I shut them down in an instant.

Not the time Keaton, not the fucking time.

"I did, yes," I finally manage now I have caught my breath.

"I trusted you!" I wish his tone was softening, but if anything, it was getting more and more angry.

"I know," I roll onto my front and slowly push myself up but then he gives me a blow to the ribs with his perfectly polished shoe. "Deserved that," I grunt, pushing up again and this time, he lets me push to my knees.

"Seven and a half billion people in the world and you set sights on my daughter, why Keaton? WHY?!"

And I've had it.

I stand, squaring up to him, chest to fucking chest.

"You want to know why?" I seethe, eyes pinned on him.

"Yeah, I do."

"Because I wanted to, because unfortunately for you, I love her. I'm *in* love with her. That's it. No bullshit. No excuses. I LOVE HER!" and now it's my turn to shout and shove him.

"You're dead to me," Titus growls, shoving me back a little harder, catching me off guard.

"Fine, that's fine," I shake my head, rage coursing

through me now, but I can't help but feel the hurt of Titus's words. Slicing through my heart with a sword. Bloodied and wounded, I knew I wasn't going to recover from this one.

Dead to him.

After everything we've been through.

"I never want to see you again!" his tone is sharp.

"Bit hard seeing as we work together."

"Then I'll leave," and Nate's head pops up over his computer.

Silence fills the room.

Both of us are angry. Chests rising and falling.

Sadness simmers my anger for a moment as Arizona pops into my mind.

"Do you know what Arizona thinks?" I pause, his angry gaze meets mine. "She thinks you don't love her anymore. That's why she hasn't contacted you."

"What?" Titus's voice softens, his eyes locked on mine, and he looks as if the wind has been taken from his sails.

"Yeah man…" I pause, running my hand round the back of my head, my whole body aches. "She thinks you're not going to love her anymore and feels like she is going to be replaced and left behind…" I pause, swallowing the large lump. "Just like her mom left her…"

Titus stumbles, falling back into his office chair, mouth a gape and shocked.

"That's what she thinks?" and I can hear the defeat in his voice.

"Yeah man," I repeat and tuck my hands into my pockets and we all just stare at Titus.

"Shit, I didn't… I mean… fuck," he scrubs his face with his hands.

"You did what I've done to you, sort of, in a nutshell."

Nearly slipped up.

Fuck.

"Sorry?"

"Went away, got married, come home and sprung it on everyone..."

"Yours was plastered all over socials."

"My bad, we had no idea..." it was the truth. We didn't.

"Also, wasn't your daughter I married, was it?" He seethes.

"No, but it was mine," the gruff British accent that belongs to Xavier floats through the office and I bite the inside of my lip to try and stop the laugh coming out. Xavier continues forward and slaps Titus on the back, hard.

"Isn't that right Titty?"

And he sighs, rolling his eyes.

Xavier continues forward and sets up camp in my office. Not ideal.

Titus's eyes find mine again and I give him a lopsided smile. I reach for my house keys and remove my car key before tossing the bunch towards him which he catches with one hand.

"She's at home, go and see her." I offer and he stands up, walking towards me and I open my arms ready to embrace him, but he plants a punch right on my jaw and it knocks me for six causing me to fall to the floor.

"That's for marrying my kid," he growls, pointing at me angrily before turning and walking away.

"Am I still dead to you?" I call out on a half laugh, half choked sob, but he just flips me off.

Standard.

Kaleb and Nate rush up and help me to my knees, Kaleb is angry as he goes to run after him, but I shake my head.

"Leave him, I deserved it." They look at me with furrowed brows, exchanging looks.

"He'll be ready for round two in a few hours no doubt."

"Whys that?" Nate asks.

"No reason," I sigh, "no reason."

CHAPTER TWENTY-NINE
ARIZONA

Pulling our clean laundry out the dryer, I sit on the floor and fold it into a neat pile and place it into the laundry basket before pulling the last of the clean washing out of the washer and popping it into the dryer, turning it on.

Standing, I carry the dry laundry up to our bedroom and put it into piles.

Our bedroom.

It's not ours. It's Keaton's.

I just sleep in here and have done since before Vegas. Leaving Keaton's clothes out, I take mine and start putting it away when I hear the front door go. My brows pinch when I look at the time, it's just past eleven.

"Babe?" I call out, walking out into the hallway then get halfway down the stairs when I see my dad standing there looking a mix of angry, sad and defeated. "Dad... I..."

"Ari... Sunshine," he chokes, stepping forward and I slowly begin to walk towards him and off the bottom step. "Can we talk?"

"Depends... are you going to shout at me?"

And he sighs, dropping his head for a moment and after

what feels like a lifetime, he shakes his head from side to side slowly.

"Then yes, we can talk," I keep my head high, nose slightly lifted as I walk past him, ignoring the urge to throw myself into his arms and let him cuddle me. But I continue forward, moving towards the living area. "Take a seat, can I get you anything? Tea, coffee, water, a dash of betrayal."

"Ari..."

I sigh, sitting down in the one seat armchair, crossing my legs under myself and wait for him to speak.

He doesn't. Silence fills the room, and the tension grows until I can't take it anymore and I hate it.

"What did you want dad, you obviously came here for a reason so just speak or if you can't find the courage to talk, then you might as well go back to work," I cross my arms against my chest and eye him.

"Keaton told me..."

My heart races in my chest, eyes widening as I sit and wait for him to explain further because I do not want to trip myself up. But the explanation never comes.

"Told you what?" I finally give in and ask him.

"That you feel like I don't love you... that you think I am going to leave you just like your..." and he pauses, closing his eyes for just a moment before he swallows and I watch as his throat bobs. "Mom did," he finally says, and I feel a small pain sear through my heart. Not at the thought of my mom, I don't remember her at all, and she is irrelevant in my life to be honest, but at how much that must have hurt him to hear from his best friend.

"Ari, I will never replace you, I will never leave you... you are my daughter, and you will always be my daughter. Just because I am having a baby with Amora doesn't mean that I am going to replace you with that baby..."

My eyes are watering and there is an ache in my chest that runs so deep I am worried I won't be able to rub it out even if I wanted to.

"I'm just..." I pause because I don't even know what I want to say to him, I just feel so overwhelmed by the conversation and a mix of emotions flood me, water cascading over me until I am unable to keep my head above the surface.

"I know... and I went about all of this in the wrong way, and I know that, I never planned to tell anyone before I told you, but then Kaleb took me to the bar and I don't know, it all just went in a different direction. I was nervous about you finding out and I had it all planned out on how I was going to tell you. But everyone was there apart from you and I don't know why, but I just... I suppose, I panicked."

I nod, a tear rolling down my cheek.

"I know you can't just forgive me, but I will be waiting for you when you're ready."

"Dad..." I pause for a moment and suck in a deep breath. The thing is, I have so much that I need to tell him too, but I am not ready for that conversation yet and honestly, I don't know when I will be. It's not just that I married Keaton and it was both of our ideas and not a drunken mistake. It's the fact that I have dropped out of med school, I am soon to become a manager for the gentleman's club I work for and lastly, I am pregnant with a baby and I am not sure who the dad is, so yeah. Now honestly is not the time for my truths just yet.

I stand up just as he does and this time, I do throw myself into him, waiting for his arms to fold around me and keep me close so I can listen to the sound of his steady heartbeat, only it is not steady. It is racing under his skin and it makes me smile knowing that he is no doubt feeling as nervous as I am.

We break away and I sit back down, my dad sitting a little closer to me.

"How's work?"

I swallow.

"Going well."

"I'm assuming you passed your exams?" he is smiling so wide and my stomach knots.

"With flying colors."

"Just like I knew you would," and the pride is seeping out of him, and guilt crushes me whole. I was such a bad daughter.

"Just put me out my misery... was your marriage a black out drunk moment?" I could say yes and make it easier for him. But I don't.

"No; we were drunk, but we planned it before we got drunk and well, you know what I am like and you know what Keaton is like, neither of us wanted to back down and well the rest is history."

"Oh god," he places his face into his hands and scrubs his face.

"Look, you can't judge, you married your client and got her pregnant so..."

"Fair." He smirks and silence fills the room, and we just stare at each other. Somehow fixing the broken parts of our hearts, letting them sew themselves back together.

"We good?" he asks.

"Yeah dad, we're good." I smile at him before we lose ourselves in easy conversation as we catch up on each other's life over the last three months that we have both missed out on.

WE BOTH STAND, IT'S LATE AFTERNOON AND I AM JUST SEEING HIM out the door.

"Thank you for coming by," I lean against the front door as he steps out into the cold winter's breeze.

"You can thank your..."

"Husband," I wink.

"Keaton," for that, "he threw me the keys and told me that you were at home."

"Of course, he did."

"Hey, it was the least he could do, plus I did plant a fist to his jaw just before I walked out..." and my eyes widen at my dad.

"No, you didn't."

"Yes, I did, it was the right thing to do," he smiles too proudly for my liking, stepping closer to me and giving me a kiss on the top of the head. "You're my baby, he overstepped the mark."

And I nod, because he is right. But he wasn't the only one who overstepped the mark. We both crossed that line.

"And please, can I sort a date out for you to meet Amora soon, you really would like her. I promise."

"Can I think about it?"

I just felt so overwhelmed by everything over the last couple of hours that I just needed to have a few hours to let everything settle down.

"Sure," and I can hear the pain in his voice, but he brushes it off like he always does.

"Thanks dad, I love you."

"Not as much as I love you, Sunshine."

He wraps his arms around me again and gives me one last cuddle before he turns and walks away.

I watch him drive into the distance and I rub the ache out of my chest that has presented itself and set up camp.

Closing the door, my back presses against the cool door and I have no idea why, but I crumble into a pool of tears.

THE DAY HAS FLOWN, AND I AM NOW ON A COUNTDOWN TO Keaton walking through the door. It has just turned five. I don't want to be his keeper and I definitely do not want to be the kind of woman that cooks his dinner and has it ready for him and waiting every day, but I also would like to do something as a thank you for him sending my dad around. He didn't have to do that and I know it must have been awful for him as my dad would have been furious with it all and the fact that my dad punched Keaton because of what we had done... I owed him it all.

Once my dad had left, I got myself showered and changed into weather appropriate clothes and walked towards the small store on the corner of Hamilton Heights to grab stuff for dinner and a bottle of red. I got carded, I mean, of course I did.

Walking out onto the sidewalk, the city air was cold and had a nip to it now the evening was drawing in. Walking a little quicker to keep warm, I could see the light on outside Keaton's and I can't wait for him to be home. Letting myself in, I kick my boots off and place the grocery bag on the side table and hang my coat up. Closing the door of the cupboard, I walk down the hallway and into the warm kitchen. Turning the stove on, I fill the saucepan with water and bring it to the boil then add the spaghetti. Heating a pan, I throw in the onions, carrots and garlic before tossing in the mince, cooking it until its browned and then adding the meat sauce. I'm not going to lie, it smells divine.

I hear the front door go and I give myself the once over in the reflection of the glass and I am glad that I decided to put on an apron with nothing underneath. Once we're finished with dinner I am going to show him how thankful I am to him.

"Baby?" he calls out, his deep voice floating down the long hallway to the back of the house where I am waiting for him.

The table is set, his wine is poured, and dinner is ready to be dished up.

He walks down towards me and clings onto takeout.

"Wanted to surprise you with dinner," he smirks when he looks at the candlelit room and drops the takeout bag on the countertop. "But this looks a lot more appealing," he wraps his arm around the back of me and his brows lift when he realizes that I am completely bare underneath.

"I wanted to surprise you with a homecooked dinner," I trace my finger over his shoulder and run them along the stubble down his jaw line. He winces. Redness blemishes across his cheek and jaw.

"Well, you definitely surprised me," he smirks, his arms locking round my body as he pulls me close, his lips hovering over mine.

"How pissed would you be if I said let's skip dinner?" his lips brush against mine and my whole body reacts.

"Pissed..." I smirk, locking my hands round his neck.

"Fine, let's eat, then I want the whole evening with you."

"Deal," I wink before he gives me one last kiss then lets me go and I instantly miss him.

Hate that.

I plate up and he is sitting at the table, his hungry eyes pinned to me the whole time and I feel my skin flame under his heated gaze.

"Stop staring."

"Can't help it, my wife is just too hot," and my cheeks pinch crimson. Facing him, my brown hair sits in loose waves just past my shoulders and I saunter my way over to where he is sitting, placing his food down in front of him.

"This looks delicious."

And I am sure he is just being kind.

Sitting next to him, his hand rests over mine and my heart thrums in my chest.

"I just wanted to say thank you."

"For?" he asks, but a knowing smirk tugs at his lips as he spins his spaghetti onto his fork and pops it into his hot mouth.

"You know what, don't make me say it," I blush, and I have no idea why.

"Look, it was the least I could do. It was even worth the kick to the ribs and the fist to my jaw."

My eyes widen.

"I'm kidding," he winks at me but I know deep down he isn't.

I know my dad.

And I know Keaton.

And the ache in my chest is back, and this time, I can't rub it out.

———

"Wish I could be with you today," Keaton says between kisses, his hands clasped round my face.

"I know," I whisper against his lips, "me too, but you

have your big work meeting," I sigh, shoulders sagging forward slightly.

"I can always play hooky," he smirks, his arms looped round my waist, and I never want him to let me go.

"You're forty-seven, not seventeen. Hooky," I laugh, shaking my head from side to side.

"Fair." He sighs, "Any problems, you promise you'll call me?"

"Of course," I nod, and I don't want him to see how nervous I am feeling. I am petrified.

"Okay, I..." he pauses and his brows furrow as if he is trying to fathom how to speak the words he wants to.

"I know, me too," I smile, pressing onto my tip toes and letting our lips slant once more before he steps away and walks out of the front door. Once he is gone, I let out a heavy exhale of breath and walk towards my bedroom. I needed to get ready for my appointment with my OBGYN. Keaton found the best of the best, and luckily, she is still in Manhattan and just off sixth avenue. I may even get a chance to have a little look around the shops.

Sage gave me three weeks off after we flew home from Vegas, I think she was worried about me and wanted to give me some time to let it all settle in. I mean, married and pregnant all before my twenty-second birthday in a few weeks. Dad has been amazing and has arranged for an intimate dinner with Nate, Killian, Keaton (of course) and Kaleb. I said he could bring Amora, but I would like to meet her by myself first before being thrown into the deep end without a float.

I dress in mom jeans, sneakers and a long-sleeved tee. Casual. Comfortable. Everything feels tight around my stomach after lunch time, so I am making the most of wearing jeans until I am home from my appointment and stripping into sweatpants. Reaching for my NYC cap, I place it over my head and push my glasses up my nose. I wasn't feeling contacts today and my head was hurting. Grabbing my keys, I jog down the stairs and fill up my insulated cup with water and drink a few mouthfuls. You just can't beat the first few sips of water.

Stopping in front of the long mirror in the hallway, I rub some lip balm into my dry lips thanks to the lovely cold New York weather that seems to be blasting through the city this week. We're nearing the end of October, and we have a cold spell hanging over the city and I am hoping it's gone by thanksgiving. I like the crisp autumn days, not the bitterly cold. Grabbing my long black puffer coat, I shrug it on and toss my phone, lip balm and keys into my shoulder bag. I didn't feel too good this morning with a bout of sickness but luckily, it subsided after an hour or so, but the flush of nausea still swept over me every now and again.

Inhaling deeply, I open the front door and brace myself for the coldness that welcomes me once I step out onto Keaton's front step. Locking the door behind me, I pull my coat close to my body, wrapping it round me like a duvet and start my walk up to sixth avenue to the clinic for my eleven a.m. appointment. I would be lying if I said I wasn't nervous, but also, a slither of excitement bubbled inside of me. The thought of having a little baby growing inside of me and being all of mine and hopefully Keaton's. But the way my luck goes, it'll be the asshole from my cam chat. That reminded me that I needed to log on and delete it all. I couldn't face it. That one moment scarred me for life and though the evening could have gone a lot worse, I am so angry at myself for agreeing to go. I knew it was wrong, but I was craving something, chasing something, but I didn't know what it was. Maybe where I was so alone, I felt like I was already at rock bottom and just wanted to feel something other than hurt and betrayal. I just wanted to *feel*. How sad is that? I sounded pathetic. Letting my head drop, I keep my eyes down as I walk, lost in my thoughts to the clinic.

Climbing the steps, I walk into the clinically clean clinic and past the receptionist who buzzed me in and sent me up to Doctor Kyra's waiting room. Pushing through the door, my eyes scan the room at the artwork on the wall, scattered with the odd poster of babies, pregnant bellies and families with their bundles of joy. The seats were decent cloth armchairs on black wooden frames, a large square coffee table sat in the middle with a few magazines and a pretty plant sat potted on the glass. It didn't smell like a typical doctors waiting room; it was warm and smelt of citrus. I took a seat in the corner, a few eyes scanned over me. Some ladies were by themselves, some with partners and a couple with their surrogate who I overheard talking about how grateful they were and my heart warmed. And never did I want Keaton here more than I did now. Sage did offer to come with me, but I said I was okay going by myself. I wasn't. But I didn't want to be that girl. I had to get on with it by myself, because, truthfully, Keaton might not be here through it all. I know he has promised that he will be, but promises can be easily broken. If this baby turns out not to be his, he has every right to walk away. Who would I be to force him to stay just because I love him.

I reach for a magazine and begin flicking through the pages, not reading, just trying to keep myself busy so I don't drown in my thoughts. I'm not sat long when an impeccably dressed woman steps out, looking down at her notes and calling my name out. I stand, pushing a false smile onto my lips and walking into the room.

"Hey Arizona, I'm Kyra. Nice to meet you." She sticks her hand out and I shake it softly. She's British. Kind eyes, cold hands and a warm heart. Or that's how the saying goes.

"Hi," I manage, mumbling my words as I take my seat.

"How have you been feeling?" she sits at her desk, clicking on her mouse and tapping on her keyboard.

"Yeah okay, had some sickness, but nothing too terrible," I give her a nod and lock my fingers together in front of me.

"And when was your last period?" She asks, looking up from her screen now.

"I know I had one last month, around the third of the month," I blush, "I think," and I am annoyed that I can't remember the exact date.

"And the test said two to three weeks, is that correct?" her eyes are back on the screen and her fingers dance over her keyboard.

"Yes," I swallow the thickness and suddenly, I am feeling hot. Too hot. I strip my coat off me, running my finger round the neckline of my crew tee.

"You okay?"

"Just a little hot, I think where I have been outside in the cold weather and now in the warm room," I give her a weak smile and reach for my water, taking a sip.

"Just take a moment," she crosses her hands over and waits for my hot flush to pass.

"I'm good," I nod, taking another mouthful.

"Perfect," she flashes her toothy grin at me, "and is there a father involved?"

Her question feels a little too personal. I know it's not and I shouldn't feel like she is judging me, but I totally feel like she is judging me.

"Yes," I nod, "there is a father."

"And you have a good support system around you?" she continues, and nerves cripple me.

"Yes, I have my dad, my friends," my voice is filled with confidence when on the inside I feel like I am dying.

"Okay, I want to get some bloods done and then we will get you on the table for your ultrasound. I'll call the nurse in then send you back outside for ten whilst I go through the results, is that okay?" she asks, but I don't actually feel like I have a choice.

"Yes."

I hate blood tests. Never liked taking them at work either. I know why she is asking all of these questions, this is my field, well, sort of. But I'm not a silly twenty-one-year-old.

She presses a button on her phone, and an older lady walks in with a trolley with a tray on top filled with everything she needs.

"Hello love," she smiles sweetly at me as I roll my sleeve up to give her access to my vein. She presses a couple of times with her gloved fingers, her eyes moving from mine to my arm. "Are you nervous?"

"A little," I admit, "shouldn't be, I'm a first-year med student," I say a little too proudly seeing as I am a fraud.

"You've achieved a lot for such a young age," Dr Kyra states as she looks at my date of birth, I'm assuming.

"I was an over-achiever, really clever actually..." I pause for a moment when I feel the scratch on the crease of my elbow, "probably wouldn't think it seeing as I am sitting here at the age I am and pregnant."

"These things happen," Kyra smiles, "birth control isn't always one hundred percent, you know that though don't you," and I nod. She wasn't being condescending, she was quite nice actually. Not a bitch. Maybe a little judgmental but hey, I would be the same if I was her.

"Okay," the nurse says as she places a cotton ball on where she took blood and tapes it in place, "that's all done, go and take a seat in the waiting room." She gives me a kind smile and I stand up, moving towards the door and back into the busy waiting room.

Pulling my phone out, I smile when I see a message from Keaton.

> **Keaton**
> Hey baby, this meeting is a snore fest. All okay? x

I scoff.

> **Me**
> Hey, all okay. Just had bloods to check my hormone levels, then will be ultrasound time xx

I see the three dots pop up.

> **Keaton**
> Does that mean something is wrong? Your dad has just left, he got out of it. Lucky bastard. xx

I sigh.

> **Me**
> No, they sometimes do it to work out how far along you are. Stop worrying, everything will be okay. Now, go, enjoy your meeting and I'll call you when I am out xx

Keaton
Okay wife, xo.

Wife. My heart melts. Keaton replaced my tacky pink diamond ring with a thin gold band, and I love it. I did protest a little, but it's perfect. He still has the one from Vegas and he told me he is never taking it off.

"Arizona?" I hear Dr Kyra call me forward again and I push out of my seat and back into her office.

I re-take my seat as she pulls up my file on her computer once more.

"Okay, so your HCG levels are a lot higher than they should be for how far along you are. Could you be a little further?" My heart sinks, because if I am further, it will more than likely be my mystery man and not Keaton's baby.

"I mean, there is a possibility. I know you can still have periods and be pregnant," I breathe out, my voice quiet.

"Come lay down, let me take a look at your womb," she smiles a bit too happy at the thought of that. I shake it off, laying on the bed and tucking the hem of my tee under my bra wire.

She squirts the cool gel on my belly, then takes her seat, reaches for the probe and she presses it against my lower stomach. I can hear her clicking the buttons as she takes measurements and I pray everything is okay.

"Well, I suppose this explains the high HCG levels," she smiles as she spins the screen around and my eyes widen as soon as they land on the black and white fuzziness that is in front of me.

"No way," I whisper.

And there on the screen in front of me is two sacks and two little beans.

"Twins," me and Kyra say in unison.

"One placenta which means they're going to be identical..." she beams as she starts printing out pictures of the inside of my womb. "You're around six weeks. Due date 28th May, but as you know I am sure, twins normally come early. We will try and keep them inside as long as we can. Ideally..." and I switch off, I am too busy staring at the two little flickering heartbeats on the screen.

"Can't believe I can see their heartbeats," I mutter to myself.

"I know, a little early but amazing for you," she stands and wipes the gel from my stomach before helping me up. "I will get you some prenatal vitamins and we can book your next appointment and ultrasound in," she sits back at her desk, drying her wet hands on a hand towel then sanitizing them.

I just nod.

I am numb as I try and work out in my head the dates and who the father may be.

"How does the beginning of November sound?"

"That works," I rub my lips together as I lift my eyes to meet hers.

I have no idea how I am feeling in all honesty. I was excited when I walked in, and now, well...

"That's all booked in, I also booked another scan for December, your vitamins will be at the front desk," she stands and shakes my hand once more before seeing me out into the waiting room.

We both say goodbye and I walk towards the front desk where a young girl smiles at me.

"I need to pick up some prenatal vitamins," I lean my elbows on the light wood surface.

"Name?"

"Arizona King," she nods, tapping on her computer then

opening her drawer and pulling out my medication. I thank her and turn, when I see a pretty redhead woman standing in front of me. Pale skin, eyes different colors. One ice blue, one dark brown and freckles scattered across her nose. Of course.

"Arizona," she says softly, and I know before she even introduces herself who she is.

"Amora," I stand a little taller, my eyes falling to her round stomach and my heart skips a beat.

"Your dad is just parking the car, we have an appointment..." and her words are like a warning, giving me the heads up to get the fuck out of this clinic before he walks through the door.

"Hear you loud and clear," I give her a weak smile and step forward, "thank you," I whisper just as I pass her and disappear out onto the streets before I bump into my dad. I don't want to have to explain that not only did I marry Keaton, I was pregnant with his babies. Maybe. I hoped.

Fuck.

Walking onto the sidewalk, my mind was occupied with everything and anything to do with the baby, but there wasn't just a baby. There were two. Twins. Identical twins. And I wish that it would have made it official that the babies were Keaton's by being twins, but identical twins are not genetic. Keaton and Kaleb were not identical. They were a genetic set of twins. I just got lucky, or unlucky, I suppose it's how you look at it. Cup half full, cup half empty and at the moment I was feeling more like a cup half empty kind of girl. And I shouldn't. I should be elated that I have two healthy babies inside of me and growing, but I just feel dread and fear. I want these babies to be Keaton's and not the mystery guy's. Keaton says he doesn't mind, but will he once the babies are born and they look nothing like him? Will he reject me and them? Maybe he would feel like he has bitten off more than he can chew when he finally comes to the realisation that this is really happening. That I am having a baby, sorry, two babies and that he may or may not be ready for this huge change in his life. Because let's face it, everything is going to change once these kids are in the world. He never wanted kids from my understanding and from what I eavesdropped when he and my dad used to speak about him and Satan.

Sighing when I walk onto Hamilton Heights, my head lifts from the floor and my eyes settle on the light outside Keaton's house. My heart feels heavy, and my chest aches with an unbearable weight that I can't seem to shift. I stall for just a moment, the fine rain beginning to dampen my dry skin and I try and figure out what I am going to say to him, figure out how I can tell him that he doesn't have to be here if this is not what he really wants. Even though we're married, even though he probably feels he needs to be by my side throughout just because we got drunkenly married in Vegas. My legs begin to move, and I know once I am inside the front door, all of this becomes a little more real and I will be on countdown until he gets home.

Until I tell him I am moving out. Until I tell him that this isn't going to work and I don't care how much he begs and pleads, I need to do this for me. I was moving out before Vegas, nothing has changed on that part. We needed this. We never discussed an *us*. I don't think there would have been an us if it wasn't for Vegas and now my pregnancy. This was the right thing to do, I knew that deep down and so did he. And once my head was straight and I was settled in a new apartment, I was going to make a new appointment with Doctor Kyra and see if I can find out who the dad is. I knew this could be done, I had seen it done at hospital when I was shadowing and learning for my internship, but for some reason, I felt like I was doubting myself.

Pushing through the front door, my clothes felt heavy and the water from my hair dripped down my face, running down my nose and off the tip. I hang my wet coat up, slipping my shoes off before I carry myself upstairs and climb into the shower, letting the hot water wash the day off of my tired body. Wrapped in a fluffy towel, I walk into my room and my eyes find my laptop that has collected dust over the last month. Guilt pangs through me for some reason and I have no idea why, but it makes me feel uneasy, my stomach knotting and swirling with apprehension. Moving forward, I grab my laptop and place it on charge, leaving it for ten whilst I get changed and towel dry my hair.

Dressed in leggings and an oversized tee of Keaton's, I bring it to my nose and inhale deeply. I will never tire of his smell. Falling onto my bed with a sigh, I reach for my laptop and open the lid. I wait for it to load then pop my password in and open my cam page. Nerves drum in my chest, my stomach swirling at the thought of signing back in and that's when I see a message from *TallDarkandHandsome*.

I hope you enjoyed Vegas... seems I have more of a hold on you now than I did before... you might run Vixen, but you can't hide. I'm coming for you.

My blood runs cold and sickness swarms in my stomach, goosebumps prickle at my skin and my palms are damp. I delete my account before slamming down the lid of my laptop. I am up and moving across the floor to the bathroom where I fall to my knees and hurl the contents of my stomach up and now, I am not sure if this is pregnancy sickness or sickness out of dread and fear. What the fuck did the cryptic message mean? I can't tell anyone. Just need to keep my head down and my wits about me. I can't run from work, I needed this and truthfully, I needed the money more. Wiping my mouth, I stand and splash my face with cool water. This was not happening.

I hear the front door close, followed by Keaton's voice travelling down the narrow, long hallway.

"Baby?" he calls out and I run to the top of the stairs, his eyes on mine in an instant and he looks frantic. Worry is etched all over his face and all I can do is run to him, letting his arms envelope and fold me into his chest, my head against his racing heart. "Are you okay? I never heard from you after your appointment."

Realisation smacks me in the face at his words. I was meant to message him and let him know that everything was okay, but I was so focused on myself that I forgot.

"I'm so sorry," I whispered, clinging onto him like he was my lifeline.

"Is everything okay Ari?" he asks me, and I lift my head to look at him, wide eyes blinking as I do.

I nod, tears pricking my eyes but I'm not sure if they're happy or sad tears. Mixed emotions swirl deep inside of me, and I can't decipher what's what.

"Let me show you," I whisper, because he deserves to know, and I want to feel some of the excitement that he will feel once I show him the ultrasound. I reach for my bag and slip out the ultrasound before lacing my fingers with Keaton's and leading him towards the living room. He looks at me confused, brows furrowed as his beautiful green eyes settle on mine, bouncing back and forth with anticipation.

I hand him the ultrasound and his large hands reach

forward, his long fingers gently taking the corner of the picture and I watch as he studies it, and then the crease lines that were deeply dug into his skin slowly start to fade, softening within seconds before his eyes are back on mine.

"Twins?" he blinks at me, and my eyes are streaming, nose running as tears roll down my cheeks. I nod my head yes, hands clasped together and pressed to my lips like I am praying. He stands, wrapping his arms around my waist and lifting my feet off the floor, his face buried in the crook of my neck, and I feel wetness on my skin.

He's crying. *Oh be still my heart.*

"Baby this is..." he whispers, placing me down and pressing his forehead against mine.

"Scary,"

"It's amazing," his lips press against mine and my heart soars like a phoenix rising from the ashes.

"They're identical," and I feel him stiffen against me only slightly before his smile creeps onto his lips.

"Ari," his tone a little edgier, "these babies are mine, blood or not. You're mine, this, us... we're a thing. It's real. You're my wife and I am your husband. I know you probably think I won't love these babies if they aren't mine, but that's where you're wrong. I will love them with all I have, I love you with all I have..." and that's the first time he has ever said the words out loud and my heart crumbles in my chest.

I love you too.

CHAPTER THIRTY
KEATON

I HATED THAT I HAD TO GO TO WORK TODAY BUT WE HAD A BIG meeting with Killian, Xavier, Kaleb and Nate. Titus was meant to be in on it, but he bailed last minute, said he had some appointment that he couldn't miss but kept very vague.

He was in and out like a bat out of hell, so it was a quick hello and goodbye. I shoot a message over to Arizona, hating that she is there by herself when I should be there holding her hand at least and keeping her calm. She probably isn't nervous. She used to work in the field, it's not unfamiliar to her.

I mean, she didn't want to be an OBYGN, she wanted to be on trauma, God knows why. I've watched enough ER programs to be put off for life, but hey, that's just me.

Kaleb and Killian are talking amongst themselves, Xavier chatting to Nate, so I slide my phone from my pocket and text her.

> **Me**
> Hey baby, this meeting is a snore fest. All okay? X

I mean, it wasn't a lie. I was bored shitless and I have no idea what they're even talking about. Honestly, I am getting a little sick of hearing the name *Wolfe*.

> **Wife**
> Hey, all okay. Just had bloods to check my hormone levels, then will be ultrasound time xx

Blood test? Fear pricks at my skin and I feel my stomach knot.

> **Me**
> Does that mean something is wrong? Your dad has just left, he got out of it. Lucky bastard. Xx

Why am I panicking? Do I have anything to worry about? No, it's normal right? Fuck, at times like this I would turn to Titus, but I can't because then he will know that I have in fact got his twenty-one-year-old daughter pregnant. Hopefully. I mean, I can't just assume that the baby is mine, can I? I can pray, wish and hope. But that's about it.

> **Wife**
> No, they sometimes do it to work out how far along you are. Stop worrying, everything will be okay. Now, go, enjoy your meeting and I'll call you when I am out xx

She knows me too well. I was worrying, still am. No point lying.

~~Me: okay wife, love you xo.~~ *(scrap that)*

> **Me**
> okay wife, xo.

Placing my phone screen down, I feel eyes burning into me.

"Back with us?" Kaleb furrows his brows and I'm not going to lie, it fucked me off.

"You finished putting people to sleep?" I crack my fingers and lean back. Not even sure why I am here. I'm just the accountant.

I hear Xavier chuckle, his hands in his lap, fingers locked together.

I liked Xavier. My kind of guy. Sure, he is only tolerating this bullshit because of Titus.

"As I was saying, Wolfe was in Vegas a couple of weekends ago."

That has my ears pricking and me sitting up tall in my seat.

"What?"

"You heard me; now, we have no idea why he was in Vegas, just know he was. We have no idea what his game is, we know he wants blood and for some reason he is infatuated with Amora."

What the fuck was that weasel cunt doing in Vegas?

"He is up to something; he is a clever man. I am hoping to have a meeting with his brother Hunter soon from prison. Was hoping he wouldn't take the fall but..." Xavier pauses and licks his lips, "as long as Amora, Royal and the rest of the girls have eyes on them at all times then they'll be okay. There is something about Wolfe Knight that doesn't sit right with me, and the fact that we know that he has been in New York and now Vegas... well, seems a little coincidental don't you think?"

I don't know why but it freaks me out. What if he turns his attention to Ari? What if he wants to get back at Titus and he would by not only taking down Amora, but Ari too?

"Fuck," I whisper.

"What?" I see Nate turn his head to face me, Kaleb's eyes burning into mine.

"What if Wolfe is trying to get to Arizona?" saying it out loud makes me feel like it's a stupid idea, but it's not. I know it's not.

"Sorry?" Nate shakes his head as if he didn't hear me, not quite sure if it was a 'sorry, fuck how didn't I think of that', 'sorry, I didn't hear you', or it could have been a 'sorry, you're out of your mind'. Either way, I find myself explaining.

"What if he is blindsiding us? Thinking he is going for Amora... she's the easy target..." I pause when I hear Xavier suck in a breath. "Sorry man, just stating the facts," he gives a tight shrug of his shoulders before I continue, "but Arizona is as much of a target as Amora is. Ari is connected to Titus and Amora in Wolfe's eyes. He knows if he gets to Ari..."

"He gets to Amora, Titus, me..." Xavier pales for just a second, his hand stroking over his beard.

"Bingo," I slam my hands down on the table making Nate jump though didn't mean too. Just always wanted to do it I suppose.

"Well fuck," Killian whistles.

"Where is Ari now?" Kaleb asks.

"Home," I lie, I do need to tell him though. It's eating away at me.

"Go home, don't leave her side. Titus is with Amora; I'll get to Connie and Killian to Reese."

"Shall I just keep down the fort then?" Nate says and I don't miss the sarcasm that drips from his tongue.

"Yeah, better do that buddy," I stand, patting him on the back. "I'm just going to finish up this month's books and then I'll head home," I talk to the room before swiping my phone from the table and walking into my office, slamming the door as I do. Oops.

I blast through what I needed to do in about half an hour, a little longer than what I wanted but isn't that always the way with accounts. Pushing up, I lock my computer. Opening my phone, my brows pinch when I see that she hasn't text me. I open the cam app and search her name, it's not there. She deleted it. What?

I close the app and reopen it again, but she isn't there. The fuck? It's not like I can ask her about it, she would go mad if she knew that I knew about her cam job. It's bad enough I know she works in Prestige.

Skimming my hand down the side of my hair, I sigh when I see Kaleb walk through the door.

"What's eating you?" he asks.

"Not a lot, just about to head out," and I watch as he slowly closes the door.

"Is everything okay? I know you've got a lot going on, but we haven't spoken properly in what feels like forever."

I drop my head and a pang of guilt bolts through me.

"Why don't you and Connie come for dinner tomorrow? I'm sure Arizona would like that. She has been feeling a little down I think." I mean, I don't think she has but I know she would be happy to see Connie, so maybe me throwing that in there might help.

"Okay, sounds good." Kaleb steps back, placing his hand on the handle and pushing it gently but not opening the door. "Everything is alright though yeah?" he checks again, and I give him a heavy nod.

"Everything is perfect," I force a smile as I pick my briefcase up off the floor and walk towards him. He gives me a pat on the back and a squeeze on the shoulder before opening my office door and following me out towards the elevator. "Let me know when you're home with Connie, same goes for you, Killian. Let me know when you're home and know the girls are okay."

They all mutter something in the way of a 'yeah we will' and then I turn to look at Nate. "You okay?"

"Yup," he doesn't bring his eyes to meet mine, just focuses on the computer.

"You sulking?"

He snaps his head up. "Go home."

I let out a soft chuckle and step into the elevator. Time to get home.

Walking through the door a little cautiously, I find the house is quiet. Too quiet. Placing my briefcase onto the floor beneath me.

"Baby?" I call out and I see her at the top of the stairs, her eyes on mine and I cannot hide the relief that swarms me when I see that she is here and safe. I'm sure worry is etched all over my face. She runs to me, my arms enveloping her and folding her against my chest. I needed her close. I wanted her to hear the sound of my heart racing beneath my skin as her head rests on me. "Are you okay? I never heard from you after your appointment." It's not a complete lie, I was more concerned about this Wolfe thing and annoyingly the whole drive home I was doubting myself.

"I'm so sorry," she whispered as she tightened her grip around my body.

"Is everything okay Ari?" I ask her, she doesn't seem okay. Her head lifts from my chest and her eyes find mine, blinking for a moment as she just looks at me.

She nods slowly, and I don't miss the tears pricking in her beautiful blue eyes. That breaks my heart. And then worry floods me once more that something may have happened that she is keeping from me. Maybe she had bad news and didn't want to tell me over the phone, and suddenly, everything that I was worrying about before is replaced with fear.

"Let me show you," she whispers, but her voice is so quiet. She pulls away from me and I instantly miss her. She steps back, reaching for her bag off the side table and pulls out a black and white square bit of photo paper. Her fingers find mine, linking our fingers and entwining them together. She leads me towards the living room and she ushers me to sit down. Shit, this must be bad. Maybe she knows that the baby isn't mine? Doesn't matter if it's not. There is no way in hell I am letting her out of my grasp. She stays standing, fingers pinching the edge of the paper and I look at her confused, brows furrowed, and I allow my eyes to settle on hers, bouncing back and forth with anticipation as I wait.

She hands me the ultrasound and my hand reaches out, my fingers gently taking the corner of the picture and I let my eyes cast down and I study it. It takes me a minute or two to realize what I am looking out. My once creased brow line is now smoothed out, eyes widening when I look up at her. My wife.

"Twins?" I blink at her as if in disbelief and her eyes are

streaming, nose running as tears roll down her pretty pink cheeks. She nods her head yes, hands clasped together and pressed to her full lips as if she is sending a prayer up to the heavens. I stand slowly, stepping forward and wrapping my arms around her waist, lifting her feet off the floor, and I bury my face into the crook of her neck, inhaling her scent and I feel my emotions consume me as I shudder against her.

I'm crying. There is no doubt in my mind that these are tears of sadness, I am overjoyed and so excited for the next chapter in our lives.

"Baby this is..." I whisper, placing her down gently and pressing my forehead against hers.

"Scary," she murmurs, and I can see she is scared. Can feel it too.

"It's amazing," I correct her, my lips pressing against hers and I feel my heart race in my chest, skipping beats as it does.

"They're identical," she tells me, and I ignore the way I feel a searing pain through me, knowing full well that these won't be genetic and another indication that this does not help whether I am the father or not. I stiffen against her, but only slightly so I know she would have missed it, and a smile graces my face as I focus on her and only her.

"Ari," my tone is thick, and I feel like I am explaining something that doesn't need to be explained, "these babies are mine, blood or not. You're mine, this, us... we're a thing. It's real. You're my wife and I am your husband. I know you probably think I won't love these babies if they aren't mine but that's where you're wrong. I will love them with all I have, I love you with all I have..." her mouth pops open ever so quickly before she closes it and I realize why.

It's because I have finally said those three words, those eight letters out loud instead of thinking them in my head.

"I do Ari, I love you."

CHAPTER THIRTY-ONE
ARIZONA

KEATON INSISTED ON COOKING, AND I WASN'T GOING TO ARGUE with him because honestly, I felt exhausted. I've not long been out of the shower and I am dressed in a black skort, denier tights and a red long-sleeved bodysuit. My hair is straight, and I opted for my glasses. My make-up is done and I finish off my look with red matte lipstick. Spraying my *Si* perfume, I leave my phone on the dresser and disappear downstairs when the smell of dinner floats through the room and my stomach grumbles. Rounding the corner of the kitchen, I see Keaton standing over the stove, fitted jeans, mid sleeved gray tee and a hand towel resting on his shoulder. He looks every bit handsome.

"Hey there good lookin', whatcha got cooking?" I hum as I close the gap between us, my arms wrapped around his body from behind, my head resting between his shoulder blades.

"Hey baby," he looks over his shoulder at me and his scent consumes me whole making me feel warm and fuzzy on the inside, my heart galloping in my chest. Linen mixed with leather and cologne, and I am ready to dissolve into a puddle on the floor.

"I am so hungry," I groan, reluctantly letting him go and picking a breadstick from the counter and popping it into my mouth.

"Not much longer," he spins, placing the lid on his saucepan and walking towards me, his hands scooping my face up so I have no choice but to look at him.

"I never had you for such a sweet man... you were always such an..."

"Asshole?" he laughs, our noses touching, lips parted.

"Something like that," I hum, my fingers wrapped around his wrists, and I never want to step out of this moment, but I know I have to.

"I had never been in love before," and it's not the first time he has said that.

"You must have loved..."

"Don't," he shakes his head from side to side, when the door chime goes just as he covers my lips with his.

Breaking away, I float down the hallway towards the door, grabbing the handle and swinging it open to see Kaleb and Connie.

"So, you are alive then," Kaleb chuckles deeply, swooping me in for a cuddle and a kiss on the cheek before Connie wraps her arms around me and squeezes.

"I am, don't worry, your brother doesn't keep me captive," I roll my eyes in a playful manner and close the door behind them as they shake off their coats which I take and hang in the closet.

"Chef's down in the kitchen," I tease as Kaleb begins walking forward, Connie next to me.

"Why does it feel like it's been forever since I last saw you?" She asks, her brown eyes on mine and my heart drums in my chest. She is wearing her long brown hair down, straight. Her skin is glowing, cheeks pink and rosy and as always, dressed a little edgy. Oversized tee, cycling shorts, fishnet tights and her platform *Dr Martens*.

"Because it has, I suppose?"

And then she swats me on the top of the arm just as we join Keaton and Kaleb in the kitchen.

"Ow," I half laugh, half groan. "What was that for?"

"For getting married without us," she hisses, placing a brown paper bag on the set table.

"Look, it wasn't planned," I sigh as I walk to the glass cabinet and grab four glasses. "It just kind of..." I pause and Keaton looks at me, a beautiful smile on his face.

"We both wouldn't back down," he takes over the conversation.

"Shock," Kaleb smirks, a chuckle leaving him.

"It was kind of a 'last one standing' thing I suppose, like who was going to back down first but then... well, neither of us did and hey, here we are."

"Husband and Wife, never had that on this year's bingo card, maybe a wild card many years down the line but you always vowed after Satan that you would never marry again," Kaleb continues and my stomach flips, heart pounding.

"Things change, so do people..." he hums, checking on the steaks, his brow raising as he looks over at me, his gorgeous eyes sweeping over me, and I feel myself burn.

"So, it seems," Kaleb smirks just as Connie pulls out a bottle of wine.

Damn, and it's my favorite.

Cabernet Sauvignon.

"Let me pop that in the fridge for fifteen while dinner finishes," I smile widely, wrapping my fingers around the neck of the bottle and walking it towards Keaton's fridge. I know one glass probably wouldn't hurt, hell, I was intoxicated the night before I found out I was pregnant and spent most of the afternoon searching for stuff on the internet to make me feel better.

It didn't.

But now I know the twinnies are safe and sound inside of me, it's made me feel better, but not completely. I still feel guilty.

Connie sits at the table, Kaleb helping himself and Keaton to a glass of scotch on the rocks from Keaton's cabinet.

"Thanks man," Keaton takes the glass from his brother's hand and takes a sip, groaning in appreciation. Fun fact, Keaton hasn't drunk since I found out I was pregnant, and I love him a little bit more for that.

Plating the steaks up, he checks on the Mac 'n' cheese, cobs and baked potatoes in the oven before turning off the stove for the string beans.

"I hope you guys are hungry, this was always a favorite when me and my brother were growing up. A simple but delicious dinner in my opinion," he smiles as he dishes out the food he has cooked and I help him walk it over to the table, placing it on the place settings.

Connie jumps up and grabs the wine from the fridge and I swallow the large lump. We discussed telling Kaleb and Connie, but now it was getting closer, I was nervous.

I'm sat next to Keaton; Kaleb and Connie are opposite us. She sat back down, popping the cork then hovering it above my glass but I covered it with my hand then shook my head, just as Keaton's hand slipped between my thighs.

"But it's your favorite?" She chimes, confusion evident as her brows furrow.

"I know," I smile weakly, swallowing down the bile that is threatening to spill.

Connie looks at Kaleb, and he shrugs his shoulders up softly before their eyes are back on me.

"I'm..." I pause for a moment and ignore the burn that radiates through my chest, "we..." I swallow. *Just rip the band aid off;* Sage's words echo through my head, and I lick my lips, "we're having a baby, well... two actually."

And I watch as their eyes widen, mouths a gape and Kaleb can't stop the burst of laughter that echoes around the room.

"You're so fucking screwed," he shakes his head from side to side, "Titus is going to kill you."

"I'm aware," Keaton sucks in a breath.

"Pregnant?" Connie repeats and she hasn't taken her eyes from me. "Is that why you both got married?"

And now it's my turn to widen my eyes.

"No, no..." my head shakes quickly, "I didn't find out till the morning, plus my body was intoxicated with alcohol," I hide my face as shame slaps me across both cheeks. "None of this was planned..." I whisper, trailing off for a moment.

"Things happen for a reason though," she is quick to add in, her voice laced with softness.

"I know, but pregnancy was not one of them. How the hell will we cope with twins?" my elbows are on the table, and I feel the reassuring squeeze on my thigh from Keaton.

"You'll have us... all of us," Connie smiles and I smile back at her.

"Not only is Titus due to become a dad again... he is going to be a grandpa," and Kaleb has lost it again, laughing until tears roll down his cheeks.

"Yeah, he isn't going to be happy is he."

"Not one fucking bit," Kaleb mutters before cutting into

his steak, "I wish you good luck, both of you," he nods before popping a forkful of steak into his mouth and gentle conversation and laughter fills the room as our evening continues like nothing has changed.

It was perfect.

WE SAID OUR GOODBYES AND I ARRANGED TO MEET CONNIE AND Reese for lunch tomorrow at *SaraBeth's*. We loved it there. Now Connie and Reese knew, I somehow felt like I could breathe a little easier, silly, huh? Next on my list was my dad, but that wasn't going to go as smoothly. We both knew that. He would blow a fuse and honestly, I don't blame him. I'm close to twenty-two and I am pregnant with twins. Still none the wiser who the dad is, yet I have his best friend promising to be by my side either way.

Sad thing is, not only am I going to break my dad's heart, I am going to break mine and Keaton's in the process. I need to move out, I needed to stand on my own two feet ready for when the wrecking ball hits. Like I've said before, I know he has promised to be here whether the twinnies are his or not, but I just can't see it. Maybe I am being a negative nelly, but still, I have to be realistic. Once I am sitting with Connie and Reese tomorrow, I'm going to ask them about Killian's apartment and if it is available for me to crash in. I don't have much in the way of money, but I know he will help me out for a short interim. Just to get me settled. Just until I know what the hell is going on.

I was desperate to get back to work next week and have agreed with Sage I will still work the floor and hold dances, but I won't be doing any pole work for obvious reasons and then when I am too pregnant, I will sink into the shadows and work in the offices because let's face it, no one will want to watch me then. I'll be damaged goods.

A pain radiates in my chest, and I press the palm to my skin to try and alleviate it, but it's no use. It doesn't help. What if Keaton does up and leave me? What if we end up ending our farce of a marriage and I am a single mother to twins. No one is going to want me. Really, who in their right mind would want to choose me, a young, single mom who is a stripper.

Where did it all go so wrong? My perfectly planned life that I had since I was a little girl is nothing but rubble on the floor beneath my feet. I always knew what I wanted. Straight 'A's, graduate, college, med school, internship, beautiful house out of New York with a white picket fence and a yard where my three kids could run wild with the most perfect husband. Ironically, I have a perfect husband and two out of three kids on the way. But this is not the dream I had painted for myself. I wanted to be at least thirty before I had kids. And yet here I am...

I climbed into bed, snuggled under the duvet when Keaton falls into bed next to me. Tugging the covers off me, his head on my stomach, fingers drawing little love hearts on my bare legs as my fingers find his hair, twirling strands between my fingers and I have never felt more content than I do right now.

"Did you enjoy your evening?" I ask, *Desperate Housewives* starting up in the background.

"I did, I feel like I have pulled away from my brother recently." He admits, his voice lazy.

"And that's partly my fault," his head lifts as he turns to look at me.

"What?" he scoffs a laugh.

"I feel like I am the reason, you have been so consumed

by me and my problems that you have dropped everyone else," I admit, and I don't know why, but I feel teary.

"Blossom." The use of the nickname makes my heart soar and I love that it isn't overused because when he does say it, it makes it even more special. I blink at him, his body rolling round towards me now.

"You are definitely not the reason. Have you held a gun to my head and made me stay here?" he asks me, brows raised in his forehead.

"No."

"I have been here because I have *wanted* to be here. You know me baby, no one can force me to do anything I don't want to... let that sink in for a moment," he licks his lips all cocky and I am desperate to kiss him, but I know I need to pull back a little because he is consuming me whole, and I don't think my heart could take it when I walk out that door.

"I feel so out of depth," I admit, my fingers back in his hair.

"You're not alone. We can both wade through these rough waters hand in hand. We have no idea what is coming, but we will get through it because we're together." He pushes up and places a kiss on my lips, and as much as I want to push him away just to cause a scene that'll make it easier to walk away, I don't.

"Just don't let me drown," I rasp.

"Never."

And instead of being strong, I let him send me to heaven and back again after vowing like aways, that this, is in fact, the last time.

I'm a liar. I know.

Just call me Pinocchio.

CHAPTER THIRTY-TWO
ARIZONA

Walking into *Sarabeth's*, I see Reese sitting at the table alone. Brows pinching as I walk towards her, but I am grateful it's warm in here. Unwrapping my scarf and shrugging my coat off when I get to the table, she looks up from her phone.

"Oh hey," she smiles, locking it and popping it into her bag.

"Hey," she stands as she places a kiss on my cheek, and I kiss her back.

"No Connie?"

"Running late," she rolls her eyes, fingers playing with the rainbow necklace that sits on her neck.

"How's Celeste?"

"She is perfect, just feel like she is growing up way too fast," she sighs, and I give a knowing nod even though I have no idea.

"How are you feeling? Has it sunk in yet?" she reaches for her sweet, iced tea and holds it up to the waitress to order another.

"Well," my smile is lopsided as I shuffle in my seat, "it

had, until I found out that I am expecting identical twins." Her lips pop open, the straw of her drink resting on her bottom lip.

"No fucking way."

"Way," taking my drink from the waitress I thank her with a nod.

"Shit, wow, that's huge."

"I know," I sigh and my shoulders sag a little.

"It's amazing though, you and Keaton must be thrilled," her British accent is still strong and no signs of it ever fading out.

"We are, it's just not quite what we expected," my cheeks burn, I can't tell them that the twinnies might not even be Keaton's.

"When are you back at the hospital?"

My stomach knots. See. Full of lies.

"Monday," I sigh, "it's been so nice being off work and just doing what I want." That is not a lie, it has been nice.

"Were they okay? I know they can get funny with leave, but you know, you've had a lot on." All I do is nod, taking a sip of my tea so I can't run my mouth like I want to. I really don't think Reese would judge me, she hasn't got a judgmental bone in her body, but still... she would tell Killian, and Killian being how Killian is, would no doubt slip up at some point and tell my dad.

No one knows apart from Keaton.

"Yeah, they were fine, doctor signed me off due to my sickness," a lie. Again.

She nods as if she understands.

"Were you sick with Celeste?" I ask, trying to get the attention off me.

She shakes her head, "I felt a little sicky I think at the beginning, but I had a pretty smooth pregnancy."

"I am hoping for a smooth pregnancy too. The sickness is so much better; I just need to eat as soon as my eyes are open. Seems to keep it at bay for a little while," I smile at her and that's when I hear the heavy footsteps of Connie's iconic Dr Martens. I honestly don't think I have seen her in anything but them.

"Look who finally arrived," Reese chimes, standing up to greet Connie. But as I go to stand, Connie tells me to sit then wraps her arms around me, kissing me on the cheek.

"I've had a morning," she huffs, falling in her seat with a thud and grabbing the cocktail menu.

"That bad, huh?"

"That bad," she calls the waitress over and orders a margarita.

Jealous.

"Oh, go on, I'll have one too," Reese claps her hands together.

Bitch.

"Can you make me a virgin one?" I bat my lashes and the waitress nods, and my little heart is happy.

"So, care to elaborate?" Reese asks Connie.

"I came on, flooded the bedsheets. I mean, this is not out of the norm for me. It happened back when I had to hide away with Kaleb at the lodge in the Hamptons," she rolls her eyes, "so I stripped the bed."

"Standard," I pipe up because I love a worked up Connie.

"Idiot," she scoffs. "Went to put the washing in the machine, it's full. Go to unload it and place in in the dryer..."

"Let me guess?" Reese smirks.

"You don't even need to," she shoves Reese a little hard.

"Where is Doris?" I ask, taking another sip of my iced tea.

"Kaleb gave her the week off," she crosses her arms against her chest.

"Damn, how dare she have a well-deserved break," Reese giggles into her drink and Connie side-eyes her. Man, she is pissed.

"Anyway," she snaps, "I sort that out and put the dryer on too so I have half a chance of getting the blood-stained sheets into the washer before I leave, so I thought I would make myself a coffee only to find that my wonderful boyfriend has used all the creamer then put it back into the fridge... empty!"

"Oh dear," I roll my lips and Reese is sniggering.

"So, you didn't get your coffee?" I ask.

"No, I didn't and the fucking dryer didn't get it done in time so now I have one wet load still waiting to dry and I have period sheets on the floor of the laundry room so Kaleb can deal with that once he has finished his gym workout. Tosser."

My brows lift. "Tosser?"

"Yeah, it's a British word, picked it up from," and she thumbs beside her to Reese.

"Tosser is a brilliant word," she sighs as the waitress brings the drinks over and Connie downs it in one.

"I'll have another," she licks her lips as I sip mine.

"Food?" The waitress asks.

"Three lobster rolls and fries."

"Of course," she smiles at us all, collecting our menus and walking away.

Standard Sarabeth's lunch.

Reese slipped away to the restroom, and once I knew

she was out of earshot, I lean across the table as my eyes narrow.

"Connie," I whisper, and I have no idea why.

"Yeah?" She leans in, a girlish grin on her face, her hands splayed against the table like she is waiting for some juicy gossip.

"Is your dad's penthouse still empty?"

Her brows furrow, the smile slowly slipping away.

"I think so, why..." she pauses for a moment then leans in a little closer, "is everything okay between you and Keaton?"

I sigh, letting my head fall for a moment.

"Yeah, everything is perfect..." my eyes meet hers and I can see the confusion on her face.

"Then why do you want to move out?"

"I think it's the right thing to do, I was meant to move out weeks ago but then..."

"I'll speak to my dad," she nods when she eyes Reese walking back towards us and I sit back in my seat, lifting my virgin cocktail to my lips and taking a mouthful.

"So, who fancies a walk around central park before we head back home?" Reese smiles between me and Connie and we both just nod and smile.

CHAPTER THIRTY-THREE
KEATON

12 Weeks
Size of Babies: a lime

THE WEEKS HAVE PASSED IN A BLINK OF AN EYE AND FOR SOME reason, Arizona is pulling away. I was hoping it was just an off day, but the off days turned into weeks. We had her second scan today, the twelve week one and I get to see the twins on the screen, and I would be lying if I said I wasn't excited. My chest aches with nerves and my stomach knots tight, but excitement beats every other emotion that is currently swarming through my veins.

I'm sitting in my office, tucked away in the corner with my book. Not usually one for reading, but I need to silence the noisy voices in my head. Arizona is upstairs getting dressed and all I want to do is sit and watch her, basking in her beauty. I'm a sap, you don't need to tell me. She has my heart, wholly. I would shout it from the rooftops if I could.

Who would have thought, playboy Keaton head over heels for his best friend's daughter.

Sickening.

But it's true.

I love her so fucking hard.

My thoughts wander back to two weeks ago when we last slept together. It wasn't just sex with us. It was so much more; it was a connection that I had never felt before. Something tying me to her, pulling me in constantly. But since then, she hasn't let me near her. I would never force her into something she wasn't feeling. We're married but it still doesn't feel real. We went from a hook up before getting drunk and married. Running my index finger across my bottom lip, my book half closed on my lap and my eyes are pinned to the door, wishing for her to walk through.

But she doesn't.

My phone pings and it takes me a while to actually let my eyes fall and my hands to move before I even slip it out of my pocket, and when I do, I sigh.

> **Lucy**
> Hey stranger, I've missed you. Come see me tonight? It's been far too long. X

I mull over my answer for just a moment, fingers hovering over the on-screen keyboard.

> **Me**
> Not tonight, Luce, maybe another.

Eyes are back on the door. My skin crawls and my palms sweat at the thought of not being close to her, an addict waiting for his next hit but knowing full well it's unobtainable. Out of reach. So, so far out of my reach.

Get a grip.

I finally let myself out of my head, then my face falls and I lose myself in my book for just a while, well, long enough for me to let the minutes slip by.

I am so desperate to talk to my friends about it, but I can't. The only one I could talk to is Kaleb but honestly, I don't want to. I don't know why, but I feel judged by him. He has always been so put together. He was never a playboy, a drunk, a loose cannon... he was level-headed and grounded. His job was everything to him, dedicated his life to it until Connie. He always swore off love after watching my mom and dad's shit show of a marriage, whereas believe it or not, when I was a kid, I wanted to be married and have the big family. But as I got older, that dwindled to nothing, The thought of starting a family scared me. I am just grateful I never had kids with Satan. That would have been a disaster. Marriage ruined me... until it didn't.

I married Arizona King. Sure, it wasn't ideal, but it felt pretty damn perfect and that factored with the twins... well, I feel like the luckiest guy in the world.

I had it all.

The dream that I once wished for that dwindled to nothing for years was slowly turning back to the way I always wanted it, where now, suddenly, I felt like I was going to lose it all again and I had no idea why.

The minutes slip by and she walks into the living room like a god damn goddess dressed in a soft white dress with knee high heeled boots. Black knitted jacket thrown over her arm, bag hooked over her shoulder.

"Hey," she smiles, and I let my eyes do one last sweep over her body.

"Hey," I stand slowly, placing my book down and closing the gap between us in four long strides. Four strides too long in my opinion. "You look beautiful as always," I lean in, placing a soft kiss on her cheek. She smells delicious too. Fresh apples and elderflower and all I want to do is sink my teeth into her skin.

"You don't look too bad yourself hubby," she winks, stepping away and walking towards the door.

Hubby. I liked that a little too much.

I follow her out like a lost dog, not looking back as we walk along the sidewalk. My hand skims round her back as I gently move her over to the inside of the sidewalk so I can walk closer to the road. The urge to protect her is too strong. She gives a sweet smile, dimples presenting themselves in her cheeks.

"You excited?" she asks me, slipping her hand inside mine and everything feels right in that moment and the doom that once stormed deep inside of me slowly melted away with every step we took hand in hand.

"I am, a little nervous too," I admit, my heart heavy for just a moment.

"Don't be nervous. Everything will be perfect."

It didn't take us long to get to the Doctors office and I kind of wished it did. The walk was too short. I wanted to walk it three times over just so I could enjoy a little more of us time. Buzzing us in, we walk past the reception where Ari checked in. My eyes scanned round the waiting room, looking at the posters on the wall. Mad to think this will be us in a few short months. Two babies to love and cherish. Me and Kaleb didn't have the best childhood, but I was going to make sure I tried my hardest to give my children the best damn childhood. That's the thing when you come from a shitty background, you vow to never put anyone through what you had. You constantly try to do better. Sure, I am a sarcastic selfish prick when I want to be, but I still have a heart that beats and a body that bleeds. I still care. Deep, deep, down in the crevices of my heart is the light. Arizona is slowly pickaxing away at the ice that surrounds the warmth, edging closer and closer to finally releasing me from my iced heart.

"Arizona King."

I lean across to her, my lips pressed against her ear, "You need to change your name to Mills." A smile slips across her lips before we stand at the same time, fingers brushing as we walk closer towards the brown-haired doctor.

"Hi," Ari says as the doctor steps aside, letting her walk into the room with me following. Nerves cripple me but so does excitement.

"Nice to see you again, how are you doing?" the doctor asks as she sits at her desk, Ari and me taking our seats and my face is turned towards her, eyes watching as she speaks to the doctor, answering her question.

"I feel okay, still some sickness lingering of a morning."

"That should ease off in the next few weeks," she gives Ari a warm smile before her eyes lock on me. "And you must be Keaton?" I blink a couple of times.

"Yeah," I'm a little hesitant as I answer.

She constantly smiles, this woman. I haven't seen her lips turn down once.

"Nice to meet you, I'm doctor Kyra. Just in case you hadn't realized," her eyes fall to the name plaque on her desk.

I nod. What am I meant to say back to that?

"Okay, another round of bloods today and scan. What do you want first?" her fingers lock as she focuses on Arizona.

"Bloods," I watch as she rolls her lips and my hand slips onto her lap, rubbing my palms over her thigh.

Kyra pushes a button on her phone and an older nurse walks through a door to the side, pushing her trolley through with a tray topped with everything she needs.

I'm not queasy, but there is something about drawing blood that doesn't sit right with me. It makes my stomach flip before bottoming out and my skin goes clammy.

"You okay?" Ari looks at me concerned as she shrugs her cardigan off, and letting the nurse get to the veins in the crease of her elbow.

I nod. How do I tell her that I am, in fact, not okay.

"Okay, you ready?" The nurse asks as she tightens a strap and taps the vein.

"Ready as I'll ever be," she focuses on me and that right there is when everything around me disappears into nothing but calmness. All I see is her and only her because she is all I care about.

Her.

Only her.

The nurse finishes up and exits out the same door she came from. Ari has a small cotton ball taped where they drew blood. Hated it. Hated that they marked her beautiful skin.

"Come lay down, let's get a look at the twins," Kyra stands, ushering Ari over towards the bed. I move behind her, following her footsteps before taking a seat next to the bed. She lifts her top and Kyra squirts clear gel onto Ari's little swollen belly. I feel like she's only really started to pop over the last week or so and it makes my heart swell inside my chest.

My fingers lock with Arizona's, her head turned to face the screen that the doctor is currently looking at, the probe pushed onto her lower stomach and that's when I hear it. The sound of galloping horses.

"They've changed so much," Ari whispers towards the screen, my eyes fixed to the flickering heartbeats. Two hearts. Two babies. Tears sting behind my eyes and as I blink, a tear rolls down my cheek.

"Wow," is all I can muster, Arizona lets out a soft laugh as she squeezes my hand.

"It's something right?" her voice floats over me like silk, my skin pricking in goosebumps as I focus on the two babies on the screen.

"It really is," and only then do I pull my eyes from the screen and look at her. My wife. The love of my life. I have fallen hard. God damn, so fucking hard.

My eyes well and I tear them away from Ari and back onto the screen. I never want this moment to be over.

Right here, right now. Everything is just... perfect.

"Twins are measuring good, Twin A is a little bigger but that is normal. We will keep a close eye on them both to make sure each is growing, but right now, I am happy. Do you have any questions?" Kyra asks as she freezes the screen on the image, then hands Arizona some tissue to wipe the excess gel off her belly which means she has to drop my hand and I miss her touch already. I help her sit up, and she twists round to face Kyra. I watch as her brows furrow slightly, fingers locked but her face drops as she looks at her stomach before they're back on the doctor.

"No, everything is fine," she breathes out, but the tone of her voice is not convincing. At all.

She hops off the bed and walks towards the doctor's desk to grab her bag and coat.

"Is everything okay?" I say quietly as I stand next to her, and she looks at me giving me a solid one nod response.

"Okay, so I'll see you in December for your next scan, this one takes a little longer as we check all the babies heart, chambers, spine, neck fluid...." she rambles off but I know the doctor is telling me over Arizona because she already knows.

"Plus, you can find out the genders if you wish," and my ears prick.

"Thank you, Kyra, I'll see you soon," Ari shakes Kyra's hand then turns for the door.

"Oh, Ari," Kyra calls out just as she gets to the door, she spins and waits for the doctor to continue. "If you have anything you want to ask before your next appointment, just give me a call and I'll be happy to answer any questions you have," she gives a soft nod and Ari nods back before walking out the door and there I am just standing there wondering what the fuck is going on.

Following Arizona out to the front desk, she talks quietly to the receptionist as she confirms her next appointment.

"Does that date still work with you?"

"Yes, fine," her tone is clipped as she takes her files back and slips it under her arm.

She looks at me, and I don't know what her eyes are telling me. They're erratic but sad, searching my face for something, anything.

"Ready?" she asks before she turns on her heel and walks out the door, me right behind her. Only when we're out on the sidewalk do I reach for her elbow, pulling her back into me.

"Hey, hey..." my voice trails off and I see the tears in her eyes. "Baby..." I pause and she shakes her head from side to side. "What's wrong?" My fingers softening on my grip.

She looks away for a moment, arms folded across her

chest. "You can talk to me baby, you know that." My voice is calm, my eyes soft but when she looks at me, her eyes are red rimmed and filling with fresh tears.

"I wanted to ask about finding out who the dad was but then I freaked, because what if the twins are not yours Keaton? What if they're the mystery guys?"

"I told you I don't care, these babies are mine Ari, I know it."

"You don't!" she raises her voice at me, and I feel my heart crack. "You won't love these babies like they're your own if you find out they're not yours. There will always be a voice in the back of your mind constantly thinking 'I wish they were mine'," she pauses for a moment, angrily swiping a tear away with her palm. "I don't blame you Keaton, I don't blame you not wanting to be by my side through this, bringing up another man's babies. I get it. So please, don't hang around for my sake," she scoffs and turns away from me, head down as she walks away.

And what do I do? I turn in the opposite direction and walk.

Because honestly? Maybe she is right.

CHAPTER THIRTY-FOUR
ARIZONA

I sit in the warmth of Connie and Kaleb's penthouse. Connie sits on the chair next to me, I'm curled up on the sofa like a little ball. Hot chocolate sits in my lap, warming my hands and my eyes are dry. I have cried so much I don't think I have any more tears left inside of me.

We've sat in silence for most of the time I have been here, I have no idea what to say. Kaleb is here, pottering somewhere. He doesn't want to encroach, I get it. It's his brother. I'm his best friend's daughter. It's messy. Real, fucking, messy.

Kaleb walks into the room, hands folded into his pockets of his suit pants, and I hear the heavy sigh vibrate through him. Connie turns to look at him, a weak smile gracing her face.

"I'm sorry, I've taken up so much of your evening," my own sigh leaving me as I go to stand, and Connie places her hand on my knee.

"Don't be silly, you're always welcome here."

"I don't know what to do..." I pause, my eyes moving from Connie to Kaleb as he strolls across and sits in a chair, but next to Connie. His long finger rubs across his lips, ankle crossed over his knee.

He is smart. Handsome. I see similarities between him and Keaton, but they're so different. Dark brown hair with shimmers of grey, tousled and styled. Beautiful striking green eyes and warm sun kissed skin. Both have structured cheek bones, and strong jawlines. Sharp enough to cut through diamonds. Always wrapped in the perfect designer suit, timeless. They're both devastatingly handsome.

"Tell me what's going on? I might be able to help," he offers, his voice soft like cotton.

"I'm worried," I half shrug, admitting.

"Of?"

"Keaton leaving me," I blink away a tear, placing my cup on the coaster and twist my wedding band around.

"Why would he leave you?" Kaleb looks at me utterly confused and I swallow the large lump that has formed in my throat, tightening by the minute. How can I admit that I may be pregnant with another man's baby? How can I tell them that I work in a strip club and because of that, I went to a private room with someone I pleasured myself to over a webcam? I'm a fraud and as my story develops, the lies become harder to cover, harder to remember.

Silence fills the room once more and I can feel their eyes burning into me and suddenly I feel like I can't breathe.

"Ari?" I can hear the panic in Connie's voice as I swing my legs round and stand from the sofa.

"I can't breathe," my hand pressed to my chest as it rises and falls, tightness crushing my chest like someone is tightening a belt, hole by hole and sliding it through the buckle.

"She's having a panic attack," Connie rushes out the

room and next thing I know, Kaleb's arms are wrapped round my trembling body, as he holds me.

He slowly lowers me to the floor, sitting behind me so I am between his legs as Connie drops to her knees in front of me, brown paper bag being placed over my nose and mouth.

"Deep, slow inhales." Connie's voice echoes in the distance but I am too consumed with my own thoughts.

I nod, ignoring the way my lungs are burning, my eyes stinging with tears that have escaped and rolling down my reddened cheeks. Humiliation scorns my face, my heart racing like galloping horses deep within my chest. It aches and almost feels hollow. My heart crumbling in Keaton's hands and it doesn't matter what I try to do, we're always going to destroy each other. And if these babies are not his, how can I be selfish to expect him to stay with me? How can I expect him to raise kids that aren't his. He may be here for a month or five, but he will soon grow tired and want out of whatever fucked up relationship we are in. I should have never crossed the line, and neither should he.

The tightness in my chest eases, my breaths shallow and my heart begins to calm to a slow and steady rhythm.

"You okay?" Kaleb asks me just as the elevator doors ping open and I see an angry Keaton storming towards us, brows furrowed, lines etched into his stupid handsome face. His lips are dropped, his eyes erratic as they search my face. He lowers himself in front of me, pulling me from his brother's grasp and onto my feet as he encases me within his arms, his heart racing under his chest and that's what I focus on.

"What the fuck?" his voice ruins the moment in an instance, his words hurling towards his brother like bullets ready to pierce Kaleb's skin.

"She came here to talk to Connie, then she had a panic attack, so I did what I used to do to Connie..." he pauses and I hear the sharp inhale of breath rattle in Keaton's chest, his body vibrating.

"You should have called me," he is pissed off.

"Why should I?" Kaleb retorts. Connie stepped up from beside Kaleb, her eyes bouncing between Keaton's. I push away from his chest, slowly turning to face Kaleb and Connie.

"Because she is my wife."

Connie holds her hand out to stop Kaleb from answering. "And she's my friend. She was my friend well before anything happened between the both of you. She's not your possession. She came to speak to me because I am her friend."

She crosses her arms across her chest and Kaleb rests his hand on her stomach, pulling her back and towards him so her back is against his chest.

Keaton says nothing but I hear the rumble of a growl that deepens as the seconds go on.

"I'm fine," I admit, trying to diffuse this hostile situation. I didn't want to cause any issues. Especially not between Kaleb and Keaton.

"Are you?" Kaleb asks, one brow raises, and I watch as the corners of his lips lift, his eyes not on me, but on Keaton and I know he is trying to get a rise out of him.

"Yes," my tone is clipped. I feel Keaton's hand rest on the slight swell of my lower stomach and my heart flutters in my chest.

"You can stay here anytime you want," Connie interjects, and I stiffen against Keaton as his hand that has now curled round my hip tightens.

"She doesn't need to stay here; she lives with me. It's her home."

I sigh, dropping my head and shaking it from side to side.

"And that's fine, I am just giving her the option. If things ever get too heavy or you need time out then you know where we are," and that riles Keaton up even more than he already is.

"Is there something you're not telling me?" Keaton asks, letting me go and stepping in front of me, his beautiful eyes volleying between mine and I shake my head.

"Are you sure Ari? Because I feel like I've walked into something that I shouldn't have..." he trails off and my heart thumps hard against my ribcage. "You have distanced yourself from me over the last week or so, then in the doctor's office..." I step back but he closes the gap between us. "I told you, I'm not going anywhere..." he lowers his voice, his lips inches from mine and all I want to do is edge forward so I crash into him. "I'm all in."

"You don't know that," I counter back in a whisper.

"I do," he nods softly, fingers gripping my chin and holding my head in place, so our eyes connect, his gaze deepening as I lose myself in his. "I promise you..."

"Don't," I nibble my bottom lip to stop the choked sob that is threatening to escape.

"Don't what?" he asks, edging me back against the wall.

"Promise something you can't keep," a tear rolls down my cheek, but his thumb pad catches it and wipes it away.

"I don't break promises..." and I feel it, the truth seeps out of him.

"We will see," I choke out, and with that he stumbles back as if I have winded him and my heart throbs inside my chest, my bottom lip wobbling. "I'll see you at home?" I sort of ask, sort of say before I dip out, head down, and walk towards the elevator of the penthouse and press the button.

I give one look over my shoulder and see all three of them standing there, staring at me. A small smile graces my lips and I mouth *thank you* as the doors ping open and I step inside and only when the doors close, do the tears cascade down my cheeks once more.

CHAPTER THIRTY-FIVE
KEATON

I STAND AMIDST THE CHAOS, KALEB'S VOICE LASHING AGAINST MY skin and opening up wounds causing them to bleed slowly.

What the fuck just happened? How did we go from what we've been to this? It doesn't make sense.

I stumble back and sit on the sofa where Ari was not long wrapped in my brother's arms, and I am staring straight ahead when Connie places a tumbler of scotch into my empty hand. I slowly look up at her, eyes full of sympathy and bitterness runs through my veins, my tongue coated in harsh words that I swallow down.

"What's going on?" Kaleb asks as he sits next to me.

"I have no fucking idea," I admit, bringing the thick rim of the glass to my lips and take a swig, the warmth consuming me in an instant as the amber liquor slips down my throat.

Kaleb sighs beside me and I turn to look at him. I know that sigh. That's the sigh of '*I have something to tell you but shouldn't't'*. It's the sigh of '*I probably know the reason for her outburst, but it's not my place*', and so on. But he does this knowing full well I am going to ask.

"What is it?" and he will reply with....

"Nothing."

Before I begin to get agitated and huff. And like clockwork, he will respond with...

"I mean..."

"What?" and now I snap because he is beginning to piss me off.

"Well," he sucks in a breath, leaning back into the sofa and stretches one of his arms over the back.

Then I roll my eyes.

He is such an annoyance.

Love him though. I do. But he pisses me off. It's a sibling thing. Would love to plant one on his jaw, bust his lip maybe. But if someone else thinks about it or does it... well, then it's outright war.

"Kaleb, spit it out man," frustration is evident in my voice, I sit forward, fingers wrapped around my glass tightening, but I close my eyes for a moment to calm myself. I don't want to shatter the glass.

When my eyes open, Connie is walking out the room, no doubt annoyed at her significant other who is about to blow the friend code. We all know if one of your girlfriend's friends divulge with you in the room, she trusts you. That means what you hear in that moment goes no further.

But to Kaleb. It's a point scorer.

He may be the decent one out of us both, and I mean that honestly because I am trash. I know that, but fuck, he loves to gossip.

"She thinks you're going to leave her man," he puffs his cheeks out, ankle sitting on his knee and his whole demeanor is relaxed.

"What?"

"Yeah, she is scared you're going to leave her... I did ask

267

her why but then she had a panic attack and that's when you walked in," he whistles through his teeth before he stands and pours his own glass of scotch out.

"I'm not going to leave her, I have told her time and time again..." I feel defeated. It's like she doesn't want this to work out, like she wants me to give up on us.

"I would have told her the same if I had a chance... you wouldn't leave the mother of your children without a dad now..." he turns to face me, tumbler in his grasp, amber liquid poured over ice. "Would you?"

"Fuck, of course not..."

"Then why does she think it Keat? There must be a reason?"

This is where I should have kept my mouth shut. This wasn't only my story to tell, but yet I couldn't keep the secret that has been burning a hole through my heart any longer. The fear that these kids aren't mine and may be someone else's guts me to my very core. But I love her. With every fiber of my existence. I am irrevocably in love with her.

"Because there is a chance the twins are not mine." And even saying the words out loud leaves a bad taste in my mouth and it doesn't matter that I just downed the remainder of my scotch, the taste still remains.

"What?" the disbelief is evident, and it makes me feel sick to my stomach.

"You heard it," I scowl, pushing up and pouring myself another glass.

"I did, but..."

"There was a guy before... just once but... timings and shit." I take a sip of my drink, eyes closing for just a moment as the warmth coats my throat.

"Well shit."

"Yeah... shit."

"I mean... you've done it more than once right?"

I scoff a laugh, "Yeah."

"So, chances..."

"Chances. But it's just that. A chance. A slim fucking chance and you know, it only takes once," I nod, bringing my glass to my lips again.

"Slim."

"Yup, but still."

"Shit," he murmurs again then pats the space next to him. I stroll over, sitting and letting my head rest on the back of the sofa, I feel Kaleb's hand on my shoulder, giving it a reassuring squeeze before we just sit in silence.

Complete and utter silence.

We're fucked.

CHAPTER THIRTY-SIX
ARIZONA

I slept in my own room last night. Keaton didn't come to find me, and I didn't find myself wandering towards the place that feels like home. In his arms. Head on his chest as I listen to the steady beat of his heart. Instead, I woke up feeling alone and abandoned and I only have myself to blame for that. I kept pushing and pushing until I had put a wedge between us because I am so scared of him leaving me and walking away.

Nothing about the last six months has gone the way I wanted. This is not the dream I had envisaged.

Pulling myself from bed, I shower and dress in sweatpants and a loose, oversized tee. Nothing fits and I need new clothes but that's not on the top of my list at the moment.

What's on the top of my list is moving out and focusing on earning as much money as I can, but without the stage and eventually, the private dances, the money is going to dwindle into nothing.

How the fuck am I going to bring up two kids?

My head is in my hands for just a moment when I internally slap myself. *Pull yourself together.*

Pushing my glasses up the bridge of my nose, I pull my hair into a messy pony and walk towards the kitchen. The coffee pot is hot, so I pour myself a decaf with creamer and do myself a bowl of cereal with cold milk.

I'm not alone long when Keaton walks into the kitchen looking as handsome, if not even more so, than usual and wearing the perfect Tom Ford suit.

"Morning," his voice is gruff and he can't even look at me.

"Morning," I whisper, my eyes on my bowl of cereal and suddenly I am not hungry anymore. I hear the sound of him reaching for a mug and I ignore the urge to peek a look at him over my shoulder.

My phone beeps, my brows furrow and I turn it over to see a message from Lucy. Shit, I have really neglected her.

> **Lucy**
> Hey beautiful, you working tonight? xo

Then another.

> **Lucy**
> Sorry to ask, but what's Keaton's problem? I messaged him a few days ago asking to see him and he replied with 'not tonight luce, maybe another'. Is he seeing someone else because the last time we were together he sounded pretty adamant that he wanted us to be a little more than fuck buddies... but yeah, do you know anything? xo.

My heart jack hammers in my chest and the rage slowly seeps into my blood stream.

I spin on my stool, one leg over the other, arms crossed against my chest.

His eyes lift, brows raised as he leans against the surface. Phone in one hand, coffee in the other.

"Heard from Lucy at all?" I ask, and that gets him standing a little taller.

"Not in a while, why?"

"Just wondered whether you had told her we were married or not?" He says nothing, just looks at me in confusion. "Only reason I ask is because she has just messaged me asking if all is okay with you because she text you for a hook up and you replied with *'sorry luce, I'm married to Arizona. We're a thing now so this can't happen anymore.'*"

And I watch as his jaw laxes slightly, lips popped open.

"Ohhhh wait, my bad, you *didn't* reply with that, silly me. No, no, you replied with *'not tonight luce, maybe another'*" and I am fucking angry.

"Ari... wait."

But it's too late.

I sweep my phone off the countertop and walk away but Keaton is hot on my tail. He grabs my elbow, pulling me back and turning me to face him but I am in blind rage mode. My hand connects with his cheek and the echo of the slap fills the quiet house.

"Don't you fucking dare," I seethe, tugging my wedding band off and throwing it at him as I walk towards my room, grab my suitcase I came with many months ago and begin to dump my belongings inside of it.

When I look up, he is standing at the door, a red mark across his face and eyes glassy.

"I didn't mean what I said to her, it was a quick-fire response."

"I don't care Keaton," my tone is harsh and a pain sears through my chest.

"You do care Arizona, why are you lying?"

"No idea, it must be contagious because I've been living with a liar, seems I have become pretty good at it too."

"What does that even mean?" his voice grows louder as he steps closer to me.

"Exactly what you think it means," I zip my case up and spin to face him. "I'm done Keaton. Here, you have your escape plan," I continue towards the doorway, so we're standing shoulder to shoulder, "I suggest you take it," and I just about manage to get the words out before the tears threaten.

I wasn't lying when I said I was getting good at it. Because what I just spun was just that. A lie. Another to add to the long list. I didn't want him to use this as an escape, but I was giving him it anyway.

CLIMBING OUT THE CAB, I stare up at KILLIAN AND REESE'S house. This felt a little too ballsy. Should I be here? No. But I needed my own escape plan, and this was just it. I didn't want to leave Keaton, I didn't, and I promise that wasn't a lie, but I needed to. For both of our sakes.

Inhaling on a shaky breath, I climb the steps to the impressive townhouse and knock on the black front door. I'm not waiting long in the cold when Killian opens the door, utter confusion on his face as his eyes sweep over me, concern is evident on his worried brow.

"Arizona," he steps forward, "are you okay?" his eyes swooping and taking in my suitcase and bag.

I nod, but shrug at the same time because honestly, I

don't know. Am I okay? Like really? When I sit and count all the ways that my life has been derailed in the last six months, I would conclude that no, I am, in fact, not okay.

"Come in, it's Baltic out there," he isn't lying. It's bitterly cold. Freezing in fact. He looks tired as he steps back, opening his home to me. And I am so damn grateful. I had no idea if they were even in, and I know I had originally spoke to Connie about having Killian's old apartment, but given my last encounter and the fact that Keaton showed up, I feel like Kaleb would spill my truths and tell him everything. And I'm not saying it would be out of choice, but maybe they coax it out of each other. Is it some twin superpower?

I step inside, and warmth blankets me.

"Thank you," I wrap my arms around myself, my coat tied at my front. Grateful I sized up before I found out I was pregnant. This bump feels like it's growing by the minute.

"Want me to take your coat?" and I shake my head.

"I'm not planning on staying long, just have a favor to ask, that's all." He nods a knowing nod. Does he know? Has Connie already brought it to his attention. He leads me down the hallway and towards the back of the house where a large kitchen-dining area sits.

"Your house is lovely," my cheeks redden slightly.

"Thank you, I would love to take credit for it, but before Reese, it was merely a shell."

"I heard my name," Reese's voice floats through the room and I smile as I turn to face her, and she looks as pretty as ever. Dirty blonde hair, beautiful opal eyes, tall and lean.

"Hey Buttercup," she walks towards Killian as he calls her nickname and embraces him, placing a kiss on his lips, baby monitor wrapped in her fingers before turning and facing to look at me.

"Is everything okay?" she asks me, her eyes doing a quick sweep over me.

"Yeah," I roll my lips, "just want to ask something of Killian."

They both just stare, waiting for my words.

"Me and Keaton need some time out..." I pause for a moment, and I see them both look at my empty left finger.

"Has he hurt you?" Killian's voice is tight, vice like. A slither of rage flashes in his eyes.

Yes.

"No, no, nothing like that," I shake my head from side to side softly, eyes cast down as my face falls forward, so my focus is on the ground.

"Then what happened?"

I can feel both of their eyes burning into me, but I don't want to look up.

"We just need some time apart. That's all... I was wondering if I could maybe rent the penthouse for a couple of weeks?"

A couple of weeks will be all I can afford.

"Of course you can, and we don't want the money Arizona. You're family." Killian says softly, "but why don't you go home? I'm sure your dad would love to have you back."

And I snort a laugh, finally allowing my eyes to look at them both.

"Killian," Reese sighs, placing her hand on his chest, "not your place," she gives him a small smile.

"I'm just not ready yet... he has no idea about..." my hands round my small bump.

Killian rubs his lips. "I want to tell him; things have just been a little ..."

"I get it," he holds his hand up to stop me from speaking, "no need to explain." And his words are not harsh, far from it. I watch as he breaks away from Reese and steps over to a small cabinet on the wall, opening the door and unhooking a bunch of keys. He walks towards me, handing me the keys and lingering for just a moment. "There is no rush, you take as long as you need, and I promise to not tell Keaton where you are... unless you want me to?"

I shake my head from side to side.

"I think it's best we both just give each other some space," and Killian nods.

"Okay, come, I'll drive you over."

"Oh, please no, honestly, it's fine. I have already taken up a lot of your evening, I don't want to take up any more of it. I'll get a taxi," I half laugh, and he smirks.

"It wasn't a question," he raises a brow and I lower my head, dropping it forward. He walks past me, cocky smile on his face and I look up at Reese who beams at me.

"You'll never win against Killian Hayes, trust me."

"No shit," I laugh before pulling her in for a cuddle as we say our goodbyes.

"I'll come see you tomorrow, that work with you?"

"Yeah."

"Perfect, I'll see you tomorrow," she gives me one last hug and follows me down the hallway. My brows pinch when I notice my suitcase and bags have already been taken. "He won't let you lift a finger," she smiles, fingers curled round the front door as I step outside and into the cold.

"Thanks for everything."

"You never have to thank us," and my heart warms. I was worried when I fell out with my dad that I would have no family left. Yet, I have all the family I need right here.

Killian helps me into the penthouse and also explains that Reese's parents, Mateo and Liz lived a couple of floors down in apartment 108 so if I had any problems I could always knock. I thanked him and after he showed me how to work certain appliances and the hot water and heating, he was out the door. Closing it behind him, it took me a moment or two for everything to sink in. This wasn't what I wanted, but it was needed. I want to be with Keaton, I love him with all I have but I needed to do it for both of us to even stand a chance.

Sure, the issue with Lucy wasn't that big, but it was big enough to cause a distraction to be able to walk out the door without him following me. He knew he fucked up; he is a stubborn headed man, I give it a couple of days and my phone will be blowing up with missed calls and messages. I felt like everything was getting a little too real. I was pregnant with twins. I married my dad's best friend. Everything was fucked up. I missed him as soon as I walked out the door, it took everything in me to keep walking until his home was so far out of sight I couldn't run back and into the safety of his arms. I was adamant we would find our way back to each other, but until then. I was on my own.

Just like I was all of those months ago.

Slipping my phone out of my pocket, I open my music app and play *you're on your own kid - taylor swift*, and never have I resonated more with a song than this one.

Because I was well and truly on my own.

And worse of all, I only had myself to blame.

CHAPTER THIRTY-SEVEN
ARIZONA

THE LAST COUPLE OF DAYS PASSED IN A BLUR, EVEN WHEN REESE and Connie showed I pretty much blanked the whole thing out. I needed to get back into my routine, and that's exactly what I was going to do tonight. I was back to work this afternoon and I wasn't going to let my heartache and pregnancy get in the way. I was going to show up, get to work and come home. I even texted Sage about taking extra shifts because I need as much money as I can get. I hadn't even started looking at things to buy yet and I know how expensive one baby is, let alone two. Keaton would help with all of that, I know he would, but I wouldn't expect him to. It's not his responsibility, I mean, it could be, but honestly, I just have this feeling in my gut that the twins aren't his.

Sighing, I finish packing my work bag and lock the door behind me.

It wasn't long before I was walking into the club, and as soon as my feet hit the locker room, it was like I had never been away.

The first half of my floor work was done and I tucked

myself away in the staff room to eat my sandwich, chicken, rocket and hummus. Couldn't get enough of it. I wasn't alone long when Lucy slumped down beside me, eyes on my stomach before they were on my eyes.

"Why didn't you tell me?" She sighs, leaning her head on my shoulder and it hits me in that moment how much I have missed her.

"Didn't know how to," I manage after a mouthful of food.

"How about, *'Hey luce, wanna meet for a coffee? Got some news'*, I mean, anything would have been better than you just walking in. You've been gone weeks and you come back sporting a small, round tummy. I mean, it looks like bloat to me, but I see it so much more now I know you're actually pregnant."

Now it's my turn to sigh.

"I don't know, I just felt a little out of sorts with it all to be honest. Pregnancy was not on my bucket list this year but here I am. Single and pregnant."

"Who's the dad?" the burning question on everyone's tongue and my heart aches.

Wish I knew. Your guess is as good as mine is what I wanted to say, but instead I say, "A guy I met at the private club..." I pause and I know she is letting her mind drift back to the night I walked in numb and let them take care of me after I had the private night with my mystery man.

"Does he know?" her head is off my shoulder now, eyes full of concern and all I do is place my hand on my tummy and let my head fall before I softly shake my head from side to side.

"Shit."

"Yeah, shit," I scoff.

"We're your family, we will all help out where we can,"

and I can hear the kind sentiment in her voice and my heart throbs in my chest. Placing my hand that was once on my stomach on her hand, I blink back the tears.

"Thanks Luce, that means the world to me," I swallow down the burning lump in my throat and ignore the sting behind my eyes that threatens to unleash my tears.

"Not a problem, I mean it."

"I know," I whisper, "I know."

CHAPTER THIRTY-EIGHT

KEATON

It had been four days.

Four days since she walked out the door and took my heart with her. I tighten my palm around the gold band that she threw at me in anger. Hated that she took it off.

Hated it.

I didn't want to love her. I really didn't, but I somehow ended up falling head over fucking heels for her. So stupid to think that this would have actually worked. Everything I touch turns to poison.

Wish I was lying.

As much as my ex-wife, Chantelle, was Satan dressed up in a pretty pant suit, she wasn't all bad. She was a good suitor, family had money, she was career driven but still wanted a family someday. We worked well together, until we didn't. She was good for me, and I mean that wholly. She was.

But I somehow turned her into a vindictive, conniving bitch. She turned on me quicker than a raging bull with its matador. It didn't matter what I did to suppress her and give her everything she could ever dream of, nothing was enough for her. I never knew what I had done to turn her into a cold-hearted bitch, but it must have been something, and then I realized it was being with me.

I offered to give her children; I never made her choose her career over motherhood. I offered to be a stay-at-home dad, a full-time nanny, whatever she wanted. But then it dawned on me, she didn't want any of that. She didn't care about my feelings and my wants for my life on this planet. She only cared about herself. She agreed to marry me out of a need more than a want. She desired nothing more than a ring on her finger and a man who came from a good name. Mills.

Bertie Mills—my father—was a successful businessman. Shrewd and cold when needed, but it got him as far as it did. It wasn't until Chantelle left that I realized he and her orchestrated it all. Even worse, they were having an affair. I found out, promised to keep it from Kaleb, but not my mom. Kaleb didn't need to know the one man he idolized more than me—jokes—was our father. My brother would have bent over backwards for him if it meant getting a *'I'm proud of you'*. It never did come. Even on his death bed. I followed through with my promise, and still to this day my brother never knew what really happened.

And for Chantelle, me outing them to my mother, the love of my life before Arizona, was the worst thing I could do. I ruined her life, ruined her chances of being happy. She would have been comfortable with me, but clearly comfortable wasn't enough. It wasn't until I signed those divorce papers years later that I realized I was the poison in her veins. She tolerated me, stayed with me because I didn't really give her a choice. It was bad enough that she brought shame to my family once, I wasn't going to allow her to do it again. But once my mom died, her wish was for me to make her as insufferably happy as I could, well, I had no reason to protect her anymore. I turned cold and callous with her, made her life hell in the end I suppose. And when I finally served her with divorce papers, she took them like a woman starved.

She cleaned me out, mostly. I tucked money away every now and then, and the house I live in was my parents. Tarnished with *Betrayal* but filled with so much love.

And since her, well, there hasn't been anyone.

Until Arizona.

I've fought with myself over the last couple of days as to whether I should message her or not. I always choose the latter. She needs space, we need space. It's been hundred miles per hour since she moved in. That doesn't mean I didn't still love her with every fiber inside my body.

If this is what love feels like, then I have never once been in love.

This is painful. It's messy. It isn't easy. But it's addicting, beautiful and scary. Loving her knocks the air from my lungs, but breathing without her is unbearable. My heart is shredded and my chest aches at the hollowness that now fills it. My heart began to heal, the crevices that were settled in so deep were slowly closing again and the weeds that buried beneath the surface we're now blossoming into flowers.

It was her.

My blossom.

Ugh, fuck, I missed her.

The house was too quiet without her.

Didn't like it.

Not one bit.

Hated it. Hate wasn't a strong enough word.

Loathed it.

Kicking my feet up onto the sofa, I lay and stare at the ceiling.

I needed to get to work. Couldn't mope all day unfortunately.

After another ten minutes of staring at the boring as fuck white ceiling, I rolled myself up and off the sofa and sluggishly made my way to the car.

Over today already.

THE DRIVE IS SHORT TO THE OFFICE; ALWAYS IS. MOSTLY. ALL three cars are here. Not sure why I was hoping Titus wasn't going to be here.

Pulling into my spot, I inhale deeply then cut my engine. I hadn't seen Titus in a while. I have avoided him at every chance I have had. I can't keep lying to him. But, for her, I have to.

I mean, I can't tell him we're having twins because I'm not sure if they're mine.

Fuck's sake man.

Rubbing my thumb on the underside of my gold wedding band, my heart aches.

Miss her.

Stupid amounts.

Literally feel like I could die without her.

So fucking dramatic.

Finally, and reluctantly, believe me, I climb out the car. Briefcase in hand, and my head is thumping knowing I have this month's accounts to go through. Busy and late night.

Blessing in disguise really. All I do at home is mope around because I miss Arizona.

Slamming my car door, the loud noise echoes around the underground garage. Walking towards the elevator, pressing the button, the doors ping open, and a heavy sigh vibrates through my chest as I step inside the elevator, inhaling deeply as the doors slide shut. The ride up is short. Too short.

My foot is out the elevator, my eyes seeking out Titus and he is sitting on the phone, leaned back in his chair, feet on his desk and crossed at the ankles. Nate is Nate. Buried in his computer and Kaleb is tucked in his office.

It's quiet.

Too quiet.

No Xavier, and no Killian from what I can see. Killian normally pops in; he doesn't work here. He works across the city with his wife, Reese at Lorde's PR. Pretty sure that's where they met, might be wrong though.

Love them together. Love just them actually. They're so good for each other. Like rays of sunshine in each other's lives. I know he has said before that he felt like he was walking around in darkness before he met Reese.

Cute. But I get it.

Placing my briefcase on my desk, I click it open and grab my piles of paperwork. Kicking up my computer, I notice a piece of paper that says *sign here*. I see Titus hovering by my door as I quickly scribble my signature where asked then toss the pen down onto the desk.

"All set for Ari's birthday next week?" he asks me like I had forgotten.

"Pretty much."

I'm not all set.

Don't want to slip up that she doesn't live with me anymore.

He would blow a gasket.

"She okay?" it's more of a grunt than an ask.

"Yup," I sigh, not in the mood for small talk today. Closing my briefcase, I place it on the floor by my feet and focus on my screen as I log into my computer.

"What's eating you?" He steps into my office like I have invited him in.

Annoyed me a little bit.

"I've got a busy day."

"Well maybe if you got here early like the rest of us instead of doing what ever it is you do..." and he trails off fully aware of what he has just said.

My lips pull into a smile as I chuckle, opening my emails. "Don't."

"I haven't done anything, pretty sure those words came from your lips man, not mine."

"I'm mad at you."

"Join the queue," I huff and his hands are pressed onto my desk, annoyingly beautiful blue eyes burning into me.

"What is that supposed to mean?"

I shrug. "Exactly that, you're not the first and surely not the last to be mad at me, so..."

"But I top everyone else surely, you did get drunk with my just barely legal daughter..."

"She's twenty-two next week, hardly *barely* legal... don't be dramatic Titus. It really doesn't look good on you," my brows furrow as I keep my eyes on my screen.

"And marry her," he finishes.

I sigh, leaning back in my chair, fingers locked and resting in my lap as I let my eyes lift to meet his.

"And what?" my brows sit high in my head, lips turned down slightly as I wait for his response.

"Well," he stands, hands tucked into his pockets.

"I'm not happy about it."

"Right?"

Silence.

"Titus, man, I am fucking busy. Have you got something to say or?"

"I want you to divorce Arizona."

My eyes widen, my back straightens, sitting a little taller in my chair.

"And why would I do that?"

"Because she's my daughter and I don't like it."

"I don't like you at the minute but hey," I shake my head from side to side and I watch as he stands up, not sure if he thinks I am threatened by him; I'm not.

"She isn't some victory, I know you told me you love her, but I have a hard time believing that," and that really gets under my skin. I scoff, clenching my jaw and the prominent ache is evident.

"Never thought she was a victory... and I do love her. Not sure when I had to start explaining my feelings to you."

"When you married my daughter while drunk."

"We planned it before we were drunk."

"I have a hard time believing that too."

"Do you? Really? Because you and Ari are really close? Bullshit Titus. Don't believe me, ask Killian, ask Reese, ask them if I dragged her down the aisle of the little white chapel of love in Vegas and forced her to marry me."

I stand from my own desk, and I am fucking raging.

"Don't."

"Don't what? I'm just stating facts Titus and you don't fucking like it." He crosses his arms across his chest tightly.

"Maybe you should spend a bit more time wanting to fix your relationship with your daughter instead of wedging yourself up my ass with your bullshit."

"Excuse me?"

"You heard me," I pace round the side of my desk so we're standing toe to toe. "You know nothing about her, so please don't come in here acting like dad of the fucking year. I get she's stubborn, but fuck, please show me how you've tried to make it right with her and don't even try and redeem yourself with her birthday dinner." I sigh, "I love you man, I really do. You're my best friend but please, back the fuck down and get out of my face. I love her and she loves me. You want her happy and loved, don't you?" He says nothing. "Fuck this, I don't care if you don't. I am done with this bullshit Titus. Just fuck off and leave me alone," and that's when he hits me.

Fist to jaw and fuck my life.

It hurt.

I swear my jaw dislocated. My eyes feel like they're spinning in my head.

"Don't ever fucking talk to me like that again. I have every fucking right to voice my thoughts when it comes to *my* daughter. Don't think just because you're married that I am going to let you both ride off into the sunset. You don't deserve her. She deserves a lot better than you. I know that and so do you. So, stop with your bullshit Keaton." His voice is loud and stern, and I know better than to answer him back.

Guy's a cunt.

He shakes his hand by his side and walks into the waiting elevator.

Kaleb pokes his head round the door, my hand is still pressed to my jaw.

Fuck that aches.

"Hit you?"

"The fucking guy has iron fists," I scoff, shaking my head and Kaleb steps into my office.

"What did you do now?"

"Not a lot... just told him to stop preaching. Wants me to leave Ari."

"I mean, he does have some right."

"Does he?" I turn to face Kaleb, resting on the desk. Jaw still throbbing. Didn't like that one bit.

"Yeah, you got drunk."

"We planned it before for fuck's sake, does no one listen," I scrub my face.

"Look, I'll always have your back and be by your side, but sometimes you do cross the line."

"We've all crossed the fucking line when it comes to our love lives, the only one who hasn't is Nate," I throw my arm up towards where Nate is sitting and he looks up at me, pure confusion on his face.

"Yeah, but Nate is..."

"Nate?" I groan out.

Silence fills the room for a moment.

"I deserve love too; I deserve to marry whom I want and when I want even if it is my best friend's daughter."

"Code and line my man..."

"Like I said, you've both crossed the line too. Maybe I need to get Xavier's take on all of this because you two are so fucking blindsided."

He sighs, hands in his pockets.

"Can you just leave? You out of everyone knows everything and you're still not taking my side so just please, fuck off."

He drops his head for a moment, shaking it from side to side.

"The sad thing is Keaton, I always take your side. That's the problem," and before I can even ask what the fuck he means, he is out of my office.

Well, fuck him, fuck Titus, fuck them all.

Haven't got time for this bullshit today.

Dicks.

CHAPTER THIRTY-NINE
ARIZONA

14 Weeks
Size of Babies: a Kiwi

I AM DRESSED BUT SITTING ON THE SOFA OF THE PENTHOUSE alone. It's my birthday and I have never felt more alone than I do today. I think of the text I received this morning.

> **Keaton**
> Happy Birthday, love Keaton xx

Not going to lie.

I didn't like it. It stung, my heart tore into shreds.

Connie and Reese called me and offered to take me for breakfast, but I blew it off.

I am wearing a long dress and luckily, it hides my bump perfectly, but I won't be able to hide it much longer. I feel like I am the size of a house already and I am only going to get bigger. I really do need to pull my big girl panties up and tell my dad that I am pregnant.

He will assume they're Keaton's. He will kill him. No point even thinking he wouldn't.

What the hell was I thinking? I wasn't. Clearly.

I know they say men think with their dicks, but I was clearly thinking with my vagina when it came to Keaton. Because it didn't matter how much I tried. I just couldn't stay away from him.

Until now, obviously.

But as much as I knew it was the right thing, I also hated it. Hated every minute and every second that I was away from him. Heart hurt. Felt constantly sick, but let's be honest, it could be the two babies that are growing inside of me.

I check the time on my phone, it is just past seven. Table is at half-past in downtown Manhattan. Yes, I am cutting it fine. But it's my party and I'll be late if I want to.

I huff, this is not how I expected to spend my birthday this year. I expected to be woken up with champagne, macaroons, breakfast in bed, presents and nothing but birthday sex all day.

But I was currently alone in my best friend's dad's penthouse, pregnant with twins, starving and no presents, no champagne, no macaroons and definitely no sex. And annoyingly, I was most annoyed with the no sex. Because my god, Keaton knew how to fuck.

And yes, I am fully aware I have nothing else to compare it to, well, apart from the one night with mystery man, but honestly, I don't think it can get much better than Keaton.

I am instantly horny and even more pissed off.

Groaning, I push up from the sofa when I get a sharp pain shoot through my stomach.

"Ouch," I whisper out to the room, my hand gliding under my small bump as I breathe in through my mouth and out through my nose.

It's fine. I just stood too quickly, I reassure myself and reach for my phone that is still sitting on the sofa. Taking a step forward, another pain radiates through me, and my legs buckle beneath me.

The fear that spikes through me is enough to make me throw up. Am I losing my babies? Choked sobs leave me, my chest heavy and my stomach tightens as the pain radiates through me.

I needed to get to the hospital. I thumb a message to Kyra and hope she can meet me at the hospital.

Kneeling up, I pull myself to my feet and I am secretly praying that everything is going to be okay.

Slowly and cautiously, I walk towards the front door of the penthouse, locking it behind me as I continue down the short hallway and to the private serving elevator. Once inside, I slip down the mirrored wall and just close my eyes. I needed a moment to let the pain reside. Just a moment. That's all I needed.

Just. One. Moment. It's the last thought that enters my mind.

CHAPTER FORTY
KEATON

It's coming up to two weeks since I last saw Arizona, since I last spoke to her. I know she is okay, Killian keeps me updated. Annoys me that he is checking in on her and not me. But what am I supposed to do? Hang around like a weirdo until she is ready to take me back?

Ha, no.

My fingers fiddle with her dainty gold wedding band that I wear around my neck, hung on a gold chain and tucked away under my white shirt. Only I know it's there.

Turning my wrist to face me, it's just gone seven. I am dreading tonight, but at the same time I am so psyched to see her. I couldn't even put it into words.

Better get going. I gaze over at the small present wrapped up. I wanted to get her something that I knew she would love and cherish. Whether she wanted it from me was another thing and that's what I had to prepare myself for.

Walking to my car, I start the engine and head for the restaurant in downtown Manhattan. If it wasn't for Ari, I wouldn't be going. Kaleb and Titus can both choke on a bag of dicks for all I care.

Ready to dust my hands of them. Hypocrites.

I'm not in the car long when an unknown number flashes on my phone. I roll to a stop at a red light and answer.

"Yeah?"

"Hi, is this Keaton Mills?"

"Yeah speaking," my brows crease, digging a little deeper into my forehead.

"I need you to come to New York-Presbyterian Emergency room."

Kaleb? Arizona? But surely her dad would be her emergency contact.

I don't even need her to tell me why, I am already spinning my car around and causing chaos.

"Is everything okay?"

"It's your wife, sir."

I hear the blood pumping in my ears, heart thumping in my chest and all I can hear is a high pitch ringing as everything blurs out around me.

I cut the phone off, not giving two fucks if she was still talking. I just needed to get to her. I booted my car the whole way and definitely jumped a few red lights but honestly in this moment, no fucks were given. I didn't care. All I knew is that I needed to get to her. I needed to make sure she was okay, she was all I cared about.

Should I call Titus? Yes.

Am I going to? Not yet.

Parking wherever I can, I cut the engine and climb out of my car, locking it behind me. I don't bother with the meter, I run towards the hospital, breathless when I get to the reception desk.

"Emergency room."

The young lady looks frantic.

"Arizona Mills, King. Fuck, I don't know if she changed her name," I bang my hand on the hard surface making her jump and now I look like a mad man.

"Calm down sir."

"I just need to know where I need to go to find my wife, Arizona."

My wife.

Fuck, that hurt my heart. Splintering it into nothing but wood shavings inside my chest.

She taps on her computer and each second drags into hours.

My eyes scan the signs and I see the emergency room to my left. I give up with her and I run. My heart is thrashing in my chest like a great white in the choppy ocean.

I don't stop. I keep running. Throwing myself through the doors, I'm met with another reception area.

What the fuck.

"Sir?"

"Arizona King," I splutter out, fuck, I am unfit.

She gives a slow and solemn nod as she picks the handset of the phone up and presses a couple of buttons. My hand is on my chest, and I can feel my heart racing under my shirt.

"The nurse is coming to take you to her."

I roll my eyes.

"Can someone just tell me if she's okay?" and I hear my voice crack but the receptionist picks the phone up again. I stand and just look at the room around me. People in beds with injuries as they wait to be seen, Doctors rushing in and out, some patients worse than others and I feel like I am in an episode of Grey's Anatomy.

This is where Arizona worked. Her friends are here. And now she is back as a patient.

"Mr. Mills?" I hear the sound of a gentleman's voice and I give him a quick once over. Mid-twenties maybe, probably one of Ari's old intern friends.

"Where is my wife?" my voice is thick and I am trying everything to keep my cool.

He doesn't respond, just leads me down a quieter hallway before slipping into a glass side room and closing the door behind me.

And that's when I see her.

Red puffy eyes, tear-stained face, but still as beautiful as ever.

"Baby," I rush over to her, careful not to hurt her as I scoop her face into my hands, foreheads pressed together, and the tears roll down my cheeks.

"I'm okay," she whispers through her own tears.

"Yeah?" I pull back and let my eyes roam over her once more.

"Well, I'm getting there."

"The babies?" and my heart is pounding in my chest.

She is silent for just a moment before she cries some more, wrapping her arms around my body and burying her face into my shirt.

"Blossom, you're scaring me."

"Arizona had a threatened miscarriage," a female British voice fills the room and I know who it is instantly.

Dr Kyra.

I look over my shoulder at her and I can see the compassion on her face as she steps towards us, sitting on the edge of the bed.

"But the babies are okay?"

"Yes," she smiles softly, "both babies are perfect."

"Thank fuck," I reach for Arizona, gripping her chin and lifting her beautiful face to look at me.

"The babies are okay Blossom; they're going to be fine..." I pause for a moment then turn my attention towards Kyra. "The babies will be okay, won't they?"

"Babies?!" Titus's voice booms around the room and I can feel the tension rolling through the thick air.

Shit.

CHAPTER FORTY-ONE
TITUS

I am fucking frantic. I got a call twenty minutes ago from the hospital New York-Presbyterian telling me that Arizona was in the emergency room. I am just grateful that she is okay.

Me and Amora walk into the hospital and head straight for the emergency room.

"Baby, I'll wait here. Just go and make sure she is okay," Amora gives me a soft smile and I place a light kiss on her lips before I turn and walk for the room where Arizona is.

The door is closed, curtain pulled, and I can hear distant voices.

I give a gentle knock before I push the door open.

"The babies will be okay, won't they?" I hear my dick of a best friend say and my fucking blood boils.

"Babies?!" my voice is loud as it bangs around the room like a thunderstorm.

Keaton turns slowly to look at me and Doctor Kyra is looking between the three of us trying to work out how we all must know each other.

"Doctor Kyra, it's nice to see you again," I say softly, simmering my rage for just a moment.

"Titus," she stands, brows furrowed, "is everything okay with Amora?"

"Everything is perfect thank you, I am here to see my daughter," my eyes narrow on my daughter who won't even look at me and Keaton's stare is burning into me.

She gives a chin lift, rolling her lips.

"Is she okay?" my voice is low and Kyra walks towards me.

"I am not sure how much you heard."

"Not a lot knowing Titus," Keaton pipes up and he should consider himself lucky that we're in a hospital because the way my anger is growing, I am ready to put him in here, permanently.

"Don't fucking push me," I growl.

"I think you should both come outside, Arizona does not need this right now."

"I'm not leaving," me and Keaton say in unison.

"Then you both need to calm down. Arizona had a threatened miscarriage," and my eyes soften as I look at my baby, my sunshine looking so small and lost in her hospital bed and my heart fucking breaks. "There are a few causes, but from what Arizona has been telling me, I think a lot of it is stress." I feel like I am being told off.

"Stress?" Keaton repeats and he looks as if he has been winded.

"Yes," Kyra says gently.

"Baby, why haven't you reached out to me if you've been feeling stressed," Keaton's hand cups her cheek, my fists balled by my side.

"I didn't want to cause a commotion. I pushed for the

separation; I didn't want to have to rely on you after I pushed you away."

Fuck. I run my hand over my chin, the stubble scratching.

"Arizona, I am going to fill out your chart but I would like to keep you in for a few days just so we can monitor you and the babies."

"Babies, you keep saying babies."

"Yes, babies." Kyra says as she opens the door to Ari's room.

"My wife and I are expecting twins," Keaton says with a shit eating grin on his face.

"Get the fuck outside now." I expect him to refuse. But the cocky fucker stands up tall and proud, leans over and kisses *my* daughter on the forehead before walking out of the room looking like he has slept with a hanger in his mouth.

CHAPTER FORTY-TWO
KEATON

"You shouldn't even be here!" I hear his voice first and my skin pricks. I turn round and see him walking towards me from her room.

"I'm her husband," I storm towards Titus, meeting his strides. I am in no mood. I am super pissed off that there is a chance I have caused her to be here, my pig-headed behavior and giving in so easily definitely has not helped.

"Don't play that card Keaton, you've been married all of five seconds."

"And what?! You harp on like you had the most perfect relationship. You fell in love with a girl that wasn't yours to love, you got her pregnant whilst she was engaged to someone else then fucking married her so do not preach to me about relationships when yours is far from fucking perfect." I am raging. Snorting hot air from my nostrils like I am an angry bull.

"You're getting on my last nerve."

"Back at you my man," I shake my head from side to side as I stare down the long and quiet hallway and can't help the small laugh that passes my lips.

"What's funny?"

"You," I turn to look at him and my lip turns up in a snarl because I am not lying.

He steps up towards me, and I'm not going to lie, he scares the shit out of me but I'm not going to let him know that. He towers over me. I'm not short. Probably around 6'3-6'4, 6'5 at a push on my tiptoes but he is an easy 6'7 and he would pummel my ass into the ground without hesitation.

"Why's that?" his voice is low and gruff.

"You know nothing," and I know Arizona is going to hate me for what is about to come out my mouth, but do you know what, I am past caring.

"Care to elaborate?"

"Ari hasn't worked in this hospital since the beginning of the year, she didn't pass her exam so instead of facing the embarrassment of having to do her first year all over again, she quit."

He says nothing, confusion laces his stupid face and I have no idea why, but I actually feel a little sorry for the guy.

"She works in a strip club; I had no idea until one night I popped in and saw her. I promised to keep her secret, but I can't do it anymore. You need to pull your head out of your ass for a while and actually focus on your daughter. She thinks you don't love her, she thinks she has been kicked to the sidewalk. She may not show it, but she is hurt inside. And yes, she is pregnant and they're mine."

I wasn't about to tell him that there was a chance that they weren't. It would break me and him in the process.

"She failed?" and he just blinks at me as if in complete disbelief and I nod.

The tension that was once an angry flame was now slowly fizzling out into nothing more than cooling embers.

We're not alone long when I hear the heavy footsteps barreling down the hallway. Lifting my head, I see Killian, Nate, Kaleb, Reese and Connie. Amora leading them to us. All dressed to the nines and here we are hanging out in the hallway of a hospital.

"Titus, Keaton..." Kaleb breathes, and he doesn't know which one of us to talk to. I give him a soft, discreet knowing nod and he turns his attention towards Titus.

"We came as soon as we heard, is she okay? What happened?" he asks, and I step back when I see Nate staring at me.

"Threatened miscarriage..." he squeezes out and I hear a few shocked gasps, but four of them are fake.

"Man, I'm so sorry," and I know Kaleb is doing this because he has to, "we didn't even know she was pregnant, who is the dad?"

And I swallow. Palms sweaty. Heart racing in my chest, skipping beats.

"My best friend," his eyes burn into mine and I shrink. Not sure why. Something just felt off with the way the words fell from his lips. Betrayal maybe?

All eyes are on me.

And I look at every single one of them.

"Fuck," Nate shakes his head from side to side, "bet you wish she stayed with me now," he chuckles trying to lighten the mood and I hear a sigh from Titus.

"Not the right time Nate," Kaleb places a hand on Nate's shoulder and gives it a gentle squeeze.

"I mean, he's not wrong," Titus snipes and my blood boils.

"Fuck off." I shouldn't have said it, but I was in no mood.

Titus is on me, hands grabbing my jacket and shoving me against the wall with force and winding me, his angry eyes bounce back and forth between mine and I can't read him at all. It's as if I don't know him anymore.

"Keep going," Titus urges me and fuck knows why he done it, because I will do just as he asks. He liked to goad me.

"That's enough," Kaleb pulls Titus off me, shoving him back and away as he tries to run for me again. "Put your fucking pride aside for one moment. This is about Arizona, not you two dumb fucks." He seethes, head turning towards me then back to Titus. "I don't give two shits, knock ten ton out of each other once you're outside, but you don't do it here, do you understand me?"

And my eyes are on the floor, looking at my dress shoes. Should have given them a polish. They look scruffy.

"Keaton?" Kaleb barks and I lift my eyes to look at him.

"Yeah, sure," and I see Titus nod.

I know this is far from over.

"Titus," Amora whispers and I don't miss the look of disgust she passes me as she walks past and locks her arms round Titus's frame.

He lowers his lips to the top of her head, planting a soft kiss in her fiery red hair.

"Are you okay?" Killian asks me and I give a small, twisted smile.

"I will be," I nod, grateful that at least one of them asked me.

I know me and Titus need to sit down and speak, hash all this out but right now, like Kaleb said, we need to focus on getting Arizona better and home.

Reese and Connie have disappeared, and I give Killian a puzzled look which only gets me a tap on the side of his nose.

My heart aches when I turn to look into Arizona's room. It's her birthday and she is here. And even worse, she could have lost the babies.

My blood runs cold, freezing over at the thought.

Titus leads Amora into the room, and as much as I want to follow, I don't. I turn and walk away.

I'm not alone long, Kaleb and Nate are by my side, but not without adding their piece in.

"What the fuck were you thinking?" Nate growls at me.

"I wasn't."

CHAPTER FORTY-THREE
ARIZONA

I CAN HEAR THE COMMOTION OUTSIDE, BUT I DON'T REALLY CARE. I feel numb to it all. I nearly lost one of my babies because I let everything, and everyone, get on top of me. Too worried about working, too busy trying to push Keaton away and for what? Because he may not be the dad to the twins? What the fuck was wrong with me? I had the most perfect man willing to step up and be a dad even if they weren't his. He married me and vowed to stay by my side, yet it wasn't enough.

The door handle goes and my eyes flit across the boring room hoping it is Keaton, but disappointment floors me when I see my dad and Amora walk in.

Not ideal this being the third time we have seen each other, but here we are.

"Sunshine," the kid nickname he called me for as long as I can remember slips past his lips. His tone is warm, his eyes soft and his fingers are laced through Amora's.

She's pretty. Freckles that look like constellations in the night sky dotted over her cheeks and nose, eyes beautifully imperfect. One brown, one blue. Skin ivory white, she looks like the pretty China dolls that sit on high shelves but are to not be played with. Never touched. Long, red hair in bouncy curls and a slim figure. Cute, neat bump with a sibling of mine.

"Dad," I lick away a salty tear that escaped. They both walk across the large room, both by my side.

"Arizona," Amora's British voice is low and sweet, her scent filling the room. Apricots and cocoa butter.

"Hi," my response is quiet.

"How are you feeling?" she lets go of my dad's hand and sits on the edge of the bed, her hand scooping mine up and clasping it tightly.

"I've been better," a snort of a laugh leaves me, my chest aching.

"I'm glad you're okay though, and the babies," her cheeks glow crimson, eyes squeezing as she smiles at me.

"Me too," I admit, it's not a lie.

"I want to wish you a happy birthday, but..."

"Doesn't seem right, does it?" I laugh, my head tilting to the side and a sad stutter of breath leaves me and I feel my bottom lip turn.

I don't want to cry.

But what I want, and what happens are out of my control.

The tears roll down my cheeks and out of nowhere, Amora leans across and wraps her arms around me as I cry into her pretty pink dress.

Damn it.

She really is sweet.

Hate that.

But at the same time, I don't.

"Please don't cry," she whispers and my chest aches. I

have so many things to be grateful for, yet I feel immense sadness.

My dad is soon by my side, his lips pressing to the top of my head as he gives me a soft kiss.

"I'm so sorry, Sunshine," he mutters, and I squeeze my eyes tight as the tears roll down the side of my face.

"I am too dad," and it's not a lie. For once in the last few months, nothing in this conversation has been a lie. I am truly sorry.

One by one, they pull themselves off of me and there isn't a single dry eye in the room. My eyes fall to Amora's bump, and I smile.

"Never thought I would be bump buddies with my dad's wife..." I roll my lips.

"I never thought I would be bump buddies with my husband's daughter..." she scrunches her nose up and I don't miss the gentle giggle that passes her lips.

"How are you feeling?" I ask with a huff of exhaustion coating my question.

"I'm feeling okay, six months pregnant and feel the size of a house," she looks down at her bump, hands cradling.

"Ha, you don't look big at all. I feel bigger than you and I am only 14 weeks," I sigh, my own hands moving to my small bump that probably does look a lot like bloat now I have seen Amora's perfectly rounded bump.

"You are carrying twins, be kind to yourself," and she gives me such a warm smile that seems to make everything feel better.

"Twins," I shake my head from side to side. "Who would have thought?"

"Well, Keaton is a twin, is that not how it works?" my dad asks, and I know it must be a bitter pill for him to swallow. I mean, none of this could have been easy on him.

"They're identical twins, the babies, they don't run in families... they just happen," I half shrug as I meet my dad's gaze.

"Huh," his brows raise, lips turned down as he nods.

"I know, Keaton didn't know that either until my scan."

"And are you happy Arizona?" and I know he means it from the depths of his huge heart.

"I will be," and it's true. I will be. I just need to get some things sorted first.

MY DAD AND AMORA HAVE BEEN GONE A LITTLE OVER TWENTY minutes and Keaton still hasn't come near or by. I don't get it. Maybe the final shove was the straw that broke the camel's back. I have no idea, but I miss him. My palm rubs the ache out of my chest and my heart sinks into the depths of my stomach.

The door opens and I see Connie and Reese walking through with black and gold balloons, a birthday cake and presents. My eyes light up at their kindness.

"How you doing?" Connie asks, dragging the handful of balloons towards me and arranging them so they look pretty.

"I'm okay," I mean, I don't think I am, but I am tired of having the same conversations.

"Sorry we're celebrating your birthday here," Reese's brows furrow and I let out a soft sigh. The sound of the babies heartbeats comforting the quiet room and drowning out the beeping from the machine.

"Could be worse," I breathe out, turning my face to look at the screen.

"Yeah?" Reese asks as she places some pink peonies in a vase on the unit beside my bed.

"Yeah, I could be dead," I say deadpan.

"Wow, that's dark," Connie blows out her cheeks as she places their presents on my lap.

"Not really, just stating a fact," my eyes move between the both of them. "Was Keaton outside?" I ask and I really do try to not sound bothered, but I failed, miserably.

"No hon," Reese says as she sits at the foot of the bed, "he walked off with Nate and Kaleb," she gives a sorry smile and my heart throbs in my chest.

"Oh," my eyes fall for a moment as I look at my hands.

"I'm sure he has just popped out," Connie joins in.

"Yeah, maybe."

Silence blankets us for just a moment before Reese is shoving a present in my face. "Here, this is from me, Killian and Celeste." I take the impeccably wrapped gift. Shiny gold wrapping paper and a huge black bow. The box is long and slim and excitement courses through me.

Slowly tugging at the ribbon, I watch as it unravels, a bit like my life to be honest, and I see a pretty box. I sink my teeth into my bottom lip as I lift the lid and I see a pretty gold bracelet. I look up at Reese, tears in my eyes.

It's a charm bracelet with delicate charms hanging off the twisted chain. A dummy, a stethoscope, a sun and my birthstone, citrine.

"Reese."

"It's just a little something," she says nonchalant.

"It's beautiful, thank you," my bottom lip trembles.

I run my fingers gently over the bracelet and I feel so overwhelmed.

"My turn," Connie says as she squeezes herself next to

312

me, legs on the bed. She passes me a small box with the same wrapping paper.

I tug at the bow. and lift the box to reveal a gold ring with my birthstone, encased with diamonds.

"Girls... this is..."

I can't even finish my words as I am a blubbering mess.

"Oh doll," Connie laughs, wrapping her arm round me and pulling me in for a cuddle. Reese is at my side as well as we stay in this embrace whilst I soak them with my tears,

I loved these girls with everything I had.

Dr Kyra popped in to see me to monitor me and the babies.

"All is looking good, how are you feeling?" she asks, taking my temperature before jotting down notes.

"Tired."

"That's understandable, you've had a busy few days. I'm going to get you moved onto the maternity ward. There will be other pregnant moms. You'll still be in your own room but be better for you to be on my floor."

I nod.

"Okay perfect, let me get this paperwork finished up and then we can take you up."

She waltzes out the room and I am left alone once more.

Keaton never came back, and it hurts me to my very core.

Reaching for my phone, I text my dad.

> **Me**
> Hey, can you get me some clothes from Killian's penthouse... long story. Don't want to get into it. Need some pajamas and be nice to have some sweatpants and tees too. Also need underwear. xo

I feel weird asking my dad, but not sure who else to text. Keaton obviously didn't care.

Frustration bubbles inside of me, my chest feels tight and anxiety floors me causing nausea to swim deep inside my stomach.

The door opens once more. "Okay, let's get you moved."

"I can walk if it's easier," I suggest, sitting up as they walk towards the gurney, kicking the locks off and lifting the sides.

"Not a chance," Kyra laughs, "bed rest for you. Depending how your stay goes, I might have you on bedrest a little longer once you're home too."

Great.

I say nothing. Just let my head fall back on the pillow.

"Can my flowers and balloons come with me?" I sound sad and pathetic, and I hate it.

"Of course, Arizona, I'll get Doctor Stone to get an intern to run them up," she smiles at me as she pages before walking beside me. "So, a little bird told me you used to work here..." she trails off for just a moment and my stomach knots.

"I did..." and I know straight away it was that no good nosey bitch, Anastasia.

"What happened?" she picks away at me as we move.

"Life?" I offer as a cheap shot but know it's not taken well. She raises her brows and gives me a *whatever* look. "Fine," I cross my arms against my chest as we wait for the elevator, "I failed my intern exams," my cheeks flame and I feel ashamed.

"What department?"

"Trauma," I lick my dry lips. Sighing heavily.

"So why not resit?" the confusion is apparent in her voice. I get it. I do.

"Pride?" not sure why I am asking her to be honest.

"Really?"

"Think so…" my heart jack hammers in my chest.

"I think you got scared," she winks. She isn't lying.

"Maybe… I just didn't like the thought of staying behind when all my class moved forward. I was top of my class, no idea what happened."

"A certain dark-haired man?" she wiggles her brows, smiling at me before letting a laugh sneak out.

"Ha, no, I wasn't with Keaton then."

"So what? Did you choke?"

"I think so. I felt so overwhelmed, and the questions that I knew off the top of my head just didn't seem to come easily. The more I thought, the more I struggled," I'm breathless, I haven't spoken about this to anyone before now, but with Kyra, it's just so easy.

"I get it." she nods, the doors to the elevator ping open as I am pushed through.

"You do?" I am surprised.

"Oh yeah," she presses the button for the sixth floor, "I failed my intern exam too. Hated it. So much so I moved across the water and started again."

"Oh."

"Yeah… oh."

"I've always wanted to be a doctor since I was a little girl, can't help but feel a little bummed out that I have fucked it up."

She rolls her eyes.

"You haven't fucked it up, you have just hit a speed bump."

I sigh again.

"Won't be going back to med school anytime soon." My hands are on my bump as we begin moving onto the maternity ward.

"You're young, take a year or two and get back on the horse, otherwise you'll be living in regret for the rest of your life. Dreams are meant to be hard, if they were easy, everyone would be living theirs, wouldn't they?" she tilts her head at me as she pushes me into my new room. This one is a lot brighter, and I have a window. Not that there is much to see. It's dark, and miserable by the sounds of the rain hitting the window pane.

"I suppose," I smile at her as she parks my bed, footing the brakes on. "Thanks for chatting to me."

"Of course, I hope I helped."

"You really did," she places her hand over mine and gives it a gentle squeeze. "Now, get some rest. I'll be in to check on you and the babies a bit later on. The nurse will be on shortly to take a food order from you."

I nod, "Thank you," I say again, and I really do mean it.

"Always," she says and she walks out the door, just as Doctor Stone walks in with a nurse, placing my belongings down.

I thank them before they close the door on me and I am alone with my thoughts, well, not alone... I have my twinnies. My babies.

CHAPTER FORTY-FOUR

KEATON

I PACE UP AND DOWN THE LOBBY. I HATED LEAVING HER WITHOUT saying anything. But Kaleb was right. I needed to calm down. I was internally boiling. I love Titus, I didn't want to lose my shit with him, but he needed to cool down too. He would have had my head if the guys weren't there. But Kaleb was right. I did need to put my pride aside. We both did. We're grown ass men, we needed to sort it like grown ass men.

Turning my wrist towards me, it's just past ten and I am debating going to see her. No idea if they'll let me in, but I can try. I reach inside my pocket and my heart flutters in my chest at the small gift-box. Don't even know if it is the right time to give her this or not.

"What are you still doing here?" I heard Titus's voice and I look up to see him strolling towards me with an overnight bag. It's Ari's.

"Pacing?" I state the obvious because what the fuck am I meant to say?

We stare each other out for a bit before his lips tug into

some kind of lop-sided smirk and he closes the gap between us in a couple of strides. Long legged bastard.

He hands me her overnight bag; my head drops for a moment as I watch the exchange like some out of body experience.

"Tell her I'll see her tomorrow and drop her present in." I blink a couple of times. Feeling like I am malfunctioning.

I say nothing, just wrap my fingers round the handles before he gives me some odd off the temple salute then walks out the door.

Weird.

I look down at the bag once more, kind of wishing she asked me to pack it. But I disappeared. Should have text her. Royally ruined her birthday. Kind of. Maybe?

Shaking my head from side to side, I close my eyes for just a moment. I just needed an extra minute or two before I went to see her.

Maybe just one more.

I walk cautiously towards where I left her, and I am still hating myself over not telling her I was leaving.

Pushing through the heavy doors and walking down the hallway, I pause outside the door and inhale deeply before walking inside. But she isn't there. My heart drops, panic sets in and claws at my fucking throat. Lungs burn, eyes sting.

Turning, I run out the fucking room and scour the area, looking for someone, anyone.

"Where is Arizona Mills? Fuck! King. Arizona King?!"

The woman behind the desk just stares at me like I am a mad man.

"Where is she?" my temper is rising. She hasn't been taken home by Titus; he wouldn't have given me the bag.

"Keaton?" I hear Doctor Kyra's voice and the rage that was simmering inside of me settles in an instant.

"Where is she?" my voice is calm like the soft ocean lapping against the shore.

"Come," she smiles at me, and I do, walking like a little lost soul trying to find my way home.

Home.

She was my home.

"I moved her to a maternity ward, thought she would be more comfortable up here," she turns to look at me as we wait for the elevator.

"I thought she left..." I feel fucking stupid.

"No," she shakes her head softly, a soft laugh passing her lips. "We would have let you know, well, when I say we, I mean I... I can see how much you love her." She steps inside the elevator, and it takes me a moment to follow.

"I do love her," I sigh heavily as if the weight of the world is on my shoulders and suddenly, they feel heavier than ever.

Kyra says nothing, just pushes the button for the sixth floor and we ride up in silence.

Following her to a side room, my eyes well when they finally land on her. She's sleeping. Hands resting on her bump. She looks so peaceful.

"Thank you," I whisper to Kyra as I step into the room.

"I'll get a bed made up for you, you're welcome to stay the night with her."

And my heart warms.

I turn to tell her yes, but she has already slipped out.

Placing her bag on the floor gently, I drag the chair quietly by her bed and scoop her hand in mine.

"Hey baby," my voice is soft. "I'm sorry for leaving, I didn't mean to be as long as I was... I just..." I sigh, dropping my head. "I freaked? I think. I got overwhelmed. Your dad and everyone rushing towards me and suffocating me. I needed out, for just a while, but I didn't expect that while to turn into hours. I wanted to spend today with you, but I didn't want to come into your space. You pushed me away Ari, and I could have been an asshole and ignored you, but I didn't want to. I want to give you everything you have ever wished for, want to be the best person for you, want you to be the best you, even if that means you become her without me. But you'll never be without me. I've always been here when you needed me, and I don't plan on giving up now. I love you Blossom, more than I have ever loved anyone before. The thought that I have never been in love before you were confirmed to me just a few days ago, baby. Because the way I feel about you is all new." I pause for a moment and bring the back of her hand to my lips. "I would have never forgiven myself if something happened to you or the babies. I know you want space and I accept that but let me be there for you if you need me," she flinches, her eyes fluttering as she slowly opens them, her beautiful eyes on mine.

"Happy birthday baby," I brush my lips across the back of her hand before kissing her delicate skin.

"You came back," her voice croaks.

"I was always coming back," I admit, blinking back the tears that are threatening. "I'm sorry I was gone for so long."

"I know, I heard you," she smirks, and my cheeks flame a little.

"Damn it," I laugh softly, standing out of my chair for a moment as I lean across and kiss her, and fuck, I have missed her.

CHAPTER FORTY-FIVE
ARIZONA

17 Weeks
Size of Babies: a Pear

I HAD BEEN HOME JUST UNDER TWO WEEKS. I WAS ON CONSTANT watch. Making sure I was taking it easy, and Sage made me get a doctor's note signing me off for a month. Hated that. I was bored. But do you know what I started to do? Study. No one knows, and that's the way I wanted to keep it. My conversation with Kyra struck a match deep inside of me, relighting my passion for doctoring. It may lead to nowhere, but it may lead to me getting my dream once more.

"Hello," I hear Keaton's voice float through the room and excitement singes my nerves.

"In the kitchen," I call back as I load the dishwasher. He rounds the corner with two covered plates, and they smell so good.

"Pumpkin pie and the scalloped corn," he places it on the oven top then tucks his hands in his pockets.

"Thank you, where is Dad with the turkey?" and he shrugs his shoulders up. They're still not on speaking terms. I am tempted to hire a boxing ring and throw them in it together until they've knocked all the shit out of each other.

"Can you maybe call him?"

"Sunshine," my dad calls out and I can smell the turkey before I even see it.

"That smells soooo good," and I know I am drooling.

He places it on the countertop, and I peek a look under the foil. Looks delicious.

"And I have pecan pie," Amora says, "I hope it's okay, my first thanksgiving and I am so excited," she places the pie dish down.

"It was agreed I sorted the pie," Keaton swoops in, lifting her pie dish up.

She furrows her brows, her growing bump pushing into him as she snatches her pie back.

"I put it in the group Keaton," she snaps.

"Well, I didn't see it."

Dad is already scrolling up the chat.

"Please, it's fine. There are fourteen of us," I huff, placing my hands on my hips.

"Fourteen!?" Keaton groans.

"Did you not read any of the group?"

"I did, but I thought it was just our little crowd," he rolls his eyes.

"Well, Reese wanted to spend it with her mom and dad as well, so Mateo and Liz were invited," I reminded him softly.

"Plus, my mum and dad," Amora says sweetly, placing her pie back down.

"It's going to be hell," he groans, kicking his toe into the floor.

"Stop being a grouch," I give him a gentle nudge in the ribs, and he chuckles, wrapping his arm around my shoulders and pulling me in for a kiss on the side of the head which gets a growl from my dad.

"Leave off man," Keaton moans, dropping his arm from me instantly and I miss it.

"Don't do it right in front of me, I know you two are... well..." he sighs, "just don't do it in my direct eyesight, I mean, have a little respect."

"Wow, it feels weird being here," Reese chimes, Celeste clinging to her mom, fingers wrapped round the gold chain that hangs from her neck.

Killian whistles as he walks through the door with piled up plates.

"We have the candied yams, green bean casserole..." Killian's voice is playful and I smile.

"And we have roast beef, cauliflower cheese and Yorkshire puddings," Liz informs in her British accent.

"You have what?" Keaton barks.

"Again man, the group," Titus places his head in his hands and Amora laughs.

"No, I'm not on about the group. What is a Yorkshire pudding?"

"Only the best side with a roast dinner; trust me young man, you are going to be changed."

"I hate to admit," Killian pipes up, taking Celeste off Reese, "they are so good, especially with thick beef gravy."

And I think we all look towards him, heads tilted, eyes

narrowed, brows dug in deep as we try and decipher what he has said.

"Gravy, it's not like your gravy. You have it sweet with chicken and biscuits, right?" Amora says as she leans against my dad, his hands resting on her bump and my heart warms. I am glad he has found someone to love him as much as he deserves, and I am glad he has found someone to love too.

"Right," Keaton nods, fingers curled round the countertop, mine too, and we don't miss the chance to let them brush occasionally.

"Well, back home in England, we make gravy with the meat juice or granules, and we serve it with roast dinners, or sausage and mash. Anything sort of like a comfort food, we add gravy."

"Like sausage in a hole."

"Toad dad, Toad in the hole." Connie barrels through the door with Kaleb, both with naughty grins on their faces.

"Yes, that, toad. Toad in the hole."

"Sausage in a hole," Reese giggles, cheeks pinching.

"This is bringing back horrid thanksgiving memories." Connie shakes her head, lip curled in disgust.

"Why?" I ask as I take the plates from Connie.

"I have made stuffing and homemade cranberry sauce." She announces.

"Ahem," Kaleb coughs, clearing his throat. "Who made the cranberry sauce?"

"Alright Chandler Bing," she rolls her eyes at him, and we all laugh.

"Okay so just Nate with his stuffed pumpkin."

"What?" Keaton scrubs his face.

"He decided to go vegetarian for November, no idea

why but," I shrug my shoulders up. Why did I decide to host thanksgiving in the penthouse. Already regretting it.

"Anyway, who wants a drink?" Connie calls out as she pops the champagne.

Reese charges forward, grabbing two champagne flutes and Connie fills them up. They both cheers each other.

"No one else want one Con?" Kaleb raises his brows.

"I'm not your maiden. Go make your own damn glass."

"Scotch?" Killian walks over with a crystal decanter.

"Where did that come from?" my frown pinches.

"My secret stash," he winks and the guys all follow him out into the living area.

"How are you doing?" Liz asks me as she pops the electric kettle on and raids through the cupboards for her Yorkshire teabags.

"Yeah okay, feel like I am getting a bit more energy now," I admit as I grab a bottle of water from the fridge and take a mouthful, then I offer one to Amora, but she shakes her head.

"I'll have a tea," she smiles at Liz, her cheeks pinching pink.

"Me too," I hear another light well-spoken brit and Amora's face lights up.

"Mum!" she chimes, running into her mother's embrace.

"Oh Amora, I have missed you so much," her mom holds her tightly and I feel a tightness in my chest. A tightness I have never felt before. I rub it out, ignoring it.

"Amora," A deep, gruff voice follows, and I can't help but stare, Amora is such a blend of the two. Her dad's eyes, her mom's skin and hair color.

"Dad," she sighs, and he kisses her on the cheek, his eyes find me and he gives a sort of smile that tugs at the corners of his mouth. A scar runs from his ear, down his cheek and ends at his nostril. I try not to stare, but it's a little hard not to.

"Hey darling."

"How rude of me," Amora's mom walks over to me, "I'm Royal, Amora's mother, and this is my husband, Xavier."

"Pleasure to meet you," I smile.

"Likewise," her eyes focus on me a moment before they fall to my bump.

"Your father has told me so much about you, he is very proud," her head tilts slightly and her cheeks must hurt from the constant smile she wears.

"I bet he is," and I know my tone is dripping with sarcasm.

I take the dish from her that's filled with roast potatoes and Xavier places an apple pie down before opening the refrigerator and placing a tub in there. *What is that?*

"Custard." he says, answering my unspoken words but my wondering mind.

"Oh."

"Tea?" Liz asks Royal.

"Oh yes, that would be lovely."

"I'm Reese's mum," she continues, and they both fall into easy conversation. I take that as my cue to walk out the kitchen and make sure the table is ready.

"Where is Nate?" I ask when I look at the time. We agreed to meet at three, it's quarter to four.

"I'll call him," Keaton says as he pulls out his phone.

"At least we have candied yams this year," Reese says happy as a kid who has been handed candy.

"No one cares for the candied yams," Connie rolls her eyes.

"Don't start this again. You purposely sabotaged them before."

"I did not!" She places her hand across her chest.

"You did," Reese nods and Killian lets his head tip back making some weird groaning noise, Mateo occupying Celeste with her toys on the middle of the rug that sits in the center of the living area.

"Not this again," Kaleb sighs, tapping his finger on the side of his crystal tumbler.

"Then I dropped them anyway, so you ruining them didn't matter anymore cos we didn't even get to taste them."

"And I can assure you if you did taste them, you wouldn't want to eat them again. I just don't like them."

"Well, I would have liked to have gotten the chance," Reese shakes her head from side to side.

"Why did you drop them?" I ask, perching myself on the arm of the sofa when Killian stands up, offering me his seat but I shake my head, refusing.

"Oh my god, have you not heard the story?" Reese sits up in her seat, eyes wide.

"No?" I look round the room and see how defeated Killian and Kaleb look. They both exchange a *'here we go'* look.

"Dearest Connie invited me to thanksgiving with her dad, and because I couldn't get back home because of a freak snow storm they had in the UK, I jumped at the chance otherwise it would have been a microwave meal for one."

"Nate is going to be ten minutes," Keaton interrupts and Connie throws him a death stare. "Sorry," he murmurs, standing beside me, hand on my thigh.

Titus coughs.

"Give over man for fuck's sake,"

"Anyway!" Reese calls out, clapping loudly to bring everyone's attention back to her.

"Jesus Christ," Killian groans.

"I decided to cook some traditional thanksgiving sides, green bean casserole and candied yams."

"Vomit," Connie wretches.

Reese ignores her and I stifle my laugh behind my bottle of water.

"So, we're walking towards this penthouse, no idea that Connie's dad lived in the building. I mean, she never once mentioned it and neither did he." She throws a dagger glare over towards Killian but he just chuckles, shrugging his shoulder up. "We go through this weird Hogwarts, platform 9/34 shit and then there's a private elevator to this penthouse."

"Rambling," Connie looks at her manicured nails, twisting her hand to face her.

"Connie lets herself in, calling out '*Dad*' as she does, and I am just standing with my candied yams. Proud as punch I was."

"What about the green bean casserole?" Keaton asks, clearly fully invested in this story.

"Think we binned it," Connie shrugs up.

"And then I hear this voice say '*Hey Princess*' and I swear my soul left my body. I was frozen and it wasn't until he walked round the corner and our eyes met, that my candied yams were falling in slow motion and I was frozen to the spot."

"Why?" Nate asks, scrunching his nose as he holds his pumpkin.

"Hi Nate," I smile, my eyes on him but he just waits for Reese.

"Because she was having relations with my dad. She didn't know he was my dad to be fair, I wasn't very forthcoming with that information."

"Forthcoming? Connie, you told me your moms used a sperm donor!"

"Yeah, well that's what they told me until...."

"Anyway! Who's hungry, let's dish up." We did not need Adele-gate bringing Thanksgiving down. If there's one story that I've heard numerous times, it's that one and I can't hear it one more time. But for those of you that don't know the story, here we go. Adele is Connie's birth mom. Adele and Killian used to have some form of a relationship I think, she fell pregnant and Adele didn't want the baby but Killian knew Lara and Katie did. So, Killian introduced them and it was a closed adoption until Adele started blackmailing Killian and well, yeah, Connie found out, shit went south, there was a sneaker thrown at someone's head but honestly, I can't remember who it hit. Now you're all caught up, you're welcome.

I walk into the kitchen, and I get shooed out.

"You go and sit down, we will get this served up," Liz and Royal usher me out and to the table. Killian and Keaton are on drinks, Titus and Nate help bring the food in and Connie and Reese place the plates down and me and Amora sit opposite each other smiling that we just get to sit and *relax*.

The food is served, our glasses are full and we're all holding hands as Killian stands at the head of the table to give thanks.

"I am thankful for my found family, friends I never knew I needed or wanted, but they found me anyway. My daughters, my wife, I love you very much. More than life itself. I am thankful for our health and thankful for every good day that comes here after, and of course, I am thankful to Elijah," and I open one eye and focus on Reese. "Because without him, I would have never made it to today, I would have never met the love of my life and I would have never been blessed with my baby girl, Celeste, and I would have definitely not have met you, all of you, so Elijah," Killian pauses, reaches for his scotch and lifts it towards the sky. "Thank you."

We all raise a glass and Reese wipes a stray tear along with Mateo and Liz and my heart constricts in my chest.

In this moment, all I feel is the overwhelming love from this new family I have fallen into. And for that, I am thankful. Truly thankful.

Keaton catches my gaze from across the table and my heart thumps in my chest.

And of course, I am thankful for him. Always.

Tall Dark & Handsome
Tick tock, Arizona, I am coming for you.
I'll take them all out one by one,
But I'll start with the one that he calls the sun.
You hurt me,
I'll hurt you,
Tick tock, Arizona, I am coming for you.

ARIZONA

THREE MONTHS LATER

30 Weeks

Size of Babies: a Cabbage

> **Me**
> Where are you?

I text Keaton. He promised he would be here at ten a.m. It's just past and he isn't here. I pace. Not sure why I am so agitated? Hormones? Probably. The intercom buzzes and I grab my purse from the side table and open the door.

"Finally," I roll my eyes in an exaggerated manner.

"Kid, I was two minutes past ten."

"Still late, *kid*." I jibe as I lock the penthouse behind me.

"You look as beautiful as ever," He leans in and places a kiss on my cheek, my skin tingling. I've missed that.

"Who paid you to say that?" I smirk, dropping my keys into my purse as we begin to walk towards the elevator. It's a Saturday. Keaton is dressed in jeans, crew neck cream tee and a navy jacket tucked under a bomber and finishes his casual look with fresh white sneakers. Me? I'm wearing maternity jeans, a black vest top tucked into my jeans and a white flowing shirt that covers my arms and is buttoned to the top of my bump as the sides fall either side. My feet are hidden in black soft pumps and it was a struggle. They're swelling at rapid speed. I debated sandals but it's still cold. I have my large coat hung over my arm because I feel like I am cooking from the inside out.

"No one," he stops, long fingers pushing the button of the elevator, my eyes falling and I see his tacky gold ring still firmly wrapped round his finger. We're not together. We never had the conversation. I threw my ring, he didn't follow, and I suppose we kind of fell into this weird, in between.

"You're a terrible liar, Mr Mills."

331

He scoffs a laugh and steps inside the elevator as I follow.

"So," he begins, "what is on your to get list?"

I mull over his question, my eyes greedily sweeping over him, and I feel a deep burn twist in my stomach and radiating down my thighs. He really is handsome. Sexy. Rugged. His hair styled and fluffy and I want to lock my fingers round the root. His full lips parted and his stubble working for him. It would be so easy to hit the emergency stop button and just let him have his way with me.

"Ari?" he cocks his head to the side and my cheeks flame when I snap out of it.

"Yup?" I try and conceal my embarrassment at being caught.

"Did you hear what I said?" his lips twitch into a smirk.

He knows.

He so knows.

I could have lied. I didn't. I just stared at him.

"No?" why am I answering in a question.

"Would you like me to repeat it?" he chuckles as the lift halts.

"Please," I dip my head as I walk out of the elevator and turn right towards the exit of the building.

"What is on your list?"

You.

"Everything?" and this time I do answer with a question for a reason. He stops dead in his tracks, head tilting ever so slightly as he looks at me, eyes narrowing. "I am freaking out," I admit, fingers locked in front of me.

"Why?" he licks his lips. I want to be his lips. Why am I so horny?

"Because I have nothing, these babies could come at any day."

"That's why we're going shopping aren't we, baby."

Baby.

"But we do need to decide where we're going to stay when the babies are born,"

I stiffen. "I would really like for you to come back home, Ari."

"But..."

"Look," he pauses for a moment and closes the gap between us with two steps. Not hard, one step of Keaton's is three of mine. "I know we're sort of..."

"On a break?" Damn it.

"Yeah?"

Oh, now he is asking me the questions.

"Yeah."

"But we have both agreed that I am going to be in the babies lives, just to help out." He nods as if trying to convince himself. I'm annoyed with myself. I have no idea why I haven't said I want to be back with him. I knew I wanted it. I'm sure he wants it. But?

"So come home Ari, give Killian his penthouse back and move home." His hand cups my face, my eyes glassy. "Move back home with me, please," and I don't miss the desperation in his voice.

Truth was, I wanted to go back home. I loved him with everything I had.

"Okay," I whisper, and I see the glee in his eyes, his lips spreading into a slow smirk.

"Roommates, of course?" he wiggles his brows.

"Of course." Small steps. This is what we need. We will fall back into each other, but for the minute, our focus is the babies. "But can I move back home tomorrow? I have a date with the girls tonight," I grimace.

"There is no rush, we can order everything to home,

then we can sort you moving back whenever you're ready," and his hand slowly slips from my face making me miss his touch instantly.

"Okay," I smile as I turn, Keaton beside me.

"Where first?" He asks, a car waiting for us.

"Cribs," and I take his hand as he leads me away.

"Cribs," he gives a heavy nod and slips in beside me.

Sitting in Sarabeth's, Keaton has a goofy smile on his face and my heart warms inside my chest.

"What you smiling for?"

"I just..." he takes a mouthful of his soda and places it down softly, "I had the best day."

"Me too," my cheeks turn pink as I take my own mouthful and our burgers come just as Keaton opens his mouth to say something.

"Can I get you anything else?" the server asks and I shake my head, Keaton dismissing the waitress kindly.

"Are you happy with everything that we got?" he asks as he grabs a fry from his plate and dips it in the ketchup and I have never wanted to be a pot of ketchup more than I do now.

"I think so," I distract myself by pulling my phone out and opening my list.

"How much can you check off?" he brings his burger to his lips.

"Most of it. We have the stroller, the cribs, the swing chairs, the bottles, pacifiers, baby slings, diapers, diaper bag, clothes, muslins..." I pause.

"We just need to get their coming home outfits and hats, right?"

"Right," I smile as I lock my phone and swipe my own fry.

"Do you need anything Arizona?" he wipes his mouth with his napkin, his burger back on his plate.

"A few bits, I need to sort my hospital bag out too, but I will sort that."

"I don't mind..."

"No, honestly, you have done so much for me, for us," my hands round my lower bump, "I will never be able to thank you enough," and I swallow the lump down that's presented itself in my throat.

His hand glides across the table, palm up, fingers pointing towards me, and I tuck mine inside his.

"I will always do everything I can for you and our babies."

Our.

Sitting in the penthouse, Connie and Reese are drinking wine, while I drink soda water. Not as exciting but still.

"So, a little birdie told me you're moving out."

"That little birdie can't help but gossip can he," I pop a brow and Reese giggles beside me.

"We tell each other everything," Connie turns her nose up to the air and I roll my eyes.

"But yes, I am. For the babies."

"Yes, of course, for the..." and Reese places her wine down on the coffee table then air quotes, "babies."

"It is for the babies!" I say a little louder than I wanted. First mistake. Defensive.

"Just admit you still love him," Connie sighs, softly shaking her head from side to side.

"I do," I shrug my shoulder up, "I won't lie about that. I do love him; it just got a little... I dunno. It was a lot."

"I get that, but do you want to sacrifice your happiness for whatever the issues were," Connie looks at Reese and turns her hands up, nose crinkling at the bridge.

"Not really, but I just think we need to find ourselves again. Take our time,"

I sip my soda.

"We've all been there, none of our relationships were easy, we all had bumps in the road," Connie nods, and Reese scoffs a laugh.

"Pretty sure mine was the biggest bump," Reese smirks at me knowing it will cause a rise from Connie.

"It's not a competition Reese," Connie rolls her eyes and I laugh, letting my head toss from side to side softly.

"Anyway," I chime, trying to diffuse the ticking time bomb that has presented itself in front of me.

"Yes, anyway," Reese beams at me.

"Is he a good fuck?" Connie asks out the blue and I choke on my inhale breath. Eyes wide as my cheeks burn.

"Connie!" Reese leans across and swats her.

"What?! I'm sure we're all thinking it."

"Definitely was *not* thinking it." Reese defends.

"Stop lying."

"Ugh," I let my head fall back and I contemplate answering. I mean, why shouldn't I? Is that not what girlfriends do? Fair, it's a little weird 'cause it's Connie's brother-in-law but... "He is such a good fuck," I blurt out and the room falls silent.

"Not that I have much to compare it to..."

Why are they so quiet?

"Wait, what?" Connie sits forward. We all know Connie is—was—the more promiscuous out of the three of us.

Reese had only been with Elijah, her one-night stand and Killian. Connie, well, she liked sex and was always up for casual sex before Kaleb. Loved that for her. Then there was me. Shameful really. Cam girl getting herself off with toys and I was always waiting for the one request of me using a dildo and taking my virginity that way... but my private client took care of that in the end.

"Yeah," I breathe out, ignoring the tremble deep within my chest.

"So was Keaton your first?" Reese shuffles to the edge of the sofa, Connie hanging off her words.

I shake my head.

"Someone at work..." and I stiffen momentarily. I don't want to slip up.

"Oh," Connie smirks, "minx."

"Hardly," crimson paints my cheeks.

"Was he good?"

"It was over before it started to be honest." okay, it was a lie, but I wanted off this conversation as quickly as possible.

"But Keaton?" Reese's lips grow into a wide grin, eyes dancing with mine as she waits for my response.

"Oh my god," I fan myself, and the girls giggle.

"Life is too short for shit sex, it's got to be hot AF." Connie reaches for her wine and takes a mouthful.

"Amen," we all chime and lean in to clink our glasses.

"How's the horniness?" Reese asks as we all settle back into our seats.

"Awful, I was so turned on earlier watching Keaton lick his lips. What the fuck is that all about?"

"Third trimester horniness," she smirks.

"I'm always horny," Connie shrugs a shoulder up.

"Shock," Reese rolls her eyes and laughs.

"So, you going to act on it?" Reese purses her lips at the edge of her glass.

"No," I shrink. "It's already complicated, I don't want to make it worse."

"How can you make it worse? You married your dad's best friend and are pregnant with his twins... please, unless I am missing something, how can you make it worse?"

And I say nothing. Just shrug my shoulders up.

"Top up?" Reese asks, sensing my mood and Connie nods, handing her an empty wine glass.

"Sorry, I don't mean to overstep," Connie leans over towards me and I can see the sincerity in her eyes.

"I know, it's just things are a little in the air at the moment and I don't want to add to that."

"When are you moving home?"

"Next week, I've got a few things to sort out with work then I should be good to go."

"You going to miss this place?" she asks, sitting back in the chair and I look round the penthouse and let out a happy sigh.

"Yeah..." I pause for a moment, "I am."

Once the girls had gone, I double checked the lock on the door for the last time and climbed into bed. I hovered my finger over my cam app, and for some reason curiosity gets the better of me. Signing in, I confirm the re-activation of my account before I am greeted with my dashboard, and I see notifications and messages. I also see *TallDarkandHandsome* is online. Always thought it was Keaton. Still think it could be. He was always online when I was, Keaton was always locked in his room. Coincidence? Maybe. But then that one night made me doubt my inkling. Keaton wouldn't have treated me like that. Would he?

A message pops up and my heart races.

Hello little Vixen.
It's been a while, I was starting to worry where you were.

I ignore it.

Don't play hard to get, I'm closer to you than you think.
I'm always watching you Arizona.

My blood runs cold. I panic, shutting off my phone and wishing it to be morning already so I could go to Keaton's.
Now I would lay wide eyed and worrying.
But sleep came eventually.

CHAPTER FORTY-SIX
KEATON

I sit at my desk clock watching. I am ready to go home. Arizona moves back home this afternoon and I am clocking off at three.

Two hours to go.

Me and Titus have avoided each other. I really thought Ari being in hospital would have mended our rift, but clearly not. He is walking round with a constant thundercloud over his head and it's starting to annoy me. My fingers fumble with the buttons of my shirt before they're clasped round the wedding band round my neck. I still have her birthday present in my desk at home, couldn't find the courage to give it to her for some reason.

Kaleb breaks me away from my clock watching and smirks when he sees what I am playing with.

"Not ready to let go?"

I drop my hand and button my shirt back up.

"Never."

"Fair," he nods, stepping into the office. "I wanna talk to you about something," he says, pulling out the chair in front of my desk and flopping down.

"Yeah?"

"I want to propose to Connie. Everyone is shacked up, well, apart from Nate."

"Nate's Nate, though. He could be married for all we know, and he wouldn't tell us. He would be one of those that would elope to some exotic country and swear he dropped it into conversation."

Kaleb laughs as he rubs his empty wedding band finger.

"You're not wrong," and I laugh.

"I just feel like I want to take the next step with Connie. We don't want kids. We're happy with our lives, but I do want her to be my wife. Titus is married, you're married..." he pauses, "well, kind of," he adds, smirking.

"Cunt. I am married."

"Killian and Reese... and then there is me."

"And Nate," I throw in.

"Fuck Nate."

"Harsh," we hear Nate's voice and Kaleb spins round to see Nate standing in the doorway.

"Hey, come in a minute," I say and he does, hands tucked in his pockets, dirty blonde hair messy as always, the odd curl showing.

"Yeah?" his brows raise.

"Kaleb wants to ask Connie to marry him."

"Really?" he sounds shocked.

"Yeah, why wouldn't I?"

"Dunno, she doesn't really seem the married type?"

I watch as Kaleb sits a little taller.

"Well, neither do you."

"No?" Nate cocks his head to the side, and I know he is playing with him.

"No." Kaleb rolls his lips and I can see him thinking over Nate's words.

"I mean, has Connie ever said about wanting to get married?"

He pauses for a moment, Kaleb's eyes on me before they move back to Nate. "Don't all girls want to get married?"

"Nope," me and Nate say in unison.

"Well, fuck."

"Maybe you need to have a little chat with Connie before you ask her such a question." Nate gives a solid nod and turns on his heel before stopping at the threshold. "You shouldn't just assume these things," he winks then disappears back to his desk.

"So..." I click my fingers, leaning back in my chair, pushing back. "What you going to do?"

"No idea." he sighs, rubbing his chin, his stubble scratching at his skin. "Fucking Nate."

"Fucking Nate," I shake my head from side to side.

Silence rolls through my office, and I take a moment to look at my older brother, by only a couple of minutes may I add. Similarities mark both of us, but we're so different. Eyes slightly different shades of green mixed with hazel, skin tone similar, my lips a little fuller than his. Kaleb has grey scattered down the side of his thick, dark hair. I haven't had a single grey. Both have stubble. I could probably grow a beard, he couldn't. His would look more like bum fluff. He never had stubble when he met Connie. He was cleaner shaved. Killer jaw. High cheek bones. Handsome. Like me. But I was a little rougher around the edges, maybe?

"Looking forward to having Ari back?" Kaleb interrupts my thoughts and I blink a couple of times.

"Yeah, house has been too quiet."

"Make the most of it, soon you'll have two screaming babies to fill the silence."

"Yeah," I half laugh, eyes drawn to the picture on my desk of me and her in the little white chapel. Both smiles wide, eyes glistening with what I think was happiness, maybe a little alcohol and to think my babies were already inside of her. Madness.

And yes, they might not be mine. But I don't care. They're mine. They will always be mine.

"You seem really happy."

I puff out my cheeks.

"I mean, I could be happier. I'm basically celibate and the woman I love is pushing me away but hey, I'm happy," and I laugh, no idea why. Nerves? Realization?

"You? Celibate?!" Kaleb roars.

"Wish I was lying. Haven't been with anyone since Ari walked out. Desperate..." I pause for a moment and duck my head to look through my office window to see if Titus is sitting at his desk. "But no, no one but Arizona."

"Well fuck," he runs his hand over the stubble on his chin and whistles.

"Are you happy?" I sit up, elbows on my desk.

"Extremely. I never thought I would find love... but then she came into my life like a damn wrecking ball," he laces his fingers together and chuckles softly.

"The best way man."

"Did Ari wreck you?"

I sigh. It's not heavy. It's not light. It's not happy and it's not sad. It's just a sigh.

"Completely."

CHAPTER FORTY-SEVEN
ARIZONA

It's just past seven and I am home. *Home*.

Sitting on the sofa, the babies are kicking and Keaton's hands are resting on my bump.

"Wow," his eyes light up, watching as my stomach morphs and shifts.

"I know, imagine how it feels," I smile as I watch him.

"Weird?"

"Yeah, but also comforting," I nod, my hands resting on top of Keaton's now.

"I really missed you," his voice blankets me in warmth, his eyes penetrating through mine and my heart bangs against my rib cage, trying to escape and eclipse Keaton's.

"I really missed you," it's not a lie. Far from it actually. Things just feel right when I am with him. He is home. My lungs burn, my throat aching with the want to tell him how much I love him. But I don't.

I ignore it until I feel like I am suffocating.

Don't care.

I can't be vulnerable yet. Maybe soon. Just not yet.

Everything in my head is a mess and I need to declutter.

Reluctantly, I move. Well, try to. Keaton helps me up like the doctor showed him. A soft grip round my elbow as he gently pulls me to my feet. I give him a small smile, his eyes not leaving mine.

"I'm going to draw a bath."

"No, I'll go and do it. Then you can relax, and I'll start unpacking," he smiles at me before disappearing out of the living room and upstairs. I waddle towards the kitchen, reaching for a glass and filling it with water. I drain it, then fill it again. Shouldn't have, because I will need to pee in about thirty seconds. Climbing the stairs slowly, I feel out of breath. The babies are still sitting high and are squashing every organ in my torso. We decided to keep the babies gender a surprise. I think boys. Keaton thinks girls. Cravings are a mix between sweet and sour. No old wives tales are leading me in any direction of which sex they could be. We agreed as long as they were healthy, that's all that mattered.

I walk into my room and Keaton comes out of my bathroom, shirt sleeves rolled round his elbows, veiny, thick, muscly arms on show and I am weak. Hormones are killing me. I am soaked. Can feel it. He can probably see it in my light denim maternity pants. His hungry eyes rake over me and my cheeks flame. I drop my head. Can't look at him. It's too much. I walk past him and into the bathroom, pushing the door shut behind me and only then do I breathe easier.

Stripping my clothes from my body, my brown hair has grown longer since being pregnant and now falls past my shoulders. I let my eyes lift, looking at my reflection in the mirror in front of me. Caramel skin glowing, eyes full of hope, hair thick and glossy, boobs full and round and a cute, but large, swollen bump. I turn to the side, crinkling my nose when I see my stretch marks that bite into the skin on my hips. Love to hate feeling with them. Love them because of my twins, hate them because I miss my perfect skin. Turning away, I dip my toe into the warm water and my body relaxes in an instant. Sinking under the water, my bump pokes out and I smile as I watch for the little hands and feet that press out of my skin. This pregnancy has flown by and it's bittersweet. I have had such an easy pregnancy since the hospital; it's just not how I would have planned it. Wanted to be well in my thirties before I had kids. But destiny chose this for me. For us. Twenty-two and nearly a mom of twins. Wow.

Towel wrapped—just about—around my body, I rough dry my hair with a towel. I brush my teeth and cleanse and moisturize my face before padding into my room. I reach for a little two piece. It's still cold, but I feel like a furnace. Even more so after my bath. I dress in a white ribbed cropped top and matching frilly shorts that sit under my bump. Soft cotton material and covered in cherry blossom.

I brought them because Keaton calls me Blossom.

Love the nickname. Only heard it a handful of times but it's a favorite. My hair is dry, my skin is moisturized, and I debate going back downstairs, but just as I walk out of my room, Keaton appears on the landing with my suitcase.

"Oh, hi," I whisper, my eyes glued to his as I watch them fall down my body. My heart. I have missed the way he looks at me. Adoration. Want. Lust. Like I am his forever.

"Wife," his lips twitch and my skin burns.

I step back, letting him pass with my bag and watch as he bends and places it at the foot of the bed.

Slowly turning I look at him, his hands are folded into his suit pants, head tilted slightly with a boyish grin on his face. I step closer and back into my room.

"What?" my cheeks blush and I hate it. Maybe. Maybe not.

"God," he pauses, voice low with a hint of rasp, "you're beautiful."

"Keat..." I trail off, dropping my face to the floor and focus on my feet before his are there too.

Two steps and he is here.

His finger and thumb find my chin, gripping and tipping my face up so I have no other choice but to let his soul burn into mine, taking me as prisoner and I didn't care that he threw away the key. I was ready to burn for him, calming into embers before withering out into nothing but ash. Only for him. Captured and bound in the depths of his heart and I never wanted to leave. He had all of me.

I knew where this was going. It shouldn't, but we both know that as soon as we're together, an invisible string, an invisible force, pulls us together until we orbit eternity intwined as one.

"Keat..." I repeat, breathless, my eyes on his lips and my whole body trembles.

"Blossom," and my heart flatlines for just a moment, arms around his neck before his lips are on mine and that's when my heart rate picks up. Bit by bit we piece each other back together until there is nothing left but us, as one, whole.

KEATON

I stand at the foot of the bed, hands enveloped into my suit pants, head slightly tilted to the right as my eyes roam over her. Pretty little pajama set. Cropped tank, frilly shorts.

White, ribbed with cherry blossoms. Perfection. A grin slips onto my lips, and she catches it. Of course she does.

"What?" her cheeks pinch with that pretty pink that I love and my heart flutters, dick instantly hard. Fuck's sake.

"God," I pause, inhaling deeply and when I speak, my voice is low and raspy. "You're beautiful."

"Keat..." her voice is soft and I fucking love it. Innocent until she's naked. Her face drops, and I miss her eyes on me. I step towards her. It took two steps if you're wondering. My neck cranes, head dipped, and my finger and thumb grip her chin. Tipping her beautiful face up towards mine, my heart stutters in my chest at just how perfect she is. Perfect is too less of a word. Our eyes lock, souls blend and our hearts knot and wrap around each other in a matter of seconds. The undeniable force field that consumes us as soon as we're together wrapping around us like an invisible string, pulling us together until we have nowhere else to go. Free falling into infinity, the world disappearing around us when all I can focus on is her. It's always her. It will always be her.

"Keat..." *Keat.* She's breathless, chest rising and falling, her blue eyes on my lips and I am starved of her. Desperate. Sick, so sick and she is the only antidote that will heal me.

Her. Mine. Forever.

"Blossom." Fuck, it feels good to let that name slip from my tongue, her eyes widen for a moment before her arms are wrapped around my neck, pulling me towards her and as I gently tip forward, our lips lock, tongues entwine and dance to a song only we can hear and I know that as long as we're together, we fix each other. Bit by bit. Piece by piece.

Hands clasp her cheeks, turning my face as our kiss deepens and I know this is wrong, but I couldn't stop. My lips greedily trail down her jaw to her neck as I let them linger a little longer over her pulse point and smile. Grazing across her collar bone before I am on my knees.

"Keaton, we shouldn't."

"I know baby, but it's too late. We shouldn't have crossed the line all those months ago," my hands are on her bump as I drag my lips over her warm skin, the smell of honey and vanilla engulf me from her moisturizer, and I groan. "But we crossed the line, we would have always ended up here, wife, we're destined. Written in the stars. You know the truth; you know that this," I fall back onto my knees, "this is everlasting, Blossom. You were made for me. It doesn't matter how much we try, we will always find our way back to each other." She whimpers as my long fingers slip inside her shorts, letting them glide through her lips and she is already wet.

"Keaton," she whispers, eyes glassy and I know there are a thousand words she wants to say but she won't. Not yet.

"I know," my lips press at the top of her thigh, finger teasing at her opening. "I just need tonight, this moment, I need you Ari. Let me worship you, let me *love* you. I need to show you how much you mean to me, tonight, tomorrow, infinity."

Her breath catches as I fill her with two of my fingers, just as my other hand skims her shorts out the way, my lips edging closer to her as my tongue flicks her clit. Her fingers dig into my shoulders as she steadies herself.

"Bed," she breathes.

Normally I would argue, but not tonight. I stand, satisfied with the small taste I have had but I need more. Desperately. Before she can stop me, I lift her into my arms and guide her to the bed, laying her down gently, hair fanned out underneath her and looking as pretty as ever.

If someone told me a year ago how soft I would be for this woman, I would tell them to go suck a dick. But here I am. Hypocrite. Always hated men that acted like this, until her.

Her.

My universe.

My constellations.

My galaxies and everything beyond. I was cocky and condescending—still am—but not with her.

Soft.

So fucking soft.

My fingers dust over her skin and I am addicted to everything about her. The way she feels beneath my fingertips, the way she melts on my tongue, the way she tastes on my lips. My eyes connect with hers as I hook my fingers into the waistband of her shorts and slip them down her thighs and off her ankles. Her toes pressed against my shirt covered chest, and my thumb rubs her archway, neck craned, head dipped as I plant soft kisses on the top of her foot, across her ankle and up her calf, her knee, her thighs until I am knelt between them.

"I will never tire of you, baby." Her eyes glisten at my words, lips parted and her tits overspilling her tight crop top. I lay over, careful not to put any weight on her bump, hands either side of her face as I kiss her softly.

She wriggles beneath me, and I smirk.

"You're not going anywhere."

"I feel so unattractive," she whispers and my heart falls heavy in my chest, aching.

"Blossom," I lick my lips, slowly pushing up but staying on my knees. "Don't you ever feel anything but beautiful." I kiss over her bump, and I know it must be hard for her, the way her body has changed to accommodate and grow two babies. Her skin stretched; belly swollen but she has never looked more beautiful to me than she does now.

"I will love you till the end of time, until the world is nothing but ashes, nothing but a million particles disintegrating through the infinite of galaxies. And even then, it will never be enough Arizona. I am weak for you my love, I adore you. More so now than ever."

"Keaton," she chokes out a sob, slowly trying to sit up but I shake my head and place her hand on my chest, so she can feel the way my heart beats for her.

"This is yours Arizona, it'll never beat for another woman the way it beats for you." A tear rolls down her cheek and I swipe it away with my thumb.

Lifting her hand from my chest, I place a kiss on her palm then rest it back on the duvet of the bed.

Twisting her slightly, I seek out the purple stretch marks on her hips and cover them with my lips, kissing away any worries and insecurities she may feel in this moment. I know it won't last, but for now, it's all I can do.

"I love you," she whispers to me and my fucking heart leaps in my chest. My fingers dust up the inside of her parted thighs, slowly letting her roll on her back just as I slip them inside of her, her back arching, hips lifting and that's when my mouth is on her, tongue rolling over her clit. Fingers curl in the bedsheets, her body writhing beneath me and I don't stop until I taste her on my tongue, the way she moans my name as she comes. Eyes roll, body trembles and I feast on her until she is spent.

Crawling over her, her eyes bounce back and forth between mine. Her thumb brushes across my lips, wiping her arousal from them and I groan. Fingers fumble with my shirt and I am desperate to have her hands on my skin. She leans up slightly, pushing my shirt off my shoulders and her eyes focus on my gold chain and my heart stops for just a moment. Picking at the delicate chain, her eyes find mine and no words even have to be spoken. Her pretty blue eyes are watery, as they search for something, anything.

"Always been with me, Blossom." And she shoves me up, panic courses, pricking at the base of my neck but there was no need to panic. She takes control, pushing me onto the bed underneath her. I fumble with my pants, she pulls them down my legs and then she's on me. Legs either side of my body, my hands are on her hips, and I am fucking desperate to be inside of her.

Her lips are on mine, tongue dipping past my lips and I moan into her mouth. Gliding fingertips up her ribs, I tuck them under her cropped top and pull them over her head. Hands on her full tits, my lips lock and suck and my cock throbs beneath her. She's on her knees, hands wrapped softly round my thickness and rubs the thick head of my cock over her clit then glides it through her soaked cunt.

"Fuck, please, sit on me. Let me fill you, fuck Ari, *please*," I am fucking begging her. My balls tighten, my cock pulses and I won't last long as she teases me, rocking her hips back and forth, tip pressing just inside her tight pussy and I bite the flesh on her breast, eyes rolling in the back of my head as it tips back. "I need to sink into your pretty pussy," I choke.

She smiles down at me, wild brown hair framing her face, covering us, lips teasing over mine but hers are parted so I couldn't even kiss her even if I wanted to. Pressing the tip of my cock into her cunt, she hovers, and slowly, ever so fucking torturously slow, lowers herself over me as I fill her to the hilt, pausing for just a moment, jaw wound tight as I fight with myself not to come now I am inside of her.

"You okay baby?" she purrs, and I want to fuck her so

hard. My hand curls round the back of her head, grabbing the curls at the nape of her neck and I tug her head back, exposing her beautiful throat. My hand fits perfectly round the base of the neck like a pretty necklace, and my lips dust up the column on her throat, bobbing as I make contact.

"Don't tease me Ari," I smile against her warm skin and that's when her hips roll over me, hands pressed against my chest and her fingers play with her wedding ring that hangs from my neck. She lifts herself up and down and I help her, curling the hand that was once at her throat round her hip.

"You feel so good," she moans, her tits bouncing, pussy tightening around me.

"It's all you baby," I whisper against her skin. It's the truth.

"I need more," she begs slowing her hips, "fuck me from behind," and my eyes light up, cock thickening inside of her.

Lifting her off me, I gently roll her onto all fours and kneel up behind her. Giving myself a moment to just appreciate the delectable sight in front of me, I line myself up at her cunt and pound into her with one, hard, thrust.

And I give her what she wants.

More.

I fuck her hard and fast from behind until our moans are mixed with the scent of us as we come together.

I let her catch her breath before I fuck her two more times before she passes out, head on my chest and curled up at my side.

Just where she has always belonged.

Listening to the way my heart beats to a rhythm that only she knows.

CHAPTER FORTY-EIGHT
ARIZONA

I HAVE NEVER FELT MORE CONTENT THAN I DO NOW.

Keaton is asleep next to me; my fingers play with the chain around his neck as I listen to the way his heart beats in his chest. If I could pause on a moment, it would be this one here. Always.

My eyes begin to feel heavy when my phone vibrates on the side table. Panic swarms me when I see my dad's name flash up.

"Dad," I answer, keeping my voice low, "is everything okay?" I squint at the time, it's two thirty a.m.

"Amora is in labor."

"We'll be right there." Cutting the phone off and placing it back on the bedside unit, I gently wake Keaton up after I am dressed and tell him to stay in bed. Of course he doesn't. He dresses half asleep and with numerous yawns before we're both stumbling down the stairs. He grabs his keys and phone, and we walk to his SUV. He traded his old car in a few weeks back and now we have a *Jeep Grand Cherokee*. It's gray and looks pretty parked at the sidewalk.

The drive is short. Amora is under the same hospital as

me and has the same doctor. Kyra. Keaton yawns most of the way, scrubbing his face.

"Tired?" I ask, my hand resting on his thigh.

"Yeah, some minx kept me up far too late," he turns to look at me, eyes hazy and his lips slowly turning into a smirk.

"I think you had more to do with that than me," I wink, his hand slipping between my thighs and giving my skin a gentle squeeze.

"Innocent until proven," his voice is slow, sleepiness still thick in his tone. Yawning, he turns his blinker on as we pull down the side road towards the carpark for the hospital.

"Hmm," I hum, leaning forward to grab my bag when Keaton slams on the brake pedal and I hit my head on the dash. Hard.

"Fuck," Keaton shrieks, putting the handbrake on and unbuckling himself.

"I'm fine," I lie. I'm not fine. My head feels like it's split in two, throbbing pain at the base of my neck, head is pounding, temples ache.

"You're bleeding," I can hear the panic in his voice as I brush my fingertips up round my hairline and feel the wet stickiness coat them.

My intake of breath feels short.

"I'm fine," I reassure him, turning to face him and his face is drawn, eyes hollow.

"Baby, I'm..."

"Keaton," I place my hand on his cheek, trying to pull his eyes to mine. "It was an accident, please don't worry about me."

Thing is, he probably does need to be worried. I can feel

how deep the cut is. Annoying when there is nothing to cause it, maybe it was just the force.

"Let's get parked, I can get checked out while here," I reassure him once more and he just nods, silent.

He pushes into drive, and within minutes, we're parked up and he is throwing coins into the meter.

Walking around to my side of the car, he opens the door and takes my hand in his, grabbing my bag from the footwell.

He looks horrified.

I take his hand, linking my fingers through his as we walk towards the hospital, bypassing reception and heading for the labor ward. I can feel eyes on me, a few hushed words and I know the blood is trickling down the side of my face. Tugging the sleeve of my sweater over my hand, I press it to my small wound and keep moving forward.

"I am so fucking sorry," his grip tightens on mine, "I think I dozed off," and I see how the guilt suffocates him in that instant.

"I shouldn't have made you drive; we should have got a taxi."

"It could have been so much worse," he whispers, and I know what he means. We could have crashed. One of us could have died. I shouldn't have made him drive. The blame for that one was on me.

"I'm okay," I stretch my fingers out beside me, desperate to have his link with mine but he pulls away, hand rubbing over his tired face. Guilt consumes me.

We reach the labor ward and my dad steps out of the side room and seeks us out instantly, happiness soon turning to worry when he sees my bloodstained sleeve, eyes instantly narrowed on the man beside me. His best friend.

"What the fuck happened?" my dad roars, and he is toe to toe with Keaton.

"Dad, I'm fine." I step in between the two men I love most in the world and press my hands against my dad's chest, ignoring the stained blood on my hands and I feel the trickle once more.

"You're clearly not," his brows pinch when he looks at the gash on my head.

"I'll get checked out, but please can you just...." I exhale heavily, dropping my head.

"Fine," his tone is clipped, and I can feel the way Keaton's chest vibrates against my back, the low rumble of a growl present.

"Thank you," I whisper, sleeve back against my head. "Is Amora okay?"

"Yes," he sighs, his own head bowing for a moment, "slow labor, but she is bossing it. Just waiting on Xavier and Royal," he pauses, his head lifting just as Xavier walks through the door. "Talk of the devil and he shall appear," his voice is a low grumble and I nibble the inside of my lip.

"Titty, where is my daughter?" Xavier says as he owns the room, shoulders back, head high, back straight.

"Come, I'll take you."

"Oh, well, hello..." he pauses as he stands at my side. I slowly turn to face him, blink a couple of times then look into his eyes. Exactly the same as Amora's. "Arizona," he smiles.

"Hey."

His eyes scan my face then lift to where my sleeve is pressed. "What happened? Are you okay?" his strong British accent fills the room.

"She's fine, thanks," Keaton wraps his arm around me, hand on bump.

"Hi," Xavier rolls his eyes, shaking his head at Keaton. "Arizona, it was a pleasure seeing you again, but if you would please excuse me," he gives a gentle but curt nod as he breezes past me and over to my dad. Royal gives me a small smile as she walks past, catching up with Xavier.

"Keaton," my dad's voice is loud as he walks away, giving him a look over his shoulder, "get her seen, now."

I hear the deep sigh leave Keaton and I shake my head from side to side.

"Come," he links his fingers through mine and walks me away and to the emergency room.

"Honestly, I think you're making a bigger deal out of this than needed."

"Ari, please. I am wracked with guilt; please can I just get you checked out? If not for you, but for my own peace of mind."

I nod, rolling my lips and choosing not to respond.

We're not waiting long until I am called forward and see one of my old work friends, Taylor.

"Oh my god, Ari," her eyes scan over me, widening a little more when she sees my bump then they're back on my face. "Are you okay?"

"I'm fine," I hum, hands linked under my bump as twin B kicks away.

"How far along are you?" one of her brows lift as she gloves up.

"Thirty weeks, pregnant with twins."

"Wow," she smiles, "you must be thrilled."

Is it wrong that I feel a stab of jealously course through me? This was my life. This was what I wanted. I love Keaton and I love my babies, but I miss the old me. The old Arizona. The one with her nose stuffed into a textbook. Not the one that swung round poles for a living and lost her virginity to a stranger off her cam app. Nausea rolls through me.

"I am," I keep my answer short, eyes finding Keaton's. I know he can read me. He knows exactly what I am thinking.

His hand scoops one of mine into his and squeezes it tightly.

"How did this happen?" Taylor asks and I hear Keaton about to answer.

"He hit the brake too hard at the barrier. It was open when we were pulling up but came down a little too quickly which caused my husband to hit the brake a little too heavily," I laugh it off, my stomach tightening, my heart racing.

"Oh man, those barriers can be a real nightmare can't they." She shakes her head from side to side in a knowing manner as she examines the cut on my head.

"I have told him I am fine, but he wanted me to get checked out." I throw my hand up as if it's not a big deal.

"Well, he is right to have brought you in. You need stitches," she pulls her gloves off, stepping back and furrowing her brow.

"What?" I scrunch my nose.

"It's pretty deep. What did you hit it on?" she asks me, taking notes.

"The dash," I sigh, my eyes looking at my bloodstained sleeve.

"Let me get you cleaned up then Dr Trent will be over shortly to get you stitched up."

I nod. Turning to look at Keaton. His eyes are fixed ahead, jaw tight and teeth no doubt clenched.

"I'm okay," I whisper, but he doesn't respond. We just sit in silence whilst we wait.

Ten stitches later and an awkward goodbye with Taylor and Dr Trent and we're back on our way to the labor ward.

"Fucking stitches," Keaton curses himself and I know he will beat himself up. They even checked for concussion and pediatrics were called down to check the twins' heartbeats. Both okay.

I want to fight against him, try and make him feel better, but it's pointless.

We walk hand in hand as we round the corner and towards Amora's room. I knock softly, letting myself in whilst Keaton hangs back in the hallway.

"Hey," I squeak, Amora looks fed up.

"Hey," she presses a smile against her lips, and I walk across to her. "How you doing?"

Stupid question, yes.

"I've been better," she smirks, hands resting on her bump as she begins to pant. My dad is there holding her hand as she squeezes it and I'm glad it's taken his attention off of me with my stupid band aid on my head.

I am not looking forward to this. I want to opt out.

Royal approaches from the restroom with a damp washcloth and she glides so elegantly over to her daughter, placing it over her clammy head. Her red hair stuck to where she is sweating. The moment suddenly becomes too much when I grieve for a mother daughter moment I will never have.

I step back, backing out of the room just as Amora's contractions ease and that's when my dad's eyes lift and land on me, widening and I don't miss the thunderous scowl that marks his face.

"Don't tell me you had stitches."

I nod, locking my fingers in front of my stomach.

He closes his eyes and inhales before breathing out his exhale nice and slow.

"Dad, I know you and Keaton have..." I pause for a moment, "issues."

"They're more than issues Sunshine," he half laughs, rubbing his hand over his stubble and my heart throbs.

"You need to get over it." my tone is blunt, and I hate that I've said that.

"That will never happen," he shakes his head from side to side.

"Then get over me," my voice trembles, on the verge of tears and his mouth falls lax with the words that have just spilled from my lips.

"Ari..." he chokes.

"It's your choice dad."

He stays silent and I give a sad, heavy nod. Turning I reach for the door handle when I hear my dad's footsteps, his hand reaching for my elbow and pulling me to face him.

"He isn't good enough for you," his beautiful eyes bounce between mine and I feel the imaginary slap across my cheek, my heart plummeting.

"No, you're right," and I see the confusion on my dad's face, "he is better."

He is speechless and with that, I look over towards Amora and give her an apologetic smile. "I hope everything goes okay and I can't wait to meet my new little brother or sister," and I mean that. I am beyond excited, but I can't keep doing this.

"Tut Tut Tut," Xavier whistles as he enters the room, eyes burning into dad and that's my cue to walk out the door and not look back.

Keaton stands as soon as I am in the hallway and I keep

quiet, just walking past him and towards the exit of the hospital, him on my heels.

He keeps asking me what's wrong, but I can't tell him.

I can't tell him that my dad, his best friend, thinks he is no good for me. Keaton will agree but that's where he'll be wrong. They're both wrong. I meant what I said to my dad. Keaton is better. He makes me better. Wholly.

I love who I have become with him. Sure, things haven't been easy. But I love him.

With every nerve ending, every fiber, every skip of my heart beat and every solid pump of my heart.

And that will never change.

Whether we choose to be together or not.

I will always, without a doubt, love Keaton Mills.

Cross my heart and swear to die, I'll love him till the end of time.

CHAPTER FORTY-NINE
ARIZONA

SLEEP DOESN'T COME EASY WHEN WE'RE HOME. MY HEAD IS thumping, I am replaying the conversation between me and my dad and I hate that's where the evening took us. I honestly thought he would be okay, but he can't seem to let it go. I know it isn't ideal. I get it, I really do. But, I also don't. Sighing, I'm bored at staring at the ceiling. Climbing out of bed, I pad downstairs to the living room and turn the TV on. Moving towards the kitchen, I pour some milk into the pan and let it simmer. It's quiet and peaceful. The sunrise is just around the corner, ready to greet the day, but I'm not ready for morning yet.

Turning off the gas, I reach for a mug and pour my milk then drizzle a little honey before stirring it. Cupping it, my hands slowly warm. The hum of the freezer draws my attention and I suddenly have a craving for ice. I am salivating just thinking about the crunch. Placing my mug down on the countertop, I tug the freezer drawer and my eyes light up when I see the ice compartment full. I pick a piece, popping it past my lips and crunch down, and it was too satisfying. I needed more. What the fuck. I hadn't had one single craving, but here I was, raiding the freezer like an addict. I grab a plastic jug from under the stove and fill it to the brim. Holding my ice in one hand, milk in the other, I quietly walk towards the living room and sink onto the sofa. I have one of Keaton's oversized tees on, I smile when his scent drifts up and fills my nose. Placing my jug and mug onto the glass coffee table, I tug the sofa throw up and over my body then like a happy kid who has her candy waiting, I reach for my ice, popping another piece into my mouth as I flick through the streaming app. I settle on *Something Borrowed* and drop the control into my lap. I'm not alone long when I hear the heavy footsteps of Keaton.

"Hey," sleep masks his usual gravelly tone and my skin prickles. His thick brown hair is sticking up in numerous places, eyes puffy and full of sleep. Wearing low rise pajama pants, his Adonis belt proudly on show. A dusting of brown hair forms from his pants waistband and up to his belly button, breaking for a while until more is scattered across his broad, toned chest.

"Hey," I say as I crunch down on more ice and I see his lips pout, one eye closed, the other watching me.

"What you eating?"

"Ice," I say in a mocking tone. I mean, surely, he can see it's ice right?

"I can see that, but why?"

Don't make sense.

I shrug, smiling when I see Kate Hudson and Ginnifer Goodwin dancing on the large screen in front of me. "Craving?"

"Yeah?" he hums, sitting down next to me.

"Yeah," I nod.

"I've got a craving," his voice is slow, and I know that

tone. My mouth is open, ice between my fingers and the ice water is running down my wrist.

"For ice?" I act dumb and he shakes his head from side to side, leaning over and lowering his mouth over the ice and licking it erotically, his hot breath on my cold fingers and pleasure ripples deep inside of me, I press my thighs together just as he sucks the ice from between my fingertips.

Lifting the blanket from me, his eyes rake over me and tired Keaton is long gone. He clicks the TV off then leans across me, turning me to face him then pushing me back gently so I am laying on the sofa.

He looks at the nearly empty and melted jug of ice and tuts in a disapproving matter.

"This will not do," he shakes his head softly, his hair flopping forward, and it takes everything in me to not run my fingers through it and fix it. His long fingers dip into the jug and pulls the last piece of ice out and purses it between his lips. He stands, and I watch, lips parted, chest heaving at the sight in front of me. It doesn't matter how much I see this man with my own eyes, I will never tire of how beautifully sexy he is. And he is all mine.

One step, two step and his leaning down, the gold chain that has my wedding band on dangling and my fingers wrap round the delicate metal.

Our lips inches apart, breaths heavy and eyes dipping as the quiet teasing between us intensifies. We always say we won't do this anymore, but it's pointless even wasting breath on saying the words. Because as soon as we've entered this force field that surrounds us, we're doomed.

Iced water drips from his mouth onto my lips and I know how it feels yet I gasp as if surprised, and that's when he kisses me, passing the ice through his lips, his tongue rolling it around my mouth, and I am hot and ready for him. His fingers are not touching me, hands not grabbing and his body isn't even on top of me yet I am writhing beneath him because I can't get enough. I need more. Within seconds the small ice cube has disintegrated into nothing but water that I drink down like I'm dehydrated. Desperate.

"Be right back," he smirks against my lips, breaking away and I swear I could come from just him looking at me like he wants to devour me. I say nothing, just brace myself with panting as I wait for him to return. I look down at myself, wish I would have changed but why does it matter because within minutes he will have this tee off and over my head and I'll be naked under his touch, his lips, his body.

My body stiffens when I hear his footsteps hitting the hard floor in the hallway, knowing he is seconds away from sending me to seventh heaven.

"Look at you," he groans, and I don't miss the chance to sneak a peek at him in the lowly lit room. He is a God.

"Look at you," I raise my brows and it's a cheap come back but honestly, I just want him. I eye the jug of ice and I clench my thighs together.

"Still craving ice, baby?" he asks, looking at the jug then back to me and it takes me a moment to register what he has asked. I nod, eagerly. God, I am *so* needy.

His lips pull into a sexy smoldering smirk, and I am wet. Who am I kidding? I was wet when he first walked into the room. The sofa cushion dips slightly, his knee between my legs as he hovers over me, one hand beside my head, the other hooking out a cube of ice. He pops it into his mouth for just a second before pursing it between his lips and pinching it with his finger and thumb. I watch with intent, the way he moves towards me, his eyes hazy as the ice cube meets the skin on my thighs. Water runs between them as his other fingers play with the hem of the sage green tee. Lifting the cube from my skin, I instantly miss it.

"Open," he orders softly, and I do, I pop my lips open and welcome the cube into my hot mouth. His hands are back on the hem of my tee, sitting me up gently and pulling it over my head before discarding it to the floor.

"So fucking beautiful," he whispers, lips on my collar bone, hands kneading my heavy, aching breast.

My eyes flutter closed, my body heating up under his touch when I feel an iced coolness dance over my skin. Letting my lids open, his beautiful green eyes are on me and only me. He drags the ice cube lazily over my collarbone, then circles it round my hardened nipples whilst his mouth blows warm air on my other breast. He moves the fast-melting cube across and gives my nipple the same attention and my skin covers in cold goosebumps. Water pools on my skin and my breath catches at the back of my throat.

"I have plenty more, don't you worry Blossom," he croons and I lick my lips. He reaches for another and continues from where it melted, but now he runs it across my sternum, down to my navel then glides into my groin, wetting my cotton panties in an instant.

He hooks a finger round the waistband and gently pulls them from my legs and off my feet.

Water drips down my inner thigh just as one of his fingers tease at my soaked pussy.

"So wet," he moans, eyes falling to my spread thighs, and I hate that I can't see because of my bump.

A light moan vibrates in my chest as he plunges a finger

deep inside of me and slips it in and out at a slow, teasing pace.

The ice is no more, but before I can take my eyes from him, his finger has hooked another cube of ice, this one a little larger than before. Dragging it over my other thigh, water drips between my thighs and I clench around his finger just as he curls it and rubs my g-spot.

"Oh," I moan, head tipping back and that's when I feel it.

Ice cold.

Right between my legs.

Fuck.

KEATON

She is a fucking vision. Naked beneath me, skin glistening, tits swollen and full, legs parted and her cunt so fucking wet. I tease her with the ice, dragging it up and down her thighs as one of my fingers rubs the spot I know she so desperately needs relieving. I smirk, a boyish fucking grin on my face. Once the ice melts, I hook another from the jug. And honestly, I have never enjoyed ice as much as I do now.

Popping it into my mouth, I ignore the way my tongue burns from how cold it is. Lowering myself between her pretty thighs, I push the cube between my lips and onto her swollen clit.

"Oh," she moans, the breath being snatched from her lungs when the coldness hits her clit, fingers twisted in my hair whilst the other grabs the sofa cushion as if she is bracing herself. My tongue rubs between her lips as I keep the ice pressed against her clit. It melts quickly, water running down her pretty cunt and I make it my mission to lap it up. I don't give her a second to enjoy just my tongue, another ice cube is in my mouth and back on her, two fingers slip in with ease and I slowly fuck her, sliding in and out at a torturous rhythm and the sound of how wet she is making my cock pulse. Gliding the ice cube up and down her pussy, rubbing it over her clit whenever I reach the top and her moans fill the room.

"It feels so good," she whimpers, her fingers tightening in my hair.

Water trickles over my fingers, my tongue there to clean up.

Another ice cube down, but it's straight in my mouth and on her. Pulling my fingers from her, I drag the ice down and using my tongue, I push it inside of her. Two fingers slip in just as my tongue flicks over her clit and her body trembles. Sucking on her clit, my hand reaches up to her tits as I grab and grope her. Burying my tongue deeper, my fingers fuck her and her whole body stiffens.

"I'm going to come," is all she manages.

"Come for me baby, come all over my tongue and fingers," I beg, moaning as ice water trickles from her cunt, my tongue sucking on her clit once more and that's when she soaks me, her arousal dripping down my hand and wrist, her body trembling as she cries, pleasure ripping through her.

"Such a dirty girl," I smirk, kissing her clit and slowly removing my fingers but not before having one more taste.

I kneel up, looking down at her and I love it when she's just came. Eyes all heavy and hazy, chest blotchy, skin shimmering and her lips are parted. She has the *'just came'* look down perfectly.

"You okay?" I ask, my cock aching between my legs and

she nods. I help her up and place a soft kiss on her lips and I expect her to cuddle into me. What I don't expect is for her to be on her knees in front of me as she fists my cock from my pants and flicks her tongue over my thick head.

"You don't have to do this ba..." and she fucking sucks me into her mouth, cock sliding down the back of her throat with ease. "Fuck," I grunt, hands in her hair and I am mindful that she is pregnant with my babies. As much as I would love to throat fuck her right now, it's not the one.

I ease back, pulling the tip of my cock to her lips and her wide eyes bat up at me. Slowly pushing my hips forward, she swallows me down and my head tips back and I know it won't be long before I am coming down her pretty throat.

"I need you," I moan, pulling out again, and this time, she leans back.

She stands, her hands on my chest as she pushes me back onto the sofa. I watch her, hair framing her face as she climbs onto my lap, knees either side of my legs. Her fingers wrapping round my cock as she rubs my head through her folds, pressing against her clit as she works herself up.

"Fuck, baby," I groan, and she presses me at her opening. Eyes pinned to mine as she lowers herself over me, and I watch as her eyes roll into the back of her head, and I will never tire of how good she feels. I guide her, rocking her back and forth over me. It's not going to be long, I can already feel my orgasm building, her pussy tightening and her moans sound like a symphony to me. Her nails dig into my chest, clawing at my skin, marking me and that's when I lose it. My hands tighten on her hips, fingers digging into her skin as I lift her up and down my cock. Her trembling fingers circle her clit and her body trembles, head falling back and the sight of her being close to coming tips me over the edge, I skim my hand up her spine and wrap it round the back of her head as I guide her lips to mine. And that's when we both lose it, both moaning into each other's mouths as we come together.

CHAPTER FIFTY
ARIZONA

I wake hot and sweaty. It takes me a moment to work out where I am. We're on the sofa. Me and Keaton entangled, and I have no idea how we have both fit. Well, Keaton is right on the edge. And I am naked. Brilliant. I sit up slowly, trying not to wake him as I look for his tee. It's bunched on the floor over the other side of the room. I sigh, walking over and grabbing it. Pulling it over my head, I turn to look at Keaton and a small smile graces my lips. We really are good together.

I'm showered and feel a lot better than I did last night. I ache though, my stomach feels tight, and I feel exhausted. But I didn't sleep much and the hot as fuck man on the sofa definitely worked me out. Padding across the room, I sit on the edge of my bed wrapped in a towel as I use the smaller one to rough dry my hair. I see my phone light up and I contemplate reaching for it, but decide I better. Scooting up the bed, I grab my phone and see three text messages from my dad. Hovering my thumb over the message notification, I inhale deeply as I open them.

> **Dad**
> Did you get home okay? xo

> Ari, Sunshine... please, I don't want to fall out with you over this.

> Look who's arrived.

My heart swells at the photo he has sent. Amora is holding the most precious, tiny baby and all the animosity has faded in an instant.

> **Me**
> Dad, what a cutie. Congratulations. How is Amora? x

He reads it instantly and types a response.

> **Dad**
> Amazing. If you get a chance, come down and see us. We would really like that. Xo

A small smile lifts the corners of my mouth and suddenly, I am desperate to get to the hospital. Locking my phone, I dress in maternity khaki cargo pants, a tight white tee that sits neatly over my bump. I brush my hair into a tight, slick bun and scowl at the band aid still stuck to my head. I spray down the stray hairs and smooth it out. I moisturize my face then add a layer of foundation and concealer to hide my dark eye bags. Dusting a light pink blush across my cheek bones, I finish my look off with a flick of mascara and soothing lip balm. Grabbing a crew neck white sweater, I slip my feet into my white sneakers and grab my phone.

Placing the coffee pot on, decaf of course, I wait for it to warm before lifting it and pouring myself a large cup.

Adding creamer and sugar, I sit in the kitchen and enjoy the silence. It's not often I sit in complete silence, but when I do, I feel at peace. Relaxed. Tranquil. I hate being alone, but to sit in your own company when it's on your terms and you can enjoy silence, well, there is something so different about that. Taking a mouthful, my soul does a happy dance. Once finished, I reach for a bowl and grab some granola, yogurt and strawberries. My eyes fall to the freezer drawer and my mouth waters at the thought of ice, my stomach knotting and my clit pulsing at the memories from last night. My cheeks burn. Balancing my bowl on my palm, I use my free hand to pull the drawer open and grab a cube of ice, popping it into my mouth like a naughty kid snatching something they've been told not to touch.

"Still craving?" I hear his voice and annoyingly not his footsteps.

I spin to face him quickly, guilt all over my face but I play it down with a wide, toothy grin.

"Seems that way," I say around the ice, letting my eyes drop and giving into the blood that runs to my cheeks.

"You're dressed, are you going out?" he asks, walking past me and the smell of sex consumes me. He reaches for a cup then pours his coffee, drinking it black.

"Amora had the baby," I say as I try and sit at the breakfast bar, huffing and getting frustrated. He gives me a sympathetic smile, walking over to me and he shouldn't look this good in the mornings. Just fucked hair, toned and sculpted body wearing nothing but low hanging pajamas. Even his feet are sexy. Nothing like a half-naked man bare foot in your kitchen. He drags the stool out a little further and lowers it before helping me on, then, like the child I clearly am, he tucks me back in.

"Thank you," I nod, taking a mouthful of my granola.

Don't even fancy it anymore, should have gone with cereal. My favorite. I pinch my brows.

"That's amazing, boy or girl?" he asks, leaning across the breakfast bar and all I can think about is him leaning over the back of me whilst he pounds into me. Obvs, without my huge bump. What the fuck is wrong with me.

"Didn't say," I shrug, "I'm going to go to the hospital."

"Want me to come?" He asks, and I can hear the vulnerability in his voice.

"I would love for you to come, sure dad would to," Liar liar, pants on fire, "but please, if you don't want to, I won't be offended and I'm sure dad wouldn't either." That's not a lie. Dad would definitely prefer his best friend, who happens to not only be fucking his daughter into next week, but also married her drunk in Vegas and possibly knocked her up with twins, to not come.

"You sure? I don't want to encroach."

I scoff a laugh, waving him away with my hand. "Of course I am sure."

"Perfect, I'll go and get showered," he smiles, walking over to me and placing a soft kiss on the top of my head, mindful to not brush across the band aid.

"Cool," I say through a mouthful of granola and now, because of my own stupidity, my anxiety hovers around a solid eight. Perfect.

———

WALKING INTO THE HOSPITAL, I FIGHT WITH MYSELF TO NOT TAKE Keaton's hand in mine. I mean, I want to, but feel like I shouldn't? Labor ward is quiet, and we can easily sneak through to where Amora was last night. The blinds to her room are shut so I gently knock on the door. We're not waiting long before my dad opens the door, eyes all glassy and a wide smile on his face. He looks exhausted. Won't tell him that though.

"Hey Sunshine," his voice is quiet as he places a kiss on my cheek. Want to have it out with him. Won't though. Wouldn't ruin this moment for Amora.

"Hey Dad," I whisper, stepping past him and making a beeline for Amora. "Wow," I smirk, "it should be illegal to look *this* good after giving birth!" Shaking my head from side to side. I'm not lying. She looks radiant and glowing. Skin all dewy. Eyes glistening. Hair wavy and long.

"You're too kind," she smiles at me, a blissful sigh leaving her as she looks at me.

"How was the labor?" Why did I ask.

"Horrific," her smile slips for a millisecond. Blink and you would have missed it.

"Oh," because, what am I meant to say to that.

"But, all went well," she nods, reaching for a tissue off the side unit and wiping a stray tear. "Damn hormones."

"Hey, hey, no tears," my dad says, walking over and kissing the stray tear away as he sits on the edge of the bed. "I love you so much."

"I know, I just keep thinking about how perfect she is," Amora sniffles. "And I love you too," her voice whines as she begins to cry again.

"She?" I blink, eyes batting between both of them.

"Yup," they say in unison and my heart swells.

"Can I go and see her?" Excitement fills me as the question rolls from my tongue.

"Of course, I'll take you down to see her," my dad says as he stands up from the bed and walks towards the door.

"Grandpa," I hear Xavier say to my dad as he walks through.

"I'm dad, not Grandpa, that's you," my dad scowls, wrinkles apparent on his face.

"You will be, might as well get used to it," he chuckles as he walks over to his daughter and gives her a gentle kiss on the forehead, lingering for a moment, "anyway, I want to be called gaga, and mum wants to be called nanny, not grandma. I am under very strict orders to tell you that," and Amora laughs. My dad on the other hand just rolls his eyes.

"Idiot," I hear him rumble as he steps outside the room. "Won't be long," he calls out to Amora, smiling proudly at her.

She returns his smile with a nod.

Stepping out into the hallway, I side eye Keaton who is sitting on the chair, elbows resting on his knees, head dipped.

"What is he doing here?" my dad growls and I roll my eyes.

"I drove Arizona," Keaton rolls his shoulders back, cocky smirk on his face as he sits back into the chair.

"Surprised you didn't crash and hurt her again."

"Low blow," Keaton shakes his head.

"Didn't want you here."

"Dad," I snap, swatting him.

"It's fine *baby*," and the way my dad fucking stiffens when he hears the pet name roll off Keaton's tongue.

"What did you just call her?" he steps over to Keaton, towering over him. Keaton doesn't move or flinch. I move quickly, well, as quick as a heavily pregnant woman can move and step in front of Keaton once again.

"Dad, please." I press my hands to his chest and that's when Keaton stands up behind me in some form of protection.

It takes my dad a hot minute to break his angry gaze

from Keaton and finally settle on me, anger and frustration melting away within seconds.

"Can we go and see my baby sister?" and the words cut a little deeper into my heart, a weird warming sensation coating any other emotion that was currently pulsing through me.

"Sure thing, Sunshine."

Keaton places a soft kiss on the top of my head before stepping aside and resting his hand on my dad's shoulder and suddenly, I can't breathe.

"Congratulations," and my weak heart breaks, cracking into pieces and crumbling into my hollow chest. I watch as Keaton squeezes his shoulder then walks out of the labor ward.

My dad doesn't move. His jaw is clenched, eyes gazing forward into Amora's room, and I know how much that meant to him. He just wouldn't admit it.

He says nothing, just turns on his heel and begins walking and I take that as my cue to follow him. We don't talk. Just walk the narrow hallways. Nerves vibrate deep in my stomach, he has never once asked about work since I have been married to Keaton, yet he would always ask me before. This is where I did my internship, well, in his eyes, should still be doing my internship but he hasn't asked a single question about how it is going. Keaton wouldn't have told him? Surely? No, of course not. He would have told me. I shake the negative feeling that settles deep inside my chest as we round the corner to the nursery. My heart swells when I see all the beautiful newborns wrapped and swaddled in their plastic cribs.

My dad stops outside, looking through the large glass window and just stares.

"All okay?" I ask, turning and looking up at him. I can't read him. His face full of emotion but his eyes emotionless.

"Yeah," he rolls his lips, snapping out of it and pushing a smile onto his lips. "Ready?"

"More than ready," I nod, and he opens the door before we're dressed in shear pink gowns.

I watch as dad talks to the nurse before leading me towards my little sister's crib and my heart swells in my chest as he scoops her up delicately and holds her in his large arms.

"She's so tiny," I whisper, eyes welling. Little button nose, and full lips. She's a mini Amora.

"Susan," my dad calls out to the midwife, "could you follow us to my wife's room?"

"Of course, let me just get Bree in," she gives a sweet smile as she slips out the back door.

I stroke her tiny hands with my finger and she locks her grip around it and I feel my throat thicken as I choke out a tear.

"Okay, you ready?" Susan asks as she pulls the baby's crib out and my dad nods, eyes on his newborn and I reluctantly pull my finger away. Missing it instantly. We walk slowly towards where Amora is resting and her eyes light up when she sees her husband walk round the door with their little bundle. I look down the hallway, but Keaton is nowhere to be seen and I rub the ache from my chest.

"Amora," I breathe, walking into the room, "she is beautiful."

"She really is, isn't she."

I nod. "And so tiny," my voice is a little higher as a permanent smile graces my face.

"She weighed six pound four." Amora tells me as dad

hands their daughter into her arms. Amora kisses the top of her head, and she stirs, a little squeak leaving her.

"And her name?" I wait.

"Twyla," Amora says softly and I look at my dad then back at her.

"Twyla?" I repeat.

"It means Twilight," and then it clicks. My dad's favorite time of the day and Amora, his wife's, nickname.

"Oh, it's perfect," I clasp my hands and Amora turns her face towards me.

"Would her big sister like a cuddle?" and I have never held my arms out as quick as I just did.

"Do you even have to ask?" I laugh, scooping her up and making sure to hold her head as I let her rest in my arms.

"Hey princess," I coo, sniffling. I hadn't even noticed the tear that escaped is now rolling down my cheek. "I'm your big sister, I promise to always be there for you, promise to always be the cool one when your mum and dad say no..." and as I flick my eyes up to my dad he raises his brows, "I'll be your best friend," and my heart thumps against my rib cage.

"Plus, you will have some friends to play with soon," I blink back another wave of tears and swallow the apple sized lump.

I stroke the soft and delicate skin of her cheek with the side of my index finger and an all-consuming love prickles over me.

"I love her so much," I look at my dad and Amora, "thank you for taking the job dad and thank you for doing all the stuff I don't want to think about you doing, so you could have her," they both laugh, and my dad is at Amora's side, scooping her hand in his and planting a soft kiss on the back of it.

"Bet your mom and dad are over the moon for their first grandchild," I sigh, slowly rocking from side to side.

"They are, I mean, it's not what they wanted for their twenty-five-year-old but," Amora laughs just as Xavier and Royal step into the room.

"What didn't they want?" Royal's brows raise, "Hey Arizona."

Amora ignores her mother's question.

"Hey," I nod and Xavier knocks my dad out the way and presses a kiss to the top of his daughter's head and I let out a low chuckle.

"Morning Arizona," Xavier stands, folding his hands into his pockets, "where is your husband?"

"No idea," I throw a scowl at my dad, "he was sent away, was told he wasn't welcome," venom seeps through my voice.

"Well, that's not ideal is it." He turns to face my dad. "Titty, you should treat your son-in-law with how you would expect to be treated by your own father-in-law," and I don't miss the condescending tone.

"I do, I treat him like shit because that's how you treat me," my dad snipes and Amora sighs, Royal shakes her head from side to side.

"Now, now *boys*," she mocks, placing her hand on her husband's forearm, giving him a look that only he knows.

"Fine," Xavier rolls his eyes in an exaggerated manner. "As far as son-in-laws go, you really aren't that bad. It could have been a lot worse."

"No shit," my dad scoffs and that's when the room fills with a piercing little cry, and everyone falls silent. I step towards Amora and hand her over to her. She soothes her and Titus is there helping her remove her top so Twyla can latch on.

"Titus, close your eyes, stop looking," Xavier booms across the room as he turns away from his daughter so she can nurse in peace.

"Dad!" Amora shouts at him and Titus chuckles, shaking his head.

"I'm going to take that as my cue to leave," I smile, reaching up and undoing the tie on my gown and discarding it into the bin in the corner of the room.

"Sunshine," my dad looks at me confused, Amora facing me too, perfect brows pinched. "You don't have to leave."

"I know," I smile, rubbing my own bump, "but I'll see you a bit later yeah? thanks for inviting me to meet Twyla."

My dad stands tall and walks towards me, pulling me in for a hug, lingering for a moment or two.

"Love you baby," he kisses the top of my head and I give him a squeeze.

"You too," I step back and give Amora a kiss on the cheek. Waving to Xavier and Royal, I walk out the room and that's when I see Keaton.

Standing at the end of the hallway with a crooked smile on his face and looking as handsome as ever. We walk towards each other, my arms throwing around his neck as his lips slant over mine.

"Take me home," I whisper.

"Always, Blossom," he kisses me once more, "always."

CHAPTER FIFTY-ONE
KEATON

Sitting at my desk, I am lost in my spreadsheet when Kaleb knocks on the door.

"Got a minute?" he asks, and I nod, locking my screen and sitting back in my chair.

"What's up?"

"We've got an update with Wolfe; I'm pulling everyone in for a meeting at lunchtime. Work with you?"

I check the time and sigh.

"Yeah, fine. We have a doctor appointment at three so as long as we're wrapped up by then."

"Yup that will be fine." I nod. "Cool, see you at twelve. Lunch is being ordered soon."

"Perfect," I nod as he walks out the room, closing the door behind him.

I get I need to be kept in the loop, but I do feel I am kind of irrelevant in it all. Sure, the man is an absolute cunt. Granted. Will die on that hill, happily. But me and Arizona are not involved. I just want to stay in the bubble that we're currently in. Sighing, my eyes cast to the photo of me and her on my desk, the night we got married in Vegas, and for just a moment, I want to go back to that night.

My heart thumps, ignoring the way it skips a couple of beats and I bury my head back into my computer until I am called.

ARIZONA

Pushing through the doors of the small coffee shop, the sweet pastry smell mixed with coffee beans makes my stomach grumble. Why am I hungry? I haven't stopped eating this morning. Sage seeks me out before I notice her in the busy shop. Her hand waves me over and I make my way through the crowd. A small smile purses against my lips and she stands, kissing me on the cheek.

"How do you look so good?" I groan. Her bump is small and round, figure curvaceous and thick. She is stunning. Drop dead. Then there's me. Swollen hands, feet, stomach feels double the size.

"I don't, I am just wearing a black dress. Hides all my lumps and bumps," she laughs as we take our seats and I wrap my hands round the hot chocolate Sage has already bought me.

"I'm just going to grab a muffin; do you want one?" I ask, pushing myself away from the table but she shakes her head from side to side. I choose a chocolate chip muffin and my mouth is already watering. Heading back to my seat, I smile. "So," I let out a breathy sigh, "what's new?" I pick at my muffin, popping it past my lips.

"Not a lot," she smirks, "missed you. I'm ready to have

this baby now though, aren't you?" she sips her hot chocolate.

"Sort of," I shrug, "a bit scared," I admit.

"You wouldn't be human if you weren't," she reaches across the table and places her hand over mine.

"It's just gone so quick hasn't it."

She nods.

"How's work been?" I ask and guilt consumes me. She made me manager and then I handed my notice in. I just couldn't face it anymore. Being pregnant and flaunting my body for greedy eyes and hands.

"Busy, I have pulled back now and left Dex in charge," she smirks, "he is enjoying it."

"That's good, how are the girls?"

I only care about one. Well, not sure if care is the right word anymore. Me and Lucy fell out after I found out about her message to Keaton. He messaged her and told her that we were married and to leave him alone. She didn't. Then she took it upon herself to start harassing me. I blocked her and cut her out of my life. Snip snip.

I have enough going on, what with the messages from *TallDarkandHandsome*. I really need to tell Keaton but it just doesn't feel like the right thing to do at the moment.

"Yeah they're good, all keeping busy. It's not the same without you..." she pauses and places her mug on the table. "Will you be back?"

It takes me a moment to answer, but not because I don't know what to say, but because I feel guilty. I shake my head from side to side, dropping my eyes as I watch my fingers pick away at the muffin.

"That's fair," and I don't miss the sadness in her voice, "but we will still stay friends, right?"

"Of course," I lift my eyes to look at her, head tilted to the side and now it's my turn to reach for her hand, brushing my thumb back and forth over her tattooed skin. "You're stuck with me now, plus, our kids will be the best of friends."

"I really hope so," she rubs her lips together, "we have Dex's half-brother, but he won't be interested in the baby when it comes. He's six, he is more interested in football," she scoffs. "Plus, Rhaegar, Dex's dad, still lives in England with his wife, Shay." She casts her gaze down, crossing one leg over the other as she flicks her long, black hair over her shoulder.

"Well, ours will be the best of friends," and I mean it.

"I really do hope so."

Both of our smiles reach our eyes, and we fall into easy conversation before I have to leave to meet Keaton for our scan. I was always excited before, but we have to have them every two weeks to make sure that the twins were growing well and numerous other checks.

Stepping onto the sidewalk, Keaton pulls up just like he promised. Walking forward, I open the door and he gives me the most handsome smile.

"Hey baby," his voice is low as I slip in beside him, "how was Sage?" he asks as I buckle myself in and he pulls onto the road.

"Yeah good, was nice to see her. I've missed her," I rest my hand on my bump as twin A kicks into it., my other hand rubbing my temple, my head is pounding. "How was your day?"

"Boring," he smirks, turning to face me, "but I am excited to see the babies, are you?"

"Yeah," I breathe, my heart racing, "I am."

"Are you okay?" he asks.

"Yeah, fine, just had this splitting headache since last

night and I can't seem to get rid of it," I sigh, rubbing my belly. Truth was, I was worried about pre-eclampsia. Swelling, headaches... I mean, it could *just* be pregnancy, but I knew the signs.

"Well, when we're done, how about movie and snacks on the sofa?"

"With ice?" I blush, resting my head on the car seat.

"Definitely," he reaches for my hand and brushes his lips against the back of it.

CHAPTER FIFTY-TWO
KEATON

THE MEETING WAS DRAWN OUT. WOLFE IS GETTING CLOSER, AND Titus and Xavier are getting jumpy. I know how he treated Amora and I get they want his blood, but I'm not sure if this is the right thing. Is he a threat? Yes. Do I think he will come for Arizona? No, and that's all I care about.

Arizona and the babies.

They're my world. All I care about.

Titus is trying to put provisions in place like moving Amora and Twyla into her mom and dad's home on the upper east side. They can hide her tracks from Wolfe, the hunter. He has some obsession with her, maybe it was because they were due to be married, maybe because she was part of a transaction. Xavier fucked up. Big time. I'm sure you know the story so I won't bore you with it again.

I find a parking spot a couple of blocks away and put some quarters into the meter. We walk hand in hand towards Dr Kyra's office and I don't miss the little spring in Ari's step.

"You're in a good mood," I scoot her over to the inside of

the sidewalk, so I'm roadside. Don't like the thought of her being near the road.

"I am looking forward to seeing the babies," she admits, a glint of something in her ice blue eyes. I could lose myself in them, drown in them completely. Never wanting to resurface, even if that meant I had to give my last breath. For her, I would. Every single time.

Climbing up the steps to the doctors, we buzz through and check in with the receptionist. We sit and wait in the clean office, and for some reason, nerves float through me and cramp my stomach and she senses it in a heartbeat. Of course she does. My leg is bouncing up and down, but her palm is pressing against my thigh and a calmness crashes over me like a wave against sand.

The door swings open and an impeccably dressed Dr Kyra walks out into the quiet waiting room and calls Arizona's name. She stands first, then me. Her fingers brush against mine and I link mine through hers. Desperate to feel the rush from her touch, to feel the way my skin tingles from my head to my toes.

"How are you both?" Kyra asks but I keep quiet. I am fine. It's not about me. It's about Ari.

"Yeah okay, achy. My stomach feels so heavy."

"Well, that's understandable. You're what, thirty-one weeks now?"

"Thirty, plus five," I correct her and give Ari a slow wink.

Kyra smiles at me and starts tapping on her computer.

"But apart from what you mentioned, you're feeling well?"

Ari nods.

"Okay, let's get your blood pressure checked as-well as your sample."

I shuffle out the way, not wanting to get in Kyra's way. I tap my fingers gently on my denim covered thigh to keep my mind busy. No idea why I worry when I'm in here. Always do.

"Your blood pressure is quite high, mind if I do it again?" and my ears prick at Kyra's words. I turn to face Ari and scan her face for something but I'm not sure what.

"No," Ari says softly, as Kyra presses the button, and the band begins to inflate.

I watch as Kyra looks at the numbers and pinches her brows.

"Okay, let's give it a minute."

"Is everything okay?" I ask, Ari stays mute.

"Arizona's blood pressure is 145/90, it's very high. I worry about pre-eclampsia. I would like to see if she has any protein in her sample, then re-do her blood pressure."

I nod. I am trying to keep calm, I really am. Slipping my phone from my pocket, I look up at Ari and give her a reassuring smile. She smiles back, but it's forced. She's worried.

"It'll be okay," I say softly as Kyra walks out of the office.

"Will it?" she blinks at me, waiting for me to tell her yes.

"Yes baby," my hand is on her thigh, and I give her a gentle and reassuring squeeze. Now it was my time to calm her down.

Hate that I have lied to her.

She looks away, and I type a quick google search. Shouldn't have done that.

Definitely shouldn't have done that.

Early delivery.
High risk of complication.
Stillbirth.

I lock my phone; fear strikes through my chest like a lightning bolt.

The door clicks and Kyra is back in the room and walking towards her desk.

"Okay, so you have protein in your urine, along with the high blood pressure..." she pauses for a moment, "I would like to do a blood test, just to see if it could be pre-eclampsia."

Moving my hand over hers, her fingers slip through mine, and I squeeze her hand tightly. She nods, and I can see the glisten of the unshed tears in her eyes.

"It'll be okay baby," I say again but I feel awful because I have no idea if it will be okay.

"If it is pre-eclampsia, we will monitor it. If we need to intervene, then your babies will be delivered earlier. It's a lot safer for us to do that then to let you carry to potentially full term and expose yourself and the twins to risks."

She says nothing. Just stares ahead.

Kyra buzzes through for the nurse and the same lady toddles out with her trolley, trays and needle.

"Hello Ari, how are you?" the older woman's voice fills the room. Ari looks up at her and smiles through the unshed tears that are threatening.

"I'm good, are you okay?" she asks as the nurse slips the needle into her skin and draws two tubes of blood.

"I am wonderful, thank you," she nods, placing the needle down then putting a band aid over the crease of Ari's elbow.

"Good, that's good to hear," she nods, and the nurse says goodbye before walking back out of the room.

"Please try not to worry, we will keep a very close eye on you if it turns out be that. I know it's easier said than done, but it's better to catch it now, then to catch it a few weeks down the line."

My heart aches in my chest.

"We will have to wait a bit for the results so let's get you scanned so you can see your babies, yeah?" Kyra tries to keep her tone upbeat for Ari's sake but it's not helping. I stand, Ari's hand back in mine as I walk her over to the bed. She looks numb. Completely numb. I can see her trying to process all that Kyra has said, but honestly, I think it is going in one ear and out the other.

Arizona lays down, lifting her oversized tee up and under her chest. Kyra squirts the gel onto her belly and an uncomfortable silence fills the room. Tension brews and I hate it for Ari. This is not what she was expecting today. But within seconds, that silence has gone, and the room is filled with two heartbeats galloping. I lean forward, my hand still linked with hers as I look at the screen and see our babies wriggling and moving which causes Ari's belly to move and pulse.

"They've got so big," she whispers, eyes glued to the screen, but my eyes are glued to her. The way the worry washes off her face in an instant, her lips parting and forming a beautiful smile and bearing all of her teeth. She has the most picture-perfect smile. I wipe a stray tear that runs down the side of her face away with my thumb pad and my chest tightens.

"All is looking great Ari, the babies are growing nicely. If I was to estimate, they're probably around two pounds, maybe. Twin B is a little smaller, but that is normal with twins," she places the probe back into its holder and wipes Ari's belly.

"How long will you keep them in for if my results come back showing I have pre-eclampsia?"

"Ideally, a few weeks. But it'll be weekly monitoring, and if things are getting worse then we will deliver the babies," she smiles sweetly at Arizona and I help her sit up.

"And they'll be okay? If they had to be born early?" we wait on bated breath for her to answer.

"We can't promise anything, but we would hope they would be perfectly fine being born early."

And that's when she breaks. All I can do is pull her into me and comfort her.

<hr />

ARIZONA

The wait feels like a lifetime. I know it's probably thirty minutes if that, but still, right now, thirty minutes feels like a lifetime.

I knew it was pre-eclampsia. As soon as she said about my blood pressure, all my symptoms made sense

"You're being so brave," Keaton whispers, sitting as close as he can to me, hand wrapped around mine. Normally I would find a comment like that condescending but not now. Not since being with Keaton because I know he generally cares about me.

I turn my face to look at him, a weak smile playing against my lips.

I don't feel brave. I feel like a scared little girl.

My eyes lift and find Kyra as she walks into the room with my notes folder.

"So?" Keaton asks the question for me and squeezes my hand.

"Arizona, you do have pre-eclampsia," I see the grimace on her face and my heart drops. "You will need to go onto bedrest until we decide to intervene. I would like to admit you tonight."

"Can I bring her in tomorrow? Just let her have one last night at home. I promise to keep an eye on her," he pleads and my heart flutters in my chest.

"If by tomorrow you mean eight a.m. sharp, then yes, for you two... I will allow it," she looks up through her lashes at Keaton and he glides his finger over his heart in a *'cross my heart'* gesture.

"You've got a promise."

"Good," she gives him a nod then turns to face me, eyes soften, and a ghost of a smile on her lips. "And Ari, I know it sounds scary, but I am hoping the twins can stay inside as close to your due date as possible. We will be monitoring you daily, blood work, urine samples, blood pressure tests and of course more scans." She closes my notes. "And if we get to the point where we need to get the babies out, then we will carry out a caesarean to remove them safely."

"A caesarean?" my blood pumps loudly in my ears. I start to panic, my chest tightening, eyes widening as they stay pinned to Kyra. I have insurance, but what if they don't cover it.

"Yes, it's the safest way, even if you didn't have pre-eclampsia I would have pushed for an elective c-section for the twins delivery."

All I can do is nod.

"Think of the babies," Keaton reminds me and I breath out a shaky breath.

I nod again.

"Do you have any questions?" She asks, turning her attention to her computer.

Millions.

"No," my voice is quiet.

"Okay, well you have my number," she looks up at me and smiles before averting her gaze to Keaton, "and we will see you and Arizona at eight a.m. tomorrow morning?"

"We will be there, New York-Presbyterian?"

She shakes her head from side to side.

"No, can you bring her to Ancien St. Clair's? I would like her monitored there."

"Of course."

"Wonderful," she stands as we do, Keaton's fingers linked with mine as Kyra shows us out. "Enjoy your evening and I will see you tomorrow."

"Thank you," I say, dipping my head as we walk out of the doctor's office and onto the sidewalk. I pause for a moment, closing my eyes and inhaling deeply as I fill my lungs with the cold, fresh air. The winter sun on my face and honestly, it's never felt as good as it does now.

"You okay?" Keaton asks.

"Perfect," I grumble.

"Let me date you tonight, we have never been on a date. We're married, well... at least I think we are," Keaton's words slice through me, bringing me back down to reality with a thud.

"We are... it's just been a little..." I pause.

"I know."

My eyes fall to his chest and my heart aches knowing he is wearing my wedding band around his neck.

"I'm sorry I have never spent the time actually dating you though, we sort of just skipped that part," he runs his hand round the back of his neck, his lips lifting at one side.

"We did, didn't we," I scrunch my nose as I focus on him. Green eyes soft, hair wavy and styled, brown stubble with flecks of grey scattered through like salt and pepper, high cheek bones and devilishly handsome as always.

"Ari," he pulls me back to him.

"Mmhm," I hum just as his fingers lace through mine, his body pressed against mine.

"Be mine? In every single fucking way, *please*," the last word drips off his tongue like a beg, "Be my girlfriend, my wife, my soulmate, my best friend."

My eyes dance with his, my heart beating along to the same rhythm as his.

"Always," I smile through my whisper of an answer.

And right there, on the sidewalk of sixth avenue, Keaton Mills, my dad's best friend finally asked me to be his. It didn't matter that we were both already legally bound. This moment right here meant so much more.

I was his. He was mine.

Always. Infinite. Forever.

CHAPTER FIFTY-THREE
KEATON

ARI IS DRESSED TO THE NINES. BLACK MID LENGTH DRESS THAT hugs every single curve and high black stilettos that are enough to make me weep.

She perches herself on the edge of the seventh step, and I am knelt on the bottom. My mind flashes back to our night on the stairs, the night she told me she was moving out, the same night she told me to fucking crawl and I did it. I'm not even ashamed. Not even now. I would fucking crawl anywhere she asked me to.

Her foot presses against my chest, white shirt between my skin and her shoe. My fingers fumble with the delicate strap that wraps around her ankle and once buckled, I lean down and place a soft kiss on her exposed ankle. I repeat with her other foot. Helping her up, I guide her down the stairs but stop her from stepping off the bottom one.

I kneel once more, my mouth pressed against her bump.

"I love you two so much," my hand rubs gently, and I feel one of my twins kick my hand.

"They love you too," she smiles down at me, and I

stand, an arm wrapped around her back, the other cupping her face, "and I love you."

"I love you," she smiles at me, just as my lips press against hers and for just a moment, the world slips away from beneath us.

———

WE RIDE IN A TAXI DOWN TOWARDS COLUMBUS CIRCLE AND THE evening is busy. I pay the fair then open the door and once I am on the sidewalk, I lean down and hold my hand out for her to take. Slowly, she steps onto the sidewalk and I steady her once both of her heels are firmly on the ground.

Her poor feet are already swollen but she was determined to wear her heels and dress up pretty for date night.

Fingers linked, we head towards The Museum of Art and Design.

"Where are we going?" she asks quietly as I get the door.

"For food," I smile at her, wiggling my brows as I state the obvious.

"Duh," she swats me as I lead her to the elevator, and we ride to the top of the museum in silence. Stepping into the dimly lit but tasteful restaurant, we're taken to our seats, and we have the most beautiful view of Central Park. We're handed drink menus, and we browse whilst the waiter hovers.

"May I get you both a drink?"

"I'll have a glass of the Two Rows cabernet sauvignon please," I hand him back the menu before he turns his attention to Arizona. And I take this moment to just look at her.

I don't think I have ever felt as overwhelmed with love than I do now. All the worries of this afternoon have slowly slipped from me. I bask in the moment. She is breath-taking in every sense of the word but seeing how she glows, the way her body has changed into something truly breath-taking whilst she is carrying two babies is just beautiful. She is beautiful. Truly.

"I'll have a scarlet glow iced tea please," and she hands him back the menu.

"Certainly, I'll be back soon with your drinks," he says before walking away. My hand reaches forward to take hers in mine.

"Thank you for this, I never realized how much I needed a date night," she smirks, eyes glistening.

"No need to thank me, I'm annoyed at myself for not doing this sooner." I admit and guilt twists my gut. "I'm also sorry for not giving this to you sooner," I rasp, leaning back for a moment as I tuck my hand into the inside of my pocket and pull out the small box that was sitting in my closet for far too long.

Her eyes fall to the ribbon wrapped box before they're on me.

"What's this?" she whispers, fingers playing with the ribbon.

"You'll have to open it and find out," I tease, tongue in cheek.

Her cheeks flame as she gently tugs on the ribbon and lets it unravel. She picks at the black wrapping paper a little too carefully and reveals a black velvet box.

I'm hoping she likes it. Well, loves it.

Connie and Reese gifted her a pretty ring with her birthstone and a delicate charm bracelet and suddenly I feel like my gift will be underwhelming.

She opens the lid, slowly, agonizingly slowly might I add, and I see the way the tears pool in her eyes.

"Keaton," she whispers, her blue eyes find mine and all I can do is smile. My heart is racing in my chest as I focus on nothing but her. I blur everything else around us out for a millisecond.

"Marry me," I smirk and she laughs, "okay, so yes, I know we're married but we did it ass way up. I wanted to at least be able to give you an engagement ring."

She nods, tears rolling down her cheeks. I reach for the box and pull out the engagement ring. A teardrop shaped three carat diamond that sits on a thin gold band. I turn it slightly so she can see the engraving on the inside.

'10.22.2023 – the date time stood still.'

"Keaton," she chokes as she holds out her trembling left hand and I slip it on with ease, and I hold her hand for a while longer, brushing my thumb across the back of her fingers.

"And when you're ready, your wedding band is yours."

She cocks her head to the side and smiles.

"Here are your drinks." The waiter returns, and our hands slip apart as he places our drinks onto the table, he pulls out his pad ready to take our order, but I'm not hungry anymore.

I am obsessed with her. Wholly.

My wife. My soulmate. My best friend.

CHAPTER FIFTY-FOUR
ARIZONA

I WANT TO SAY I HAD THE BEST NIGHT'S SLEEP LAST NIGHT, BUT I would be lying. Shock.

I slept awfully but I think a lot of it was to do with nerves. I had to go into hospital for a couple of weeks so they could keep me monitored and I hated the idea of being away from everyone. And when I say everyone, I mean Keaton.

I needed to tell my dad and the girls, but honestly, I just didn't want to at the moment. My dad was in his newborn bubble and I just feel like everything that has my name attached to it is drama.

"Ready?" Keaton asks me as he loads my bag into the trunk of the car, and I nod.

I'm not. But I have to do what is best for me and the babies. I need to stop being selfish for a moment.

Kyra said that Keaton is welcome to live in the room with me, but I told him not to. The odd sleepover, yes, but he is so busy at work, and I don't want him to fall even more behind because of me.

Climbing into the jeep, Keaton leans over and straps me in and makes sure the seatbelt sits under my bump.

"Do we have everything?" I ask as he pulls onto the road.

"Yes baby, we checked the bag three times."

"What about the babies' stuff."

"It's all prepped, remember? Let's just focus on you yeah. Everything else can be handled when it needs to be," his hand slips between my thighs and I know he is right.

I sigh as I watch the trees blur past the window and anxiety swarms in my tummy, my heart thumping harder with each mile that brings us closer to the hospital.

"Everything will be okay," Keaton says as we pull into a space outside the hospital. I feel a little at ease already seeing that where I will be staying doesn't look too much like a hospital. Pushing the car into park, Keaton is out and by my side within seconds as he helps me out.

"I am hungry," Keaton rolls his eyes, laughing softly as he shakes his head from side to side.

"I have spent all morning asking what you want and you told me nothing because you were not hungry, and as soon as we get here, you choose to be hungry now?"

"It's not my fault, it's the babies," I shrug my shoulders up.

"Let's get you settled then I will go and get you whatever you want," he steps towards me, placing a soft kiss on my forehead and I tame the butterflies he makes me feel every single time.

Hand in hand, he leads me into the hospital.

"Okay, so checks are done, one of my nurses will be back in a couple of hours to check on you," Kyra smiles as she pops my chart back at the foot of the bed.

"I'm going to run out and grab Arizona some food and snacks, is that okay?"

"Of course," she turns her body towards me and smiles, "of course, Ari will have the option to eat here too and I swear, the food is really good. Plus, the chocolate pudding is to die for," she winks at me, "I'll see you soon," and then she's gone.

"You okay?" Keaton sits on the edge of my bed and tucks a loose strand of hair behind my ear.

I nod.

"Do you want me to call your dad?"

"No, leave it for the minute. He has enough going on with having a new born at home. You tell him, he will panic and then be up here. I don't want to stress him out."

"Okay," he leans in and kisses me softly. "What do you want to eat?"

My stomach grumbles on cue.

"A decaf oat latté, tomato soup and grilled cheese," and I am drooling at just the thought of it.

"Of course, Blossom," he stands and I already miss him.

"And snacks. Chocolate, fruit, chips and cereal. Please don't forget cereal."

"I would never," he winks, "if you need anything you call me, okay?"

"Okay," my eyes flutter, he smiles and my heart melts in my chest. He walks towards the door, pressing his hands to his lips as he blows a kiss. I reach up, catching it and tuck it against my heart.

"That ring looks real pretty on your finger, wife."

I giggle, shaking my head and once he is out the room, I look down at it.

"It really does," I sigh.

I'VE NOT BEEN ALONE LONG WHEN THE CALMNESS I WAS FEELING listening to the sound of the babies heartbeats soon fizzles into sheer panic.

We have nothing done at home. Things have been ordered. The cribs are not arriving for another two weeks. The nursery isn't painted. None of their clothes are washed. Fuck.

Unfortunately, by the time Keaton walks through the door, I am in full panic mode. My heart rate is through the roof, eyes streaming and snot bubbling from my nose. Really not my finest or most attractive moment but it's real.

"Baby, what's happened?" he drops the bags, and then my coffee and cartons on the bed table and rushes towards me. His large hands cup my face, eyes flitting back and forth as he searches for anything to give him a hint. "Are you okay?" he asks as my breath shudders on my intake, and I nod, but soon move from a nod to a shake.

"Talk to me Blossom, I can't help if you don't tell me."

I sniffle, trying to drop my head but he doesn't let me.

"Eyes on me, breathe baby," he whispers, and I do, for the first time in what feels like hours, I breathe.

"There's a good girl, slow breaths in and out for me."

"I panicked."

He lets out a low laugh, "I guessed that." He drops one hand from my face and places it on my bump, "But it's no good for you or the babies, why were you panicking?"

I swallow the thickness away.

"We have nothing ready; the nursery is full of boxes and hasn't been decorated, the cribs aren't coming for weeks, none of their clothes are washed..." and my bottom lip trembles. His thumb brushes against my bottom lip, head tilting to the side but not once dropping his gaze from mine. "Baby, I promise everything will be ready for when they come home," and it takes me a moment to realize what he said.

Then it floors me.

They won't be coming home with us straight away. If the twins are born early, they will have to stay in neonatal until they can breathe on their own.

"They won't be coming home," I whisper because saying the words out loud are too raw.

"They will, they just won't be coming home with us straight away," he corrects me, and I nod, head tipping forward and this time he lets me. Keaton pulls me into him, and I have no idea how long we stay in this embrace, but it feels like forever.

I HAD BEEN HERE FOR FOUR DAYS, AND I WAS ALREADY LOSING MY mind. Keaton had popped down to grab coffees and I missed him. A smile graces my face when the I feel twin A kick, and I place my hand there wanting to feel it again.

"Hey," my head lifts and Keaton rounds the corner with warm drinks and cakes.

"Hey," I drop my head and continue to feel the baby kick. Keaton places the bag and coffee cups on the table over my bed and places his hands on my stomach, his face lighting up when he feels the kicks and wriggles beneath his hands.

"I will never be over this," he says, smile wide and I think I may have fallen in love with him a little more.

"Me neither," I admit. We stay silent, enjoying the sound of the twins' heartbeats and the movements they're giving us and at this moment, everything feels perfect.

"Sir, you can't just go in there," we hear Becca, our midwife call out into the hallway. Keaton is up off the bed and rushing to the door and I sit up in my bed, eyes wide and frantic, heart racing beneath my skin.

"Yes I can," and my blood runs cold. Fuck.

My dad bolts through the door, and he is seething. Nostrils flared, eyes bloodshot and bulging and his fists are balled at his side.

"What the fuck?" Keaton steps forward to try and barricade the tornado that is my dad off but it's useless. He knocks him out the way causing Keaton to stumble back and fall onto the sofa.

"You're dead to me," his jaw clenches, his voice tight and venomous as he angrily points his finger at my husband.

"What?" Keaton rolls himself up, standing toe to toe with my dad.

"Can we get security please, labor ward." Becca stands in the doorway and the blood is pumping in my ears harshly.

"You're quick to tell me that my daughter dropped out of med school to become a fucking stripper, but you didn't think to tell me that she was in hospital?" my dad shoves Keaton in the chest with force and my heart fucking drops into the pit of my stomach being disintegrated into nothing as my stomach acid burns all that's left of my broken and weeping heart.

"She didn't want to tell you," Keaton says, not budging when my dad is chest to chest with him.

"*You* should have told me."

"You told him?" my voice is a whisper, my lungs burning as they heave, craving for air but I can't breathe. The beeping of the monitor quickens, and all I can hear is screaming and shouting. There's commotion, things smashing on the floor, but I can't see any of it. Everything is a blur.

"Get your fucking hands off of me," I hear my dad shout, a high ring silencing them out for just a moment before my eyes re-adjust and focus. My dad is being dragged out by two security guards, but he is fighting them with everything he has. Keaton is standing, panting, hands on his hips but his head is turned towards me. His hair is a mess, eyes filled with regret and a busted lip and nose. He doesn't wipe the blood away; just lets it trickle.

"You told him?" the crack in my voice is evident, my tears rolling down my cheeks even though I didn't want them to fall. I'm wilted like a rose, losing all hope and the will I had left inside of me has slowly been taken from me. He was the sun I so desperately needed but he didn't care. He tucked himself away and left me when I needed him.

"Ari... baby," he takes a step towards me.

"Don't," my voice is hoarse as I shout at him.

"Let me," he takes another step.

"Get out," I turn my face away from him and point to the door.

"Please," his own voice cracking so I squeeze my eyes shut so I don't have to look at him. Because I am weak. Hot tears escape and run down the side of my face.

"Just go," I choke out, a sniffling weak mess crying over him.

Silence fills the tension that suffocates the room for a few seconds before I hear the sound of his footsteps skate across the tiles and then the closed door follows, and only then do I let myself turn towards where he just was.

Coffees spilled; table knocked over, pure devastation caused in short five minutes.

He broke my trust, snapped the tie between us in a second.

He told him.

CHAPTER FIFTY-FIVE
KEATON

IT ALL HAPPENED SO QUICKLY.

I knew I shouldn't have said anything, but in that moment weeks ago, it seemed like the right time. Idiot. I was a fucking idiot.

I walk towards the exit of the hospital, head dropped, lip throbbing, nose feels like it's broken. Probably is. Titus has a solid right hook. She told me to go. She didn't want me there. I fucked up.

Exhaling a shaky breath, the cool air hits me as soon as I step out the front of the hospital and that's when I see Titus. The security guards have roughed him up a bit and he is sitting on the curb, head in his hands.

I fold my hands into my pockets and walk across to him, perching myself next to him. Slowly, ever so slowly, does he lift his head from his hands and look at me. Eyes darkening within a matter of seconds.

"What do you want?" he hisses, face turning away from me as he looks up the quiet road.

"Nothing," I admit. And it's the truth. I don't.

"Then why are you out here?"

"She didn't want me in there," I shrug my shoulders up, bringing my knees to my chest and resting my arms.

He laughs.

"I didn't tell her." I lick my lip then wince as the sting presents itself.

"Figured that one out," he says sarcastically. Neither of us say a word. We get an odd look from a passer-by and I just hold my hand up, giving a small smile which has them walking that bit faster.

"You should have."

"I should have what?"

"Told her."

I scoff. Preaching to the choir.

"I should have done a lot of things," I nod, letting my head drop, my eyes pinned to the road.

"Is not falling in love with my daughter one of those?"

"Not for one second. I will always love Arizona." I roll my shoulders back and look him dead in the eye. "That will never change. But just so you know," I sniff, touching my left nostril with the tip of my index finger and wiping some blood away, "this wasn't what I had planned when you asked me to watch her. Nothing happened for a while, we were like passing ships in the night until I bumped into her at work."

I see the look of horror on his face.

"No, not like that," I shake my head from side to side knowing full well what he thinks.

Silence crackles between us and I sigh, heavily.

"I'm mad at you," he states, and I roll my eyes.

"Yeah, I get it."

"No, you don't." Titus stands and looks down at me still sitting on the curb. "You were my best friend. I trusted you to look after my daughter. Out of all the

410

women in this city, I don't understand why you had to choose her."

"I didn't choose her," my tone flat as I look forward.

"She chose you?"

A snort of a laugh leaves me.

"It just happened. Right moment, right time."

"She is my daughter."

"Yes, I know," my tone was a little condescending there, granted. "It doesn't change anything Titus," and that's when his hand grabs the collar of my shirt and drags me up to my feet.

"What happens when you get bored of her and decide to go back to your playboy ways?" his eyes bounce between mine.

"Playboy ways?" I crinkle my brows, scrunching my nose up and ignoring the throb that pulses across my face.

"Yeah, 'cause let's be honest Keaton. You're hardly husband material, let alone da..." and he doesn't have a chance to even finish his sentence. I launch myself at him. My hand is on his stupid face as I push it, Titus's hands are on my shoulders as he tries to shove me back. Sliding my elbow back, my fist jolts forward and lands on his jaw causing him to lose his stature for a moment. Anger seeps out of me with every fist I throw, but he blocks every single one thereafter. I step back, panting as I shake my head.

"What the fuck gives you the right to even say that to me?"

"I am looking out for Arizona, I will always protect her..." he steps towards me, "even if that means from you."

"I have never once hurt her or upset her until you, you big, tall, idiot came into the hospital room like a raging bull," I laugh a little, "so maybe I should be protecting her from you?"

And that winds him up.

"What?"

"Yeah, we were fine until you came in all angry and shit," I stand tall, as he steps towards me.

His eyes burn into mine, but he doesn't scare me. Never has. He can throw a punch, sure, but that's about it.

"I will never leave her, the only time I will is when she tells me to leave. But you? Nate? Kaleb? Killian?" I laugh, "fuck no, she's *my* wife, the mother of *my* children. I love her with everything I have and if that means losing you as a friend after all this time?" I pause for a moment, and I can see the rage filling Titus's eyes. "Then fine."

And that's when he unleashes his anger on me. But I don't take it this time. No, this time I fight back until we're both bruised, bloody and sitting back on the curb like two naughty schoolboys.

"Do you feel better?" I ask, poking the bear.

"Not remotely."

"That's a shame," I nod.

"I am done with this, with us," Titus groans as he stands up.

"Yeah?" I ask, looking up at him.

"Yeah," he nods before he turns and walks away.

Not going to lie, fucking broke my heart.

CHAPTER FIFTY-SIX
ARIZONA

He told him.

After everything we had been through, he told my dad my secret. A secret that wasn't his to tell yet he done it anyway no doubt for his own gain. My chest now hollow, where only moments ago my heart beat along to the pretty song that only he could hear. A song that only played for him. And now there was nothing. My chest ached. Emptiness caving in and cracking where he had once filled. Everyone I love in my life leaves. Whether that be my fault or theirs, they always leave and I am the only one it hurts.

My mom.

My dad.

Lucy.

Keaton.

Things will go back to normal with my dad eventually, but our wounds have only been patched up with band aids. But still. He left me, replaced me and now it's just me and my babies.

Alone. Again.

I catch the glisten of my engagement ring and hold it up in front of my face, a weak smile trembles across my lips.

How did it all fall apart that quick?

Letting my hand slowly fall into the duvet, I sink under it and cry myself to sleep. Because honestly, as much as he has hurt me, I've hurt myself more by telling him to leave.

I wake, eyes blurry and they feel swollen. I can hear movement in my room and slowly sit up to see a figure at the side of my bed, checking my monitors. I turn to look at the time, it's ten past ten. Not late, but also not the usual time Becca comes in.

"Hello?" I say to the gowned figure, the bottom of his face hidden behind a mask.

"Hello Arizona," dark eyes shimmer with a glint of uneasiness and my blood runs cold. I have no idea who this man is, but he isn't anyone I have met before.

Panic claws at my throat as I reach for the buzzer, but his hand is on my wrist, stopping me.

"Get off of me," I shout, before screaming but it doesn't help. He slaps his hand across my mouth and turns me to look at him before he rips his mask off.

And that's when I recognize the eyes.

His face.

Everything about him.

"Don't make a fucking sound, do you understand me?" his eyes bug, jaw sharp like glass and cheek bones hollowed.

I nod, eyes watering and I try my hardest not to cry in front of him.

"Good girl," his chilling voice sends shivers up and down my spine. "Now, I am going to lift my hand... you're not going to make a peep, are you?" he asks and I shake my head quickly.

He lifts his hand from my mouth, and I roll my lips. They hurt. He was forceful. My fingers spread on top of the covers to try and feel around for my phone but it's not there.

"Looking for this?" he catches me, and my phone is in his hands.

A whimper leaves me and just when I think he is going to hit me, or kill me, he smothers my mouth with a muslin cloth and it doesn't matter how much I try and fight it, it's useless. My body feels heavy, lungs burning, eyes closing and that's all I remember before my world goes black. Silent. Empty.

CHAPTER FIFTY-SEVEN
ARIZONA

MY EYES FINALLY OPEN AFTER TRYING CONTINUOUSLY, BUT MY head is groggy. I feel sick to my stomach and I have no idea where I am. I blink a couple of times and see I am in a white, sterile room. But it's quiet. There are no machines beeping, no babies' heartbeats, nothing.

I try to sit up, but I can't. I am strapped down to the bed by my ankles and wrists. Panic blankets me, heart racing frantically.

"Help!" I scream, my voice cracking where my throat is dry. "Please," I cry, "someone help me."

I see the door open, my heart skipping beats and that's when a tall, scrawny, black haired man walks in. Brown eyes seek out mine, an evil grin on his face.

"Well, good morning Arizona," he is next to me, fingers digging into my cheeks as he turns me to look at him. I have no idea why he chose me. The only link to him is through Dex and Sage.

"Stay away from me," I grit, but all he does is squeeze tighter.

"Can't do that *Vixen*."

And I feel my once warm blood turn to ice instantly, chilling me to my bone.

"Allow me to introduce myself," he leans closer to me, "I'm Wolfe, or, as you know me Tall Dark and Handsome."

I laugh. Hysterically laugh which causes him to drop his hand from my cheeks.

"I'm sorry, but you don't suit your chat name; for one, you're not handsome. In the slightest."

And I feel it. The skin on skin contact as he slaps the back of his hand across my cheek with an almighty blow.

My eyes sting with burning tears, my throat bobs and I struggle to catch my breath.

"Don't you dare, slut."

A name I have heard more than once, it doesn't sting like it used to.

"I've watched you long enough to know how you work, hard exterior most of the time, but inside, you're nothing but fluff. I will rip you limb from limb and pull the stuffing out of you. I am ready to make those who wronged me feel pain."

Confusion lays heavy over me.

"What have I got to do with any of that shit you're spilling?" I suck in a breath, my cheek bone and jaw throbbing from the contact.

"Well, for one, you're carrying my babies," he grins, dimples presenting in his cheeks and my stomach rolls with nausea. "Thank you for giving me your purity..." he rubs his hands together, "after being promised a virgin and given a whore, it was only right I took from you what was taken from me."

"You're talking in riddles," my voice trembles, but I know deep down where this conversation is going.

"Am I, Arizona?" he cocks his head as he walks to the

foot of the bed. "For someone who was well ahead of their class, you're pretty thick," he narrows his gaze on me, running his tongue over the front of his teeth.

I choose to ignore him, and instead, goad him. I want to hear the words come from his mouth.

"Pretty scar you have on your neck, shame they didn't cut a little deeper. I wouldn't have missed. I would have watched you bleed out at my feet and felt no remorse," I smirk, and I see how angry he becomes. He slowly steps around the bed and leans over me so his face is inches from mine. His hand is back round my cheeks, forcing me to look at him. The taste of copper fills my mouth, but I ignore it. Focused on looking at this coward in the eyes.

"You've kidnapped me for what reason? To prove something? To get the person who sliced your throat back here so you can take everything from him?"

A slow sickening smile pulls at the corner of his lips and my stomach rolls.

"I see you've worked it out." I swallow down the bile that is threatening to come up.

"Your dad did say how smart you were," and that's when I realize how this all loops back to my dad and Amora.

Promised a virgin.

His throat was cut on his wedding morning and left for dead.

But here he is. In front of me and with revenge in his blood.

I spit in his face, and he growls, wiping it off his face before another slap crashes against my skin.

"Enjoy the last few hours with those precious babies of yours, because soon, I will be cutting them out of you," he pushes my face back into my pillow with force and I am trying my hardest not to cry. "And don't think your daddy is coming to save you, he has no idea where you are."

I wince when the bedroom door slams shut and realization seeps in.

I am going to die here.

CHAPTER FIFTY-EIGHT
KEATON

I WENT HOME LAST NIGHT AFTER EVERYTHING WITH TITUS AND Ari. I needed to give her space, and honestly, I needed some thinking time, so I got started on the nursery. I cleaned the room of the boxes and placed them in the spare room. I stripped the wallpaper and painted the walls with an off-white paint. I had no idea how Ari wanted to decorate but I thought if we had a blank canvas, it would make it easier for her. I worked through the night and ignored the way my body cried for sleep. I wasn't giving in. I couldn't. I had too many emotions plaguing me. And now, I was driving to the hospital with Ari's favorite coffee and pastry. I'm nervous but excited. She won't forgive easily, she is her father's daughter after all.

Pulling into a space, I pull the sun visor down and slide the little cover across and wince when I see my face. One eye purple, lips swollen, and nose bruised and crooked. He definitely broke it. Sighing, I grab the coffee and slam the car door shut. Paying the meter, I slowly walk into the hospital and ignore the way people stare at me. I have no idea if they're even going to let me in the ward after yesterday, I mean, I wouldn't. Me and Titus were possessed. Anger got too much, and we snapped. It was going to happen. Of course it was. But I never thought he would walk away from me; I never thought our friendship would be over that quickly, but here we are.

Walking into the ward, I head for her room. I don't look at anyone, don't speak to anyone, just keep my head down but as I approach, people are standing outside her room. Two of them people being Kyra and Becca. Their voices quieten down as I approach, and I see worry etched into Kyra's face.

I ignore it, pushing down the gut feeling that something is wrong and walk into the empty room.

"Where the fuck is my wife?" I turn out of the room and my eyes are on Kyra.

"We have no idea, I thought after yesterday you or her dad may have taken her."

"Why would we take her out of hospital when we know she has to be here?" It doesn't make sense.

But then it does.

Fucking Titus.

I knock Kyra out the way, throwing the coffee and pastry in the bin as I run out of the ward.

"Where are you going?" Kyra calls after me.

"To find my fucking wife."

I boot my car all the way to Titus's house. No fucks were given. Pulling curb side, I rush out and bang on the door.

Bang. Bang. Bang.

I am frantic with worry, but I'm also so fucking angry.

He doesn't answer.

Bang. Bang. Bang. I thump my fist against the door. Amora opens the door, wide eyes filled with shock.

"Keaton, what is it?"

"Let me in." My tongue is harsh and I don't mean for it to be, well I do, but not with Amora.

"Calm down, you're scaring me." Her voice is quiet.

"Move out the way Amora or I'll...".

"Or you'll what?" Titus roars from behind his wife, moving her out the way and tucking her behind him. "Finish what you were going to say."

I let the anger simmer for a moment, wanting to be careful how I respond.

"Where's my wife?" I am desperate, you can hear it in my fucking voice. Titus's concrete facade soon softens, brows furrowing.

The longer this goes on, the more frantic I become.

"What?" Titus's voice softens slightly.

"Arizona. Where is she?" panic claws at my throat and I can tell by the way he is looking at me that he has no fucking idea what I am going on about.

"In the hospital?"

I shake my head from side to side, heart racing beneath my chest.

"What?" and the realization hits him. He is grabbing his keys and shoving me back but not before giving Amora a kiss.

"She's not there." I swallow the bile down that is threatening to spill.

"Not my Sunshine, fuck," he shouts.

Titus closes the front door behind him and we jog down the steps towards his parked Jeep. Titus's phone is pressed to his ear, and I know he is on the phone to Kaleb.

"We've got a problem, Arizona's missing, meet you at the office. Get Nate," he cuts the phone off just as he slams the car door shut. I climb into the passenger side and my fucking heart is thumping so hard.

My phone buzzes and I see Kaleb's name.

Kaleb
It'll be okay, brother.

I lock my phone and my throat thickens when I see the photo I snapped of her a few weekends ago in the kitchen. She is standing in front of the large window, wearing a cream cropped tee and black leggings that sat under her bump. She's holding a bowl of cereal and smiling at the camera, and I choke back, not wanting the tears to fall. Especially not in front of Titus of all people. I've got my own shit going on in my head, I would hate to know what is going on in his.

He punches his finger on the screen of his car as it dials Xavier's name.

"What?" the bite to his British accent makes me stiffen in my seat.

"Arizona is gone," Titus just about manages. He chokes up, fist balled and pressed against his lips.

"That cunt," Xavier growls

"Meeting at the office."

"I'll be right there," I can hear him moving around, "I'll grab Killian too," and then the phone cuts off.

The drive is short and quiet. Both of our minds are in overdrive, and I don't know about Titus but I am terrified.

Titus abandons the car in his spot and we're the first ones here. I follow Titus to the elevator, and we ride up in silence. There is so much I want to say but I don't. I stay mute and keep my thoughts on Arizona.

She will be okay. She has to be.

I stroll into the office, hands in my pocket and Titus rushes to his computer. I feel like a spare part. I have no idea what to do. I don't get involved in their operations much. I offer up a hand when needed but I crunch numbers. Not the same in working out a kidnapping. That's Titus and Kaleb. Nate too I suppose. He is the brains behind it. Will know the ins and outs.

"How certain are we that it's this Wolfe guy?" I squeeze the words out my tight throat. Wish my heart would slow. Feel like I can't catch a breath.

Titus is bent over his desk, fingers on his keyboard when he turns his face to look at me.

"One hundred fucking percent."

I grab the bin from the floor and empty the contents of my stomach.

"Shit," Titus groans, tutting as he walks past me to grab me a bottle of water from the fridge. He passes it to me and gives me a solid, hard, pat on the back and I swear he shifts a lung.

"Thanks," I grumble, opening the top and drinking half the bottle.

I feel like such an idiot for acting like this. She is Titus's blood, and he is cool and collected. Or is he? Beads of sweat appear on his brow, the vein in his neck throbs at a fast pace proving that his heart is racing just like mine is. He is agitated and fidgety. Fingers keep tapping, foot keeps shuffling and when he eventually takes a seat, his leg is bobbing up and down.

Kaleb bursts through the elevator and paces himself over to me with four long strides, wrapping his arms around my shoulders.

"We will get her back," he breaks away, hands on my cheeks as his eyes burn into mine and all I can do is nod. I heave in a deep breath and flashbacks from when Reese was taken plague me. My chest is hollow. Have never felt an emptiness like the one that consumes me in this moment.

He moves to Titus and gives him a shoulder squeeze and only then do I see the facade slip, the tears spilling in his eyes and when my brother consoles him, he breaks.

"Come on now lads," Xavier chimes walking in with Killian, "it aint a fucking funeral, is it? We will find the weasel cunt and end him before he can even lay a finger on Arizona."

"Would he hurt her?" I ask as Killian gives me a pat on the shoulder.

Titus and Xavi look at each other before their eyes land on me. They don't even have to say anything. I forgot Titus had to live with him and witness how he treated Amora. The man was as evil as they come.

I hadn't even noticed Nate sneak in. He was already deep in his computer.

Titus sits back down, and he looks wrecked all of a sudden.

"What time did you last see Ari?" Nate asks me and I hear a breathy sigh from Titus.

"Last night, me and Titus got into..."

"He didn't tell me Ari was in hospital, I only found out because Amora had an appointment with Dr Kyra. Conversations were had and *that's* how I found out my daughter was on bed rest in hospital."

"Wait," Killian stammers, "she's in hospital? Is she okay?"

"She's..." and I am cut off by Xavier.

"Enough of the pleasantries for fuck's sake, so, Nate, in answer to your question it was last night."

"Time?" Nate scrubs his face.

"Four? Maybe? I don't know," I slide down the wall and drop my head.

"Well, this is fucking brilliant. Nate, bring up the CCTV from four onwards. Kaleb, call Kyra."

"I'll do it, I already have her number saved," Killian says, and he already has his phone to his ear.

Kaleb just stares and Xavier gives a shrug of his shoulder.

"Okay, so yeah, both tweedle dee and tweedle dumb were at the hospital at four thirty," Nate says and Xavier and Kaleb walk round to the screen. Me and Titus don't move. What a sack of shit we are.

"Fucking hell," Xavier laughs, shaking his head.

"What a punch," Kaleb pushes his tongue into his cheek, "nice for not hitting back brother, top man."

I roll my eyes, side eyeing Titus.

"I did wonder how you got the shiner Keaton," Xavier looks over the desk with a soppy smirk on his face.

I flip him off.

"Fast forward," Kaleb says, leaning down so he can look at the screen closer. "Okay, so I am assuming that's Kyra?" and I stumble to my feet and walk across the room to look.

"Yeah," I sigh and all I focus on is his Arizona. She looks so sad.

"Okay, so Kyra leaves and that's around eight. Then Arizona goes back to sleep."

Kaleb is giving me a run-by-run commentary and I know he means well, but it just makes me feel even more of a dickhead than I already feel.

"Stop," Xavier bellows and we all freeze. "Nate, skip to the hallway camera for a second."

Nate does as he says and starts the recording again. I have no idea how our little whizz kid even knows how to hack into the computers and CCTV. Freaks me out to be honest.

"Do we know if Ari had any way of meeting Wolfe before without realising?" Kaleb asks, rubbing his chin just as we see the cunt walk down the hallway of where Ari's room is.

And I know I am going to get beaten again as soon as these words leave my mouth.

"She was a cam girl."

All eyes are on me, along with Killian who walks over at the right time.

"What?" Titus is up from his chair and raging.

Fair.

"She was a cam girl," not sure why I am repeating it. I'm sure they didn't need to me to say it again.

"The fuck," Titus spits coming for me but Kaleb steps in front of me, pressing his hands onto Titus's chest.

"Not now," he growls at Titus, but Titus is too far gone. Eyes stuck to me.

"I never interacted with her on there, I was tempted, but didn't." and Kaleb turns to look at me as if to say *what the fuck are you doing*. "But I did used to sign on to keep an eye on her. She had two followers. Me and someone called *TallDarkandHandsome*."

Seeing as I am spilling all, I may as well continue with my downfall.

"I didn't connect the two when I bumped into her in Prestige."

Three. Two. One.

"Prestige?" Killian asks, Kaleb's eyes widen.

"Thought she was in med school?" Xavier asks.

"So did I," Kaleb slowly lets go of Titus but as soon as he

does, Titus tries to run for me again. This time Killian and Kaleb hold him back.

"So did I until I didn't," I rub my lips together and my chest aches. "I had no idea, decided one night to pop in and that's when I saw her. I was so fucking angry and shocked. Dragged her away to one of the private rooms where she explained all. Made me promise not to say anything..." I pause and level my eyes on Titus's, but his are still filled with rage. So much rage, hate and venom and it's all aimed at me. Can't blame him. He will hate me after this, but to be fair, if I was in his shoes, I would hate me too.

I would loathe me.

I've betrayed him. We both have.

"Weeks passed and one night she comes home and she's out of sorts. Spooked even maybe," I run my hand round the back of my head when I think back to the night where she gave everything to me. The night that everything changed. "She made a comment..." and I pause, this is too far even on my account.

"What did she say?" Killian asks.

I look round the room, they're all staring at me, waiting for me to tell them but I'm not sure if I can. Not even for my sake or Titus's, but for hers.

"It's not really something that I think she, and Titus will want you all to know."

"Tell us," Titus grits, jaw clenched and fuck his jaw must be killing him. He hasn't unclenched it since he came for me.

"She came home marked from work; I went feral. Hated that someone had laid hands on her, but she assured me it was nothing. She wanted to drink herself into oblivion. I told her I was always there for her if she needed someone. I made her promise that she would talk to me if something happened. She agreed," my stomach knots, "we ended up drinking, we played some stupid truth or dare game I think."

"What are you, fucking twelve?" Xavier bursts out but I ignore him.

"She told me that she lost her..." and I watch as Titus's eyes close and I know this must be awful for him to sit and listen to.

"Thinking back, not long after that she stopped going online and after Vegas, she deleted her account."

"Do you think the private client was Wolfe?" Kaleb asks and he and Killian have both let Titus go now.

"I think he was," I swallow the large lump that has formed in my throat and my stomach drops at the realization.

"Here!" Nate shouts, pausing the screen.

And on the screen is Wolfe, pushing Arizona out in the wheelchair. The most chilling thing is he knows we would watch this. Because he is staring straight down the lens of the CCTV camera, smiling the most sinister and evilest grin I have even seen in my life whilst my wife and the mother of my children is unconscious.

I fucking screamed, scaring myself. My lungs burning. Sadness turned to fucking venomous rage and I was ready to burn the fucking world to ashes to get her back. And I knew I would have these men behind me every fucking step of the way, ready to destroy anything that stood in our way.

Hell hath no fury like a man who is about to lose the love of his life.

CHAPTER FIFTY-NINE
ARIZONA

Is it morning or evening? Who knows. It's always bright in this small room. Clinical and minimalistic. No windows. The room is stifling.

The days have disappeared and worry etches itself deeper inside of me knowing that the babies haven't been checked. I am just relieved that I can still feel them kicking.

Wonder if Keaton has even noticed I am gone. I wouldn't blame him if he didn't. I told him to go. Didn't want to. Hated it. But I was so angry. Angry with my dad and the way he stormed into the room and knocking Keaton about. He thinks he has the right to do that to the man I love. My chest trembles on my intake of breath, then Keaton telling my dad about me working at Prestige. It wasn't his place. I know that when I speak to him about it, he'll say he done it for me. That's the thing with Keaton. He is fiercely loyal. He would do anything for anyone he loved. Never used to think that before I got to know him. He was always so cocky and full of himself but then he changed. I saw a glimmer of something no one else did and I fell hopelessly in love.

Turning my face, I try and ignore the tears that pool in my eyes. My dinner is sitting on the table next to me, which means Wolfe will be in any moment to spoon feed me and the thought makes me gag.

I have no idea what he wants from my dad and why I had to be the pawn, but I suppose he failed with Amora so now he is going to take the next best thing. If I had to, I would sacrifice myself for him. And I would do it in a heartbeat. If it meant that I would save the ones I loved. My family.

I would sacrifice myself for them. Because that's what you do for the people you love, right? Even if it means you're the one to die.

Blinking, the tears roll down my cheek and I am desperate to palm them away, but I can't, so they drip off my jaw and into the pillow as it absorbs. Just like it has since I have been here.

The door unlocks and I feel my pulse quicken. With each day that slips by, more my hope dwindles of them finding me. But if this piece of shit is as clever as I think he is, he will have planned it out so they follow the breadcrumbs that lead them here. That's when he will attack. One of them will lose. But who?

"There she is," Wolfe smiles, closing the door behind him and locking it, he walks towards me, hands deep in his pocket. "How are we this morning?" he asks as he sits on the edge of the bed, and I stiffen. His hand lifts as he tries to stroke my cheek, but I turn my head. How silly of me. He grabs my face and forcefully turns me towards him and my eyes are welling. "No point fighting me *mostriciattola*," and the way the words roll off his tongue make me sick to my stomach. "I will do what I want with you, I've had you once,

I can have you again. After all, you let me take your virginity."

I can't argue with that.

I did.

He didn't force me.

But do you want to know why? For some reason, I thought *TallDarkandHandsome* was Keaton. How fucking foolish of me. I gave myself to this man willingly, shared my most intimate moments and it was Wolfe all along. The one that tried to kill my dad, tried to hurt Amora and Twyla. My bottom lip trembles. I didn't stand a chance.

"You will submit to me, you can fight all you want, but being bound to a bed gives you little to no chance," he laughs, pushing his hand into my face so the back of my head dips further into the pillow.

He sits tall, running his hand down the side of his black, slick hair before he reaches for the dinner plate and spoon.

I force my lips shut, rolling them under my teeth and praying I can fight him off.

He spoons mash and peas onto the spoon and hovers it in front of my lips.

"Arizona, if you don't open your mouth, I will force it in," his tone is sharp as he runs a finger across his brow, "and I will continue to do so until you choke."

I breathe heavily out of my nose.

"I will kill you Arizona, don't think I won't. It would give me great pleasure when your dad turns up and your lying dead in the bed."

Tears prick behind my eyes.

"Don't tempt me *mostriciattola*."

My lips are still rolled tight, so what does the cunt do? He pinches my nose, holding it tightly so I have no option but to open my mouth and I fucking hate myself.

He feeds me, praising me as he does, and I have never felt more humiliated then I do now.

"Then after this, I am going to bathe you. Wash every inch of your body and then, you're going to let me fuck you and fill you." I gag, just as he shovels another spoonful of food into my mouth. The sound of the spoon hitting the plate echoes round the room.

"Then, maybe, I'll leave you alone. It all depends." His hand reaches behind my head, grabbing the hair at my nape, dragging my head all the way back and his mouth is on my skin, and I feel repulsed. My scalp burns from how tight he is grabbing, and I want to die. His tongue glides up the column of my throat and I shudder. The growl vibrates in his throat, and I squeeze my eyes shut, willing myself to black everything out. But I don't have a chance. He shoves me away from him in disgust before undoing the restraints from the bed, but my hands and feet are still bound. He drags me off the bed, then knocks my ankles out and I fall to the floor in a heap. Everything aches. He is going to kill me. Grabbing my hair from the root, he proceeds to fucking drag me along the concrete floor towards the bathroom, slamming the door behind us.

Tossing me in the shower like I am trash, he turns the water on and it's freezing cold. He strips me down and all I want to do is curl into a ball and hide myself, but I can't.

So, I close my eyes and black everything out.

It's the only way I can get through this.

The only way where I don't want to rip my skin from my bones and burn it.

I am tarnished, and it's all because of him.

CHAPTER SIXTY
KEATON

DAY FIVE

FIVE DAYS.

Five days of no sleep.

Five days of no food.

Five days of no leads on where the fuck Wolfe has taken my wife.

Five days without her.

And as each day slips by, our worry grows.

I am frantic. My stomach is in bits and my nerves are shot.

The guys are the same. All putting our heads together to try and work out where the fuck he is.

Xavier is struggling. His already short temper is non-existent.

"What are we missing?" Xavier paces. Up and down. Back and forth. "He wants us to find her, he wants payback."

Titus shakes his head from side to side.

"This is your fault," Xavier jabs his finger at Titus and Kaleb steps up towards him.

"Don't."

"If he had actually checked to make sure he was dead before running off to marry my daughter then we wouldn't be in this situation," his tone is harsh.

"Fuck off Xavier," Titus roars and that's when I step in. I stand, shoving Xavier.

"Don't you fucking dare. Either drop the blame and help us or just fuck off. Because whilst we're fighting and bickering, Wolfe is doing fuck knows what to my wife and Titus's daughter. I can do this on my own if you're too busy pointing fingers," I throw my hands up and pace towards Nate. Heavy eye bags, narrow eyes, dry lips. We're all fucked.

I rub my fingers across my brow and Nate scales through CCTV recordings.

"It doesn't make sense, it's like he just disappeared." Nate sighs, leaning back in his chair and tipping his head back.

I fall to the floor, my legs giving out beneath me, and I crumble.

Kaleb is over me, crouching down beside me as he wraps his arm around my shoulders.

"We will find her, I promise."

CHAPTER SIXTY-ONE
ARIZONA

I am numb.

I am broken.

I am ruined.

And the final thoughts that settle in mind, causing a depressing emptiness in my chest is; they're not coming.

CHAPTER SIXTY-TWO
WOLFE

I KNEW IT WAS GOING TO TAKE THEM A WHILE TO FIND HER, BUT this is taking the piss.

I am bored.

I need to ramp it up a little.

I sit with my feet on the desk of the club, bourbon in hand as my long finger taps on the crystal glass, my eyes focused on the CCTV of the club and Arizona's room.

Maybe I didn't leave enough clues? Maybe they're not as clever as they say.

All I want is to sink a bullet between Xavier Archibald and Titus King's eyes, but maybe I need to threaten them with Arizona.

A smirk pulls at my lips as I knock the rest of my drink back and slam it down on the desk.

Storming out of my office, phone in hand, I head towards her room. Fishing the key from my pocket, I unlock her door and let myself in.

She recoils instantly and I know she will be sore from earlier. I don't care. I am going to break her until she feels so unloved that she crumbles to nothing in front of me before

Keaton and Titus can sweep her up into their hands only for her to be so broken nothing will fix her.

What she doesn't realize is I am going to cut those bastards out of her stomach to destroy her once and for all.

"Hello Arizona," my tone is cold as I walk towards her bed, and she tries to protect herself but it's pointless. She is wrapped in a new hospital gown; the other was destroyed. My lips twitch when I play the memory back and I feel my cock stir in my trousers.

"Get away from me," she spits, and it lands in my eye. My temper rises but I calm myself down and glide my fingers across my eye, wiping it away.

"Oh, *mostriciattola*, I will never do that," I kneel on the bed and grab her cheeks, lowering my lips to hers. "I will do whatever I want to you, do you understand me?" I whisper and I watch as the fear strikes in her eyes. Love that. I am slowly breaking her.

I step back, kneeling off the bed as I slip my phone out of my pocket. I need to send them something that will make their blood boil and I know exactly what.

Undoing her restraints, I pull her to the floor. She's on her knees in front of me and fuck does she look pretty. All teary eyed and bruised from my hands and mouth. She's a picture.

I lean down, pressing my fingers into her cheeks.

"I am going to take a picture of you to send it to daddy dearest, hopefully it'll make them want to find you because honestly, I don't think he wants to."

She whimpers which makes me smile.

I love that she fears me. I feed off of it. Pushing her away from me, she falls back, and I tut. Leaning down and picking her back on her knees.

The back of my hand connects with her cheek which leaves a pretty mark on her already bruising face.

I grab her chin, tilting her face to look at me as I rub my thumb over her cracked and split bottom lip, cocking my head to the side as I smirk down at her. Pushing my thumb between her lips and into her hot mouth, I lick my lips just as she sinks her teeth into my thumb and bites down, hard.

I roar, ripping it from her mouth and dragging her up by her hair which causes her to cry out.

"Shame it wasn't your dick," she smiles, blood from her split lip coating her teeth and rage consumes me.

"You little slut," I slap her round the face again. "I was going to save this for later, but do you know what, I changed my mind."

I toss her to the bed and my blood is boiling. I storm from the room and root around in my desk drawer for the paperwork. She's fucking made me bleed. Little bitch. She'll pay later for that. Grabbing the pile of papers, I move towards her door and slam it behind me. Hitting the papers down on the side table, I reach across and wrap my fingers around her neck.

"Oh, the restraint it's taking to not fucking strangle you to death."

She smirks at me which angers me more.

I pull her up by her throat and slam her face down on top of the papers, hoping she has seen Keaton's signature.

"Now, you nasty little whore, you're going to sign these divorce papers, but not before calling Keaton and telling him you're leaving him. I want him to think you don't love him anymore. Then I will take a photo of you that will degrade you in the worst way and make your dad fucking furious.

She wriggles beneath my hand, but all that does is make me press harder.

"Do you understand me?" She whimpers a yes. "So, fucking, weak," I laugh as pull her up by her hair. "And just so you know, if your babies are still alive, I'm cutting the little bastards out of you. After all, they're half mine so I get a choice too."

Her eyes widen.

"They're Keaton's," she goads me.

"Are they? Because the DNA results said different," and I see the way she pales.

I throw her a pen, then dial Keaton's number—on an unknown number of course—and turn it onto speaker. I hold it against her ear, and I watch as the tears fall down her cheeks.

"Hello?"

She chokes on her tears, her breath stuttering at the back of her throat. She looks so pretty when she cries.

"Hello," she inhales.

"Oh, baby," you can hear the relief in his voice.

"Fucking spit it out." I grumble, getting annoyed already.

"Are you okay? Where are you? Has he hurt you?" And she cries silent tears. Wish I felt sorry for her. But I don't. Not even an ounce. Always swore I never had a heart. Even when I murdered my mum and watched the life seep out of her eyes. Didn't cry. Felt no remorse. Even putting the call into Xavier about killing my dad. Would have done it myself, but I wanted someone to owe me something and he was perfect. Silly old cunt.

"I am divorcing you." She forces out, hand over her mouth to stop the sound of her cries from filling the phone line.

"Ari..."

"I'm done. I can't forgive you for betraying me."

Interesting.

"I didn't mean it, I did it for you, for yours and your dad's relationship."

"I don't care."

Liar.

"Blossom, please, I'll do anything, what do you want?"

Blossom. Sickening.

"For you to leave me alone, the papers are signed. It's over."

"Ari," but I snatch the phone off her.

"It's done," and I cut the phone off. "Now sign the fucking papers."

And once she is done, I drag her back to her knees and take the fucking photo that will break her daddy's heart.

CHAPTER SIXTY-THREE
KEATON

M<small>Y PHONE RINGS WITH AN UNKNOWN NUMBER AND</small> I <small>ANSWER IT</small> on the first ring. I press it onto speaker and twist my finger at Nate to start tracking the call.

"Hello?"

The line is silent for a moment, and I hear a sniffle.

It's her.

"Hello," I hear the sharp intake of breath, the way it shudders on her inhale and my chest caves in.

"Oh baby," relief swarms me in an instant and then I hear him in the background.

"Fucking spit it out."

And my blood boils.

"Are you okay? Where are you? Has he hurt you?" Titus is on his feet, fire in his eyes waiting for Nate to pick something up. He tells me to keep the conversation going.

My heart is racing against my chest.

"I am divorcing you." her tone is curt, but I can hear the sadness in her voice and then the speaker gets muffled. She's crying.

"Ari..." I whisper, because I don't believe her.

442

"I'm done. I can't forgive you for betraying me," she sniffles, and my heart is crushed.

"I didn't mean it, I did it for you, for yours and your dad's relationship." It's the truth, I wanted Titus to know and her too.

"I don't care,"

You do care. I know you do.

"Blossom, please, I'll do anything, what do you want?"

Thump. Thump. Thump.

"For you to leave me alone, the papers are signed. It's over."

"Ari..."

"It's done," Wolfe's voice seeps down the phone and my blood runs cold and the phone goes dead.

I turn to face Nate, and he shakes his head from side to side.

"Fuck!" I throw my phone at the wall and watch as the screen flickers on the floor.

A beep fills the hostile room, and Titus's eyes widen as he looks at his phone.

"What is it?" I rush over and I have never felt anger like this before, this is an anger that I have kept buried for as long as I can remember, but it's finally erupted on seeing the image of Arizona on his phone. Gagged. On her knees. Bloodied and bruised and being forced to do something no one should have to witness.

"I'm going to fucking kill him," Titus roars.

"You'll have to beat us to it," Xavier says with Killian, Nate and Kaleb standing behind him.

CHAPTER SIXTY-FOUR
WOLFE

THE FRONT DOOR BUZZES AND I RADIO THROUGH TO SECURITY TO let him in.

Dexter Rutherford.

Nice to keep people close. Was easy to keep tabs on Arizona through Dex. Not that he would know. Clueless bastard.

A knock on the door pulls me from my thoughts and I sit up in my seat.

"Come in," I call out and Dex and his little stripper whore walk through the door. Pretty face, reckless body. Would destroy her.

"Dexter, Sage, so nice to see you again," I stand, leaning across the desk and shaking his hand.

Would have had a hard on from the sight of Sage but got my fix from Arizona before my meeting so I am all good, for now anyway.

"Dex, please," his gruff British accent grates on me.

"Of course," I sit down and minimize the CCTV screen. Don't need them finding Arizona now do I?

"So, I am assuming our meeting is all good? You've

444

looked over the contract and wish to buy the club?" My eyes move between the both of them, hands clasped, and index fingers pressed together. He already signed on one dotted line but I changed a few of the terms and needed another signature.

"Yes, I think so. Few little things that I would like to discuss with you, but nothing that will turn us away from this club."

"I think that calls for a celebration, don't you?" I say, standing and grabbing the crystal decanter full of bourbon.

"Certainly does," Dex smiles at his whore who stands from her seat.

"I am just going to use the ladies room, you two talk business."

"Sixth door on your left," I tell her, wanting to make sure she doesn't try to go snooping.

"Thank you," she leans down and kisses Dex on the cheek and I don't miss my chance to let my greedy eyes roam over her.

Fuck, I would love to sink my cock in her. Maybe I'll swipe her next, make Dex work for her. Lips twitch, cock stirs.

"Here we go," I hand Dex a crystal glass and clink them together.

"To new business,"

"To new business," Dex repeats just as Sage walks out the door, my eyes on her ass until she disappears.

Definitely getting her next.

CHAPTER SIXTY-FIVE
SAGE

I WALKED DOWN THE NARROW CORRIDOR TOWARDS THE SIXTH door on the left, just like Wolfe said. Looking around the club that is soon to be ours, I get an unnerving feeling in my lower stomach. There is something about Wolfe that I don't trust. The way his eyes rake up and down my body when I walk into a room. Makes my skin crawl. I am distracted when I open the door on my left and walk into a white clinically clean room. I don't remember seeing this when we had our tour.

And that's when I see her.

Laid on a bed, strapped up and restrained.

Bloody and bruised.

My heart sinks in my chest, panic coursing through me as I rush over to her as quickly as I can to make sure she is okay.

"Oh my God Arizona, are you okay?"

I shake her gently, trying to wake her from her sleep.

"Ari, please wake up," my voice cracks and I am terrified.

She stares, and it takes her a moment to open her eyes

and realize that I am standing beside her. She blinks a couple of times, and that's when I see how bruised her face really is. Both eyes purple and bruising, her nose, swollen and bloody, and her lips are cracked and split and covered in dry blood.

"Sage?"

I brush her hair from her forehead gently, minding not to hurt her at all, she has a Band-Aid on her head, and I'm not sure if that is from now or before she got here.

But I don't understand why she is here.

Why has nobody come to find her?

Why have we not been told?

It seems she's been here longer than a few days, and that makes me worry even more.

"Is it really you? Or am I dreaming?"

"It's really me". I choke on my words.

"How did you find me?" Her voice is hoarse, her eyes darting around the room in a panic as she looks for Wolfe I'm assuming.

"Me and Dex had a meeting with Wolfe. Do you remember the club that we looked out whilst we were in Vegas?"

She nods.

"This is where you are. We flew to Vegas to sign the paperwork for the club. I needed the toilet, so I excused myself in the meeting and Wolfe told me where to go," I pause for a moment and just stare at her. She is a shell of herself. "But I got so distracted when I was walking, I must've opened the fifth door and not the sixth."

She's placid and dopey. Has he been drugging her? Fear prickles at the top of my spine and my worried eyes sweep over her body, her bump, then I am back on her eyes.

"Does anybody know that you are here Arizona?"

She shakes her head from side to side, and I don't miss the way that her bottom lip trembles, her chin wobbles, and her eyes are filled with unshed tears.

"It's okay, I can get you out of here, I'll get Dex to distract Wolfe and then I can sneak you out."

"You won't be able to do this, he has eyes everywhere." She sucks in a breath, And I don't miss the shudder on her intake. I turn around and see the flashing camera. Shit.

"If you want to help me undo my restraints loosely and give me something that I can attack Wolfe with," she sucks in a breath, "but don't make it obvious," her eyes skitter to the corner of the room before they're back on mine.

I don't like the idea of leaving her here, but she is right if I get involved in it I have no idea what Wolfe could do to me or Dex or worse, Arizona.

"Go back to your meeting with Wolfe, pretend that this didn't happen and get Dex to call Keaton or my dad." Her voice is trembling, her hands shake. "Promise me, Sage, promise me that you will do as I've asked, and that you will walk out of here and forget that you ever saw me, but please get the message out."

I give her a confirming nod.

Loosening her restraints, we make it look like she is still attached to the bed, but she's not. I pull out the bottom drawer of her bedside unit and find a mixture of silver surgery tools. My blood runs cold at the thought of what they're in there for and it's not even worth thinking about. I slip the scalpel into her hand, and she tucks it up the sleeve of her gown.

"Are you sure you're going to be okay?"

"I am," is all she replies with, and I can see the fire in her eyes. She's got the hunger in her belly, and I know that she will not let him win.

Walking out of that room was the hardest thing I have ever done. Hated that I had to leave her, but she was right. I needed to get back to my meeting. I had already been gone too long and I'm sure Wolfe would've been getting suspicious by now. I gave Arizona one last look before slipping out the door. I walk into the correct one for the ladies room. Rushing in and out, I wash my hands and then make my way back to where Wolfe and Dex are waiting.

"Did you get lost?" Wolfe asks me and I don't miss his snarky tone. I give him a kind smile.

Kill the fucker with kindness.

"No, not lost, just took a little longer than I expected," I take my seat back next to Dex and waited for them to finish up their conversation. The paperwork was signed, and we walk out of the club hand-in-hand with a date to take over the club within the next three weeks. Wolfe follows us out and says goodbye at the door with a firm handshake of Dex's hand and leans in to kiss me on the cheek. I stiffen as soon as his lips meet my skin, the way he makes me feel is indescribable. Lingering a little longer than he should, and I don't miss the way his lips brush against my ear and I'm half expecting him to whisper something in there so only I can hear but he doesn't. Dex tightens his grip on my hand, softly tugging me away. Wolfe steps back and away from me, clearly reading Dex's silent warning, his eyes raking up and down my body once more, and that feeling of uncomfortableness resumes deep in the pit of my stomach. I hated walking away, knowing that I was leaving Arizona in that hellhole with him. But I promised her. I promised I was going to get a message to Keaton or her dad via Dex. As soon as I'm out of the club, I lead Dex outside the stuffy building and into the warm air of Las Vegas.

"Dex," my voice is urgent as we continue walking

towards where we parked. I needed to get far enough away from him.

"What is it babe?" His eyes bounce back and forth between mine.

I can't help but look over my shoulder to make sure that I'm not being followed by Wolfe, and once I know the coast is clear, I stop in my tracks and place my hands on Dex's chest.

"We need to get a message to Keaton," the panic burns deep within, clawing at my throat, my heart is racing under my skin, it thrashes inside the depths of my chest.

"Temptress, you're scaring me, what's happened?" The concern is etched onto Dex's handsome face, but I'm struggling to get the words out. I know what I want to say, but the sheer fear of leaving her in the hands of that monster is enough to cripple me with paralysis.

"Sage did something happen when we were in there?"

I shake my head from side to side, and I know that is a lie, but nothing did happen to me whilst we were in there.

"I need you to text Keaton and please do not panic when I tell you this," I can hear the blood thumping in my ears, the noise sickening and my stomach twisting with anxiety at the thought of the words that are about to leave my mouth.

"Text Keaton what?"

"When I was walking to the toilet, I took the wrong door, when I pushed through it, there was a clinically clean white room with a bed, and it took me a moment to realize that there was somebody in that bed." For just a moment, my eyes catch Dex's as they bounce between mine, "Arizona was in the bed."

I see the shock that masks Dex's face, his eyes widening as the seconds pass, and silence consumes us for a second.

His brows furrow, and I don't miss the way he looks at me as if I'm telling him a lie.

"Are you sure?" Dex's hands are on the side of my face as he tilts me up to look at him. My silent tears roll down the side of my face and his hands.

"I swear," I swallowed down the bile that is threatening my throat, as I try to push the lump that has formed itself there back down. "It was Arizona laying in the bed, but she didn't seem herself. She had bruises and blood, and she looked as if she had been drugged. She was in and out of sleep, and I promised her that I would get a message to Keaton. I have no idea how long she's been in there for. I don't even know whether they know that she's missing. I mean," I laugh, but I think it's more of fear than hysteria. "Of course, they know she's missing right? Especially Keaton, But I don't understand how they've not found her yet..." my chest heaves, "they do know right?"

Dex pulls me close, my head resting on his chest, and I hear the sound of his erratic heartbeat racing under his skin.

"I offered to get her out, and she told me all I had to do was loosen her restraints," I suck in a breath, "he has her tied to a bed, legs and wrists bound to a metal bed frame. She couldn't move even if she wanted to." Tears flood my eyes, my mind flashes back to the memory of Arizona, laying on that bed.

"All she asked me was for us to get a message to Keaton, and for me to slip something into her hand, so when Wolfe goes into her room, she can attack him." I whisper the words out, because saying them out loud feels too harsh. It makes it all real.

"What did you give her?" He asked, concern lacing his voice as he presses his lips to the top of my head.

"I could only find a scalpel…" I pause and swallow the acid that burns my windpipe. "I don't even want to think what it was doing in there, but I'm scared Dex. I'm worried for her. We need to get her out of there. Please, please can you text Keaton and tell them where she is. And if for whatever reason they don't come, then we need to bust her out."

Dex is already slipping his phone out of his back pocket, opening his messages and typing a text. Of course they would come, especially Keaton I mean the whole crowd would come for Arizona, I'm just hoping it's a 'we couldn't find her' more than 'I didn't want to find her' situation. I know how these men can make deals for selfish reasons, and I just hope that Arizona was not at the center of one of them deals.

"The message has been sent," Dex slips his phone back into his pocket and wraps his arms around me, enveloping me. "We will stay in Vegas just in case anyone needs our help, and if for whatever reason they don't come, we will get her out of there."

I look up at him, my eyes glisten with unsheathed tears, and I feel helpless in that moment. "You promise me?"

"I promise you." And I know that Dex Rutherford never breaks a promise.

CHAPTER SIXTY-SIX
ARIZONA

I HAVE NO IDEA HOW LONG IT HAS BEEN SINCE SAGE WALKED OUT of the room, but Wolfe hasn't been near or by and that makes me panic even more. What if he found out? What if he saw on the cameras that Sage was here, and she helped me loosen the restraints that were tight around my wrists and ankles. What if he noticed her slip me the scalpel from the bottom drawer, and then watched me slip the scalpel up the sleeve of my gown.

Fear prickles at the base of my head, travelling down my neck, causing goosebumps to explode over my sensitized skin. I let my head fall back for just a moment, my eyes closing as a single tear runs out and down my cheek. It dissolves into the pillow beneath my head, just like all the others have before. A small smile slips across my lips, when I feel the most subtle kick from twin A, still trying to reassure me that they are still here, and I'm not alone. I will do anything for these babies, and I will not let Wolfe anywhere near them. He can try and I mean he will give it a good try, but that's as far as he will get.

WOLFE

Slipping the paperwork that Dex signed, making this club now his, in the drawer of my desk I close it and lock it behind me. Standing, I push a button through my suit jacket and make my way to my favorite girl's room. Okay maybe not favorite girl but she's my favorite at the moment.

Walking the narrow corridors, my heart races with excitement when I know that I'm going to be with her in a matter of minutes. I have no idea why Keaton and Titus, or even Xavier, haven't managed to find her yet. If they would've looked at my tracks and noticed the breadcrumbs, they would've at least found a clue by now, but they're probably too busy sitting by their computers trying to track me that way because of course, that's the only way they know how.

They've got their little computer whizz who thinks that's how he will find me.

Silly, silly, boys.

I go to unlock the door and find that it is already unlocked. I must have been so distracted earlier I forgot to lock it when I left. I pinch my brows and push the handle down. I stand a little taller as I walk into the room and find her awake and waiting for me. Broken and bruised. Just how I like her.

"Hello, little Vixen. Have you missed me?"

She says nothing, just glares at me with an absent look on her face. I stalk over to her, the whole time my eyes are pinned to hers. And only when I get close to her, do her eyes move to focus on me.

"So, I have decided that today is the day that I cut those bastards out of you. It seems that nobody is coming to save you and honestly, I'm over the thought of having heirs."

Her body stiffens, and I see the way her body pulls against the restraints.

"No point fighting me little monster, the babies are coming out of you whether you like it or not." I run my finger across her cheek, and she turns her head away from me, as if completely disgusted by my touch. It only turns me on more when she fights me.

I kneel on the bed, cock hard and I'm ready for my release, and only when I have filled her, I'll cut them fucking kids out of her and honestly, I don't even care if she bleeds out.

I'm bored.

It's been nine days and nothing. Not a single sign that they're even trying.

My hate isn't with her. It's with her cunt of a father and Xavier.

But spilt blood is still spilt.

I'm at the point where I don't care who it comes from.

She goes to scream but I cover her mouth with my hand.

"Now, now, little Vixen, I need you to be quiet." I smirk as I look down at her, and she fights against me with all she has, but she'll never win.

Ever.

CHAPTER SIXTY-SEVEN
KEATON

I AM GOING OUT OF MY MIND. IT'S BEEN NINE DAYS. NINE LONG, horrific, grueling, torturous days. We've had nothing else from Wolfe, and for some reason that scares me more. Nate is working day and night to try and find the missing piece. We need to work out where Wolfe has taken Arizona. We've replayed his steps, we even checked his laptop that he left in the hospital room, and there is nothing apart from his chats with Arizona when she used to be a cam girl.

He has left sloppy clues, but still nothing that will indicate where he has her hidden.

Xavier walked into the room with fresh coffees and food, placing them down on the large conference room table. But the thought of eating food makes my stomach turn. I can't think of anything other than finding Arizona. I can't sleep, I can't eat, I don't even feel like I can breathe without her. I inhale a sharp intake of breath and I feel the rattle deep within my chest, reminding me just how hollow it has become since Arizona was taken. I fear for my unborn babies lives, but I fear more for Arizona's.

I can't stand to be here anymore. I pace towards the elevator and Kaleb is hot on my heels.

"Where are you going?" he asks me, concern lacing his voice, and I let out a heavy sigh.

"I just need a moment," I admit, as I press the button for the elevator and call it to our floor.

"Let me come with you, I don't like the thought of you being out there alone."

I want to protest and fight against him, but it's pointless. Even if I said not to, Kaleb would still follow me. He always has and he always will at the end of the day. He is my big brother.

"I don't have a choice, do I?" He lets out a soft chuckle, and I have no idea how we can even laugh at a time like this when I feel like my world is ending, I feel like my heart has obliterated in my chest, and there's nothing more than dust, crumbling through the crevices. Once there was a full and strong beating heart, and now there is nothing left, but a few remains of what once was. Arizona was the reason my heart beat the way it did. She was the reason my heart beats so ferociously within my chest, making me feel things I have never felt before, but now, without her, I was empty, numb, a shadow of myself. My eyes were hollow. I was dead behind them, nothing left and all my soul has done since she disappeared is weep. Without her, I was dead.

I can only breathe with her, I am only able to live with her, I am only able to exist with her in my life because without her I am nothing.

We have walked for what feels forever. My tired and heavy feet beating against the sidewalk. The heavy rain is hitting my skin and it stings. But I don't care. I would like to say it's nice to feel something other than a shattering pain but I don't feel anything, I am numb.

There is nothing that could make me feel any worse than how I am feeling now. My whole world has crumbled around me and it didn't matter how much I tried to pick up the pieces and glue them back together, they would never look the same. I would never be whole again.

I had to learn to live with a broken world, a broken heart and a shattered soul.

The silence is comforting after being in an office for nine days, listening to voices constantly talking about what may have happened, or where she may be, and even worse what he has done to her. It was too much for my mind to comprehend. It was nice to have some silence, so I could gather my thoughts, but who was I kidding? My thoughts were dark and gloomy with a thunderous cloud hanging over me, but I have kind of gotten used to that now. I've got used to feeling how I have. She was my ray of light, and without her my world was gray.

I have no idea out of all the places in New York why my legs have taken me to the hospital where I dropped Arizona off. I didn't want to be here, I didn't want to be reminded of the last conversation that we had, where I broke her trust, and no doubt her heart but here we are. I'm standing outside, the rain is cascading over me and I'm taking it all in. I'm letting the rain wash every ounce of guilt that I feel away.

"Did you wanna go inside?" Kaleb asks me and I can see the concern all over his face. He's worried about me. I know he has been here; I know he'll be feeling the indescribable pain that is searing through my heart, but I don't care how he felt. I don't care that he has been through this. I don't care that even Titus had been through this with Amora. Well, let's be honest his situation was completely different to mine. He was still with her. Still got to watch her. Make sure she was safe because he was to never leave her side but me? I did leave her side, I walked away again. Instead of dealing with it, I ran away like a coward to lick my wounds when it wasn't even my wounds that needed to be licked. I had to focus on her, but I was too childish to even do that.

Before I answer him, I walk up the steps and into the hospital. I don't stop to talk to anyone, I just head for her room.

Fear cripples me as I step closer to where I left her ten days ago.

I made Kyra promise that she wouldn't go to the police because we were working privately to find her. I just hoped she stuck to it.

Whispers echoed around the ward as I walk towards her room, my chest aches and I heave.

Kaleb rests his hand on my shoulder as we step into her room. Everything has been left where it was. The room has not been touched and it scares me.

I walk slowly towards her bed, my fingertips brushing over her cotton pillowcase. Everything still smells of her and I crumble. Falling to my knees I reach for the pillow and pull it towards my chest as I hold it tightly.

This is what I have become.

A broken man.

I hear Kaleb's footsteps, but I can't look up at him.

"Keaton..." his voice rumbles through the room but I ignore him. "Why is there a poker chip on Arizona's bed?"

My head snaps up just as my phone beeps.

Kaleb holds the chip between his finger and thumb and my eyes widen, heart falling out of my chest.

"I know where that's from..." my heart stutters. Pulling my phone from my pocket I see a text message from Dex that simply says *'Arizona'*.

"Fuck!" I shout, all self-wallowing dissolving in an instant as I push to my feet.

"What is it?" Kaleb asks, narrowing his gaze on the chip.

"Tell the guys we're heading to Vegas."

WE DON'T FUCK AROUND. WE LAND AND ARE ALREADY IN TWO cars heading for the strip. My heart has been racing since we landed, and I am desperate to get to her. I just hope we're not too late.

Nate is already on his computer searching the hotel CCTV. I have been trying to call Dex but he isn't answering.

I leave another voicemail.

"Dex, please, call me. I'm in Vegas," I cut him off just as my phone screams in my hand. It's him. "Hello," I pant, feeling like my heart is in my throat and I can't breathe.

"I'm so sorry man, I didn't mean to ignore you and when I tried to call you back, your phone was going to voicemail and it makes sense now, you were already in the sky."

"Yeah." Is all I manage. I feel sick.

"How did you figure out Vegas?" Dex asks.

"Kaleb found a casino chip under her pillow when we went to the hospital where she was last seen," I swallow the thickness down, the lump so far lodged into my throat I am desperate to throw up to just try and ease it a little.

"Fuck," Dex whistles.

"Look, I don't mean to rush you off the phone but where was she? Was it you that found her?" I have a million more questions, but I don't have time. Nate is giving me eyes from the front seat of the escalade we're currently cruising in.

"I didn't see her, it was Sage."

"Why didn't she get her? Why did she leave her?"

"Arizona told her to. She didn't want to put Sage at risk."

I suck in a sharp intake, hand covering my mouth and even in all of this hell, she still puts others before herself.

My selfless, beautiful Arizona.

"Where is she?"

"*Laced Promises*."

"Thanks for everything Dex."

"Look, before you go. Me and Sage are still in Vegas. We promised each other we would stay here until we knew she was safe. Sage worried you weren't coming, Sage thought there may have been an ulterior motive," and that feels like a knife in my back, but I get it. Look what Xavier done to Amora.

"I get it," I sigh, and I am struggling to keep my emotions in check.

"We will be here if you need us."

"Thank you," I mutter before cutting the phone off.

I tell Nate the name of the club and the driver heads there, the second escalade following behind us.

It's time to rescue my baby.

WE SIT IN THE SUITE OF THE HOTEL, WE'RE RIGHT WHERE WE NEED to be. Just across the strip and our eyes are settled on the entrance of the building. Nate is going to stay back and watch our moves along with Kaleb. Killian stayed back home in New York, so Amora had someone there if she needed, at least that way she has Connie, Reese and Royal. I sigh, pinching the bridge of my nose as I feel a migraine building at the base of my head, my temples throb. I am exhausted, but I won't be able to sleep until I know she is safe with me. Connie and Reese are pissed at me for not telling them that she was in hospital, I get it. But she didn't want a fuss. I done as she asked and yet I am the bad guy. Kaleb rubs my shoulder in a reassuring way and a small smile forms on my lips.

We agreed that me, Titus and Xavier would be the ones to find Arizona. I felt sick to my stomach, what if something bad had happened to her? What if he had hurt her? Rubbing the ache from my chest, my palm presses against the wedding band that hangs around my neck. My eyes close and my mind flashes back to the call. She was so scared, I could hear the fear in her voice when she told me we were divorced. He made her sign the papers. We haven't been able to work out why he done it, but it doesn't matter why in the grand scheme of things. He still made her do it.

I pace the room, waiting for Nate to give us the green light. He has managed to hack into the hotel security where the club is situated and has been spending the last hour trying to break down the walls for *Laced Promises* but to no avail.

"We need to make our move before it gets too dark," Xavier rumbles from across the room, standing in the window like a peeping Tom.

"Xavier is right, Nate, we're going to have to go in blind and hope that luck is on our side," Titus sighs as he pushes off the end of the bed and walks to where Xavier is hovering.

I hear the groan that escapes Nate and I know he is

agitated. Nate hates not being able to finish a job, so this will be rubbing him up the wrong way.

"Fine," he stands from his desk and walks across the room to the closet. He grabs two black briefcases and places them on the bed. Unbuckling them, he opens the lid to reveal three handguns with silencers on the barrel.

"Do you think these are needed?" I ask, brows furrowing when I hear a deep laugh coming from Xavier.

"Oh, we do, you don't know what Wolfe is like," he shakes his head from side to side.

"He is a monster," Titus swallows, his throat bobbing and I know he is scared. I am terrified of what we're going to find when we eventually find her. I just hope that Wolfe didn't intentionally leave the door open knowing that Sage would find Arizona and in doing so, would make Wolfe move her on once more and out of our grasps.

"I've come across some nasty pieces of shit in my life..." Xavier turns, hands folded into pockets as he walks towards where the guns are sitting in the briefcase, "none of them compare to Wolfe."

Dread buries itself in my gut.

"Can we just go now; I need to get her. I need to know she is safe," my eyes bounce between Titus, Nate, Kaleb and Xavier. Nate gives a very soft but stern nod. He fixes our guns, and we slip them into the waistband of our suit pants.

"Kaleb will distract the security guard..." Nate begins and I watch as confusion smothers Kaleb.

"Sorry? I thought I was staying here with you."

Nate just smiles at him, nose crinkling and a low chuckle passes his lips.

"You need to be the distraction," seriousness blankets the room and Nate is not fucking about.

"Great," Kaleb rolls his eyes, "and how am I going to do that?"

"I'm sure you can work it out, you're not just a pretty face." Nate chuckles then opens the hotel door. "Now go, I'll be watching you and if anything goes sideways, I'll be sure to let you know."

Anxiety cripples me, but I need to focus on the end game and that is getting Arizona. Dead or alive.

I told my brother in private that if I die, not to be sad. Because if dying for her meant taking my last breath and that she got to live then I would happily go. I would sacrifice myself for her over and over.

Giving him a firm nod, I walk out the door behind Xavier and Titus. Kaleb follows behind a couple of steps back and as soon as we're out on the strip, we part ways. I hang back, Kaleb keeps walking and Xavier and Titus move to the right.

We all have reason to put a bullet through Wolfe's head. I just hope I'm the first to pull the trigger.

The strip is busy already and it's only five p.m. Vegas never does sleep. We wait for Kaleb to disappear into the club and then we hear Nate in our ear.

"Start making your way over, try and stay apart. You don't want to draw attention to yourselves."

We all look each other, and I give a firm nod.

"Kaleb is just walking up towards *Laced Promises*, only one security guard," Nate continues and I try and silence him a little. I am trying to keep my head in the game and not go into a panic.

I'm not panicking in case something happens to us.

I am panicking that we're too late.

"Kaleb is approaching the guard. Hang back," Nate

464

orders us and we do. We fall back just in front of the club, the three of us spread through the crowd.

Silence fills our ears and my heart is rushing in my chest.

After five minutes I hear the static in my ear, the sound of Nate's heavy breathing. We wait with bated breath for his command.

"Move."

We walk into the building and follow Nate's instructions, when we see Kaleb and the out cold security guard.

"What the fuck happened to distract?' I hiss, looking over my shoulder as we surround the guard who is on the floor.

"Wasn't working, now get the fuck in there before the cops show up."

"Already got it covered," Nate says as three men dressed in uniform walk towards us, dragging the body away.

"Let's go," Xavier rasps as he pushes through the red door.

"What about me?" Kaleb asks, hope in his voice.

"Go across to the restaurant and get yourself an iced coffee princess," Nate mutters in our ears.

"Are you serious? You're cutting me out again? Just like you did with Connie. I'm relevant!" he shouts out and I twist my lips and bite the inside of my cheek to stop myself from laughing.

His eyes bounce between the three of us but none of us say anything.

"We don't have fucking time for this," I grit, teeth clenched, and jaw wound tight.

"Fuck you," Kaleb sulks, turning his back and walking away. Xavier's low chuckle vibrates through me.

"Is he always like that?"

I sigh.

"Pretty much," Titus says, following Xavier and only when I am inside the club, does the fear prick at my skin again. What makes it worse is that no doubt Wolfe the weasel is watching our every move.

"Move upstairs, you need to slip into the corridor which is tucked between room three and four. It's narrow, but once down there you want the eighth door on the left."

The three of us keep mute. I slip my gun out the back of my suit pants just as Xavier and Titus do. I pull the safety catch and make sure it is ready to shoot if needed.

Titus slips down between the rooms and uneasiness coats my skin. Xavier nods for me to follow behind Titus, then he stays close behind me.

"Perfect," Nate talks quietly in our ears. We have small bodycams on so he can see where we're going. "Sixth door on the left," he reminds us.

We all stop outside the door, all eyes locking on each other's, and I inhale heavily. Titus gives one final nod as he reaches for the handle and twists it slowly. He pushes the door open and my jaw goes lax when I see Arizona in front of me, covered in blood. My heart drops in my chest, my knees weak and I feel like my legs will buckle at any moment. I edge forward, but am stopped in my tracks when everything moves too fast because the next thing I hear is the sound of a gunshot, echoing around the room.

CHAPTER SIXTY-EIGHT
ARIZONA

TWENTY MINUTES BEFORE

WOLFE IS ON TOP OF ME, HAND OVER MY MOUTH AS I SCREAM OUT. I am ready to fight, I needed to make sure he did nothing to hurt the twins.

"Now, now little Vixen, I need you to be quiet." He smiles down at me, and my stomach rolls with nausea.

It's now or never.

Fight or flight mode.

If I let this moment pass, I'll be dead within a matter of hours. There is no way I will survive if he cuts the babies out of me.

I gently loosen my left hand out of my restraint, then use my fingers to slide the scalpel out of my gown.

Wolfe unbuckles his pants and I heave against his hand. He is rough and unforgiving. He has humiliated me and broken me in ways he never should, but I am still breathing. And that's all that matters for now.

I don't care that I am starving, no doubt dehydrated, I just needed to end this once and for all.

Keaton and my dad are coming for me, I know they are. Sage promised me that much and that's what has kept me going.

"Don't fight me, you'll lose every fucking time," his fingers wrap around my throat as he begins to squeeze the life out of me. I try and gasp, my eyes widening as his fingers tighten.

And that's when I make my move.

My eyes lift at the corners as I smile behind his hand and I catch him off guard as he looks down at me, brows furrowed and I swing my arm up, stabbing the scalpel into his neck and slicing through his carotid artery.

His eyes widen, his hand slipping from my throat, and I gasp for breath, burning my lungs. I watch as he tries to stop the bleeding from his throat, but he can't. I watch as the life slowly drains from his dark and evil brown eyes, the death rattle loud as the last ounce of breath escapes before he collapses on top of me and all I do is lay, still.

Frozen almost.

I'm a doctor. I know how much blood pumps round the human body, but until you physically see a body drained of every ounce of it, you just can't quite comprehend those numbers.

Wolfe bled out pretty quick and once the realization hits me, I freak. With the last ounce of strength I have, I shove his corpse off me and hear as it hits the tiled floor. I fall off the bed, knees hitting the floor and I shove his body away from me, his blood leaving a trail. I pat him down, and find a gun slipped in the inside of his suit jacket. I have no idea who is in here and I don't want to not be prepared. I grab the gun, then wipe the hair out of my face. I let my head fall back and close my eyes, I have never believed in

God, but at this moment, I am doing nothing but throwing prayers his way.

Bracing myself for what is about to come.

But what I expected was not what I got.

No.

The door opens slowly, and I fire the gun.

My body stiffens when it opens fully, and there in front of me, eyes wide and jaws laxed are Keaton, my dad and Xavier. My dad shouts out as the bullet hits his shoulder and I throw the gun in shock.

"Who would have thought it aye?" Xavier rumbles and side eyes Titus, "Even your daughter knew to make sure he was dead."

My dad groans, "Fuck off," as he covers his bleeding shoulder. And I am hoping it's only a flesh wound.

"Arizona," Keaton chokes as he runs towards me, scooping me up on my trembling legs and as soon as I am in his arms, everything goes black.

CHAPTER SIXTY-NINE
KEATON

WHY IS SHE STILL ASLEEP?" WORRY CONSUMES ME AS I LOOK AT Arizona. She looks nothing like my Blossom. She is bruised, bloody and malnourished.

"She has been through a lot. She has been starved and is severely dehydrated. Her cheek bone is broken, and her wrists are bruised and cut from being tied." The doctor sits down beside me, I can see the worry on her face. I turn to look at Arizona. She looks so small without her baby bump.

"I drew some blood and gave her an internal examination..." she pauses, and my eyes graze across to hers. She doesn't have to say what she found. I can tell by the look on her face.

Anger boils deep inside of me, fists balled to my side.

"Her blood work is clear, along with her swabs. She will be okay Keaton, she will heal from this."

"Will she?" I drop my head, trying to hide the tears that creep over me. How do I tell her that because of *him*, she lost her babies.

I shake my head side to side.

Kyra's hand is on my shoulder, and I take comfort that she is with me.

The sound of someone clearing their throat has me lifting my head and turning to look behind me. Kaleb stands in the door, and I can see the heartbreak etched into his expression.

"I'll give you some time alone, I'll be back in a couple of hours," Kyra stands, her lips turned down as she looks at Arizona then slips past my brother.

"I am so sorry," Kaleb just about manages as I stand, throwing myself into my big brother's arms. This was not the life we planned. This was not what was supposed to happen. But life is a cruel mistress, sparing no one. I choke, his hand rests on the back of my head as he comforts me like a lost little boy and only then, do I let the tears I have been fighting, fall.

CHAPTER SEVENTY
ARIZONA

I swallow, my throat tightening as I do. I am gasping. My lungs burn when I inhale deeply, my eyes fluttering open when I see a male doctor standing over me. My hand is being held, a thumb rubbing back and forth. I slowly turn my throbbing face to see Keaton, eyes glassy and my heart somersaults in my chest.

"Arizona," the male's voice floats across the room and I lazily drag my eyes to him. "Can you hear me?"

I nod. The pain that shoots through my body makes me stiffen in the bed.

"I'm just going to do a few checks," he says, leaning across me and my chest tightens as sheer panic strangles me. My eyes well and I shake my head from side to side.

"Don't touch her," Keaton growls from beside me and I see Kyra gently move the male doctor out of the way.

"Hello Arizona," Kyra's voice is soft and I feel the panic slowly seep out of me. "Can I just give you a check over?"

I'm struggling to find my voice.

I nod again.

She leans across me and lifts a torch over my face,

shining in my eyes as the male doctor hovers over her shoulder and he gives her a curt nod.

He turns to face the young nurse that walked into the room and asks her to collect some water and some bland food.

My stomach tightens and a burn rips through me.

"The babies," is all I manage to croak out, and I see as Kyra's eyes drift towards Keaton. Slowly, I roll my head, turning to look towards him and he gives a soft nod. Kyra walks from the room and it's not until I allow my eyes to follow her, I notice that my stomach only has a small swell. No rounded baby bump.

Tears prick my eyes as Keaton sits on the edge of the bed.

"Baby," his voice is soft as his eyes settle on mine. He looks broken. His hands cocoon mine, and my stomach drops.

A single tear escapes, running down my cheek as I close my eyes and brace myself for the words that are about to leave his lips.

"Dr Kyra tried... she just... it was..." he stammers over his words and my heart breaks.

"Please," I beg, still not having the strength to look at him.

"She couldn't save them," and my whole world comes crashing down on me. He took everything from me, my purity, my dignity, my pride, my soul and my babies. He ripped me to pieces, shredding me into nothing and destroyed me in the worst way.

"I tried so hard," I whisper, allowing my eyes to open as I look at the man I so desperately love.

"I know baby, I know," he leans gently across me, and places a soft kiss on my forehead, lingering for just a moment.

"How's my dad?" my voice cracks as I brace myself for another blow.

"Recovering."

Relief coats me like April showers.

I turn my face away and play his words on loop until my chest is hollow, my heart is disintegrated, and my eyes run dry.

I lost them.

Even I couldn't save them.

SIX MONTHS LATER

I say goodbye to Dr Combes and walk out onto the sidewalk. I was reluctant to go to therapy when Dr Kyra suggested it, but once I was out of hospital and back home living the life I lost, the grief really took a hold of me and that's when I booked my first appointment. The last six months have passed by in a blur and I honestly cannot remember most of it. I lost myself in the process. The days slipped into weeks, the weeks into months and here we are.

Six months to the day I was found, and it still isn't any easier taking each breath. Grief works in funny ways, some days I feel like I am the best version of myself. A constant smile is worn on my face proudly, I feel a little stronger and I know I have my babies in my heart, and on other days, I can't function. I can't get out of bed, so I don't. On top of grief, I have the PTSD of the assault that Wolfe carried out. My whole world stopped on the day Keaton told me the news, but for everyone else, it kept turning. Life has to move on. I can't be stuck, frozen in the worst moment of my life. I would do anything to go back in time, try and change the outcome, but this was all mapped out. If it wasn't then, it would have still happened.

My fingers pinch the pendant with my daughter's fingerprints that I wear with pride around my neck. Primrose and Posie.

They were perfect in every way, far too perfect for this cruel, cruel world.

Today was a good day. The sun was shining, the birds were singing, and the cherry blossom trees were in full bloom. Me and Keaton were hosting a dinner tonight for our friends and family. Keaton thinks it may be too soon, but I am ready to step back into the real world. I have been so far away from the day to day that it was time to come back down to earth.

My phone beeps in my purse and I slip it out and see a message from Keaton. A grin tugs at my lips when I read the message.

> **Keaton**
> Look up, beautiful.

I do, just as the cherry blossom petals fall, my eyes find his across the road, as he stands on the sidewalk. My heart skips a beat. I have never loved someone as fiercely as I loved Keaton Mills.

He holds his hand up to me and my heart sings in my chest. Walking to the edge of the curb, I get ready to cross when he shakes his head from side to side. He steps into the road and picks up a light jog before he is in front of me. His hands are at the side of my face, his eyes burn into mine just as his head tilts and his lips slant across mine.

"God, I missed you," he whispers against my lips, edging me back and away from the road.

"I missed you too," I admit as he kisses me again before he crouches down and places a kiss on my swollen tummy.

"And I missed both of you too," he smiles against my bump and kisses it. A flutter of a giggle bubbles out of me as he stands and links his fingers through mine, and we walk hand in hand down the blossom lined sidewalk towards home.

The table is set, Keaton is finishing up with dinner and nerves bubble deep inside of me. This isn't *just* a dinner. This is where I tell my dad, his wife, my friends and my brother-in-law that I have been accepted into the hospital of my choice again. This is where we tell my dad, his wife, my friends and Keaton's brother that we're expecting twin boys. This is where we tell our families what the next few months hold. This is where we put the devastating six months behind us and look to the future with Primrose and Posie tucked inside our hearts, where they're safe with me until my last dying breath.

Keaton's arms wrap around me, and I smile as he nuzzles his face into my neck as he whispers against my skin.

"We have thirty minutes," and I feel the smirk on my skin, my pulse racing.

"We can do a lot in thirty minutes..." I admit, turning and placing my hands on his chest.

"Want to prove to me just how much?" and I don't get a chance to even catch my breath. He lifts me and my arms wrap around his neck, legs circling his waist as he carries me up the stairs and places me on the bed.

I smirk up at him, my fingers fumbling with the buttons of his shirt. He is between my legs, lips on mine as I push his shirt off his shoulders and let my fingertips roam over his skin. He pushes off me, his hungry eyes ablaze with fire as he looks down at me and my cheeks burn. He gently pulls me up and lifts my pretty lilac summer dress over my head and drops it to the floor.

"God, you're beautiful," he rasps, cupping my full breasts into his hand, his mouth lowering as he sucks my hard and sensitive nipples into his hot mouth. Dusting his lips across my chest, he gives the same attention to the other.

"We don't have long," I whisper, my head rolling back.

"I know baby," he groans, dragging his lips across my skin as he sinks to his knees. "But I just need one taste," his fingers swirl at my opening, his tongue flicking across my clit and a moan escapes me, my body smothers in goosebumps. This man tore me into a million pieces and spent the last six months piecing me back together, bit by bit. I was far from perfect, but to him, I was.

His lips are pressed into my groin, my hips, across my bump. His fingers digging into my hips as he stands, towering over me.

"I will never tire of you, baby," he rasps, my hands clasping his face as I pull his lips to mine. A gasp leaves me when he spins me round and gently knocks my knees, so I fall forward, my hands breaking my fall.

I hear the sound of his belt unbuckling and I clench my pussy.

"Hold onto the headboard, this is going to be hard and fast baby."

My breath shudders as I do as he asks, my fingers wrapping round the top of the headboard. Back arched, legs parted. He kneels up behind me, his soft kisses trailing across my shoulders, down my spine just as his fingers curl round my hips. I feel his cock nudging at my soaked opening, and with one roll of his hips, his cock sinks into me with ease, stretching and filling me.

"Fuck," I whisper, eyes rolling in the back of my head, and I will never tire of how good it feels when he is deep inside of me.

He slips in and out of me, his pace slow and I am loving it. I turn my face to look over my shoulder at him, the man who holds my delicate heart in his hands, the one who fixed me back together again more times than I would care to admit, the man I love with every fibre of my being. I give a sultry smirk, eyes hazy as pleasure consumes me.

"You promised me hard and fast," I taunt through a moan, and he growls, his fingers digging in a little harder as he does just that.

Fucks me hard and fast until we're both coming, our moans filling the room as our orgasms collide.

WE CLEAN UP AND HEAD BACK DOWNSTAIRS JUST AS THE DOORBELL rings.

"Close call," he whispers in my ear, kissing my cheek before he steps around me and opens the door to my dad, Amora and Twyla.

"Sunshine," my dad beams at me, stepping into our house and embracing me.

"Hey dad," I smile, Amora giving me a sweet smile as I break away. Walking towards her, I place a kiss on her cheek then turn my focus onto my baby sister, Twyla. Six months old and beautiful, red hair and ice blue eyes. I bend down, unbuckling her from her car chair and cradle her in my arms.

"Hey baby, I've missed you," I place a kiss on the top of

her head and walk towards the kitchen. I hear Keaton and Titus talking and my heart warms. They're still not how they were, but they're getting there and that's all I can hope for.

Amora walks straight through and puts Twyla's food into the fridge along with her bottle then pops the kettle on.

"Tea?" she asks, and I nod, all whilst watching my sister.

It's not long before our house is filled with everyone, and I have never felt more content than I do right now. We all fall into easy conversation, Celeste is toddling around, Twyla is taking everything in and baby Dexter is sound asleep in his travel cot. He is Sage's double. Jet black hair, pale skin and stunning green eyes. He is going to be a heartbreaker when he is older.

Xavier grumbles from the other side of the room and my dad rolls his eyes and that's when I find Keaton staring at me, so adoring and like I am sitting on the pedestal he has put me on from the moment he came into my life. He gives a gentle nod and I know that's our cue.

I stand, tapping my knife on my glass and draw everyone's attention to me. Keaton is standing by my side, one arm tucked round my back, the other resting on my bump.

"May we have a moment," I blink through the tears that are threatening, my smile so wide.

The chatter soon fades into nothing, and I take this opportunity to look around the room at my family.

My dad, Amora and Twyla. Kaleb and Connie. Nate. Killian, Reese and Celeste. Sage, Dex and Dexter. Xavier and Royal. This is not the family I was born into, it was the family that was made for me.

"We just wanted to say a few words and thank each and every one of you for everything you have done for us all over the last year." I sniff, my eyes locking on my dad's for a moment. "We couldn't have gotten through the last six months without out any of you," I swallow the lump down and I feel a kiss on my temple which makes me smile. "We wanted to let you know a few things before we dish up dessert," nerves flutter inside my tummy, my chest tightening and my heart races. "We found out a few days ago, that our beautiful rainbow babies are boys," I blink back the tears and the room cheers. "We're going to have sons, and dad," a lone tear escapes and I palm it away, "you're going to have grandsons," I sniff and Keaton pulls me closer to him. "Also," I say a little louder over the chatter and cheers, "I am going back to medical school next year," my dad's eyes are glued to me and I can see the tears brimming in his eyes. "I passed my exams and will be starting my internship again," I choke out a laugh and feel Keaton's arm slip away from me. I turn to look at him and there he is, on one knee, holding onto my wedding band that has hung around his neck since the moment I threw it at him.

"Ready to marry me yet?" he smirks, and I burst into tears, laughing as I nod my head.

"Always stealing my thunder," Kaleb shouts across the kitchen and the room falls deafly silent.

"What?" Keaton says as he stands up and takes my hands into his.

Kaleb pulls Connie to her feet then sinks to one knee and I hear the room cheer.

"What the fuck?" Killian grumbles and Reese swats him.

"Connie..." his voice cracks, "darling," and she is crying.

"Let me be your husband, please," and she is nodding her head yes, and he lets out a sigh of relief.

"Is asking the father's permission not the done thing anymore?" Killian seethes, but we all ignore him. We're too focused as Kaleb slips a beautiful platinum band on her finger, a huge solitaire diamond. Plain and classy.

"Don't worry old man," Reese taunts him.

"I never got asked either," Xavier rolls his eyes, his voice deep and serious. "He just stood at the end of the aisle, ambushed the planned wedding."

"Oh, fuck off," my dad lets out a loud laugh and the room laughs along with him.

The rest of the evening is filled with nothing but love and laughter, oh, and matching tees for the men. All picked out by me and Keaton and we think they're pretty spot on.

Killian - Mr Steal your daughter's best friend.

Titus - Marries the job.

Kaleb – Pussywhipped.

Keaton - Mr Steal your best friend's daughter.

Xavier - Mr Stockholm Syndrome.

Dex - Stalker.

Nate - Secretly Kinky.

And yes, Nate's was a complete fluke, but there is something about that dark horse. He keeps his cards close to his chest for a reason and I'm sure in time, we will all find out. But until then, he is just Nate.

We're all sitting in the living room, soft music playing, and I feel complete. I lose myself deep in my thoughts for a moment to when I came home from hospital. I was broken in every sense of the word. Keaton found a parcel and handed it to me, and I knew what it was as soon as my fingers touched the box.

"WHAT IS IT?" KEATON ASKED AND I SWALLOWED DOWN THE tears.

"Some books..." I paused, the lump in my throat burning.

"Oh," is all he responds with. My trembling fingers pull at the tab, and I slip the two books out.

I choke on my inhale of breath, hot tears rolling down my cheeks as I hold the two parenting books in my hands.

"I was terrified that I wouldn't know how to be a mom," I sniffled, palming my tears away, "I wanted to be the best I could be, but growing up without one made me think I would fail. How could I be a mom when I didn't know what having a mom was like?" I looked up at Keaton and he stood in front of me, his hand cupping my cheek as he catches a tear with his thumb pad.

"You didn't need a mom, because Ari, you would have been the best damn mom in the world. You fought so hard, you done everything in your power to keep those girls safe. And you did." He crouches in front of me, "I have no doubt in my mind baby, you are a mom. You were a mom from the moment you saw the two lines on that pregnancy test so don't ever fear you don't know what it's like. Your mom was a coward, and you, my love, are not."

YES, I MAY HAVE NOT HAD MY MOM AND I WAS RAISED BY A SINGLE dad, but now, sitting here and looking at everyone, I've realized that they're my family. Not blood, but family nonetheless.

They found me when I didn't know I was lost.

Keaton sits beside me, hand on my bump and my head is on his shoulder and right now, everything is perfect.

"I love you blossom, thank you for guiding me out of the darkness."

I lift my head as I look at him, unshed tears glassing my eyes.

"And I am so glad that your dad took the job in England."

"Me too baby, me too," his lips lower over mine and my heart leaps in my chest. "I love you Keaton Mills, until the end of time, forever and always."

"Forever and always, Blossom, forever and always."

EPILOGUE
ARIZONA

I NEVER THOUGHT MY HEART WOULD BE AS FULL AS IT WAS NOW.

Two sons.

Smith and Sebastian.

Two little terrors but my god, they're amazing.

The last year has whizzed by, and I have loved every single minute of it.

But am I ready to go back to work? It's bittersweet.

Today is my first day as an intern but under a different hospital, and I changed from trauma to pediatrics. It was the right thing to do, and I know it was my guardian angels that I have to thank.

"Are you ready?" I hear my husband's voice echo down the hallway, a boy in each arm and my heart melts. He has never looked more handsome than he does now.

"I think so," I nod, and check the time.

"Are you?" I ask, and he gives me such a sweet smile.

"I have been ready for you to pick your dream back up again from the moment I bumped into you," he steps closer to me, placing a soft kiss on my lips.

"I don't deserve you."

"Of course, you do," he kisses me again and Seb grabs my face, putting a sloppy kiss on my cheek.

"Oh, baby boy," I scoop him from Keaton and snuggle him for just a moment before I tuck myself under his arm and that's how we stand when there is a knock on the door. I look up at him, our eyes filled with anxiousness.

"We're doing the right thing aren't we?" I whisper and Keaton nods.

"Yes baby, we are," he places a kiss on my forehead before he steps aside and opens the front door.

"James," he smiles, and I peep over his shoulder at our new nanny.

Twenty-three, just out of college and ready to take on the challenge of two boisterous boys.

She steps inside the house and the boys are already holding their arms out for her and she scoops them both into a hold, a huge smile on her face.

"I don't think we're going to be missed at all," I sigh as Keaton wraps his arm round me and pulls me into him, my head resting on his chest, my hand splayed against his shirt.

"Yeah, we will," he kisses the top of my head and my heart stammers in my chest.

After a minute or two, I break away from Keaton and grab my bag.

"Okay, any problems I have left a few numbers, but you can reach me and Keaton at work."

"We will be fine," she smiles, reassuring me.

"I know," I promised myself I wasn't going to cry. Liar. Tears are streaming down my cheeks.

"I'll send updates throughout the day, I promise," she smiles sweetly. She is an angel.

"Okay," I sniffle, stepping towards the boys and placing

a kiss on the top of their brown hair, lingering a little longer with each kiss, inhaling their scent. "Bye my babies," I choke, then press onto my tiptoes and kiss Keaton on the lips. Turning quickly, I head for the door when I bump into Nate.

"Oh, Nate, hey," I place my hand on his shoulder as I pass him, "would love to catch up but I don't want to be late."

He nods and smiles at me, "Have a great first day," he calls out as he steps into the house.

"Keat?" he calls out and I turn to give the boys one last wave when I notice how Nate is just staring at James.

My brows furrow for just a moment, and Keaton walks into the lobby with a huge smile on his face.

"Nate, this is James our Nanny; James, this is Nate. The boy's uncle and my best friend."

"Lovely to meet you Nate, I would shake your hand but..." James shrugs her shoulders up, arms full with Smith and Seb, and Nate just nods, turns on his heel and walks towards me, knocking his shoulder into me. He doesn't apologize, just keeps going until he is in his car.

Keaton looks at James, to me then back to Nate. I shake my head, lifting my shoulders and Keaton looks back at James who looks as confused as us.

"Right, okay," he sighs, "any problems..."

"I'll call," she smiles, and her cheeks must be hurting from the constant smile that is plastered on her face.

"And their routine and stuff is all listed out in the kitchen."

"Got it!" she says as she closes the door, and I am sort of glad she did otherwise I wouldn't have left.

Keaton steps beside me as we walk towards the sidewalk.

"What the hell was that about?" I whisper as we get to Nate's car.

"I have no idea," he mutters, leaning down and giving me one last kiss. "I'll find out though."

I scrunch my nose up, and smile.

"Have the best day," he whispers against my lips.

"You too," I edge forward and kiss him, really, for the last time.

"Be safe, I love you."

"I love you more," I smile, eyes a little watery. I stand and watch as he gets into Nate's car and once he is tucked inside, I get into mine.

I wait until he drives away before pulling out onto the road. I was ready for my new adventure. I was finally where I wanted to be.

And most importantly, I was happy.

Immensely.

NATE

They say the quietest ones have the biggest secrets.

Well, mine are about to be spilled.

THE END

The Revenge, book four in the Illicit Love Series will follow Nate. Yes, I am keeping his book more of a secret. After all, isn't that what Nate has been up until now? Mysterious.

. . .

Keaton, Arizona, Titus, Amora, Kaleb, Killian, Connie, Reese, Royal, Xavier, Dex and Sage will all return in the final instalment of The Illicit Love series.

Want to know more about Killian and Reese:
Mybook.to/DHYSM

Want to know more about Kaleb and Connie:
Mybook.to/TheResIL

Want to know more about Titus and Amora:
Mybook.to/TLo

Want to know more about Dex and Sage:
Mybook.to/SomethingWS

ACKNOWLEDGMENTS

Dan. My best friend. My husband. My world. Thank you for pushing me to start this crazy journey. I love you to the moon and back. If it wasn't for you, this dream of mine would have never come true.

Robyn, thank you for everything. I would be lost without you.

Leanne, thank you for always being here for me. You're a friend for life. I am grateful for you coming into my world when you did.

Lea Joan, thank you for editing The Betrayal, I love that we can work together.

My BETA team, thank you.

And lastly, my readers... without you, none of this would have been possible.

My loyal fans, I owe it all to you.

Made in the USA
Columbia, SC
29 June 2024

37882344R00300